MURDER
AND
MAYHEM
IN MANAYUNK

A JACK REGAN/IZZY ICHOWITZ NOVEL

Hi Kathy,
    Hope you enjoy the book!

                Neal

BY

NEAL GOLDSTEIN

DEDICATION - *FOR MARILYN*

ACKNOWLEDGEMENTS

———◦◦◦———

The author would like to thank everyone who assisted in the research, reading, editing, promotion and publication of this novel. Special thanks to my editor, the wonderful Anne Johnson Kram, for her insight and gentle hand with this novice writer, and her husband, the award winning journalist and author Mark Kram Jr., for generously sharing his time and encouraging me to pursue my passion. To my assistant, Margaret McGrath, for her patience and technical expertise in repeatedly showing me how to utilize the word processing programs so that I could throw away my pencil and legal pad.

To my mother Helen who introduced me to the joy of reading and love of literature so many years ago, and my brother Steve who set such a great example of how to be a man.

Most of all, thank you to my amazing wife Marilyn, and my sons and best friends Matthew and Benjamin, whose love, support and encouragement make all things in my life possible.

PROLOGUE

———◆———

The light from a weak sun was breaking over the mountains as the stranger approached the building at the end of the village path. He could see his breath as he looked down trying not to trip over the stones and debris that littered the ground, the last vestiges of a drone attack the previous spring. He could feel the weight of the watchers' stares. He was tall and walked with a slight limp. He had traveled throughout the night. His keffiteyeh was stained with perspiration. When he entered the building the stranger smiled and bowed to the old man who sat crossed leg on the prayer rug in the center of the room.

"As-salamu 'Alaykum," the old man greeted the stranger.

"Wa 'alaykumu s-salam," he responded as he took his place at the opposite side of the rug.

The meeting had been arranged by the head of the Al-Qaida cell in Aden, the legendary leader of the December 29, 1992 bombing of the Gold Mohur hotel.

The old man stared at the stranger. The stranger waited. The old man could read nothing in the stranger's face.

"You have traveled a great distance," the old man spoke in Farsi as he signaled one of his tribesmen to serve the tea. In keeping with their custom, the serving of tea was a sign of respect.

The stranger nodded. He accepted the cup that had been offered to him and held it in both hands in front of his face as the man poured the tea from the dented metal kettle. He nearly gagged from the dung-like odor of the brown liquid. He held the cup above his head and nodded his thanks to his host and his entourage. He took a full sip and bowed his head as he struggled to keep it down. He looked up and smiled at the old man. He waited for the others to be served.

"So you will destroy the bell?" the old man finally asked.

The stranger nodded.

"But of what value is that?"

"It will demonstrate our reach, and our dedication to the destruction of all things they hold sacred."

"Is that all?" The old man was not impressed.

The stranger stared back at him, with a gleam in his bottle green eyes. He shook his head and smiled. "No there will be more, much, much more."

"So what do you want from us?" the old man asked.

"The sleepers," the stranger replied.

The old man nodded.

PART 1.

THE MURDER

ONE

She kissed him and smiled as he pulled her close and thrust his hips into her body. She moaned and parted her lips accepting his tongue as she gently pushed him against the wall.

"I want you," he said breathlessly.

She pulled away and smiled at him. "But you said you had to leave to attend some important meeting. Didn't you?"

He nodded.

She pressed her body into his and felt his reaction. "Poor baby; go to your business meeting and when you're done I'll be here, waiting for you."

She kissed him again and opened the door for him to leave.

She smiled and said, "Remember, I'll be waiting. And when you come back, I've something very important to share with you."

"What is it," he asked.

"I'll tell you later," she teased.

She closed the door and shook her head. It had been so easy to make him fall in love with her. She didn't tell him her secret yet. She loved to tease him and keep him off balance. Soon everything she had worked for would be hers. All the sacrifices and disappointments would soon be nothing but distant memories.

She walked towards the fireplace and slowly gazed around the room. Someday soon she would own a place like this, she thought. No, not like this-someplace with a commanding view of the city - a place where the power brokers of the town would come at her beck and call.

She heard the noise and looked out the back door that opened to the canal path that ran along the Schuylkill River the length of Manayunk.

Christ. She thought she had made it clear that it was over.

"What are you doing here?" she asked as she opened the door.

"May I come in?"

She sighed and stepped aside. She was determined to leave no doubt that whatever they had once been was now over.

"I saw what you were doing. Do you really think he'll leave his wife for you?"

She shrugged and turned away.

"Listen to me, you belong to me."

"Get your hands off me," she said and continued to walk away.

Before she had taken two full steps she felt the cold iron strike the back of her head. Pain exploded from the top of her skull throughout her entire body, causing her to convulse in paralyzing muscle spasms through every limb. The excruciating white hot electric shock that cascaded through every centimeter of her body was beyond any pain she had ever experienced.

She felt the wind from the force of the second blow before the cold metal actually made contact with her skull. Her body was unable to respond to her brain's signal to evade the assault. She tried to scream but was unable to make a sound. *How could this be happening,* she wondered as her body fell to the floor.

The third blow crushed her skull and she lost consciousness. Her lifeless body laid on the floor six paces from the fireplace in a slowly expanding pool of blood.

The killer stared at the body. "Fucking tramp," the killer said and walked out the back door.

TWO

——◆——

egan ran up the steps of the entrance to the Union League. The building took up an entire city block of what was once again the focal point of yet another renaissance of center city Philadelphia. The League had presided over South Broad Street since 1865, a bastion of the City of Brotherly Love's power brokers. The classic French Renaissance – styled building, with its brick and brownstone façade, and the dramatic twin circular staircases that lead up to the main entrance, looked out of place-a relic of the past in contrast to the cool exteriors of its closest neighbors the Bananna Republic and F.Y.E. record store.

The only blemish in the otherwise august image the League projected, despite all the wealth and power of its members, was the aluminum food cart on the northwest corner of Broad and Samson streets that an enterprising street vendor, with the help of the ACLU and a local columnist had won zoning board approval to sell falafels and soft pretzels a mere one hundred feet from the building's entrance. The League's founding fathers must surely be rolling in their graves.

Even though his mother's family had belonged to the League for over a century, he found it ironic that his father, the son of a Philadelphia police officer from Manayunk, who, but for a fortuitous marriage to the daughter of a Main Line aristocracy, would never have been allowed admission to the elite club on South Broad Street despite his office, was now one of its most prominent members. Regan was certain that if offered the opportunity, his father would prefer to hang out with the falafel crowd rather than eat the over-priced, over-cooked fried oysters and tasteless chicken salad, a combination that defied explanation, served to the pretentious members of the club to which he now belonged.

"You're late, mother will be furious." His sister Annie greeted him. She straightened his tie and brushed an errant curl from his brow. He hugged her and kissed her cheek.

"I know Sis."

Annabelle, the eldest of his three sisters, the one who always ran interference for him, flashed one of her radiant smiles. She looked exactly like their mother. She was beautiful in a quiet, almost aristocratic way. She still looked like she was twenty-one years old. It was impossible to believe she was forty and the mother of three.

As they approached the reception line he saw the entire Regan clan, all three generations. His twin sisters, their husbands and children in tow, stood to the right of his parents. Annie's family covered his parent's left flank leaving a place for him immediately next to his father.

"Jack, good of you to join us." His mother gave him a frosty greeting, as she also straightened his bow tie and brushed the same errant curl from his forehead.

"Love you too, Mother," he said and kissed her proffered cheek. "Dad, all present and accounted for," he hugged his father in greeting.

John Hogan Regan, Commissioner of Police of the City of Philadelphia, stood with his family as the movers and shakers of the city and the Commonwealth of Pennsylvania, including both United States Senators and several members of Congress, paid him tribute. The annual fundraiser for The Children's Hospital of Philadelphia, that Commissioner and Mrs. Regan chaired, was one of the most prestigious events on the social calendar.

Patricia Maxwell Regan maneuvered her son to a quiet corner for a mother and son chat after the receiving line had dispersed.

"Jack, your father and I are concerned… We all loved Susan…but it's time to move on."

He was both moved and frustrated with his mother's interest in his social life, or perhaps more accurately stated, the absence of one.

"Mother, I…"

"Jack, you have to start going out, to really live… Susan wouldn't want you to be alone. Come on, why don't you give some of those gals a chance?"

"I promise, Mother."

"Oh, Jack, don't patronize me. You know your father and I only want you and your sisters to be happy."

"Come on, Mother, do you want me to be just like the Marx Brothers, Groucho, Chico and Harpo?" he gestured at his three brothers in law. "Mother don't you find them a bit boring? I mean it's like they're all made of the same DNA. Members of silk stocking law firms, they serve as board members on all the right charities, good hair, good teeth, hail fellows, one and all."

Jack's remarks were intended to deflect his mother's anticipated diatribe about his job with the District Attorney. In truth he really liked his brothers in law. They were good men, good husbands who adored and respected his sisters.

"Jack, you're impossible… Is that Courtney standing by the bar? You know she just went through a difficult divorce. She reassumed her maiden name. Weren't the two of you… you know, rather close when you were in college?"

"Please Mother, let's not go there. As I recall, you were not that fond of her back then."

"Jack…Mrs. Regan…Sorry. I didn't mean to intrude…"

"Courtney, don't be silly. It's wonderful to see you again. Jack and I were just having one of our mother and son talks. He's so busy with his work, I don't often have the opportunity to… well you know. Why don't I let the two of you catch up?"

"Court, that was rather awkward, don't you think?" As he hugged her Regan caught his mother looking back at them. His mother looked a bit too happy, and Jack got the feeling this reunion with his old flame was more than happenstance. His reaction was reinforced by Courtney's expression.

Courtney Wells was the heiress to one of Philadelphia's Main Line banking dynasties, and she looked the part. It was as if she had stepped out of the pages of *Vogue* magazine. Her air of casual elegance, perfect features, with the bluest eyes you ever looked into, to Regan her beauty was almost intimidating.

"Jack, I feel, I don't know, a little embarrassed. Your mother did call to make sure I would attend tonight. She told me you weren't seeing anyone. Oh God this is …I mean I meant to call you after Susan's funeral… but I didn't know what to…"

"Courtney, it's OK. How are you doing?" He stopped and shook his head. "You know, you and I were never very good at chit chat. I'm really sorry things didn't work out for you and Greg, the two of you looked like, I don't know- the perfect couple."

"Well, sometimes things aren't always what they appear to be on the surface."

They stood in awkward silence.

"Dju know, dju really look marvelous." His lame imitation of Billy Crystal's imitation of Fernando Lamas broke the tension of the moment.

"I must confess, I went to some lengths to make myself attractive," she blushed in response

"Well Court, it sure worked, not that you really have to, I mean every guy in the room is staring at you."

"Jack, there's only one guy I really want to take notice."

"Who's the lucky guy?" He could tell from her reaction that this was not what she had expected him to say.

"Jack, duh! You can't be that dense. I mean really," she rolled her eyes as she grabbed his arm. "Let's go say hi to your sisters. Annabelle looks like she's about to run over here and rescue you from my evil influence."

Jack did not know how to react to Courtney's directness. He had grown comfortable with his situation. He wasn't sure he was ready for the emotional turmoil that came from involvement with the opposite sex. At thirty-four, he wasn't interested in casual relationships, and yet he was afraid of anything more substantive.

He floated through the remainder of the evening at Courtney Wells' side. He marveled at the way she worked the room. Her natural grace in maneuvering them in and out of mundane conversations, and the ease with which she had overcome his sister Annie's initial resistance was truly impressive. It was as if the two of them had remained a couple, and had not gone their separate ways the last ten years.

"Earth to Jack?"

He blushed. "I'm sorry, I was…"

"Jack, you will call me? After all, you monopolized my entire evening." She flashed him one of her million dollar smiles. Her driver was waiting by the rear door of her town car.

He looked at her, "Why, of course."

She hugged him and kissed his cheek. "Jack, I'm really happy your mother called."

THREE

He started out on his usual route home from Center City, the Benjamin Franklin Parkway to the Kelly Drive, to Manayunk's Main Street; as he drove his thoughts drifted back to Courtney Wells. What did she really want from him, and why now?

He entered the Parkway at the Logan Circle and took the center lane west towards Fairmount Park. Logan Circle had originally been one of the five public squares laid out by William Penn himself, the Quaker who received the land grant from the British monarch that eventually became the Commonwealth of Pennsylvania. In the 1920s Philadelphia's elite sought to upgrade the town's image and converted the square to an oval to replicate the Place de Concorde in Paris. The entrance to the Parkway and the buildings around the circle, the Free Library of Philadelphia and the Family Court House that had been modeled after the Hotel de Crillion were designed to resemble the Champs d'Elysees. Like most such attempts, Philadelphia's effort was missing something, and yet it had a quaint charm of its own.

It was a beautiful night and the Parkway's walkways were filled with pedestrians, some strolling hand in hand enjoying the early spring evening, another sign Philly was awakening from its decades' long decline.

As he drove past the newest addition to the Parkway, the soon-to-be-opened Barnes Foundation Museum, he almost laughed out loud at how typically "Philadelphia" the battle over where and how the Barnes

Foundation's treasured art collection would be housed had played out over the past decade. Millions of dollars in legal fees had been wasted as the power brokers of the region contested the legality of moving the exhibition eight miles from Merion, a Philadelphia suburb, to Center City. His mother, a former student at the Foundation, and a cadre of her fellow denizens of the Main Line establishment, were right in the center of the mess.

Regan loved his mother and respected her passion to defend the causes and people she loved. He realized her latest *cause célèbre*, her effort to reunite him with Courtney Wells, was well intended. After all she only wanted her son to be happy.

Did he really want to rekindle his relationship with Courtney, he wondered as he drove past the Art Museum and on to the Kelly Drive. They had been high school sweethearts. Once Courtney graduated from the Notre Dame Academy in Radnor and was exposed to the unsupervised life of a college coed in Boston, she became uninhibited and embraced her new found freedom with a fervor that was reckless and out of control. Regan went to Princeton, and neither of them could sustain the pressure of a long distance relationship. There had been no big breakup, they just moved on and drifted into new relationships. No bitterness; no recriminations.

As he approached Main Street, flashing lights from several parked police cruisers and news vans lit up the normally quiet side of Manayunk. This section of the city had once been an independent mill town nestled along the banks of the Schuykill River. The former borough had been incorporated along with other municipalities that bordered the city as part of Philadelphia in the early 19th century.

Manayunk got its identity from the dam, canal and locks that had been built to power the mills and factories that for nearly 100 years made it one of the manufacturing centers of Philadelphia. Even after the decline of manufacturing and the shuttering of the mom and pop businesses along its Main Street, Manayunk retained its small-town charm with its two and three story row homes that were crammed onto the hilly, cobblestone streets within walking distance of the mills and factories where generations of the workers lived. Now, because of its proximity to Center City, Manayunk like many other Philadelphia neighborhoods that had seen better days was undergoing a transformation into a gentrified, hip place for young professionals and college students to live, much to the consternation of the original 'Yunkers,' the mostly Irish and Polish descendants of the mill workers.

One of the former industrial sites, the old Shupak Pickle Works, had been cordoned off with yellow crime scene tape. As Regan slowed down he noticed a Crown Vic with distinctive dents carelessly parked with its front wheel on the sidewalk, announcing the unmistakable presence of Detective Isodore Ichowitz of the Homicide Division. Regan parked his car next to Ichowitz' vehicle and showed his ID to the officer guarding the entrance to the parking lot.

"Yo, Jack. Are you doing your James Bond thing, or is this a black tie only Homicide?" One of the local media had reconigzed him and alerted the rest.

He ignored the catcalls. "Tell Detective Ichowitz Assistant District Attorney Regan is here." The young Police Officer radioed the message and Regan was logged in and permitted access. He walked across the parking lot to Ichowitz, who was standing outside the door of the smaller of the two buildings in the courtyard.

The former pickle factory had been converted into condos. Regan was impressed with the quality of the exterior renovations that had maintained the historic character of the industrial buildings.

"Nice threads, *boycik*. To what do I owe the honor?" Ichowitz reached over and touched the lapel of Regan's tuxedo. "Armani?"

"Izz, I was on my way home from my folk's shindig at the Union League. I noticed the new dent on your Crown Vic. Just wanted to make sure you were OK."

"Well as you can plainly see, I survived. Since you're here, would you like to see how I occupy myself when I'm not testifying in one of your cases?"

Regan smiled at the big man. Isodore Ichowitz was acknowledged as the best detective in the division. He was Regan's godfather. Jack's father and the homicide detective went all the way back to their Police Academy days.

"Izz, you know I only live a couple blocks from here. We're not used to all this excitement in the hood."

Ichowitz smiled and said, "I know Jack. Except for the occasional domestic, you Yunkers play nice. But we got us a real doosey on our hands here."

Ichowitz led him into the building. In its former life it must have been where the Shupaks had stored pickle barrels for curing. It had been transformed into a dramatic multi-level living space. The loading doors at the back of the building that faced the canal path had been replaced with floor-to-ceiling windows that provided an unobstructed view of the Center City skyline several miles down the Schuylkill River. Regan, who was renovating his own far more modest home, marveled at the scope and quality of the workmanship. It must have cost a fortune, he thought.

"Izz, I had no idea that this site had been renovated," Regan said. "It must have cost millions to convert the factory and this storage area into condos."

"You're probably right. Funny thing though, despite their best efforts, the place still smells a little like a kosher pickle," the big detective remarked.

Regan and Ichowitz had donned foot covers to make sure they would not contaminate the crime scene. Blood had splattered all over the back of the room. There were bloody footsteps immediately around the corpse, leading to a partially opened rear doorway. "We haven't identified the victim yet," he said as he lifted the sheet that covered the corpse.

The victim had been a beautiful young woman. The corpse was in full rigor and there was some discoloration around her eyes and mouth, but except for the bloody wound to the back of her skull, she looked as if she were asleep.

"Jesus Christ, Izz, it's Meagan Larson. She worked for Dorothy Wiggins."

"Jack, are you sure?"

"Izz, she was scheduled to be a witness in the Wiggins' Grand Jury Investigation. I interviewed her for hours to prepare her testimony. Anyway, once you met her, if you had a pulse you weren't about to forget her."

Regan filled Ichowitz in on his history with the victim. She had been an associate attorney in Wiggins' office. She delivered documents he had subpoenaed as part of the Grand Jury investigation of Wiggins' involvement in insurance fraud and improper payments, kickbacks to local politicians and union officials. The interviews ultimately led to further investigation and her eventual agreement to provide testimony to the Grand Jury. The gossip on the street was that Larson's relationship with Wiggins was something other than that of a regular employment situation.

"Who owns this place?" he asked the detective.

Ichowitz told Regan the Nooris brothers had developed the entire complex. The Nooris were famous for their ruthless approach to the real estate development business. They claimed that the manner with which they conducted their business was the way it was done in their native Israel. The Nooris had developed and financed the Manayunk renaissance that had transformed the north end of Main Street into a collection of tony shops, expensive condos and restaurants. The redevelopment that had stalled at Shurs Lane was now moving east. They were in the unit owned by Ari Nooris, the older of the two brothers. According to Ichowitz, Ari was presently residing in Jerusalem.

"So what was Megan doing here? As far as I know, she had no connection to the Nooris brothers, or Manayunk for that matter."

Ichowitz sighed. "Jack my boy that is why we conduct investigations."

FOUR

—◆—

The next morning Regan followed his normal Saturday routine: Up at 6 AM; stretch for twenty minutes; jog south on Main Street to the Kelly Drive; pick up the pace for fifty minutes and turn back. This time he made it all the way to the Art Museum steps, nearly four miles, before he made the turn for home. He was training for the Broad Street Run, the annual event that hundreds of Philadelphians ran from Central High School at Broad and Olney in North Philadelphia to the Philadelphia Navy Yard, at the southern most part of Philadelphia, ten miles south. The proceeds from the event went to the Cancer Society. This year Regan would raise over $10,000 in pledges in honor of Susan.

As he jogged back his thoughts turned to the status of the Larson murder investigation. The Medical Examiner had preliminarily fixed the time of death between 3 PM and 10 PM, on Friday. From the evaluation of the crime scene the police had so far determined that Larson had been killed at the condominium owned by Ari Nooris at the old Shupak Pickle Works. The cause of death was severe cranial trauma. The instrument of crime was the fireplace andiron the killer had left at the scene.

Of course, they did not know who did it or why. Nor was there any apparent evidence of a connection between the victim and Ari Nooris, or how Larson had ended up at his condo. When Regan had left the scene, Ichowitz was in the process of recovering the security video from the condominium parking lot. The detectives would begin their canvas of the neighborhood later this morning. You never can underestimate what nosey neighbors, especially Yunkers, might have seen and remembered. What was Megan Larson doing at Nooris' condo?

As Regan approached the tavern at Grape and Main he saw workmen preparing to paint the exterior of the building. He looked through the open front door and saw the proprietor, Mike O'Malley, behind the bar. O'Malley was a classic Yunker. He looked like a leprechaun gone to seed. Five feet, two, a former bantam-class boxer, now many pounds over his fighting weight, he was nevertheless still a force to be reckoned with.

"Mike, giving the Grape a face lift?" Regan asked as he entered the bar. Regan noticed a red headed boy sitting at the corner of the bar using a shot glass and crayons to draw circles on a piece of butcher paper.

The boy, who looked no more than eight or nine years old, looked up as Regan entered the room.

"Not my idea," O'Malley responded. "No, it's my niece from Dublin. She says, Uncle Mike, ya better fix up the old joint now. She says, don't ya see what's happenin around you? The neighborhood's becoming the next thing. The next thing I says. What's that supposed to mean I says."

O'Malley stopped his rant when he noticed the boy at the bar staring at Regan.

"Liam, say hello to Mr. Regan."

"Lo," the boy said and returned to his drawing, while he continued to keep one eye on Regan.

"Jack, Liam's my great nephew, my niece's boy. Liam and his Ma are stayin with me for a piece. Katey, Liam's ma, knows a thing or two, or so she says, about runnin pubs. She managed the family operation in Dublin for a spell."

"Hello, Liam." Jack offered his hand.

The boy reluctantly put down the crayon and solemnly reached up to shake hands with Regan.

"What kind of a watch is that, Mister?" the boy asked.

Regan smiled. "Liam, it's a watch that can change to a compass when you press the stem. It displays the time and also lets me know the direction I'm running, so that I won't get lost. See, the arrow always points to the north. So no matter where I'm headed, I can always know how to get back home."

O'Malley poured Jack a cup of coffee and continued to gripe about the changes his niece had planned for the Grape.

As he caught the aroma of the coffee, Regan realized there was more than a new coat of paint going on at his friend's bar. The coffee had a hint of chicory, this was something new. He took a sip and was rewarded with a rich and subtle flavor that was a far cry from the normally bitter brew he had grown accustomed to at this establishment.

"Mike, where did you get this coffee? It's great!"

"Think so?"

Regan nodded as he took another sip.

Before O'Malley answered, a pretty young woman stepped out of the kitchen and said, "It's from a local brewer in Northern Liberties; they made the blend special for the Grape. Glad you like it."

"I'm Katey O'Malley, the dragon lady from Ireland Uncle Mike's been grousing about," she said as she extended her hand.

"Jack Regan, nice to meet you," he said.

There was no mistaking the fact that Katey O'Malley was Irish. She had red hair and freckles and green eyes that fixed you when she looked your way. She was tall and lean and struck Regan as a woman of substance.

She walked over to her son and mussed his hair she smiled and said, "Liam, are you minding your uncle?"

"Yes Mum."

The boy looked up from his drawing and said, "Will we be going to the park soon? I want to practice my football. Uncle Mike says there's a league I can join."

"Ah son, I'm sorry, but there's a problem with one of the burners. I'm afraid we'll have to go tomorrow."

Regan could see the disappointment on the boy's face, and his mother's reaction was also apparent.

"Mrs. O'Malley, I could take Liam to the park, it's only a block away, and I know the folks who run the soccer league. If that's all right with you and Liam," Regan said.

She fixed him with a serious stare.

"Katey, I know what you're thinkin. Jack's all right, he's not one of those perverts like you were readin about from the Archdiocese. And besides, he's got this fancy watch that will tell him how to find his way back here in case he gets lost, doesn't he, Liam?" O'Malley said.

She looked back at her son who waited for her decision.

"Liam, will you mind Mr. Regan then?"

"Yes Mum."

"Alright, when you're done I'll have lunch ready for the two of you. Make sure you have him back by noon."

Ichowitz and a squad of uniforms from the Fourth District canvassed the Pickle Works and the surrounding neighborhood looking for anyone who witnessed any of the comings and goings at the condo the preceding afternoon and evening. The old factory had been converted to twelve units, eight of which had been sold. The residents in Units two and seven were out of town. Unfortunately none of the neighbors who were at home the day of the murder could provide any leads. According to the Yunkers who lived across the street, the residents of the Works were a bunch of snooty posers who wanted nothing to do with the neighborhood folk, and that was fine by them. None of the locals saw anything that aided the investigation.

The surveillance video of the parking lot did yield a potential solid lead. Of the seventeen vehicles that had accessed the parking lot on Friday, six belonged to condo owners. Of the remaining eleven, five were identified as visitors, one was a Comcast truck. Ichowitz and his squad only had partial license plates for four of the five other vehicles and were still running them through the available data bases.

The videotape clearly showed a black Mercedes with the vanity license plate, "ILLSUEU," owned by Dorothy Wiggins, Larson's boss, entering the parking lot at 17:30. Unfortunately there was no clear view of the driver or where he or she went upon leaving the vehicle. The driver returned to the vehicle 17:55 and drove off. The techs also recovered Wiggins' fingerprints, among others, inside the apartment. Since Larson was about to drop the dime on Wiggins, the timing of her proximity to the scene of the crime might be the smoking pistol Ichowitz needed to solve the crime. He knew this was, of course, too good to be true, but at the very least it might help the investigation fix the time of death, and could ultimately lead to the killer. Besides, it would provide Ichowitz with the opportunity to question Wiggins as a "Person of Interest."

Ichowitz drove past the Manayunk Park and saw Regan standing on the sidelines of the soccer field watching the kids scrimmaging. He pulled the Crown Vic over and jumped the curb, nearly hitting the fire hydrant. Ichowitz was probably the worst driver on the force. One more crash and the Commissioner warned him that he would revoke his driving privileges and force Ichowitz to use SEPTA, the city's public transit system.

He walked over to Regan and said, "Jack, I was just thinking about you, and *voila*, there you are. I didn't know you had any interest in soccer?"

"Izz, I'm watching one of the kids, the tall red-headed boy," Regan pointed to Liam.

The two men watched the scrimmage as Liam took the ball nearly the length of the field and kicked it past the goalie. Liam was surrounded by his teammates and his coach gave him a high five as he crossed the sideline. Regan whistled and was rewarded with a rare smile from the serious boy.

"That kid looks like he knows what he's doing," Ichowitz said.

"Izz, Jimmy Mack the coach went nuts when I brought Liam over. He couldn't believe a nine-year-old has those skills."

"Jack is he one of your nephews?"

"No, he's Mike O'Malley's, you know the guy who owns the Grape Tavern, great nephew. Liam and his mother just came over from Ireland. I volunteered to bring the boy over to the park."

Ichowitz gave him a look.

"What?"

"Jack, is Liam's mother a comely lass?" Ichowitz asked.

Regan blushed and said, "So why were you thinking about me?"

"Oh yeah, I wanted to tell you that one of your favorite people in the world appears to be a person of interest in the Larson homicide."

"And who might that be?"

"Dorothy Wiggins."

"Really?"

"It's the '*emess*'- the absolute truth" Ichowitz said and filled Regan in on the evidence.

Liam ran into the Grape and hugged his mother. "Mum, I scored a goal!"

She looked up at Regan and mouthed a silent thank you. He nodded.

She had prepared fish and chips for lunch. Regan had never tasted fried fish that light and flavorful before, and the chips were crisp and delicious.

"Is this going to be on the menu?" he asked.

She nodded. "Do you think the regulars will like it?"

"I think once the word gets out that the Grape serves food like this, the regulars won't be able to get in!"

As they had another cup of what Regan thought of as "Katey's Special Blend" coffee she said, "I can't thank you enough for taking Liam to the park and introducing him to the soccer coach. That's the first time I saw that smile since we arrived."

"You're welcome. It was really a pleasure to watch Liam. Where did he learn to play so well?"

She sat quiet for a moment contemplating her response.

"I suppose his father taught him, or maybe it's in his genes. His father was a professional football player. He played for one of the clubs in Ireland."

"Will your husband be joining you in the states?" Regan asked.

"No, no. And he's not my husband. Liam's dad is not the marryin kind, not that I would even consider being wed to such a scoundrel."

Regan felt relieved to learn that Katey O'Malley was not married. He was surprised at his reaction to the fact that she was single. Could he actually be ready to get into a relationship? His mind raced back to the previous evening and Courtney Wells. Once again he wondered if he was ready for the emotional turmoil of becoming involved with the opposite sex.

As if reading his mind she said, "My Uncle Mike tells me your wife passed away. He told me she was a beautiful and gifted person. As you know O'Malley isn't very generous when it comes to giving out compliments, so that's high tribute from the likes of him."

"Yes, Susan and Mike were very close. In fact, Mike introduced us. You know, once you get past that crusty exterior Mike's a real romantic."

"Ah go on!" she said and laughed.

It had been close to two years since his wife had passed away. Regan was clearly out of practice and suddenly felt awkward not knowing what to say.

"Well, I better find out what mischief Liam's got himself into," she said.

"Will we be seeing you at the Grape? I mean, I'm sure Liam will be wantin to go back to soccer," she blushed.

"Well, I would not want to disappoint Liam," Regan said.

FIVE

The entire Regan clan gathered for lunch at the family home in Chestnut Hill on the third Sunday of the month without exception. The fact that they had all been together just two nights before for the fundraiser at the Union League did not disrupt the schedule.

Regan noticed a Mercedes convertible with the vanity license Plate "DIVA" in the driveway. When he entered the backyard he was surprised to see Courtney Wells helping his sisters put the food out on the serving table. She looked up as he approached.

"Court, this is a pleasant surprise," he said.

"Jack, I left you several messages on your voice mail. I wanted to ask you if it was alright with you if I joined your family. I mean, your mother told me you wouldn't mind, but I…"

"Court, you know you're always welcome here," he said as they embraced. She looked even more beautiful and just as elegant in a sundress and sandals as in the designer gown she had worn at the fundraiser on Friday evening. Her hair was in a pony tail and there was not a trace of make-up on her face.

"What?" she asked in response to his stare.

"You look just like you did when we were in college."

She blushed and said, "I don't know about that. I can tell you it takes a lot longer for me to create that illusion, but thanks anyway."

He continued to stare at her and asked, "Why was it that we broke up?"

She sighed and responded, "Well, I guess it was because when I went away to college I went insane. And there was also the fact that you fell in love with someone else."

"Oh yeah, I seem to recall something like that."

"There you are," his mother said. "Courtney, you know this young man is never on time. I've a mind to buy him a new watch!"

"Mother," he said and gave her a look as they hugged.

"Is Dad in the den?"

"You two aren't going to be talking shop are you?"

"I promise it will only take a couple minutes."

"Well, keep it short; after all you have company today."

His father was sitting behind the desk in his study talking on the phone. Jack knocked on the door jamb John Hogan Regan looked up, smiled and waved him in. Jack took one of the leather chairs in front of his father's desk and waited for his father to finish the call.

"Dad, I assume Izzy filled you in on the Larson homicide. Isadore Ichowitz and Regan's father knew each other since their days at the Police Academy. Both men had joined the force following their discharge from the service. Both had served multiple tours in Viet Nam. Their friendship had endured through the years, as their careers followed different paths.

Regan was a third generation police officer, destined for command rank from the day he took the oath. Ichowitz got on the force by virtue of his Veteran's preference, which increased his score on the application test, which was already the highest score even without the additional points, to number one on the appointment list. Regan was number two.

"Yes, he told me that Dorothy Wiggins had been at the crime scene around the time of the murder. He wants to question her as part of the investigation. Izzy told me you identified the victim and that she was supposed to be your principal witness before the grand jury. I suppose you want to be involved in the murder investigation."

Jack nodded his head.

"Alright, I'll have a chat with the DA."

"John." The matriarch of the family stood at the door. "This is family time. The two of you can do your business tomorrow. Now let the boy spend some time with his guest."

Regan smiled and said, "Jack, be careful. Your mother has decided it's time for you to start dating."

"Dad, I think she's already decided who I *should* be dating," he said.

"Well, you know your mother. Once she makes up her mind about something it's a lot easier if you just go with the flow. Besides, looks to me like your mother's got excellent taste. Courtney is a real beauty!"

Jack blushed.

"Uncle Jack, come see, we're all in the newspaper!" Missey, the youngest of his nieces and nephews, grabbed his hand and led him to the picnic table where the kids had spread out the Society Page of the *Sunday Inquirer*. Pictures from the Children's Hospital fundraiser took up the entire section. He sat down next to his niece and looked at the photographs. Most of the pictures were of Courtney and him. He felt her hand on his shoulder as she stood behind him looking at the newspaper.

"The two of you make such a beautiful couple!" his mother said. They both turned back at her and rolled their eyes.

"Too much?" she asked and they all laughed.

They sat under the Oak tree and watched Regan's nephews and nieces and their fathers play soccer, the dads against the kids. The kids were beating their fathers handily as his sisters and parents cheered them on. As he watched he thought of Liam O'Malley and felt guilty.

"What were you thinking just then?" Courtney asked him.

He looked at her. She was beautiful. He shook his head and said. "Yesterday I met a nine-year-old boy from Ireland and took him to the Manayunk soccer league at the park across the street from my house."

"And where did you make the acquaintance of a young boy from Ireland?"

"He's Mike O'Malley's great nephew. You remember Mike, he owns the corner pub at Grape and Main Street. Mike's niece and her son have emigrated. His niece is going to help Mike run the Grape."

"Oh," she said and gave him a stare.

"What?"

"Is Mike's niece married?"

He shook his head.

"Is she pretty?"

He nodded.

"Oh," she gave him another look.

"What?"

"Nothing."

But Regan knew that wasn't true. He couldn't believe he wasn't even dating either of these women and he was already in trouble.

D orothy Wiggins stared at her reflection in the mirror. She had long ago faced the reality that she was an unattractive woman. Her hooked nose, beady eyes and acne-scarred face somehow made her look perpetually angry. Her personality matched the image she projected to a tee. She found it more than frustrating that ugly men who acquired great wealth and power could overcome their physical shortcomings and attract beautiful young women. She had amassed a fortune and through the force of her personality and wit reached the zenith of power in her profession, and yet she found no comfort in any of her achievements. She was lonely and bitter.

The Megan Larsons of the world, the girls with perfect features and bodies to match, had it all. That bitch took her for a ride, gaining access to the rich and powerful leaders of Philadelphia as Wiggins' associate. Once she had established a presence among the power brokers, Larson dumped her. Such an act of betrayal would never be forgotten. The injustice of it all left Wiggins with a hatred that burned in her core. And yet when she confronted the tramp, Wiggins literally threw herself at her feet, begging Megan to come back, all to no avail.

"You fool!" she hissed at her reflection. "Will you never learn?"

SIX

———◦———

"Detective Ichowitz, there's a young man here who's asking for you." The officer guarding the crime scene pointed to the Comcast truck stopped at the entrance to the Pickle Works.

Ichowitz looked over and saw a young man wearing a shirt with the Comcast logo standing next to the truck. He waved the young man into the parking lot.

"You asked to see me?"

"Yes sir. I'm Ben Gold, I work for Comcast. I was at the Nooris unit last Friday evening. I saw Megan Larson there," he spoke quickly as if he was trying to unburden himself of a heavy guilt. "I was out of town yesterday and just found out what happened. I told my supervisor I saw Megan here last Friday, and she contacted the Fourth District. They told me I could find you here."

"OK, slow down Mr. Gold," Ichowitz said, trying to calm the young man. "Do you remember what time you saw Ms. Larson?"

"Yes sir, I got to the condo around six o'clock. I was dispatched there for a trouble call. The Nooris are on the VIP list, so I had to make sure I got there on time, or else they would complain. I had been there a number of times before. The Nooris always find something to complain about. I entered all the information in my log."

"OK. What happened when you got there?"

"Well, Megan, I mean, Ms. Larson, answered the door."

"Did you know Ms. Larson?"

He nodded his head. "Yes, Megan and I were classmates at Radnor High. We used to hang out together back then."

"OK. So what happened?"

"She told me that Avi let her crash at his brother's condo."

"Avi Nooris?"

"Uh-huh."

"Do you know Avi?"

He nodded, "Yes sir. He was also one of our classmates at Radnor."

"But I thought he's an Israeli?"

"Yeah, but his father was the Israeli Consulate. Avi's family lived in Radnor back then."

"Mr. Gold, could you accompany me to the Fourth District so that I can take your statement?"

"Sure, if that will help. Detective, Megan was fine when I left the Nooris condo on Friday. I'm so sorry about what happened. I mean, I've never known anyone who was the victim of such a horrible crime."

"I understand. And we really appreciate your help. Officer, will you escort Mr. Gold to the District? He's going to give us a statement to help our investigation. Please do not put him in one of the interrogation rooms. I'm using the Inspector's office. Let Mr. Gold wait for me there, OK?"

By the time Ichowitz had completed his questioning of the Comcast technician and finished checking out his story, he had concluded that Gold was legit. The Comcast tech and the victim and Avi Nooris had been classmates at Radnor High School as he claimed. Gold had logged his time at the condo and recorded all of his activities as required. According to his manager, they dispatched Gold to handle the Nooris' calls, because the Nooris were big time complainers and the young man was one of Comcast's top performers.

Gold left the Nooris condo at 6:45 PM. There was nothing amiss when he left. He told Ichowitz that the victim told him she and Avi Nooris were only friends. It was apparent to Ichowitz that Gold and Avi Nooris were not friends. However, the young man did not see Nooris at the crime scene that night. He had no reason to suspect that Nooris had anything to do with the homicide. As far as he knew there was no one else at the condo the entire time he was there that evening.

The crime scene techs had wrapped up their work at the condo and all of the physical evidence had been tagged and bagged. The Medical Examiner would conduct the autopsy on Monday morning. Ichowitz would review the security video again to see if he had missed anything the first ten times he had watched it. They were still trying to identify some of the vehicles that had accessed the parking lot. He realized that the first few hours of a homicide investigation were critically important. Even though the timing of the Comcast technician's visit to the condo had eliminated Dorothy Wiggins as a suspect, Ichowitz wanted to make sure he had all his facts straight before he questioned her. Wiggins may have seen something during her time at the condo that could be valuable to the investigation.

He was rereading his notes of the Gold statement when the phone rang. He saw from the caller ID that it was Regan.

"Jack, to what do I owe the honor of this call on a Sunday evening?"

"Izz, did my father call you?"

"Yes, I heard from the Commissioner."

"Then you know he's going to call my boss and have me assigned to your investigation. I'm sorry. I should have asked you before I spoke with him. But, with Megan Larson's murder my grand jury investigation against Wiggins looks like it's headed to the shitter."

"Fuggetaboudit," Ichowitz replied. "Besides, I can use all the help I can get." Ichowitz filled him in on the Comcast tech's evidence.

"Looks like we can't pin the murder on Wiggins," Ichowitz said. "As always, when something looks too good to be true, well you know."

"Izz, I hear you, but Wiggins going to the Nooris condo, it just doesn't feel right. I mean, Larson was going to throw Wiggins under a very big bus. Even though that wasn't public knowledge, Wiggins knew about the Grand Jury investigation. She had to assume that someone on the inside of her organization was cooperating."

"Let's sleep on it and we can deal with it in the morning. Mrs. Ichowitz is giving me that look. I think she may be getting amorous."

Regan could hear Izzy's wife say, "Dream on, lover boy, and tell Jack he seriously needs to get a life."

"Tell Aunt Ida I love her too," Regan said and hung up.

Regan turned up the sound on his system. John Coltrane's "My Favorite Things" was playing. It reminded him of happier times. Susan loved Coltrane. Regan had introduced her to jazz, bringing her along slowly from the basics like Chet Baker, Stan Getz, and Louis Armstrong and Ella Fitzgerald renditions of old Cole Porter and Gershwin standards to the avant garde of late Coltrane and everything in between.

He stared at her picture on the bookshelf and said out loud, "Susan, I miss you." She had died two years ago, less than six months after her diagnosis of pancreatic cancer. Susan had been a Fellow at the Hospital of the University of Pennsylvania. She knew as soon as the diagnosis had been confirmed that it was a death sentence. Despite her efforts to prepare him for the inevitable, Regan was shocked by the speed with which the illness overcame her.

SEVEN

———◆———

"**C**hief, you have nothing to worry about," she said.

"Nothing to worry about; my sources tell me there's going to be a series in the *Inquirer* about your fees on the Family Court House deal. The reporters are going to imply that you're kicking back to me."

"Chief, you know that's bullshit. I haven't given you a penny of my fees. Listen to me, I know the publisher. He's scared shitless of me. He knows I'll sue his ass if he prints a story like that. Just stay calm. I'm sure this is being blown all out of proportion. Let me make some inquiries of my own and I'll get back to you."

Robert S. Fogerty, Chief Justice of the Pennsylvania Supreme Court, was far from reassured by the phone call. He knew from the start that it had been a bad idea to retain Dorothy Wiggins as Special Counsel for the Philadelphia Family Court House project. Because of the favorable press coverage it would garner he agreed to step in to clean up the mess the Philadelphia Court Administration had created after it had wasted nearly a decade and several million dollars in their inept efforts to build a facility to house the Family and Juvenile Court division. Now he sorely regretted following his advisor's advice.

His political consultants had assured him this was an issue that would solidify his successful retention in the upcoming election. They told him the process had been so badly botched by the Governor and the local politicians that he had nothing to lose and everything to gain. By retaining Wiggins, Fogerty would also get the support of the union leaders whose memberships would benefit from the multi-million dollar construction project. Wiggins boasted that she could make sure all of them would fall in line. She represented the major construction unions, the Carpenters, Electricians and Laborers. She also represented the municipal employee unions whose membership would benefit once the new court house was built.

Fogerty went along with his advisors' recommendations even though he despised the woman. She had done everything in her power to oppose his election to the Supreme Court ten years before. He understood that in politics you needed to be pragmatic and have a short memory; however, he was just not made that way. He had not taken any money from her. Not even legitimate campaign contributions. Not that the stingy bitch ever offered to contribute. Perhaps she was right. If the *Inquirer* story even suggested that he had received a kickback from Wiggins, it would open itself to a libel suit that could cost the paper millions. Furthermore, any retraction of the allegation would make him appear to be a victim of a biased press and assure his retention.

Fogerty took a long pull on the two inches of Jack Daniels he had poured himself from the bottle he kept in the bottom drawer of his desk and stared at the architect's drawing of the proposed court house. Wiggins told him the unions would insist on naming the building in his honor. He was only momentarily concerned about the sweet deal he had made on the shore house in Avalon. After all, he had paid for it with his personal funds. Why wasn't he entitled to use his connections to take advantage of someone's short sale? He also paid for the renovations with his own funds. The fact that friends had fixed him up with a contractor who needed the work and gave him a good, very good, price was perfectly legal. No one involved had any cases pending before the court. No one could claim with any validity that their actions had garnered them any influence.

Regan and Ichowitz decided the best way to handle Wiggins was to appear at her office unannounced at the end of the day. According to what Megan Larson had told Regan, Wiggins always returned to her office around 5:30 to see who was still working. God help the associate who went home at a normal quitting time to be with their spouse and children. Wiggins had no life, so why the hell should anyone who worked for her believe they were entitled to one?

That morning, they attended Megan Larson's autopsy. Ichowitz was a veteran observer; Regan was not. As they gowned up for the procedure Ichowitz assured his young colleague that there was nothing to be overly concerned about.

He handed Regan a stick of wintergreen gum. "Chew this while you're watching. It will help you overcome the nausea."

Carlos Delgado, MD, the Chief Medical Examiner and one of his assistants were kibitzing when they arrived. "Dr. Locke, Isadore Ichowitz the famous homicide detective, and Assistant District Attorney John Regan will be witnessing the autopsy. We better be on our toes. We wouldn't want the Commissioner or the DA to get a negative report."

"Mr. Regan, I seem to recall the last time you were here there was an unfortunate incident where you didn't quite make it out of the theater before you lost your breakfast. I trust you ate a light breakfast this morning."

"Dr. Delgado, I haven't eaten a morsel in two days in anticipation of this morning's ordeal," Regan replied.

"Very well then, let's proceed."

Things went well for about thirty seconds until the ME used the retractors to remove the vital organs and made a horrible discovery.

"What have we here?" Delgado said reaching both of his hands into the cavity below her sternum.

"Gentlemen, it appears we have a double homicide on our hands," he said as he pulled a fully formed fetus from Larson's uterus. Regan ran out of the room in search of a place to throw up.

An hour later Ichowitz found him in the locker room, "You all right?" Regan nodded.

"Well, you don't look so good. I think we need to get you out of here and get some liquids in you. Ginger ale should do the trick. Listen, nothing to be ashamed of, the autopsy room isn't for everyone. Don't worry about Delgado and Locke. They promised me they wouldn't put your abrupt departure out on Facebook or Twitter, or whatever the hell they use to make fun of people today. Besides, I thought we should keep this development to ourselves for the time being."

"How many months pregnant was she?" Regan asked.

"Delgado figures since the fetus was fully formed she was well into her second trimester. They'll conduct a separate autopsy on the fetus later today. Hey, you're not going to be sick again are you?"

After Regan threw up again Ichowitz asked, "I thought you said you hadn't eaten anything for a couple days?"

Regan nodded.

"Well next time, don't eat for at least a week."

The receptionist smiled at Regan as he and Ichowitz entered the suite. The smile vanished the moment Ichowitz flashed his shield and said, "Miss, please tell Ms. Wiggins Detective Ichowitz and Assistant District Attorney Regan are here to see her," he said.

"Do you have an appointment to see Ms. Wiggins?"

"No, but let her know if she refuses to meet with us now, we can make arrangements to see her at the Police Administration Building later this evening."

"She's not going to like this," the receptionist said with a sigh.

"We know," Ichowitz agreed.

They could hear Wiggins shouting at the receptionist through her headset. The young woman turned beet red. "Yes Ma'am."

She stood up and said, "Gentlemen, if you'll follow me, Ms. Wiggins will join you in our conference room in a few minutes."

Wiggins' law offices were in the Widener Building, across Penn Square from City Hall and a short walk to the Criminal Court House. Recently the Widner Building had undergone extensive renovations in order to reclaim Class A status. The exterior of the building had been sandblasted to restore its original appearance.

When it was built in 1932, at 472 feet, it was the city's tallest office tower. In keeping with the city's unwritten zoning policy, however, it was seventy-six feet shorter than City Hall. It was the headquarters of the Philadelphia National Bank, and for decades the PNB sign at the top of the building could be seen for miles from any direction. As the years passed the bank had been acquired and reacquired by bigger banks and now the Widener Building and City Hall were dwarfed by taller buildings to the west. But if you tried, from certain angles you could still see the PNB sign. And even though the Widener was no longer the tallest office building in the city, none of the new skyscrapers could compete with the fact that the Widener Building housed the largest ringing bell in the world.

Wiggins' offices were on the top floor of the Widener Building and commanded an intimate view of the backside of the statue of William Penn, the founder of the City of Brotherly Love, who stood atop City Hall. Regan considered it appropriate that Penn's derrier was turned in Dorothy Wiggins' direction.

"Detective Ichowitz and Mr. Regan, to what do I owe the honor of this visit?" Wiggins said as she entered the conference room.

"Ms. Wiggins, we're conducting an investigation of the murder of your former associate, Megan Larson. We'd like to ask you a few questions, if that's all right?" Ichowitz said as he pulled a small notebook from his jacket pocket.

"Am I a suspect?" she asked, glaring at them.

"No," Ichowitz replied staring back at her.

"Am I a person of interest?"

Ichowitz sighed. "No, Ms. Wiggins."

"So then, you're not going to Mirandize me?"

"No. That is unless you insist," Ichowitz replied. "Ms. Wiggins, can we cut to the chase here and stop the charade?"

She nodded.

"We know you were at the Nooris condo last Friday evening between 5:30 and 6 PM. Can you tell us why you were there and what happened?"

"I went there to speak with Megan."

"What did you and Megan discuss?" Ichowitz asked.

"Megan had decided to resign from the firm. I went there to try to convince her to stay."

Ichowitz wrote down her response and looked up at her. "So the senior partner drives out from Center City to Manayunk on a Friday evening to convince a second year associate to remain with the firm, did I get that right?"

"Yes detective, despite my reputation, and I am very aware of what people say about me behind my back, I really do care about my staff. We spent a great deal of time training Ms. Larson. She was a talented attorney. I- we - had great plans for her. Her death was tragic."

Wiggins wiped a tear from her cheek.

For the next forty-five minutes Ichowitz questioned Wiggins about the thirty minutes she had spent at the Nooris condo with Larson.

"Where did you go when you left the condo?" Ichowitz was wrapping up his questions.

"Back to my office to catch up on my correspondence and emails, and then I went home."

"How long were you at your office?"

Wiggins flashed him a dark look, "Detective, I don't know, a couple of hours. Are we about done here?"

"Ms. Wiggins, thank you for your time. If you remember anything else about your meeting with Ms. Larson, or anything you think may help our investigation that we may not have covered, here's my card. You can call me at anytime, day or night."

As planned Ichowitz turned to Regan and said, "Jack, do you have any questions of Ms. Wiggins?"

Regan turned to her and said, "Ms. Wiggins, you were aware that Ms. Larson was scheduled to appear before the grand jury as a witness for the Commonwealth in connection with an investigation that involved your firm and certain of your clients, weren't you?"

"I was waiting for one of you to ask me about that," she said, all the time glaring at Regan.

Regan stared back at her and said, "Glad we didn't disappoint you. Will you answer the question?"

"Yes, I was aware that Megan was scheduled to testify at the Grand Jury."

"Then why did you want her to remain with your firm?"

"Young man, I wasn't the least bit concerned about her testimony or your investigation. Sometimes young associates like Megan, as bright as she was, don't fully understand what they have witnessed. Sometimes beautiful young women like Megan are persuaded by handsome young men, like you, and they just want to impress them and agree with what they suggest. I don't know what Megan told you, or what she believed, in any event, her testimony and your investigation meant nothing to me. It was a waste of time and money. Are we finished now?"

"For now," Regan said, and he and Ichowitz got up to leave.

"Next time, if there is a next time, I expect you will give me the courtesy of call before you barge into my office without an appointment," she said.

Ichowitz turned and said, "Ms. Wiggins, this is a murder investigation. If we need to talk with you again we'll be back, with as much notice, if any, as we can provide."

As they left the Widener Building Ichowitz turned to Regan and said, "Quite a performance don't you think?"

Regan shook his head. "You sure the Comcast tech was telling you the *emess*?"

"I am." Ichowitz replied.

"Well, I'm not saying Wiggins was the doer, but, I'm not buying that line of crap she was laying down up there. We had a solid case against her with Megan Larson's testimony, and there was no way Megan was going to stay with the Dragon Lady either. What's next?"

Ichowitz looked at his watch. "It's seven o'clock. I'm hungry. Let's grab some dinner and see if we can find Avi Nooris. I think it's time we had a chat."

"Good idea, I'm feeling weak after my autopsy upheaval. Since Avi lives in Manayunk, let's stop at the Grape and get dinner there."

"Jack, I know O'Malley's your pal and all, but the food there stinks."

"Izz, the Grape's got a new chef. I think you'll be pleasantly surprised."

"Now the new chef wouldn't happen to be the soccer mom from Ireland?"

"Yes Kate O'Malley is Liam's mother."

"In that case, I think the Grape's a great idea," the big detective said and smiled at Regan.

The bar at the Grape Tavern was packed when Regan and Ichowitz arrived. Regan waved to Mike O'Malley. "Mike, have you extended the Happy Hour?" he asked.

O'Malley shook his head. "Would ya look at this crowd, bunch of yuppies! They chased the regulars away," he said with a sneer. "Do ya see that young woman over there?" he pointed to an attractive woman dressed in the new style, leotards under a very short and tight mini skirt. She had blue hair all spiked up, a rose tattoo on her neck, and face- piercings on her eye brows and nose.

"She ordered a cosmo. I told her we don't serve those kinda drinks here. She says, 'Pops, let me show you how to mix a cosmo.' She goes behind the bar and mixes up some foul-smelling pinkish drink. Next thing I know all the women at the bar are askin for cosmos."

"So what did you do?"

"I'm not sure, but I think I hired a new bartender, Melody Schwartz, a girl with blue hair and a tattoo for Christ sake! I'm sure the girl's poor mother must be havin a fit! But after all, she knows how to mix a drink, and at twelve bucks a pop it seemed like a good move. Only thing is I've run out of one of the fancy liquors that she uses for these concoctions. So we're sellin them as cosmo-lites and only charging nine bucks," he said and laughed.

"Mike, do you have a table for Izzy and me?"

"Come this way. We can let the yuppies wait."

When they were seated Izzy said, "This ain't your uncle Joe's Grape."

Regan nodded. His uncle Joe, his father's older brother, had been on the force for thirty-five years. Regan moved in with his uncle when he went to law school at Penn. When Uncle Joe was diagnosed with Alzheimer disease, Regan became his principal caregiver. Joe loved the Grape and Regan brought him there as often as possible. When Joe passed away, he left the house on Cotton Street and an abiding affection for the Grape, to his nephew.

As was his custom Ichowitz always took the seat with his back to the wall. After all he was the one with the gun, so he liked to see what was coming his way, just in case. Ichowitz smiled as a young woman emerged from the kitchen and approached them. Jack turned and saw Kate O'Malley.

"I guess the word got out that the Grape has a new chef. Kate O'Malley, meet Izzy Ichowitz," Regan said.

She reached out and shook the detective's hand, "Pleased to meet ya," she said.

"I met your son the other day. He's quite a soccer player. And I can see where he got his good looks," Ichowitz said.

She blushed.

"Besides, my young friend here hasn't stopped talking about your fish and chips. I think you made quite an impression on him."

Now Regan was blushing.

"Well, I'm glad about that. It's a shame we're all out of the fish and chips, but I think you might fancy the Shepherd's Pie. I'm told it goes down well with a pint of Harp," she said.

"We'll have to pass on the Harp for now. Izzy, Detective Sergeant Isadore Ichowitz, is still on duty, and he and I have another interview to conduct this evening."

"Well, if it's not too late, maybe you can stop by for a nightcap. Anyway, let me get the two of you some dinner."

When she went back to the kitchen, Ichowitz said, "That is one beautiful soccer mom. And you say she can cook too!" He looked past Regan at the entrance to the pub and said, "Jack, I think that Courtney Wells and some of her friends just came in. Didn't I see the two of you all over the *Inquirer's* society page this weekend?"

"Jack! Uncle Izzy!" Courtney said and waved at them. She approached their table and said, "The girls and I heard the Grape has a new chef, we figured we'd find out what the buzz was all about."

She hugged Jack and kissed his cheek and then embraced Ichowitz and said, "I haven't seen you in forever. You're still the most handsome Detective in the Philadelphia Homicide Division!"

"I bet you say that to all the Homicide Detectives," Ichowitz replied.

At that moment Kate O'Malley approached the table with a steaming plate of Shepherd's Pie in each hand.

Regan said, "Courtney Wells, meet Kate O'Malley, the Grape's new chef, the one everyone is buzzing about."

Kate put the plates down on the table, wiped her hand on the towel at her waist and extended her hand to Courtney. Courtney gave her a perfunctory shake and said, "Nice to meet you," and turned her back to Kate. "Jack, Izzy, I'll let you two enjoy your dinner, before it gets cold." She hugged Ichowitz again, and then she turned to Regan and said, "Jack, your mother asked me to drive you to the Broad Street Run this Sunday. I'll pick you up at 6AM. Is that OK?"

"Sure, I guess. Court, it's really not necessary. I mean it's awfully early, I can drive over myself."

"No, it's not a problem. Besides, I'll get to see you in those sexy running shorts," she said and then she embraced him and kissed him on the lips.

"The Shepherd's Pie looks delicious Ms. O'Malley," she said as she walked away.

Kate's face turned scarlet and she glared at Wells' back and said, "Well, I have to get back to the kitchen, gentlemen. I hope you enjoy your dinners," and then she abruptly turned and walked away.

Ichowitz looked at Regan and said, "*Oy-vey boychik*, you got *truris*, very serious *truris*."

Regan shrugged his shoulders, opened his palms and asked, "What was that all about?"

"Courtney thinks something is going on between you and Ms. O'Malley, and Ms. O'Malley thinks something is going on between you and Courtney, and apparently neither thinks very much of the other."

"But Izz, there really isn't anything going on. I mean, I don't think there is, at least not yet. I think… I don't know what I think."

"Doesn't matter what you think," Ichowitz said as he took a forkfull of the Shepherd's Pie.

He smiled and said, "This is fantastic. Eat up before it gets cold. Don't worry about the girls. You'll figure it out."

Regan sat there and stared at his food; he had suddenly lost his appetite.

EIGHT

They found Avi Nooris at Studs, the restaurant and bar that he and his brother Ari, actually his half-brother, owned at the other end of Main Street. Their father had divorced Ari's mother and married a trophy wife, Avi's mother. Avi was standing at the bar with his arm draped around the shoulders of a young woman, who looked to Regan to be underage. Avi Nooris was an imposing physical specimen, six foot five, two hundred twenty pounds of sculpted muscle. He was handsome, swarthy, with Semitic features.

Ichowitz flashed his shield and said, "Young woman, we need a word with Mr. Nooris, and you look too young to be in a place at which alcoholic beverages are being served. Now, since I didn't actually see you drinking anything, why don't you just go on home, and I won't ask to see your ID. Is that all right with you?"

She nodded, grabbed her purse and left the bar without saying a word.

"Mr. Nooris, that young woman didn't look a day over sixteen. Not only could you lose your license for serving minors, but the laws in this Commonwealth are rather clear with respect to statutory rape."

"Officer, the young woman is my niece. I resent the implication. You frightened her. Now I'll have to call her mother," Nooris said with a smile. He spoke with a characteristically Israeli accent, not quite perfecting the 'R.'

"Please accept my apology. If you like, I'll call the girl's mother myself. Why don't you give me her name and phone number?" Ichowitz replied.

Nooris stopped smiling and said, "No, that won't be necessary."

"Mr. Nooris, I'm Assistant District Attorney Regan and this is Detective Ichowitz. We're investigating the murder of Megan Larson. We'd like to ask you a few questions, if that's all right. Do you have an office or someplace private where we can talk?"

Nooris led them to a small office behind the bar. The metal desk and three uncomfortable folding chairs were squeezed in the center of the room that was filled from floor to ceiling on three sides with boxes of liquor. The room had no ventilation and Regan felt slightly queasy from the sweet smell of Nooris' after shave.

Ichowitz, noticing that his friend looked pale, said, "Mr. Nooris, we know that you and Ms. Larson had been friends since you were students at Radnor High School. Can you tell us how Ms. Larson came to be staying at your brother's condo?"

"She was also Ari's friend. She needed a place to stay for a couple of weeks and Ari said she could use his condo."

"So it was your brother and not you who gave her permission to stay there?"

"My brother, me, what's the difference?" he said with a shrug of his shoulders.

"You said she was a friend of your brother Ari. Ari is several years older than you, ten years older, is that right?"

Nooris nodded.

How did he come to know Ms. Larson?" Ichowitz asked.

Nooris shrugged his shoulders again and said, "I don't know, I guess you'll have to ask him yourself."

"But your brother is in Israel."

"No he's not. He's here he came back a few days ago."

Ichowitz looked over at Regan and said, "Mr. Nooris, if your brother had returned from Israel, was he also staying at the condo on Friday night?"

"I don't know. I don't think so. I mean, he was probably at his house in Gladwyne with his wife and children. I don't think Ari's wife would like him staying at the condo with Megan," he said and smiled.

"Did you go to the condo Friday night?"

"Why would I go there?"

"Is your answer 'no?'"

He nodded.

"When did you find out about Ms. Larson's homicide?"

"The security company called me around midnight. One of their patrol cars responded to an alarm. They found the back door to the unit open and found her body."

"The security company called and told you a body had been found at your brother's condo where your friend Megan Larson was staying, and you didn't go to the condo?"

He nodded and asked, "Why would I go there?"

"Weren't you upset? After all, it was your brother's place and your friend was the victim."

"In Israel people are killed all the time," he said and stared at Ichowitz as if he were talking to a child.

"Did you call your brother to let him know what had happened?" Ichowitz asked.

"Why would I do that? What could Ari have done?"

"Mr. Nooris, can you tell us where you were on Friday night between 7 PM and midnight?"

Nooris raised his eyebrows and stared at Ichowitz, "Should I get an attorney?"

"Why do you think you need an attorney?" Ichowitz replied.

Nooris shrugged and said, "I was here at the bar until around nine, and then I went to Sweat, the gym on Main Street."

"How long were you there?"

"Until around eleven, then I went home."

"That's a pretty long work out,"

Nooris smiled and flexed his biceps in reply.

When they left the bar, Regan said, "What a cold man."

"You haven't been around many Israelis have you?" Ichowitz asked.

Regan shook his head.

"They're different from us. It must come from growing up surrounded by millions of people who want to kill them."

"I get that, but Avi grew up in Radnor."

Ichowitz told Regan he would stop by the gym and check out Nooris' alibi. Regan drove past the Grape on his way home and decided to stop in and see if Kate's offer for a nightcap was still good.

He found O'Malley behind the bar. There were still a few tables with late diners. The dinner rush had passed, and some of the regulars had returned.

"What happened to your bartender Melody?" he asked O'Malley as he took a stool at the end of the bar.

"I told her to go home, since the toffs were all gone for the night. What did you do to Kate?"

Regan gave him a puzzled look and asked, "What do you mean?"

"She's been in a dark mood ever since she served you and Izzy. Did ya forget to leave her a tip?"

"Mike, is she still here?"

He nodded his head in the direction of the kitchen. Regan stood up and walked towards the kitchen, and O'Malley whispered, "Be careful, she has sharp knives."

He pushed open the door and stood there and watched her as she cleaned the range. "O'Malley, I sent Gloria home." She turned and said, "Oh it's you." She turned back to the stove.

"Kate, did I do something wrong?"

She turned and stared at him and wiped the lock of hair from her forehead with the back of her hand contemplating her response. "No no, it's nothing you did."

"Can we have that nightcap then? There's something I wanted to discuss with you," he said.

She nodded, "I'll be with you in a few minutes. I'd like to put myself together first, if ya don't mind."

"OK, but you look put together fine to me," he said.

She waved at him and said, "Oh, I do, do I?" and flashed him a smile. "Go wait at the bar and O'Malley will draw you a draft."

"Ay see you're still in won piece," O'Malley said as Regan resumed his stool. The bar was now empty and the last of the diners were settling up.

"The chef said you'd draw me a pint of Harp" Regan said.

"She did, did she?" O'Malley turned with a full pint glass in hand and placed it in front of Regan. He pulled a bottle of Tullamore Dew from under the bar and poured a generous shot in a tumbler and placed it next to him. "Kate likes her whiskey neat."

"Thanks, Uncle Mike," she said as she walked out of the kitchen.

"I'll leave the two of you to close up if ya don't mind," he said as he walked to the stairs that led up to the living quarters.

She took the stool next to him raised her glass and said, "*Slainte*."

He repeated the toast as their glasses touched.

They sat silently after their toast, not looking at one another. She said, "You had something you wanted to tell me."

He took another sip of beer and said without making eye contact, "It's been a long time since I sat at a bar with a woman. I'm a little out of my comfort zone."

"Looked to me like you were doing OK earlier this evening when that Ms. Wells kissed you," she said looking at his reflection in the mirror behind the bar.

He looked up at her reflection and said, "Courtney and I are old friends, but believe me I was not expecting that kiss."

"Well, with those pictures in the newspaper and all, looks to me like the two of you are more than old friends."

"Yes, I know how it looks, but there's really nothing more going on. Before last weekend, I hadn't seen Courtney since my wife's funeral, and that's nearly two years ago. I like Courtney, but we are not a couple. Kate, I haven't been out on a date since Susan passed away."

"OK, but seems to me that Ms. Wells thinks there is more to your relationship than really nothing."

He sighed and said, "You're right I guess."

She turned and faced him and asked, "What is it you want from me?"

He stared at her, surprised at her question and said, "To be perfectly honest with you, I'm not sure. I guess I'm still not ready to start dating, but I was going to ask you and Liam to come to the race this Sunday. You know, meet me at the finish line, but I guess that would be awkward now that my mother arranged for Courtney to drive me to the race."

"Awkward, yes it would be that at the very least."

"Well, how about Saturday afternoon, after Liam's soccer game? We could do something together."

"We as in you, me and Liam?" she asked.

"Sure, if you like, or we as in you and me," he said looking at her reflection in the mirror.

She looked at his reflection in the mirror and then turned towards him and asked, "Just as friends?"

He nodded.

"I think that would be nice, seein as neither Liam nor I have any friends in this town."

NINE

"**D**id you see the lead story on the first page of the *Inquirer*?" Ichowitz asked Regan as he entered Regan's office the next morning.

"Uh-huh," Regan replied with a nod.

The article reported that Dorothy Wiggins, "a prominent Philadelphia attorney," had received over $10 million in fees as the attorney for the Supreme Court of Pennsylvania, in the real estate deal for the construction of the Philadelphia Division Family Court House at the same time that she was partners with the real estate developer on the project. If the allegation was true, representing both the buyer and the seller in the same transaction is a clear conflict of interest, in violation of both legal canons of ethics, and possibly criminal laws.

According to the newspaper, Wiggins claimed that there had been no breach of ethics or any criminal violation, because her relationship as counsel to the Court had ended before her partnership with the real estate developer began. She insisted, moreover, that she had disclosed all of the pertinent facts to all of the principals involved, including Chief Justice Robert Fogerty. Justice Fogerty was unavailable for comment, according to a spokesman for the Court.

"Izz, the court house project was only one of the allegations the Grand Jury was looking into," Regan said as he put down the newspaper.

"Jack, looks like Wiggins threw Fogerty under the bus. If he knew she was working both ends of the deal and did nothing about it, he's in deep doo-doo. If he didn't know about it he's gonna come off as the biggest schlemiel this town has ever known."

Regan nodded his agreement. "I'm sure Fogerty is trying to figure out how to respond. Did you check out Nooris' alibi?"

Ichowitz smiled and said, "It appears that there is a slight problem with Mr. Nooris' story. He did in fact go to the gym to work out at 9 PM on Friday as he claimed. He also left the gym at 10:57 PM."

"So his story checked out," Regan said.

"Not quite."

Regan looked at him and waited.

"Jack, you know where Nooris' gym, Sweat, is located, don't you?"

"It's on Main Street about a half mile south of where I live."

"And where is it in relation to the Nooris condo?"

"I guess it's a couple of blocks."

"It seems that for around forty minutes or so, Mr. Nooris was out for a jog along the Manayunk Canal. According to the staff at the gym, their clients often combine aerobics with the weight training, either using the equipment in the gym, or jogging on the canal path. No one could remember seeing Nooris after 9:45, so they assumed he went out to the canal, the same canal that goes past the back of the Old Pickle Works."

"I suppose a follow-up with Mr. Nooris would be in order," Regan observed.

"I was thinking that, but I want to interview his brother Ari first," Ichowitz replied. "I thought we could see him this morning."

"Izz, I can't make it this morning. I have a sentencing hearing on one of my other cases on the schedule. I'm sure you can handle this without me."

"No problem. By the way, did you have that nightcap with Ms. O'Malley?"

Regan could feel the heat in his face and realized he must be blushing.

"I guess it went OK," Ichowitz said and got up to leave. "Did you decide what you're going to tell Courtney?"

Regan blushed again.

"Looks to me like both you and Chief Justice Fogerty are going to need to make some comment on your respective *mishogas*; I'll fill you in on my interview with Ari Nooris this afternoon. This sentencing hearing, is it the Mathais kid?"

Regan nodded.

"Ichowitz sighed, "Tough one. Good luck."

Fogerty drummed his fingers on his desk as he stared at the newspaper.

"Chief, you all right?" his secretary asked. He looked up at her and said, "Not to worry," and gave her an insincere smile.

"Mr. Saunders is here, should I tell him you're busy?"

"No Martha, please show him in."

Mickey Saunders had been Fogerty's right hand man when Fogerty was District Attorney. After his term of office was up he became his law partner for the brief interlude before Fogerty's election to the Supreme Court. Saunders was his closest friend and confidant.

"Mickey, good of you to come," he said and gestured his visitor to take a seat.

Saunders sat down and said, "Bob looks to me like this time you really stepped on your dick."

Fogerty smiled and said, "Now tell me something I don't already know."

"Bob, did you take any money from her?"

He shook his head.

"Good. Did she give you anything in writing that she was withdrawing as counsel from the project?"

He shook his head again.

"OK. Did she give you anything in writing that said she was a partner with the real estate developer, what's his name?"

"Nooris. No nothing in writing."

"Good. Did you meet with Nooris, which Nooris was it?"

"Ari."

"Which one is he? Is he the kid with the muscles, or is he the older one who looks like Omar Sharif?"

"Ari's the older brother."

"Good, the kid's a loose cannon with a big mouth. The other one knows how to keep his mouth shut. So it's your word against hers."

"So what do I do?"

"You call a press conference and you act outraged and tell them you knew nothing about Wiggins being on both sides of the transaction, and that you are canceling the deal and demanding the return of both Wiggins' fee and any money paid to Nooris. You're retaining independent counsel to investigate the entire affair and based on the outcome of counsel's investigation you will decide if criminal proceedings are warranted. At the very least you will request that the Disciplinary Board consider if there has been a violation of the Canons of Ethics."

"But..."

"Bob, you're the fucking Chief Justice of the Supreme Court of the Commonwealth of Pennsylvania! You'll tell them that this news article was a revelation to you, and it validates your belief in an independent press. The reporters will eat that shit up with a spoon."

"What do I say if they ask me questions?"

"Bob, you can't answer any questions while this matter is under investigation, even though you would sincerely like to accommodate the press."

Fogerty stared at him."Who am I retaining as independent counsel?"

"Why, me of course; you OK with that?" Saunders asked.

"Yes."

"Good. Let's get this show on the road then."

"Thanks Mickey."

Saunders shrugged his shoulders. "Bob, one more question."

Fogerty nodded.

"Did you really pay that bitch $10 million dollars?"

Fogerty nodded again. Saunders shook his head and stood up.

"Remember, you didn't know a fucking thing about her playing on both sides of the deal until now."

When Saunders left the office, he pulled out his cell phone and hit the speed dial.

"How did it go?"

"He's even a bigger fool than when he was the DA," Saunders replied.

"Is there a paper trail?"

"Probably not, we'll talk about it later," he said and ended the call.

A s he approached Court Room 500, he saw Police Lt. Gary Mathais standing by the side of the door. Mathais nodded his head in the direction of the stairwell, signaling Regan away from the courtroom. Regan looked at his watch and nodded.

"Counselor, how's it gonna go in there?" Mathais asked.

Regan put his hand on Mathais shoulder and said, "Gary, your son is going to do some serious time. He should have copped a plea. The judge was prepared to accept our recommendation, but your son's attorney…"

"I know I'm not blaming you. It's going to kill the boy's mother."

Gary Mathais Jr., the twenty-one-year-old son of Lt. Gary Mathais, had been convicted of Vehicular Homicide and other felony charges three months ago. Gary was high on cocaine and other controlled substances when he ran a red light at Broad and Pattison Avenues and hit two female joggers, killing one and seriously injuring the other, and then he drove away from the accident. The two women were first-time visitors to Philadelphia who came to town from Milwaukee to watch their hometown club play the Phillies.

The young man had a long history of DUI arrests and convictions for other minor offenses for which he had received the equivalent of a slap on the wrist. As the son of a Philadelphia Police Department lieutenant, it was likely that he had gotten away with numerous other previous violations. The courtesies extended to him by his father's fellow officers and others had unfortunately fostered an attitude of arrogance and privilege that culminated in the tragic events that had ruined the lives of two innocent women and their families, and now the Mathais family.

Gary Senior was a respected member of the Department who never asked Regan or his boss for any consideration or favors for his son. Regan could see how the ordeal of the last eighteen months had aged the man.

Regan took his seat and waited for the judge to take the bench. He looked to his left and nodded to Vito Coratelli Jr., Mathais' counsel. Coratelli was the son of one of the best criminal defense attorneys in the city. Although they shared a name, Junior had only inherited his father's bombastic personality but none of his skills. Coratelli had convinced Mathais' mother that he could mount a defense that would allow her son to walk away from the charges with an acquittal. Over Lt. Mathais' objections, mother and son retained Coratelli.

The evidence against the young man was overwhelming. His arrogant demeanor throughout the proceedings must also have contributed to the quick jury verdict. Regan barely made it back to his office when the call came that a verdict had been reached. The inevitable "guilty on all counts" was pronounced over the sobs of both the surviving victim and the deceased victim's family - and Mrs. Mathais.

Now, three months later, Gary Mathais Jr. no longer displayed any signs of arrogance or privilege. He too had aged considerably, and Regan could see bruises on his face from a recent beating, no doubt from some inmate who probably took exception to Mathais' lineage. Mathais had been immediately taken into custody upon the jury's verdict which the court determined had been a violation of his probation for a previous conviction. Former police and their family members did not fare well in the penal system.

"All rise," the court officer signaled the judge's presence.

When it was over Mathais got the minimum sentence, twenty-five years. Regan assumed the judge, out of respect for the father, extended this minor courtesy. Unlike the previous "breaks" he had been given, however, this one would not prevent Gary Junior from suffering the consequences of his misconduct.

As he left the courtroom Coratelli said, "Jack, you should have done more to help the kid."

Regan looked at him and waved him closer and whispered in his ear, "You're the one who's responsible for this, you stupid fuck. Now, get away from me before I drop you right here."

"Detective Ichowitz to see Mr. Nooris," Ichowitz said as he held out his shield for the receptionist.

He waited as the receptionist, speaking in Hebrew, informed Nooris about his visitor. There was something about the young woman that struck Ichowitz that she wasn't just Nooris' secretary. After a brief discussion, the receptionist put down the receiver, wordlessly got up and led the detective to Nooris' office. Ari Nooris was standing by the door and smiled at the young woman, "Thank you Shona. Detective, please come in," he said and waved Ichowitz into his office. "Would you like some coffee or a cold drink?"

"No thank you."

"What can I do for you Detective...Isadore Ichowitz, that's your name isn't it?"

"That's right, have we met before?" Ichowitz asked.

"No, my brother Avi told me about your interview with him. His description of you was quite accurate. Except you are much better looking than he described," he said with a fifty-tooth smile. "I assume you want to ask me about Megan Larson."

Ichowitz nodded.

"Please, what would you like to know?"

"Mr. Nooris, your brother told me that you let Ms. Larson stay at your condo. Is that correct?"

"Yes detective, that's right."

"That was rather generous of you."

Nooris shrugged.

"How long had you known Ms. Larson?"

"Well, I remember her as one of Avi's high school friends. But most recently, she was Dorothy Wiggins' associate and we worked together on the court house project."

"Is that the project that's been reported about in the press?"

"Yes, that's the project."

"So how did you come to allow Ms. Larson to stay at your condo?"

"Well, over the course of six or eight months that we had worked on the project we became quite close, and a couple of weeks ago Megan asked me if she could use my condo while she was looking for a place to move."

"Did she tell you why she was moving?"

"Well, actually we didn't discuss it in person. I was in Jerusalem at the time and she texted me."

"Did you know where she was living before she moved into your condo?"

"Yes, she had been living with Dorothy Wiggins. They were in a relationship, and I believe Megan wanted to end it. As I said, we had become quite close."

"So did you or your brother give Ms. Larson permission to stay there?"

"Well, both of us I suppose. I mean, I texted her and Avi gave her the keys and the code to the unit."

"When did you return from Israel?"

"Last Thursday, the morning before…before the murder," Nooris said shaking his head as in disbelief. "She was such a beautiful and accomplished young woman. What a waste."

"Did you see Ms. Larson after you returned?"

"No, I got in very early Thursday morning. I never sleep on planes. With the time change and jet lag, I just stayed home with my family."

"How about Friday?"

"I was here all day and once again I returned home for Shabbat dinner with my family."

"And your secretary can confirm that you were here in your office on Friday?" Ichowitz asked.

"I assume so. Is that really necessary?"

"Perhaps."

"Would you like to speak with her now?"

"No, we can do that later."

When Ichowitz had completed the interview he had the distinct impression that Nooris had not been completely forthcoming with regard to the full extent of his relationship with Megan Larson. Ichowitz did not disclose his knowledge of Larson's pregnancy.

Ichowitz nodded at the receptionist as he left. He could not miss the manner with which she watched him as he walked out of Nooris' office. He turned back and saw her staring at him. This was definitely not your run of the mill receptionist. Shona whatever your last name, was someone Ichowitz should look into. Perhaps she could shed some further insight on Megan Larson's relationship with Ari Nooris.

On his way to meeting with Regan, Ichowitz stopped at the Nooris condo for another look. There was something about Nooris that bothered him. The man was a tad too smooth, too self-assured. Ichowitz stepped into the large living/dining area. Regan was right the Nooris brothers had spared no expense in converting the space from the former storage room to its present grandeur. Every amenity from the hardwood floors that looked like wood planks that had been removed from the side of an old barn and refinished, to the modern lighting fixtures and magnificent back wall of windows, had been well thought out and blended perfectly.

Ichowitz took a small flashlight from his jacket pocket and slowly examined the large room from floor to ceiling. It was in the far corner where the windows nearly met the ceiling: A tiny camera, the type of sophisticated device that only high end security companies, or government agencies could install, reflected from the beam of his flashlight. He must have missed it before because of the sunlight from the window wall, and the shadow cast from the hanging flood lights. He wondered about who had put it there and if it captured any images that would assist in their murder investigation.

"Jack, I'm at the Nooris condo. I came across something I think you should see. Do you have a ladder at your house?"

Twenty minutes later Regan was standing on the top rung of a ladder that still left him four feet below the tiny camera.

"Izz, we'll have to ask the techs to come back and remove this thing. Have you ever seen anything like this before?"

"I have back when I was in the service. The CIA used cameras like this. I've never seen private security firms using equipment this sophisticated," he replied.

"Why would the CIA put this place under surveillance?" Regan asked.

"Dunno, maybe it's not the Agency. I'd sure like to know if the camera was working last Friday night," Ichowitz said.

It took the Crime Scene techs less than two minutes to remove the camera from the wall. The apparatus was connected to an antenna on the outside that had also been hidden in shadows and had been undetected in previous inspections. The apparatus had no identifying marks and gave them no clues as to who had installed it.

"Dead end?" Regan asked.

"Maybe, but if Nooris was under surveillance by a government agency, and the fact our guys could remove it so easily, makes me think whoever installed it is pretty sophisticated. Our removing the camera may generate a reaction. We'll just have to wait and see."

TEN

———◆———

The Chief Justice's press conference was received with nearly universal skepticism by the media. How could he not have known that his counsel was on both sides of a transaction that had cost the taxpayers over $10 million dollars? Even if they believed that he taken no money from Wiggins, his complete failure to oversee the project raised serious questions about his judgment that placed his retention in jeopardy.

"Chief, don't worry, it will all blow over long before the retention election," Saunders said reassuringly.

"Mickey, that sounds just like the advice I received when I was told that by retaining that Wiggins woman it would also assure my retention. So far that hasn't worked out so well for me. Now I'm getting the shit kicked out of me by the press. Some talk show guys are calling for my recall, for Christ's sake."

"Bob, you didn't take her money, and there's nothing in writing that supports her allegations. I'm telling you soon the spotlight will be focused on her. We got the best spin doctor in the business working for you. He recommends that you lay low. I agree. You'll see, tomorrow or in another day or two, some self righteous state senator or congressman will be discovered surfing porn on the web, or a bunch of priests will be exposed as pederasts, and you'll be yesterday's news."

"What about Nooris? Won't he claim he's entitled to his money?"

"Nooris will not be a problem," Saunders replied.

"How do you know that?"

"Bob, I know, and you don't need to know," he said.

Saunders hung up the phone and smiled at the Mayor. "Looks like your plan is working out so far, Fogerty and Wiggins are right in the eye of the shit storm."

The Mayor nodded his agreement.

"So when are you going to get Commissioner Regan in the party?"

"Patience Mickey, there's plenty of time. Let's enjoy the moment."

"You're sure you have Nooris under control?"

The Mayor nodded.

"But what about the girl's murder; isn't that going to screw things up?"

The Mayor shook his head and sighed. "That was unfortunate, and unanticipated, but it won't have any impact on the plan."

The Mayor turned and looked out the window. He pointed and said, "Dorothy Wiggins' office is right over there, the top floor of the Widener Building. It's a good thing those windows can't open. Before this is over, she'll want to take a leap."

"Fuck her," Saunders said.

"I wouldn't even do that with your dick," the Mayor said, and they both laughed.

Ichowitz pointed to the chart on the wall and said, "So here's what we have so far: Dorothy Wiggins, who has a motive to eliminate the principal grand jury witness, visits the victim at the Nooris condo Friday afternoon and leaves around 5:30-5:45. The Comcast tech who responded to a trouble call at the unit at around 6 PM says the victim was fine when he left the condo a half hour to forty-five minutes later."

"Avi Nooris' alibi that he was at the gym all night has a kingsized hole in it; however, as far as we know he had no motive to kill Larson. Ari Nooris claims he did not see the victim when he returned from Israel, and like his brother also had no motive to harm Ms. Larson. Then we have the mysterious spy camera that might contain video that reveals who killed

Megan Larson, but we don't know who put the camera there or what it recorded. We still don't have a line on four of the vehicles that accessed the parking lot that night. We have a password-protected laptop computer that belonged to the victim. And finally, Ms. Larson was pregnant-the father of the unborn child is unknown."

"Izz perhaps when we find out who the father is, we'll find the killer," Regan said.

"Maybe, but why would Larson's lover murder her?"

"Dunno."

"Jack, was there anything in Larson's grand jury testimony that could lead us to the killer?"

"Sure, if the killer is Dorothy Wiggins. But Gold the Comcast tech eliminated her as our suspect. You're sure about that guy?"

Ichowitz nodded his head.

"So that leaves us with Avi Nooris and the security camera, the PC and the four vehicles," Regan said.

"And Ari Nooris I found his story just a tad too, I don't know, perfect," Ichowitz said and shrugged his shoulders.

"There's something else, isn't there?" Regan asked.

"Not sure, but there was something about Nooris' receptionist, I think her name is Shona."

"What?"

"I'm not certain; just a vibe. The way she told Nooris that I was there to question him, and the way she watched me; it's probably nothing, but she seemed way too qualified to be manning Nooris' reception desk."

"Assistant District Attorney Regan, there's a call for you on line two; caller claims she's your mother."

Regan arched his eyebrows and picked up the phone. His mother only called if someone in the family died or was seriously injured.

"Mother, is everything OK?" he asked.

"Jack, your father told me that the Mayor is going to hold a press conference this afternoon. Apparently Mayor Gallo conducted some kind of undercover investigation of the Police Department and he's going to announce that he has requested the US Attorney to look into corruption in the department. All of this is designed to force your father to resign. You know the Mayor and your father never got along."

"Mother, Dad would never be involved in or condone any corruption. This is all politics. Dad will be OK, you'll see, but why did he ask you to call me?"

"Jack, you know your father. He's so stubborn. I suggested that he call you, but he wouldn't. He said he didn't want to bother you. So I called. Do you know someone by the name of Vito Coratelli Jr.? Your father mentioned that he had something to do with this."

Coratelli was a criminal defense attorney of questionable skill and even more suspect ethics. He had skated by mainly on the reputation of his father who was a well regarded and respected member of the local criminal defense bar. Regan had most recently encountered Vito Junior in a case involving the son of a Police Lieutenant who Regan had successfully prosecuted for vehicular homicide. Coratelli turned down a plea arrangement Regan had worked out in consideration of the defendant's father. His client received a much harsher sentence as a result of Coratelli's advice. Incredibly, Coratelli blamed Regan for the mess he had created.

"Yes, I know him. Why?"

"I'm not sure but your father believes he has some kind of grudge against you and he apparently is a witness in this corruption probe."

Ichowitz reading the look of concern on his young friend's face asked, "Everything all right?"

Regan filled him in on the call.

"Jack, the PPD is the fourth largest police department in the nation, with over 6,000 officers and nearly 1,000 civilian employees. Practically all of the cops and employees are honest, dedicated, and hard-working civil servants. But there are some rotten apples among them. Since your father became Commissioner he has done a great job reforming the department and weeding out corruption. No matter what he has accomplished, a police force of this size and scope is not going to be perfect."

"The Mayor has a hard-on for your father that goes back two decades, something to do with a beef between your father and his. As I recall, John was a sergeant on the Civil Affairs Unit. The Mayor's father was a

Congressman. Your dad was instrumental in the Congressman's conviction for taking bribes from someone he thought was an Iranian businessman who turned out to be an undercover FBI agent. They got the Congressman on tape saying, 'Money talks and bullshit walks.' You were a kid back then, you probably don't remember any of this," Ichowitz said.

"Christ, Izz, that's ancient history. Mayor Gallo can't still be holding a grudge over that."

"Maybe and maybe it's because his honor had the hots for your sister Annabelle, and your parents put the kibosh to that relationship."

"What's Coratelli got to do with this?" Regan asked.

"Who knows? If all they have is that *putz's* testimony, they got *bupkis!*"

The Honorable Bruce Peter Gallo, Mayor of Philadelphia, had a chip on his shoulder the size of a small destroyer. He never forgot, and most assuredly never forgave, any insult, no matter how trivial. He was small in stature, five feet, four inches tall. He was sensitive about his height and would never allow photographers to take photographs of him with taller people, men or woman, standing beside him. He was perpetually angry, but his handsome face and quick smile hid his inner turmoil.

A reporter once quoted him in an article about his reputation for seeking retribution against political rivals as saying: "I carry around this reservoir of hate that I can dip into whenever I need to." According to the article when the reporter asked if the Mayor was joking he responded, "Cross me and you'll find out!"

Among the local heavyweights currently on the top of his grudge list, in no particular order or degree of distain, were: Pennsylvania Supreme Court Chief Justice Robert Fogerty, Philadelphia Police Commissioner John Hogan Regan and Dorothy Wiggins. Wiggins was likely on everyone's least-liked list, so her inclusion on Gallo's was a foregone conclusion, although Gallo's reasons were so trivial as to expose him as borderline insane. As to Fogerty, Gallo's grudge was almost rational since it was based on threats, or at least perceived threats, to his political future and economic well-being. Gallo's grudge against Regan was intensely personal and spanned generations.

Wiggins had once publicly referred to the Mayor as the 'runt' of his mother's litter of six children. While it was true that his five siblings, three brothers and two sisters, were all tall, all of his brothers were over six feet tall, and his two sisters stood five feet ten inches, although never next to him, Wiggin's making fun of Gallo's height was unforgivable. It's a good thing Gallo never heard the many insulting off- the-record remarks Wiggins had made about him, often referring to him as, "A mighty midget with an anatomically correct penis who no one would ever accuse of stepping on his dick!"

Chief Justice Fogerty's intervention in the Family Court House matter, of course, put a target on his back. Before Fogerty got involved, the Mayor had a sweetheart deal all set up on a site for the new facility. The Mayor now had to explain to his people that there may be no big pay day as they had been promised, or at the very least the pay day would have to be postponed until the situation became clarified.

The Police Commissioner had more or less been a permanent member on the Mayor's hit list. His decades' old grudge dating back to Gallo's father's conviction and disgrace had been lying fallow, although far from forgotten. Gallo hated the Commissioner, and perhaps more accurately the Commissioner's wife, for interfering with his relationship with the only woman he had ever loved, Annabelle, their eldest daughter. While Mrs. Regan was likely beyond his immediate reach, Gallo would make all the Regans pay dearly for interfering with that relationship.

"Jack, my chief wants to meet. Apparently, there's been a reaction to our removing the camera from Nooris' condo." Ichowitz told Regan that the Chief of Homicide had scheduled a meeting for later that day with certain parties from the feds, the particulars of which would be explained when he arrived at the Round House, as the Police

Administration Building was referred by everyone except the police. The double towered concrete monstrosity at 7th and Race Streets , that was built in the 1960's to project an image of raw power has for decades been the brunt of jokes and derision due to its peculiar design.

"Izz, there must be a full moon or something. I've been summoned to a meeting with *my* boss this afternoon," Regan replied. "I guess we'll have to compare notes."

They agreed to get together after their respective meetings to see where all the pieces of the puzzle fit, assuming they were still working on the Larsen case after whatever their respective bosses told them.

Regan was excited to learn that the removal of the security camera had resulted in a reaction. This could be the big break in the investigation that could lead them to Megan Larson's killer. Even though he and his boss had a solid relationship, he was decidedly less excited about his meeting with the District Attorney. He assumed the reason for the summons had something to do with Mayor's witch hunt.

The door to her office was opened and she waved him in, motioning to him to close the door as she continued her telephone conversation. He sat down on the chair in front of her desk and waited. Susan Romansky had been the District Attorney for nearly two full terms. She had been a tenacious litigator before she assumed the post and turned out to be a better administrator than most of the pundits had predicted. She ran an effective and professional organization that gave the citizens who elected her everything she had promised them in her campaign. There had never been even a hint of a scandal during her tenure. Every prosecution was handled competently and fairly, no matter the background, race or economic standing of the defendant.

"Jack, I suppose you already heard Gallo is on your father's case again," she said.

He nodded.

"This shit is beginning to get pretty old," Romansky said as she uncharacteristically fussed with the stack of documents on her desk, obviously uncomfortable with what she was about to say.

"Susan, you know my father runs a clean department. Whatever the Mayor thinks he has on him, I'm sure at the end of the day it will turn out to be crap." Regan wanted to relieve his boss of concern for him or his father.

"Of course, but it seems that Gallo's dragging you into the mess too."

"How?"

"According to the press release, Vito Coratelli Jr., has been granted immunity to testify before the Federal Grand Jury concerning a payoff to fix the prosecution against Lt Mathais' son. Coratelli claims you reneged on the deal."

"What? That's total bullshit," Regan responded getting out of his chair.

"That's not all. The grand jury is looking into an alleged cover-up of sexual harassment in Mathais' unit that Coratelli maintains your father directed."

"He's just making this shit up!"

Romansky motioned for Regan to retake his seat.

"I know, I know, but Gallo's from the slash-and-burn demagogue school of politics. Just throw it out there and repeat it enough times and people will believe anything. Look at the birthers and what they did to the President. He had to release his birth certificate to prove he wasn't born in Kenya."

"Who would believe Coratelli? The man's a certified jackass. He's 'shysters are us,'" Regan said.

"Apparently not for much longer," she replied.

"What?"

"Coratelli was storing what he believed to be a kilo of meth in his office. He had been set up by the FBI on a tip from one of the mob guys he represented who offered him up in return for a minimum sentence on his own drug bust. Apparently they shared the pipe a time or two, so when push came to shove Coratelli was his get out of jail quicker card."

"Geez Susan, I don't know who's scummier, Coratelli and his crack-smoking buddy, or the feebies."

"So Jack, what are you going to do about this?" she asked.

He shook his head. "For now, I'm going to ignore it and go on with the Larson investigation, if that's all right with you."

"OK. But Jack, I don't think this is going away. You'll have to confront Gallo's allegations sooner or later," she said.

Ichowitz was ushered into the Homicide Unit's conference room. His boss, Lt. Larry Jackson, was sitting at the conference table facing two men Ichowitz assumed were from the FBI or some other federal agency. Jackson motioned for Ichowitz to take the chair to his right.

"Detective Isadore Ichowitz, Simon Conway, Regional Director of Homeland Security," Jackson said as he pointed to the man who sat across from Ichowitz, "and Special Agent Monroe Ossberg," he gestured to the man seated to Conway's left, "are apparently upset with you for removing a security camera from the Larson murder scene," Jackson said, flashing the federal agents one of his patented smiles.

Larry Jackson was the first African American to become Chief of Homicide detectives. He was forty-two years old but looked ten years younger. Ichowitz had been his rabbi when Jackson first joined the unit five years before. Ichowitz, who had been the first Jew to be assigned to the unit several years earlier, understood firsthand the barriers a minority would have to overcome to survive. In the Homicide Division a member of a minority meant any detective who was not a charter member of the Emerald Society, the fraternal organization of Irish police officers.

Now the roles were somewhat reversed, and Jackson was Ichowitz's rabbi. He would not allow Homeland Security or the FBI to interfere with PPD Homicide's investigation, nor would he permit the feds to intimidate his detective. Jackson realized that Ichowitz was more than capable of handling himself; he wanted Ichowitz to know he had his back.

"Director Conway, Special Agent Ossberg, it's a pleasure to meet you. I'm so glad you're here. We really need to review the video of the Nooris condo for last Friday. It very well could lead us directly to Megan Larson's killer," Ichowitz said, smiling at the two men who stared back at him with shocked expressions.

"That's completely out of the question. Those videos contain matters of national security. There's no way we would ever release them to local authorities," Conway replied.

"So you're acknowledging that you have video footage of the murder scene during the day the murder took place. That's excellent!" Ichowitz said. "Lt. Jackson, our friends from Homeland and the FBI must have had judicial approval to put the camera in the condo. So any evidence we obtain when they share the video with us will be admissible."

"Wait a god damned minute," Conway shouted. "I never acknowledged that we had video of the homicide at the Nooris condo."

"Of course you did. You just said so. That being the case, I'm sure you want to assist us in our murder investigation. After all, withholding the video would impede our investigation. I'm sure you wouldn't want a public disclosure that your agencies would stand by and let a murderer get off, would you? Besides there's ample judicial authority that supports our right to obtain this critical evidence. Once again I am sure you're aware of the cases."

"Detective Ichowitz is correct about all of this. It really wasn't necessary for the two of you to come down to the PAB. We would have been more than happy to send someone over to get the video," Jackson said.

"Are you fucking guys out of your minds? There's no fucking way I'm releasing those videos!" Conway's face was flushed with anger and he pounded on the conference table.

"So the purpose of our meeting was not to advance cooperation of federal and local law enforcement?" Ichowitz asked shaking his head as if he was really confused. "You would really withhold this evidence?"

"Director, perhaps we should reconsider our position," Ossberg said to Conway. Unlike the Director, Ossberg did not raise his voice or express any sign of displeasure.

"But I…" Ossberg gave Conway a shake of his head.

"Detectives, can we have a moment?" Ossberg asked.

"Certainly Izzy and I will be in my office," Jackson replied.

When Jackson and Ichowitz left the room, they could hear more pounding on the table and Conway screaming at the FBI Agent.

"Sounds like the Homeland Security Regional Director isn't happy with the way things are going down," Jackson said.

Ichowitz shrugged his shoulders and said, "Jack, so maybe this time we can chalk one up for the good guys. We're the good guys aren't we?"

"Depends on who you ask; obviously Mr. Conway doesn't think so."

Monroe Ossberg knocked on the door jam and asked, "Gentlemen, can we talk?"

"Well played, Detective Ichowitz," he said as he sat down.

"Special Agent Ossberg, call me Izzy. I hope this won't cause you any problems with the Regional Director."

"Izzy, that jackass thinks he's Jack Bauer on that TV show "24," for Christ's sake. He's just a political hack who was born on third base and thinks he hit a triple. My job is to babysit him and make sure he doesn't get his lame ass in too much trouble," Ossberg responded.

"Sounds like a fulltime job," Jackson observed.

"When can we see the video?" Ichowitz asked.

"I'll have a copy delivered to you this afternoon. Gentlemen, is there anything else?"

"Agent Ossberg, can you share with us why you had Nooris' condo under surveillance?" Ichowitz asked.

Ossberg stared at Ichowitz for a moment and said, "Here's my card with contact info. After you view the video, if you need to know more, give me a call."

ELEVEN

"Ladies and gentlemen, thanks for coming on such short notice," Police Commissioner John Hogan Regan addressed the assembled media and reporters who filled the briefing room at the Police Administration Building. Commissioner Regan's formal news conferences were usually well attended because they were infrequent and always newsworthy. The Commissioner did not waste either his or the working press' time on frivolous ego trips.

"As you know, the Mayor convened a press conference earlier today to announce that he has referred a matter to the Justice Department requesting that an investigation be conducted into possible corruption of this department. He identified Lieutenant Gary Mathais as the target of the probe and implied that my office was involved in a cover up. The Mayor's press conference was the first time I became aware of these serious allegations. While that is regrettable, I wish to assure the public that this department will of course cooperate with the federal authorities in any investigation they may undertake."

"It has been the policy of this department, since I became Commissioner, not to publicly comment on internal investigations of police officers. I will not deviate from that policy now. However, I want the citizens of Philadelphia to know that the Internal Affairs Division has started an investigation of the matters referred to by the Mayor. The investigation is ongoing, and if there is any merit to the allegations, appropriate action will be taken if warranted at the conclusion of the investigation."

"The unusual manner with which the Mayor has decided to bring this issue to the public does require some comment. As you know, I was appointed Commissioner by the Mayor's predecessor. When the Mayor was elected, I tendered my resignation. I believed then, and I continue to believe, that whoever is elected Mayor has the right to appoint whomever he believes should hold this important position in his cabinet. The Mayor declined my offer to step down at that time."

"However, if the Mayor has lost confidence in me, or if he wishes to appoint a new Commissioner all he has to do is pick up the phone and let me know, or of course he can convene another press conference to say that, and I'm confident you will let me know."

"Commissioner, can you comment on the Mayor's allegations regarding your son's actions?"

"Certainly, as you know my son Jack is an assistant District Attorney. I'm proud to say that during his tenure with the District Attorney's office he has successfully prosecuted over ninety percent of the cases he has litigated. Most recently, he obtained the conviction of Gary Mathais Junior in a vehicular homicide case. The defense counsel in that matter has apparently made allegations that my son reneged on a plea agreement deal that this individual claims had been arranged and for which my son had received payment to secure."

"Defense counsel offered his testimony in return for immunity in a drug offense for which he had been arrested. There has never been any question involving my son's integrity. That cannot be said about his accuser. I believe that when all the facts are disclosed the allegations against my son will be exposed as completely baseless. I understand that the District Attorney has taken no steps to relieve my son of his duties and responsibilities. I assume she has dismissed the allegations as lacking any credibility; however, I'm sure you can reach her directly for comment."

"Thank you again."

"Jack, did you see your father's press conference?" Ichowitz asked.

"Yes."

"KYW also got your boss on the record confirming his comments. She even went further in attacking your buddy Vito Coratelli, Jr."

"Yeah Izz, but we would all be better off without this side show. How did you make out with Homeland Security?"

"Jack, that's the real reason for my call. Get over to the 4th District. Monroe Ossberg, the FBI Special Agent who babysits the political appointee putz who is the current Homeland Security Regional Director, is sending over the video of Nooris' condo. And we just got a hit on one of the partial license plates. You better sit down because you are not going to believe who the car is registered to."

"Izz you're killing me with the suspense, who already?"

"His Honor, Mayor Bruce Peter Gallo."

"Izz, you got to be shitting me!"

"Jack, I shit you not!"

By the time Regan got to the 4th District Ichowitz had already set up the monitor to play the security video. "Izz, should I get some popcorn? I guess we're going to be here for some time,' Regan said as he sat down at the conference table.

Ichowitz turned on the monitor and the screen displayed a series of views with what appeared to be people walking through the great room of the condo at a staccato like speed.

"Jack, I can stop the video at any point and watch the action in real time or slow motion. This is cutting edge stuff."

They watched the monitor, and Ichowitz stopped it at 5:32 PM when Wiggins first entered the condo. Even without sound they could see Wiggins actually begging Larson and being summarily rejected. The video confirmed Wiggins' account of the events, including her leaving the condo before 6 PM when the Comcast tech made his appearance.

The surveillance tape also corroborated the technician's account of his meeting with Larson, including a warm embrace of friends who were happy to reconnect after a protracted absence. Once again there was complete corroboration of the timing of the tech's leaving Larson at Norris' condo.

"What the hell?" Regan said when the screen went blank. He turned to Ichowitz, who was fumbling with the lap top keyboard, trying to coax the video back into life. The monitor continued to show the time at the top of the screen with no picture. Finally the monitor came back into focus showing the lifeless body of Megan Larson. The time on the monitor was 23:42.

"The video is missing over five hours. I thought you said this was state of the art," Regan said.

"It is. Something's definitely not kosher," Ichowitz replied as he pulled a card from his shirt pocket and reached for his cell phone.

"Who are you calling?"

Ichowitz waved for Regan to be quiet and said, "Please tell Special Agent Ossberg Detective Ichowitz is on the line."

Regan listened to half a conversion as Ichowitz described what happened with the security video. When he hung up Regan asked, "So, what did he say?"

"He said it must have been sun spots."

"Sun spots?"

"Uh-huh."

"Sounds like bullshit to me," Regan said.

"Me too, but I got the impression that Ossberg couldn't speak freely, like maybe the Homeland Security guy was breathing down his neck. Anyway, Ossberg mentioned buying me lunch to make sure local and federal law enforcement cooperation remains at optimal levels."

"Make him take you to the Palm."

"I was thinking more like Shank and Evelyn's or Chickie and Pete's, you know, give him a real taste of Philly cuisine. Jack, how do you want to handle the Mayor? I was hoping the video would have given us something more to discuss with him, but now we got bupkis," Ichowitz asked.

"If I'm involved he'll probably accuse us of harassment. I think we need to find out if there was any connection between the Mayor and Megan Larson, or if he had any relationship with anyone else who lives at the Pickle Works, before we question him," Regan replied.

"Good call."

TWELVE

———◆———

Liam scored the winning goal and his team qualified for the Regionals. His coach, Jimmy Mack, and all of his teammates surrounded him as Katey and Regan cheered. Katey smiled and squeezed Jack's hand as her son approached them.

"Way to go Liam!" Jack said and tousled the boy's hair.

"Mum, coach is taking the team for pizza to celebrate. Is it OK for me to go?"

"Of course, there wouldn't be a celebration without your goal!"

"After, can I go to Ryan's? His parents are taking him to the movies and he invited me to go along."

After Katey discussed the logistics of the party and movies with the coach and Ryan's mother, she approached Regan, who was sitting in the bleachers fiddling with his I-Phone.

"Must be something important, you seem concerned," she said.

He looked up. "I've been waiting for a message from Izzy, and he hasn't returned my text. I guess everything's OK."

"So where is this art museum you told me we'll be going to?"

"It's the Barnes Foundation; it's only a few miles from here. The Barnes has one of the largest collections of post-impressionist art in the world: Renoir, Cézanne, Picasso, all of them. It's really special."

"I didn't know you were such an expert on the fine arts," she said.

"I'm really not. My mother was a student at the Foundation and has been involved with fundraising for years. She dragged me, yelling and screaming, to the gallery when I was a kid. But after a while, I don't know, the serenity of the place, and the incredible beauty of the works of art, just overwhelmed me."

"And here I thought ya were just another heartless lawyer, like my Uncle Mike warned me about."

Regan pulled up to the gate of the stately mansion on North Latches Lane in Merion, a couple of blocks across the county line from Philadelphia. "Mr. Regan, good to see you," the guard greeted him.

"Harlan, how are your wife and Harlan Junior doing?"

"They're fine, thanks to you and your mother. Getting Junior in that special study at Children's Hospital, it was a life saver."

Katey shook her head once again surprised by Regan's heretofore undisclosed sensitive side.

"What?" he asked as he noticed her studying him.

"I'm beginning to see why O'Malley holds you in such esteem. There's definitely more to Jack Regan than I initially believed."

"And what was it that you first thought of me?" he asked.

"Well, I'm not sure. At the very first I thought you were trouble. Tryin to get on my good side by being nice to Liam and all, but O'Malley says I misjudged you."

"And what do you think now?"

"I'm not sure."

He smiled and said, "OK, why don't we talk about that later? Let's go inside now, and let me show you why this place is so special."

For the next two hours Regan and Kate O'Malley walked through the downstairs gallery admiring the works of art. Regan took his cues from Kate when she lingered at a painting or sculpture. She was especially drawn to Amedeo Modigliani and Auguste Matisse, two of Regan's favorite artists. Modigliani's "The Red Head" was among the impressionist's most prominent and greatest works, in Regan's opinion. He explained how the artist used angles throughout the portrait of his mistress – a technique that was often featured in his work.

"How did Barnes acquire all these paintings?" she asked.

"He was the Bill Gates of his times. He amassed a fortune after he and his partner developed Argyol, an antiseptic used to treat gonorrhea and to prevent gonorrhea blindness in newborn infants; it's still being prescribed today. Anyway, Barnes bought out his partner and then his business really took off."

"Barnes entered the art world with a load of cash and the same intensity he employed in his business dealings. It turned out he had a keen eye for art, especially young and under-appreciated artists who couldn't make a living selling their works before he discovered them. Eventually he had to use surrogates to acquire the art because whatever he purchased more or less set the market. Barnes literally made the careers of Renoir and all of the artists whose works now sell for millions. Unfortunately, many of them didn't live long enough to benefit from Barnes' discovery."

The two of them had the gallery virtually to themselves since the museum was closed to the public in anticipation of the opening of the new museum on the Parkway in Philadelphia. Regan could tell from Katey's reaction that she had fallen under the spell the collection cast on first time visitors. "When does the new gallery open?"

"In a few months; this is probably the last time we can see the collection here. The curators will be preparing for the relocation pretty soon."

As they drove back to Manayunk, Regan asked, "So now that I impressed you with everything I know about Post-Impressionists, Miss O'Malley, do you still think I'm the heartless lawyer who tried to gain your affections by befriending your son?"

She laughed and touched his arm. "No, no. I don't think you're heartless, nor do I believe you used Liam. You know Liam favors you. I overheard him ask O'Malley about you. He's borne his share of disappointments from his dad. I don't want that to happen to him ever again."

As they approached Main Street he asked, "Should I drop you off at the Grape or can we spend some more time together?"

"I suppose you have some more art history to impress me with," she smiled and touched his arm again.

"That's not exactly what I had in mind," Regan said as he drove past the Grape Pub without hearing any protest from Kate.

They sat on the deck of his house and looked out on the park across the street. "That's where I took Liam to soccer practice the day we met," he said. "He told me his father taught him how to play."

"He did."

"He told me the reason you came to the states was to get away from his father. Is that true?"

She looked at him and contemplated her response.

"Kate, look, if it's none of my business just say so."

She shook her head and sighed. "What Liam told you is partly true. It's a bit more complicated than that. I did come to the states to take Liam away from his father, but his father and I agreed it was all for the best. Is it all right if we leave it at that for now?"

"Sure, just one more question."

She waited.

"Are you still in love with Liam's father?"

She took a sip of her wine and said, "I don't know, maybe a little. Why do you want to know?"

Now it was his turn to contemplate his response, "I'm not sure. It's just that my family's telling me it's time for me to move on with my life. My mother even tried to fix me up with my girl friend from high school."

"Would that be that beautiful woman who gave me the stink eye at the Grape the other night?"

He nodded.

"Well I can't say much for her manners, but your mother's got an eye for beauty. Will ya be seein her again?"

"You already know she's picking me up tomorrow to take me to the race."

"I think she has something more on her mind than watching you run around in yer short pants."

"I think you're right about that," he laughed.

"So what are ya gonna do?"

He sighed and said, "I'm going to tell her I just want to be friends."

"Well good luck with that," she said.

chowitz greeted Ossberg as he took his seat at the counter at Chubby's on Henry Avenue in Roxborough. "I ordered you a cheese steak and an order of onion rings," he said as the FBI agent sat down on the stool next to him.

"This place smells like an onion ring," Ossberg said as the waitress brought over his order.

"What you having to drink, hon?" she asked.

"Bring him a draft of the Yuengling," Ichowitz answered for him.

"Is that a Chinese beer?" Ossberg asked after the waitress walked away.

"Something like that, only they make it in Pottsville, Pennsylvania. Don't worry. You'll like it. And by the way, there's no mayonnaise here. Put some of those hot peppers on your steak sandwich and chow down. You're not in Minnesota anymore!"

When the FBI agent had bitten off a mouthful of steak sandwich, Ichowitz asked, "What's the deal with the *farkakte* surveillance video?"

Ossberg stared at him with a blank expression, swallowed his steak sandwich and asked, "What's farrkarda mean?"

"*Farkakte*, it's Yiddish for screwed up," Ichowitz replied.

"Oh yeah, sorry about that, it was Homeland Security Director Conway's and one of the Nazis who work for him idea. They claim the video had to be redacted for national security reasons. Hey, this steak sandwich is really good," he said as he wiped the grease from his chin.

"So are you going to give me the *emess* on this?"

"*Emess*, that means the truth, doesn't it?" Ossberg said. "I was assigned to the New York office for a few months. We were investigating an international organ-selling conspiracy that involved Orthodox Rabbis in the Hasidic community in Brooklyn. They called it a real 'Shandeh,' I think that means a scandal."

"That's right. You're a quick learner. I'll have you fluent in Yiddish in no time. So are you going to tell me what's going on?"

Ichowitz waited as Ossberg took another bite of his sandwich.

For the next forty-five minutes, in between bites of his cheese steak and onion rings, Ossberg told Ichowitz the skinny on the Homeland Security surveillance of the Nooris condo.

"And you're telling me the video didn't show the murderer."

Ossberg nodded.

"But that's impossible. The camera had an unobstructed view of the front entrance."

Ossberg nodded his agreement and said, "But there's a back door. The perp must have gotten in and out using the back door."

"Jack, where have you been? I've been trying to get in touch with you for hours," Ichowitz sounded excited.

"Izz, it's a long story, sorry my phone was off. What's up?"

"*Boychik*, I met with Ossberg and he gave me some very interesting information on Avi Nooris and his little brother."

"Does it link them to the murder?" Regan asked.

"Not sure about that, but it may. It certainly opens a lot of avenues for us to proceed with the investigation," Ichowitz responded. "I think we should get together and see where this leads," he continued.

"Izz, I'm running that race tomorrow. I can't miss it, a lot of people, including you have pledged money and I have to run to get the money to the Cancer Foundation," Regan replied.

"Right, Jack I completely forgot about the Broad Street Run. Look we can meet up after. Jack what's wrong? You sound funny."

"It's nothing really. We can talk about it tomorrow."

The next morning at 6 AM, Regan waited in front of his house for Courtney Wells who his mother had volunteered to drive him to the starting point for the run.

She pulled up in her Mercedes convertible with the top down.

"Hey there handsome, need a ride?" she said.

"Court thanks for being on time. I seem to recall that mornings were not your forte," he said as he threw his backpack in the backseat that obviously had not been designed for passengers and got in the front seat.

She leaned over and kissed his cheek and said, "You really do look sexy in those running shorts. Why don't we skip the run and I can write you a check to cover the donations you would have raised? We can spend the time in more productive pursuits."

"Court, stop it; you know I can't do that."

She put her hand on his thigh and squeezed. He pushed her hand away and said, "Court, please."

She stared at him for a moment, shook her head and pulled away from the curb. They drove in silence to the registration area at Broad and Somerville.

"I'll see you at the Navy Yard, we can talk then," he said. She looked up and asked, "You alright?"

"We'll talk after the run. And Court thanks again for picking me up." Even Regan was amazed at the crowd at Central High. He overheard someone say there were 30,000 runners scheduled to participate. He gave up attempting to find his sisters and brothers-in-law in the mass of humanity and took a place well behind the elite racers and celebrities who had cued up in front of the television cameras.

It took until Hunting Park Avenue, nearly three quarters of a mile, for the crowded field to assume a semblance of order. Once he was able to pick up his pace without fear of running into someone else or being run over, Regan allowed himself to feel the energy of the crowds that cheered the runners on as they made their way on this picture perfect morning. As he got into his rhythm he let his mind wander back to the previous evening with Katey. Did he want to be more than just friends?

He made it to the finish line in eighty-seven minutes, a personal best far exceeding his previous efforts. His parents and nieces and nephews were standing in a preferred spot near the finish line, with the families of other local officials and celebrities.

"Great time Jack," his father said as he approached. "Did you see the rest of the Regan clan?"

"Dad, I was lucky to get through the throng in one piece. I've never seen so many runners."

"Jack, what did you say to Courtney?" his mother asked.

"Nothing; why?"

"Well, she dropped your bag off and ran out of here. I thought we were all going to the Merion Golf Club for lunch. Jack are you sure you didn't do anything to offend her?"

Regan met Ichowitz at the Fourth District later that afternoon. Ichowitz filled him in on Ossberg's briefing. Ossberg swore the video did not show the murder. In fact, Ossberg could not recall anything of a security significance that was worthy of being redacted. In Ossberg's opinion, it was all some ego trip Homeland Security bullshit the Director was doing to show the locals who had the bigger dick.

"So why was Homeland Security monitoring Nooris' condo?" Regan asked.

"Ari Nooris is an Agent for the Mossad, the Israeli Secret Service, or at least he was once upon a time. According to Ossberg, the word is he has gone rogue."

"What?"

"They think he has some contacts with a terrorist group. There's some chatter on websites about some kind of attack on a site where our nation was born. That could be Philly or Beantown, or even New York City. The terrorists are sometimes a little fuzzy on our history."

"Izz, why don't they just arrest him?"

Ichowitz shrugged. "According to Ossberg, there's always some chatter about attacks and it's normally a bunch of nonsense. Nooris is a big time player in this town. Before the feds take him down, they need to be sure."

"What about his brother?"

"Avi's just a thug who likes to throw his weight around and impress underage girls. Ari's the one with all the brains and clout."

"So is the real estate business just a front?"

"No, it's a legitimate business, somewhat on the sketchy side."

"So how does this tie into the Larson murder?"

"I'm not sure," Ichowitz said. He looked at the conference room wall where they had put up photos of the suspects and persons of interest and the time line of events. "So far the only name with a solid line through any of them is Gold, the Comcast tech," he said.

"That leaves both of the Nooris brothers, Dorothy Wiggins and Mayor Gallo, and who knows," he added.

"Izz, why didn't we strike Wiggins? The video confirmed that she left Larson before the Comcast tech arrived at the condo."

"Yeah, but she had motive and, I don't know, she's just so cocky. Let's keep her as a possible for now."

"What's next?" Regan asked.

"We need to question His Honor, the Mayor. Jack something on your mind?"

Regan stared at him and finally said, "Remember Kate O'Malley?"

"The really pretty chef at the Grape?"

"Uh-huh."

"You got a thing for her?" Ichowitz asked.

"I'm not sure. I mean I think we've developed a friendship. She may still be in love with Liam's father. I don't know. I really like her and Liam."

"Jack, take some advice from an old man. Don't over think it."

THIRTEEN

—————✦—————

"Courtney, it's Jack. We need to talk. Please give me a call." This was the fourth message Regan had left on Courtney Wells' voice mail since she had bailed on his family before he had completed the Broad Street Run that morning. He didn't want to lead her on. They had been friends for practically their entire lives. He did not want to hurt her.

He picked up the phone at the first ring, "Courtney, I'm glad you called," he said.

"Jack, it's Susan Romansky, sorry to disappoint you."

"Susan, I'm sorry, I just left a message …not important. Is there a problem?" Regan was unaccustomed to receiving calls from his boss on a Sunday evening.

"Not for you. It seems that our friend Vito Coratelli Jr. has already worn out his welcome with the U.S. Attorney. Coratelli was under the impression that he was receiving full immunity in return for his testimony against you and your father. Turns out he didn't read the fine print on the deal. The U.S. Attorney was only offering him transactional immunity, and it wouldn't keep Coratelli out of prison on a number of pending cases, including a RICO indictment," she said.

"Isn't that a shame," Regan responded sarcastically.

"True. Now the poor thing wants to make a deal with us."

"Susan, he's got nothing to deal. His allegations against me are crap. I'd bet everything I own that there is absolutely nothing to his accusation against my father," Regan replied.

"Jack, I'm sure you're right. But now Coratelli has something new to offer, something that may have some legs."

"Susan, the guy's so full of shit. I don't know what he could have on anybody that would hold up in the light of day."

"He says he has recordings of conversations with His Honor Bruce Peter Gallo, Mayor of this fair city and Supreme Court Chief Justice Robert Fogerty and another individual you know, Ari Nooris."

"Why would any of them have conversations with Coratelli?" Regan asked.

"Good question. Seems Vito and his father owned a small parcel on the block where the new Family Court House is being built. Apparently more than money changed hands," Romansky replied.

"Really? But even if he has the recordings and there's something there, how would any of that be admissible?"

"He was wearing a wire for the feds. It was part of a far-ranging omnibus investigation involving both federal and state crimes. If we want to press the state charges we can offer Coratelli a better deal, full immunity. Be in my office first thing tomorrow morning. I'm putting a team together to see where this goes. I figured you would want to be in on it. We'll be meeting in the war room at 8:30."

Regan immediately contacted Ichowitz to inform him of the latest development.

"So your boss thinks Coratelli has the goods this time?"

"Seems so," Regan replied.

"I don't know, Coratelli's such a slime ball," Ichowitz said. "Speaking of slime balls, I guess this means we should hold off questioning His Honor the Mayor until the DA decides what she's going to do about the Coratelli stuff."

"Agreed."

"So while you and your boss are making the big time call, I'll take another shot at the remaining cars we got on the Pickle Works parking lot video. Who knows, we may find the smoking gun," Ichowitz said.

The next morning they assembled in the large conference room on the second floor of the District Attorney's office. Regan and three other assistant District Attorneys, four paralegals and Charles Ferguson, the DA's Chief Investigator and his two top assistants. While they were waiting for the boss, Ferguson said, "This Coratelli guy's a real shyster. I just started investigating an insurance fraud case he was involved in. Coratelli was representing a woman in a medical malpractice claim, and a claim against her disability insurance carrier. Get this, his complaint alleged his client's condition, 'fatal flatulence' was a result of a botched stomach staple procedure."

"What's 'fatal flatulence?'" Regan asked.

"It seems the poor woman has uncontrollable flatulence that is so foul that she cannot work or be in confined places with other people."

"You got to be kidding?"

"Nah the complaint he filed asked the court to have gas masks available for the jury if the matter goes to trial," Ferguson laughed.

"I smell a settlement," Regan commented.

"Yeah, it will probably stink!" They all laughed.

Romansky entered the room and filled everyone in on Coratelli's recent recant of his allegations against Regan and Police Commissioner Regan.

"Boss, we all knew that the allegations against Jack were a load of crap, so what makes you think his latest proffer is worth considering?" Ferguson asked.

"Charlie, unlike Jack and the Commissioner, the new line-up of miscreants and the money that changed hands in this court house deal, I don't know but whole thing just smells bad," she replied.

The entire room exploded in laughter.

"I say something funny?"

Ferguson filled her in on the case of the fatally flatulent plaintiff.

"Look, I know Coratelli's a sleaze ball. But the way I see it, we have nothing to lose by having a serious sit down with him and his counsel. Jack you and Charlie set up a meeting for tomorrow." She then ran down the assignments for the rest of the team.

When the meeting broke, Regan asked for a one on one with the DA.

"Susan, there's something I think you should know about Nooris. The thing is, I'm not certain I'm supposed to even know about it, let alone talk about it."

Regan told the DA about the Homeland Security surveillance of Nooris' condo, and of their suspicions that the former Mossad agent had gone rogue.

"Jack, it was probably a good call not to disclose that to the team. Let's keep that off the record for now. As far as you know it's not connected to the court house mess. Do you really think Nooris is a terrorist?"

"Susan, I don't know. The Homeland Security Director, Conway, is a real jerk. He sees conspiracies everywhere. Izzy believes the FBI agent, Ossberg, is a straight shooter. I'm not so sure about him either, but I don't want to do anything that damages Izzy's relationship with Ossberg. We'll just have to see how that plays out."

Ichowitz replayed the video of the Pickle Works parking garage in the slowest speed possible to see if he could get a handle on the two vehicles they had not been able to trace. The quality of the super slow motion video lacked the definition he needed to get a clear view of either vehicle. Ichowitz decided to run the video backwards at high speed. On this view he saw a reflection of the license plate of one of the cars off another vehicle. He froze the frame and made out "AVI." It was a vanity plate. At first he thought it was the younger Nooris brother's car. A check with PENDOT had no such license plate. He was informed that Pennsylvania did not give out license plates with less than four characters.

Ichowitz tried several searches with alternative fourth letters and numbers. None of them yielded a match. This could mean that there were no Pennsylvania license plates beginning with AVI, or it could mean that the infinite number of fourth numbers or letters, or possibly more characters made further searches on this theory unworkable.

He went back to the video and searched for another clue. After staring at the frame for what seemed like an eternity, and when he was just about to throw in the towel, it hit him. He was reading the reflection of the plate! The license sequence was reversed. The plate began either IVA blank, or blank IVA. He ran a search with license plates beginning or ending with those three characters. Within minutes he got a positive response.

"Jack, I ran some searches on one of the vehicles we could not come up with."

"And did you get anything?" Regan asked.

"Uh-huh, and you're not going to like it."

"Izz, are you gonna tell me, or do I have to come over to the District and see for myself?"

"Jack, it's a vanity plate, "DIVA-2. Sound familiar?"

"Yeah Courtney Wells."

She saw Regan's car in the driveway next to his house and parked her convertible behind it. Courtney Wells thought a face to face meeting would be a better way to respond to Regan's calls. Perhaps she had overreacted to his rejection of her offer to spend a more leisurely interlude than waiting for Jack to finish the Broad Street Run. After all he had committed to participate in the event and had secured a number of pledges. Jack, the boyscout he was, had always been an enigma to her. She understood his devotion to his deceased wife. Courtney had a grudging admiration for Susan's accomplishments and truly regretted her passing.

Jack and Courtney, the golden couple in their high school years, were just too young to survive the complications of a serious relationship. Both of them needed to live and experience other people before either of them could settle into a marriage. She had no regrets over their separate lives during the intervening years. Nor did she have any second thoughts about their marriages.

Jack's marriage had ended tragically. Her marriage, more a corporate merger than a real marriage, had never been a love match. It was a business relationship, one that she was fully prepared to honor. Greg Montgomery, the scion of a Main Line family that traced its heritage to the Mayflower, unfortunately could not keep his desires under control. The divorce settlement assured Courtney a comfortable lifestyle befitting her pampered upbringing. Now, Courtney wanted more than comfort. She wanted Regan - she wanted a second chance.

As she approached the front door she could hear music from inside the house, an old recording of "Maria" from the Broadway musical *West Side Story*, featuring the trumpet player Maynard Ferguson. She remembered how much Jack loved the way Ferguson hit the impossibly high notes, and the cascading sounds of the other trumpets that accompanied his solo in the Stan Kenton arrangement. Jack had told her Ferguson was only sixteen years old when the recording was made. He had introduced her to jazz when they were teenagers. Just listening to the music made her feel young again.

She knocked on the door and heard the footsteps approach and smiled in anticipation of seeing Jack and reminiscing about the music of their youth. She tried to maintain her smile when Kate O'Malley opened the door.

"Hello Ms. Wells," O'Malley said.

Courtney stared at the woman and replied, "Kate O'Malley, right?"

"Yes. Please come in."

"Is Jack in?"

"He's out with my son Liam. Liam asked Jack if he would be his partner in some event his soccer team is in, I think it's duck bowlin, or somethin like that. They should be back any time now. Why don't you come in? I was just about to have a cup of tea."

"Really, I couldn't stay. I was just passing by and saw Jack's car. He had left me some messages," Courtney was still flustered.

"Come, have a cup of tea," Kate said as she turned and walked to the kitchen leaving Courtney at the doorway. Courtney followed closing the door behind her.

As she approached the open kitchen she watched as O'Malley stirred whatever she was cooking in the large cast iron skillet on the stove.

It smelled incredible. A Stan Getz and Chet Baker recording of "But Not For Me" was playing, another one of Jack's favorites.

The kettle began to whistle and O'Malley poured the steaming water through a filter and into the tea pot. She moved around the kitchen with the practiced air of the accomplished chef that Courtney knew her to be.

"Ms Wells, how do ya take your tea?" she asked.

"I'm not much of a tea drinker. What would you recommend?"

"Why not try it with a little cream? I think you'll like it."

Courtney nodded and watched as Kate poured the dark, still-steaming tea into mugs and topped both off with cream. She placed a cinnamon stick in each mug and handed one to her.

They sat across from each other at the kitchen bar. The aroma from the cup was almost overwhelming. She took a sip and O'Malley smiled at her reaction.

"Jack told me that the two of you were high school sweethearts, back in the day."

"Is that so?"

"Yes. He told me you were best friends and then drifted apart."

"That's true."

"Is that a picture of his wife?" she asked pointing to the photo on the fireplace mantel."

"Yes."

"She was a beautiful young woman."

"Yes she was."

"Ya know, Jack told me all about you, but he's not mentioned very much about his wife," she said.

"Well, perhaps it still hurts him to talk about her. Maybe he's still in love with her," Courtney replied.

"I'm sure you're right. I think he'll always love her."

Courtney took another sip of tea to cover the awkwardness of the silence. "Ms O'Malley."

"Please call me Kate."

"Kate, I didn't know that you and Jack are in a relationship."

"Oh no, Jack and I don't have a relationship we're just friends, and …"

Liam burst through the door carrying a trophy and shouted, "Mum, look we won the match!"

Katey smiled at her son, thrilled to see him so excited and happy. "Say hello to Ms. Wells."

"Lo."

Regan walked in and Courtney said, "Hello Jack. I was just passing by and saw your car. I didn't mean to intrude."

"Courtney, I'm glad you did. I've been trying to get in touch with you," he said.

"I know."

"Ms. Wells, why don't you stay for supper? I've made more than enough veal stew. It's almost ready," Kate O'Malley interjected.

"No thank you Kate. I really can't stay; maybe some other time. Thank you for the tea, it was delicious," she said as she got up to leave.

Regan followed her out to her car.

"Court, I wanted to tell you…"

She cut him off and said, "Jack, it's alright. You don't owe me any explanation. I understand she's a beautiful young woman."

"Court, Kate and I are just friends. I wanted to let you know that I'm not ready to start dating. I mean I haven't seen anyone since Susan died. I just didn't want you to misunderstand. I mean, I'm very fond of you."

"Jack, please," she said as she stopped at the door to her car. She turned and said, "Jack, are you sure about this woman? I mean, is it about her, or is it about her and her son?"

"What are you saying?" he asked.

"Jack, I know you. Maybe I know you better than you know yourself. You always wanted to have a child with Susan. Now, with this woman you can have the family thing. Maybe you should honestly evaluate what's going on before you get in too deep."

As she drove away Jack remembered he had completely forgotten to ask Courtney why she had been at the Pickle Works last Friday.

FOURTEEN

———⊷∘⊷———

"**M**r. Coratelli, my name is Charles Ferguson, I'm the District Attorney's chief investigator. I believe you know Assistant District Attorney Regan."

Regan nodded at Coratelli, and waited as Ferguson explained the ground rules. They had decided that Ferguson would conduct the interview and maintain a formal atmosphere throughout the process. "I understand that you have requested this meeting to explore the possibility of obtaining immunity in exchange for your testimony and cooperation with our investigation of official corruption in connection with the Family Division Court House project in Philadelphia," Ferguson continued. "We're here today to consider whether your offer is worthy of such an arrangement."

Regan watched Coratelli's panicked reaction to Ferguson's opening. Coratelli's face was flushed and perspiration beaded up across his forehead. He shifted his bloodshot eyes from Regan to Ferguson and back again, as if looking for a way to escape. He scratched his left arm below his elbow, betraying one of the telltale signs of withdrawal.

"Jack, can you help me out here? You know, for old time's sake."

"Sorry Vito, this isn't my call. Detective Ferguson will decide whether to recommend if your evidence is worthy of immunity. I'm just here to witness the process. If you don't want to continue the interview we can cancel."

"No, no. It's good. I've got information the DA will want to move on," as he replied he constantly shifted his eyes between Regan and Ferguson.

"Alright then Mr. Coratelli, the interview will be on the record," Ferguson said and pushed the button starting the video camera that was directly behind him and Regan. After noting the date and preliminary information, Ferguson asked, "Mr. Coratelli, you requested this meeting to discuss the possibility of immunity in exchange for your testimony and cooperation in the Commonwealth's investigation of possible official corruption, is that correct?"

"Yes."

"No one from this office has made any promises of immunity, or has induced you to request this meeting, is that also correct?"

"Yes."

"You have waived your right to have counsel present at this interview, is that correct?"

"Yes."

"Do you wish to reconsider your waiver of counsel, at this time?"

"No, I'm still a member of the bar and fully understand my rights."

"Are you currently under the influence of any drugs or controlled substances of any kind that may adversely affect your ability to participate in this interview?"

"No. I'm clean."

Ferguson advised Coratelli of his Miranda rights and turned to Regan who nodded.

"Mr. Coratelli, what information do you wish to share with our office?" Ferguson asked.

Coratelli took a long drink from the bottle of water Regan had placed in front of him and stared directly at the video camera and said, "About eighteen months ago, Mickey Saunders, an attorney who used to be partners with Chief Justice Robert Fogerty approached me and told me Fogerty was taking over the Family Court House project. He told me they had targeted the site at 15th and Race. He knew that my father and I owned the three story office building on the northeast corner of the block. He said that I could make a killing on this deal if I played my cards right."

Coratelli continued his monologue for the next hour and a half, laying out the particulars of the scheme that involved inflating the value of his property by several million dollars, kicking back a major portion of the excessive profit to Saunders through the Nooris brothers, the chosen developers for the project. If his description of the scam could be corroborated, the Mayor, the Nooris brothers, the former partner of the Chief Justice and others could be indicted.

"Mr. Coratelli, are you sure that Chief Justice Fogerty was not involved in the scam?" Ferguson asked.

"As far as I know, except for getting him a good deal on a shore house and cheap labor to fix it up, he got nada. Best I can figure, the 'in crowd' thought he was too stupid to be cut in on the deal."

"Vito, how about Dorothy Wiggins? She was retained by Fogerty as counsel. Was she involved?" Regan asked.

"Jack, Gallo and the rest of them would rather have cut off their left testicles than allow that bitch to dip her beak into this. They wanted the Laborers to bury her alive in the foundation of the building. The only thing they wanted to do was fuck Wiggins' associate, Megan Larson. As a matter of fact I think Gallo, or maybe one of the Nooris brothers was doin her. She was one prime piece of ass," he replied.

Regan had assumed Ari Nooris had been involved with Larson. The idea that the Mayor might have been involved was something he had not previously considered.

"Mr. Coratelli, is there anything more you want to add to your statement at this time?"

"No sir. Do I get my deal?"

"Vito, you know the routine. We have to review your statement with our boss and see if we can independently corroborate what you shared with us today," Regan said.

"You're sure about the U.S. Attorney having some of the conversations you had with Saunders and the Nooris brothers on tape?" he asked.

"Those double crossing bastards have hours of conversations. Listen to me Jack, this is solid gold."

"OK Vito. Let's take a break here. I'll have someone come in and take your order for lunch, OK?"

"Sure Jack, that'd be great. Could you do me a favor and turn down the AC? I'm freezing," Coratelli was actually shivering, another sign he was going through withdrawal.

"Sure Vito. No problem."

Regan and Ferguson immediately went to Susan Romansky's office to report on the interview.

"So you think Coratelli really has the goods on Saunders and the Mayor?"

"Susan, I know Vito. He's not smart enough to have come up with this scheme all by himself. Saunders is a scumbag from day one. This whole thing smells like something Gallo would come up with. Maybe this time he outsmarted himself by involving a junkie as one of his partners. Looks like whatever Vito made in the deal went right up his nose. He always considered himself a 'playa.' Now he's facing disbarment and God knows what else," Regan said.

"Charlie, do you agree with Jack?"

"Yeah, if we can get access to the Fed's tapes we got something to run with here," Ferguson said.

"OK. What do you want to do with our witness in the meantime?" she asked.

"We have to put him on ice, in some rehab with 24/7 projection. The Nooris brothers play hardball. If they find out he was wearing a wire, who knows what they're capable of?"

chowitz flashed his shield at the young man sitting behind the security desk at the Moravian, one of the elegant post-war buildings on South Rittenhouse Square. "Young man, please let Miss Wells know that Detective Ichowitz and Assistant District Attorney Regan are here. She's expecting us," he said.

After a brief discussion the security man hung up the phone and directed them to the elevator and said, "Gentlemen, press the Penthouse, Ms. Wells' butler will greet you."

The elevator opened onto the foyer of her apartment. Bradley Morgan, Courtney's butler smiled at Jack and said, "Mr. Regan, nice to see you again, and you also Detective Ichowitz. Ms. Wells is waiting for you on the balcony. Come this way, please."

Morgan had worked for the Wells family for as long as Jack could remember. He was, as always, dressed elegantly in a Brooks Brothers button-down blue shirt and hounds tooth slacks, an understated manner that was appropriate for the occasion. As far as Jack could see, the man seemingly never aged, and retained his straight posture and fit manner even though he must be well into his seventies. To refer to him as a butler did not accurately describe his role. He was more like a surrogate father, an advisor or mentor to Courtney; he was all of that and much more.

They followed him through the living room and out to the balcony that looked onto the square and the breathtaking view of the office towers of Center City to the west and an unobstructed view of the city east and south to the Delaware River and the professional sports teams' stadiums.

Courtney was sitting on a sofa at the corner of the balcony that provided a view of both directions. She stood up and said, "Jack, Izzy, thank you for coming to my apartment. Can I get you something to drink, coffee, ice tea, Pellegrino? No? Bradley, thank you, I think Detective Ichowitz and Mr. Regan would like to speak with me privately," she said.

"Yes ma'am," he said and retreated from the balcony.

"Courtney, I remember when your parents moved here from Radnor. The place looks entirely different, but Bradley never changes," Regan said.

She smiled and said, "Yes, after mother and father moved to Palm Beach, they insisted that I keep the apartment, and Bradley of course was part of the arrangement. After all, just because they were moving that was no reason to disrupt Bradley."

"Please sit down. What is this all about?" she asked.

"Ms. Wells," Ichowitz said.

"Izzy, please you've known me since I was a teenager, why the formality? Am I in trouble?"

"Courtney, you're not in any trouble; however, you may be able to help us with an investigation," Regan interjected.

"Courtney, can you tell us what you were doing at the Pickle Works in Manayunk on Friday, June 8th?" Ichowitz asked.

Courtney blushed and said, "Yes, I was there that day."

"OK, can you tell us about it?"

She looked at Regan and sighed and said, "I went there to see Ari Nooris, but he wasn't there."

They waited for her to continue.

"It was in the afternoon, about 3:30. I had to get back here in time to change for the fundraiser at the Union League. I thought he would be there. He was supposed to have returned from Jerusalem that morning. When I got to his condo a young woman answered the door and told me he wasn't there. That's something that seems to happen to me lately," she said and looked at Jack.

"Courtney, why did you go to Nooris' condo?" Ichowitz asked.

She sighed and said, "This is so awkward. I went there to tell him I did not want to see him anymore." She looked down not wanting to make eye contact with either of them.

"Did you know the young woman who answered the door?"

"No."

"Was anyone else at the condo when you were there?" Ichowitz asked.

"I don't know. I didn't go in. I just left."

"Jack, I had been seeing Ari off and on for a few months after my divorce. I just never felt right about it. I knew he was married. And ..."

"Courtney, you don't have to explain anything to us about your relationship with Nooris. Have you seen him or been in contact with him after that?" Jack asked.

"I sent him a text later that night, after the fundraiser. It seems so long ago, has it only been ten days?"

Jack asked, "Court, did you know Megan Larson?"

"Oh my God! Was that the young woman at Ari's apartment? The woman who was murdered? I read about it, but never put it together. Did Ari have anything to do with that? There was nothing in the newspaper that indicated a connection. Oh I feel so…Jack, Izzy, if I realized I would have come forward right away."

"Courtney, it's alright. No one is suggesting that you did anything improper," Ichowitz said.

As they drove back to the Fourth District, Ichowitz asked Regan, "So what do you think about Courtney and Ari Nooris?"

"Izz, I really had no contact with Courtney for several years. You hear things, but you know me, I don't really pay any attention to gossip. Courtney was always attracted to those edgy types. I guess that's why we went our separate ways."

"So, Courtney doesn't know about Megan Larson and Nooris?"

"Izz, we don't know about Megan Larson and Nooris, except he let her stay at his place while he was out of the country," Regan said.

"We now know that Nooris and Gallo and Saunders were in on some kind of scam on the Family Division Court House. At least we think we do if Coratelli's story holds up. That more or less confirms Nooris' explanation about how he came to be close with Larson. Sooner or later we need to get his DNA to see if he's the father of her baby. If they were lovers does that mean he's no longer a suspect?" Ichowitz asked.

"Or does that mean he had a reason to kill her?" Regan responded.

Ichowitz shrugged his shoulders. "What did Courtney mean when she made that remark about young women answering doors?"

Regan told him about Courtney dropping by his house when Kate O'Malley was there cooking dinner for him and her son the previous evening.

"Jack, you never told Courtney about Kate?"

"Izz, I was going to tell her after the Broad Street Run, but she bolted before I got to the finish line. I left her half a dozen messages. Besides, there was nothing really to tell her."

"*Oy-veh*," Ichowitz sighed.

"**M**ickey, it's so nice to see you," the Honorable Bruce Peter Gallo said.

"How's the Chief Justice doing?"

Mickey Saunders raised an eyebrow at the greeting. Gallo shook his head, signaling Saunders not to say anything of substance. "I was just about to leave for a meeting with the Chamber of Commerce. Walk with me," the Mayor said, taking Saunders by the arm and leading him out of his office.

"I've heard from a solid source that someone we know is spilling his guts about our arrangement," he whispered as they walked down the corridor. "I knew that little shit would be a problem."

"Mayor, don't worry about it our friends will know how to handle it," Saunders replied.

"You're sure about that?"

"Positive."

"Mickey, please be sure you tell the Chief I was asking about him," the Mayor said in his public voice as he patted Saunders' shoulder.

As soon as he walked outside of City Hall Saunders pulled out his cell phone and hit the speed dial.

"Meet me at the construction site in ten minutes. Something has come up that requires your special skills," he said and hung up.

FIFTEEN

Kate O'Malley was singing as she placed the order of produce into the walk-in box.

"You sound happy," Mike O'Malley said as he watched his niece work.

"I'd be even happier if you'd lend a hand," she replied.

O'Malley picked up a crate of tomatoes and followed her into the refrigerated box.

"Uncle Mike, can I ask you something?"

"Uncle Mike is it," he said. "Must be something important, I figure to be addressed in that manner."

She smiled at him, "I suppose."

"Well, what is it; you're not wantin a raise, are you?"

"No nothing like that. Jack told me that you introduced him to his wife. Is that so?"

"Yes, that I did."

"Can you tell me about her?"

"Have you asked Jack about Susan?"

"Not really."

"Why not?"

"I don't know. I just get the feeling he doesn't want to talk about it."

"So you favor Jack. Is that it?"

Kate looked up at O'Malley and said, "Maybe."

He gave her a long look and said, "Come along then," he said. "Let's have a cuppa tea and I'll tell you about Susan and Jack."

They sat at the booth near the front window with their mugs of tea. He took a long sip and said, "The story begins with Susan's parents, Helen and Norman Rothman. They owned the hardware store across the street, where the Pottery Barn is now."

"They were survivors of the Holocaust. They met in the death camp, Auschwitz. All of their people perished, but they survived. They were devoted to each other, and pretty much kept to themselves. Soon after they opened, some toughs from up the hill were giving them a hard time. I happened along when three of them were in the store tryin to shake them down. Norman refused and one of them approached Helen. Before I could jump in to help him out, he knocked two of them to the ground and those stinkin scum ran away. Norm was one tough son of a gun."

"Anyways, we became friends after that. Because of what happened to her in the death camps, they thought they could never have children. When Helen was in her fifties she conceived. They called Susan the miracle baby. And she truly was God's gift to these wonderful people."

"Susan was a beautiful and brilliant little girl. She called me Uncle Mike from when she was a wee one. I was almost as proud of her as her parents were. She won a full scholarship to the University of Pennsylvania."

"Then came the terrible tragedy. Norman and Helen, who had survived the worst unthinkable atrocities anyone could live through, were killed by a drunken driver in a head-on collision on the Schuylkill Expressway. They were driving home after dropping Susan off at her dormitory at Penn. Jack's Uncle Joe was still on the police force and knew how close I was with Susan. He sent a patrol car over for me to go to Susan's dormitory."

"Susan was devastated. I was the closest thing to family she had. After the funeral and all she came to live here, in the apartment on the third floor where you and Liam live now."

"Jack was away at college when Susan's parents were killed. After he graduated and came to live with his Uncle Joe, I got to know him.

He wasn't the spoiled preppy I thought him to be when I first noticed him hanging around his uncle's place. He was devoted to Joe, and took care of him when he got sick. He would bring Joe to the Grape and study when Joe and me caroused and lifted a pint or two."

"Anyways, when Susan came home for the summer before she started medical school and Jack had brought Joe over to the pub I says to Jack, 'Whyn't ya ask my god daughter Susan out for a date instead of the two of you just sittin around watchin the likes of us ?'"

"One thing led to another, and before you know it I'm walkin Susan down the aisle. What's that I see - a tear runnin down yer cheek?"

"Uncle Mike, I had no idea how close you were to that young woman. You must have been devastated when she passed away."

"I had to hold it together for Jack's sake. He's a good man, Katey. I think he's just starting to realize that it's alright to live again. I can tell he favors you and the boy."

Kate O'Malley went back to the kitchen to prepare the menu for the evening. She could not stop thinking about the tragic story her uncle had shared about Jack's wife and her family. She found herself thinking about Jack more and more. She swore she would never let her feelings towards any man make her lose her balance again. After all she was responsible for the well being of her son, Liam. She had left Ireland to make sure that no harm would come to him. Kate could take care of both of them. She had no need for a man in her life. Not now; not until she was sure that Liam would be safe from the trouble she had fled.

Why did she have to meet Jack Regan now? She would not fall in love with him. She would break it off before it got too serious. She had no choice. She had to protect Liam.

SIXTEEN

———◆———

The night nurse knocked on his door. She was a tall woman with frizzy blond hair. Coratelli looked up at her and smiled. He was not tolerating his withdrawal in the manner that he had been assured by the doctors. The sedative he had been given less than an hour before had done nothing to dull the agony. The junkie he was, he hoped he could con this nurse into giving him something to help him get through the night.

"How are you doing, Mr. Coratelli?" she asked as she approached his bed.

"Not so good. I was wondering if you might be able, you know, to give me a little something." He was so preoccupied with the pain he failed to realize that the nurse had used his real name and not the false name under which he had been registered at the facility.

"Let me check your chart and see if you're due for another sedative," she said as she reached for the chart at the foot of his bed.

"No, that's not necessary; no one gave me anything since I was admitted," he lied.

She smiled at him and said, "I can see that you're having a difficult time. Let me see if I can help you out."

She removed a hypodermic needle from her pocket. "Now Mr. Coratelli, this might pinch a bit," she said as she stuck the needle in his arm.

As he felt the pinch, he suddenly noticed that she had used his real name. "Hey, how do you know…" he never finished asking his question.

At 2 AM they found Coratelli's body on the floor of his room with the hypodermic needle still in his arm. The spoon and lighter and the rest of his works were near his body. No one could explain how he got the drugs into the facility. Charley Ferguson, the DA's Investigator, was notified by the facility's administrator within an hour of the discovery. Even though the facility was located in Montgomery County, Ferguson was afforded complete access to the crime scene as a courtesy by his counterpart in the Montgomery County District Attorney's office.

At 6 AM Ferguson called his boss to report Coratelli's death. The preliminary finding of the Montgomery County coroner was "Accidental death by drug overdose." At 8 AM Susan Romansky called Regan. "Jack, did Charley Ferguson call you?"

"No. What happened?"

"They found Vito Coratelli's body in his room. He died of an apparent heroin overdose. The Montgomery County coroner's office is doing the autopsy. We should find out the results later today."

"Susan, how the hell could this have happened? I mean, only you me and Ferguson knew where we stashed him. It was a secure facility with a spotless record. He was thoroughly searched before he was admitted and under around-the-clock surveillance."

"I know. It just doesn't add up. There must have been a leak at the facility. I'll see you in the office at ten. Maybe Charlie will have something for us by then."

Regan could not believe that Coratelli overdosed. Based on what he knew, Coratelli did not mainline heroin. His arms showed no visible track marks of a heavy user. Regan realized that Coratelli could have injected the drugs in other parts of his body, like between his toes, to hide the track marks, but Coratelli struck him as too lazy to go to the trouble.

Without Coratelli the court house corruption investigation was dead in the water. The preliminary interview they had videotaped would be admissible, but Regan knew that wasn't enough. Regan believed that Coratelli's death was no accident, and sure as hell he hadn't committed suicide. Coratelli was too interested in securing a deal for immunity to just throw in the cards. Coratelli had been murdered, and whoever had killed him was involved in the court house scam. Regan also believed that whoever had killed Coratelli was also involved in the Larson murder.

Regan's meeting with his boss and Ferguson further confirmed his suspicions.

"According to the preliminary toxicology report, the heroin in Coratelli's body and the residue in the spoon was pure, uncut heroin," Ferguson told them. "No one has reported seeing anything like it in this area. One of the toxicologists said it reminded him of something he ran into when he was on active duty in Afghanistan. Even the markings on the baggie looked like what he saw when he was stationed in Kabul."

"How the hell did Coratelli get his hands on pure, uncut heroin from Afghanistan? That just makes no sense at all." Regan said.

"Charley, we need to find out who knew that Vito Coratelli was the patient at the Sunrise facility. Someone on that end either leaked the information to whoever got him the drugs, or gave him the heroin himself," Romansky said. "Jack's right about this. There's no way Coratelli had access to the drugs while he was in our custody. He had to have gotten it, or someone gave it to him after he was admitted to the facility."

"Susan, I can't help thinking that the same players who are involved in the court house deal are involved in the Larson murder. There's got to be a connection between these two cases," Regan said.

"Gentlemen, do you both think that Coratelli's death was not an accidental overdose?"

They nodded.

"Jack, why don't you and Charley hook up with Izzy Ichowitz? Maybe the three of you can come up with a connection between the Larson murder and Coratelli's homicide."

They met at the Fourth District in the conference room Ichowitz had commandeered for the Larson investigation. The pictures of the suspects, some crossed out, were still pinned to the wall. The timeline developed from the investigation was written in red marker on the white board.

"Jack tells me you're not buying the Montgomery County coroner's accidental overdose theory," Ichowitz said to Charley Ferguson.

"That was no accident. The heroin was too pure, and besides, Coratelli was not a heroin addict. Cocaine was his drug of choice," Ferguson replied.

"So you think he was wacked by the principals involved in the court house scam?" Ichowitz asked.

Regan and Ferguson nodded.

"And Jack, you think the doer also killed Megan Larson?"

"Izz, I'm not sure, but I think there's a connection. Too many of the players are common to both crimes."

"OK. So let's run through the list," Ichowitz said as he walked over to the wall where the photos of the Larsen suspects were posted.

He pointed to the picture of Dorothy Wiggins and said, "So far we pretty much eliminated Wiggins as the doer in the Larson murder. The Comcast kid saw Larson alive and well after Wiggins had left the Nooris condo. Anyway, as far as your investigation of the court house scam went, the insiders hated her and aced her out. She had no motive to kill Coratelli. Agreed?"

Regan and Ferguson nodded.

"His Honor, Mayor Bruce Peter Gallo. We have his vehicle at the Old Pickle Works the evening of Larson's murder. We have not yet determined if he was at Nooris' condo, nor do we have any evidence that directly links Gallo to the victim. Your investigation ties him to the court house scam. He's one treacherous bastard, but there's no history of violent crimes. If he was involved in either murder or both, he would not likely have been the doer, but he clearly had a motive to shut Coratelli up."

Once again Regan and Ferguson nodded their assent.

Ichowitz next pointed at the pictures of the Nooris brothers. "Your investigation ties the Nooris' to the court house scam. Both had a motive to silence Coratelli. Avi Nooris' alibi for the Larson murder has a hole big enough for him to have slipped into the condo and beat Larson to death. As far as we know, however, he had no motive to kill her."

"Charley here's something that needs to remain in this room, OK?" Ichowitz asked.

Ferguson nodded.

"Ari Nooris, is a former Mossad agent, who was under surveillance by Homeland Security, for reasons still unknown to us. He also had motive to silence Coratelli, but there's no evidence that he was at the condo the night Larson was murdered, nor is there any motive for him to kill her, at least as far as we know."

Regan and Ferguson nodded.

Ichowitz removed two photos from a folder on the conference table and pinned one to the wall. "Mickey Saunders, a player in the court house scam with an obvious motive to silence Coratelli, but no link to Larson. Finally, Chief Justice Robert Fogerty, who, according to Vito, had no motive to kill him, since he was not directly involved in the scam, and no motive or opportunity to kill Larson."

"So gentlemen, what do we have?" Ichowitz asked.

"Too many players in common for there to be no connection," Regan said.

"Maybe, but not enough to make a case, at least not yet," Ferguson said.

"What's our next move then?" Regan asked.

Ichowitz stared at the wall. After a few minutes passed he said, "Why don't we approach Vito Coratelli Sr. and tell him we believe his son was murdered by someone involved in the court house scam. Maybe he will agree to help us in our investigation."

"I think we should also go back to the Nooris brothers and find out if either of them was the father of Larson's baby," Regan said.

For the next two hours they made their plans.

SEVENTEEN

———◆———

Liam walked between them and held both his mother and Regan's hands as they made their way through the crowd in the concourse at Citizens Bank Park. It was both Liam and Katey's first ballgame, and neither of them had any idea of exactly what to expect. Liam was caught up in the excitement of the crowd. When they walked out of the entrance to the field level box seats, the look of amazement on Liam's face reminded Regan of his own reaction when his father took him to his first Phillies game at Veterans' Stadium, where the Phillies played back when Jack was a little boy.

Regan got the family's field box tickets right behind the Phillies dugout. Katey watched as Jack patiently answered all of Liam's questions. She could not fail to notice her son's rapt attention to Jack's every word and how natural the two of them looked together with Jack's arm around Liam's shoulder. Jack's hand remained on Liam's shoulder as they stood for the singing of the National Anthem.

In the third inning, Jack nonchalantly caught a screaming foul ball off of Jimmy Rollins' bat and handed it to Liam. Within seconds they watched the replay of Jack's catch and Liam's look of pure joy on the jumbo screen above center field when Jack handed him the ball, as the crowd cheered. The seventh inning stretch brought the Phillie Phanatic, the baseball team's mascot, to the top of the Phillies' dugout. When the Phanatic walked by Katey he did a double take, and in his unique fashion made a funny lewd gesture, and lifted Kate out of her seat onto the roof of the dugout. When Liam reached for his mother, the Phanatic brought him onto the dugout roof as well.

The crowd cheered as the Katey and Liam tried to mimic the Phanatic's antics. Regan's phone buzzed in his pocket. His mother was on the line, "Jack, your father and I are watching the game on TV. Are that young woman and the little boy your guests?"

"Yes mother."

"Who are they?"

"Mother, I can hardly hear you. I'll call you tomorrow."

The Phillies beat the Cardinals, 8 to 1, extending their lead over the Braves to four games. Jack carried a sleeping Liam to the car. He gently placed him in the back seat and secured the seat belt around him. Liam slept through it all with a beautiful smile.

Jack opened the front door for Katey. Before she got in the car she turned and kissed Jack. She squeezed his hand and said, "Thank you."

Kate placed her hand on Jack's shoulder as he drove them back to the Grape. He carried Liam up to the third floor apartment. She noticed once again how natural the two of them looked together with Liam's head resting on Jack's shoulder. "Wait for me," she whispered, as she took the sleeping child from his arms.

As she walked back to the living room she felt a warmth flow over her that she had not experienced since the birth of her son. He took her in his arms and they kissed.

"Kate, are you sure about this?" he asked.

She looked at him and said, "I don't want to think about Liam's father or your Susan, or anything," and led him into her bedroom.

That morning Kate watched Jack as he slept. She knew that what had happened had implications that had to be confronted. Was she still in love with Liam's father, Michael Flynn? Was she falling in love with this man? How could Regan have so quickly and seamlessly become so integral in both her and Liam's lives?

He smiled at her and asked, "A penny for your thoughts?"

"Oh Jack," she said.

He pulled her down to him and kissed her.

After they made love he asked, "Should I leave before Liam wakes up?"

"Too late for that, I heard Liam whistling 'Take Me Out To The Ball Game.'"

"I'll go out and tell him you're here," she said and kissed him and got out of the bed and put on her robe.

When Jack walked out of the bedroom Liam ran to him and gave him a hug.

Jack hugged the little boy and looked over to Kate who smiled back at him.

"Hey Bub," he said. "Did you like the game?"

"Jack, can ya teach me how to play?"

"Sure."

"Will we be goin to another game soon?"

"Absolutely."

Later that morning when Regan met Ichowitz at the Fourth District, Ichowitz greeted him. "Nice catch Jack!"

"You were watching the game?"

"Uh-huh."

"So was my mother. She called and asked me about the young woman and the little boy," Regan said and sighed.

"You really like Ms. O'Malley, don't you?"

"Yes."

"And her son, you could tell from the way he hugged you when you gave him the ball how he feels about you. *Boychik*, this is a good thing, very good."

"What do you think my mother will say?"

"Your mother will love both of them. You'll see. Ida wants you to bring them over to our house soon. You know Ida, she has a nose for things like this. She's already decided that the three of you were destined to be together, '*Bashert zein*,' as my people say."

Regan and Ichowitz had arranged a meeting with Vito Coratelli Sr. at his home at 8ᵗʰ and Mifflin Streets in South Philadelphia. Despite the wealth Coratelli had amassed as one of the premier criminal defense attorneys in Philadelphia, the Coratellis lived in the modest row house in the Bella Vista neighborhood he had inherited from his parents. The house was filled with family and friends who had come to help the parents mourn the untimely passing of their eldest son.

They sat in his study. It was a small room, barely large enough for the desk and three chairs in which they sat. Coratelli looked like an older version of his deceased son. The resemblance aside, Junior could never hold a candle to his father's brilliance.

"Izzy my friend, I've missed our encounters," Coratelli said and patted the Detective's knee.

Ichowitz had been the arresting officer and principal witness for the Commonwealth in a number of cases in which Coratelli was defense counsel.

"Vito, I still have the scars from some of our duels. I can't believe you got so many of those *gonifs* off," Ichowitz said with a smile.

"Izz, don't worry, they paid dearly for their crimes. I don't work cheap. Besides, sooner or later they all have to answer for what they did."

"The *emess*?" Ichowitz asked.

"The *emess*," Coratelli nodded.

"Vito, Jack and I believe your son's death was not an accident. We think he was murdered to stop him from cooperating in an investigation the District Attorney's office was conducting."

Coratelli stared at Ichowitz, his face flushed with anger.

Ichowitz and Regan filled him in on what they knew and what they suspected. Coratelli immediately agreed to assist them in their plan to infiltrate the court house conspirators.

"I realize that Junior made mistakes in judgment. Those *schifoso, faccia di strozo*! To kill my boy, like he was a piece of garbage."

"Vito, after the funeral we'll put it together. In the meantime, take care of your family," Ichowitz said.

As they drove back to Manayunk Regan asked, "Izz, you don't think Coratelli will take matters into his own hands, do you?"

"I've known Vito for thirty years. He is one of the most rational men I have ever encountered. He is always under control, a perfectionist. If there is any way to get us an admission from that crowd, he'll figure it out."

They arrived at Ari Nooris' office at 4 PM. His receptionist, Shona, was manning her station. She recognized Ichowitz when he entered the lobby. "Gentlemen," she said. "Is Mr. Nooris expecting you?"

"No Miss, Shona is it?" Ichowitz asked; she nodded. "We happened to be in the area and need to speak with him. Is he in?"

She picked up the phone and spoke briefly in Hebrew, replaced the receiver, stood up and said, "Please follow me."

Ari Nooris was sitting at a sofa in the atrium at the back of his office. The room looked onto a garden and out to the Manayunk Canal. Regan watched as a tall man who walked with a noticeable limp made his way out of the garden. The man turned and Regan caught a glimpse of his face. The man's bottle green eyes stared back at Regan as if memorizing his face.

"Mr. Nooris, Assistant District Attorney Jack Regan and I have a few questions to ask you concerning the Megan Larson homicide, if that's alright?" Ichowitz said as they entered the romm.

Nooris nodded and asked "Detective Ichowitz, District Attorney Regan, have there been any developments in your investigation of Megan Larson's murder?"

They waited until Shona withdrew from the room and Ichowitz said, "Yes. As a matter of fact there have been some. That's why we're here."

Nooris gestured for them to take seats and waited for Ichowitz to continue.

"Mr. Nooris, were you aware that Ms. Larson was pregnant?"

Nooris looked surprised and said, "No, I had no idea." He paused and said, "Oh. That would mean that her baby was also…How sad."

"Mr. Nooris, do you have any idea as to who the father of child could have been?" Regan asked.

Nooris stared at Regan and said, "No, no I do not."

"Mr. Nooris, please understand I need to ask you this question. Could you have been the father?" Regan asked.

Nooris could not fully conceal his anger at the question, after a brief pause he replied, "Mr. Regan, Megan and I were not lovers. We were friends."

"Would you agree to a DNA test?" Regan asked.

Once again Nooris frowned in reaction to the question, "How would that help you find Megan's killer?"

"We intend to ask everyone our investigation reveals had a relationship with Ms. Larson to give us a sample of their DNA. This investigation now involves a double homicide, and we need to know the identity of father of the dead child."

"Do you consider me a suspect?" Nooris asked.

"No we do not," Ichowitz responded.

Nooris looked at them and considered his answer. "Is this really necessary?"

"We wouldn't ask you if we didn't believe that ruling out all of the potential fathers wasn't important," Ichowitz said.

"And I suppose you could get, what do you call it, a writ?"

"A subpoena, yes eventually we would obtain one," Regan answered.

"Nooris sighed, "Alright then."

"Izz, what do you think?" Regan asked as they walked to his car.

"I believe he had no idea Megan Larson was pregnant. I also think he was telling us the truth about them not being lovers."

"Did you notice the man who was walking out of the garden behind Nooris' office?" Regan asked.

"Yes."

"Have you ever seen him before?"

"No. Why?"

"I don't know- something about him."

Ichowitz shrugged and asked, "What do you think about Shona?"

"I think she's not just Nooris' receptionist," Regan replied.

"What do you mean?"

"It's the way she moves, on the balls of her feet, like she's ready to attack. I don't know; like I said, she's more than just a receptionist."

egan and Ichowitz were scheduled to meet with the Mayor at 4 PM the next day. They figured that by then they would have finished their meetings with Avi Nooris concerning the hole in his alibi and the DA and Charley Ferguson to fill them in on their conversation with Vito Coratelli Sr.

Regan had failed to return a number of his mother's telephone calls he had received throughout the day. He was trying to figure out which discussion would be more problematic: tomorrow's meeting with Mayor Gallo, or the grilling he would shortly receive from his mother about Kate O'Malley and her son Liam.

Ichowitz said, "You better return your mother's calls. She already called my wife. I'm sure she asked your father to send a squad car to your house or put an APB out for you."

"I know, Izz."

"Devil hates a coward, isn't that one of your Irish expressions?" Ichowitz said as he handed him the phone and left him alone in the Fourth District conference room. "See you tomorrow," he said as he closed the conference room door.

"Hello mother. I'm sorry I wasn't able to return your calls. We've been pretty busy today."

"Jack, are you going to tell me about that attractive young woman and that adorable little boy I saw you with at the Phillies game last night?"

"Mother, her name is Kate O'Malley, she's Mike O'Malley's niece. She and her son Liam recently emigrated from Dublin. She's helping Mike run the Grape Tavern."

"Did O'Malley fix you up again?"

"No mother, I decided to ask her out all on my own."

"But I thought you and Courtney were going to get back together."

"Courtney and I are just friends."

"Is this O'Malley woman divorced?"

"No mother she was never married."

"Oh."

After a moment of silence he said, "Mother, why don't you reserve judgment until you meet Katey?"

"So I'll be meeting her sometime soon?"

"I'm hoping she'll come to our Sunday get-together."

"Good."

Regan noticed among the missed calls was his sister Annabelle.

"Annie…"

"Jack, did you call Mother?"

"Yes Sis."

"Jack, we saw you on TV last night. The woman you were with is absolutely gorgeous; and that little boy… Jack I'm so happy for you."

"Annie, look. Let's not get carried away. We're just friends. I'm not sure how she feels about me or exactly where this is headed."

"Jack, you'll bring her Sunday?"

"I'll ask."

When he pulled his car into his parking space, his mobile phone began to vibrate. He smiled when he saw it was Kate.

"Hi Kate, I'm glad you called," he said.

"Well, Liam's been askin whether you'd be stoppin by tonight," she said.

"I wouldn't want to disappoint Liam. See you soon, if that's allright with you."

Regan was greeted by Mike O'Malley when he made his way past the crowded bar.

"Mike, I see that your bartender is still pumping out the cosmos," he said and watched the show Melody Schwartz put on twirling the shaker and filling multiple martini glasses to the brim with pink and blue concoctions.

She smiled at Jack as he approached. "Mel, wasn't your hair blue last time I was here?" he asked.

"I felt like a change, do you like the green?"

"Very you," he said.

"And I thought you only went for red heads," she said and nodded towards the kitchen.

O'Malley grabbed his arm and said, "You'll never guess who called me his afternoon."

"My mother?" Regan replied.

"Right ya are, me bucko. She wanted the complete dossier on me niece and Liam, don't cha know. She wanted all the particulars on yer relationship too."

"And I'm sure you told her everything," Jack said.

"Yeh. I told her how the two of you have been attendin St. Cecilia's classes in celibacy, and how I've heard you sayin your Hail Marys for havin impure thoughts and all. I think she bought it," O'Malley deadpanned.

"Ya better get in there before she overcooks the stew or something," O'Malley said and nodded towards the kitchen.

She was standing next to Eduardo and Miguel, the two line cooks she had hired to help since the word had spread that the cuisine at the Grape was no longer limited to ham and cheese on stale bread and beef stew from a can. The two young men from Belize were amazing cooks, grateful for the opportunity to refine their craft under Kate's tutelage.

"Hey you," Regan said as he approached.

She smiled, "Hey yourself. What's in the box?" she asked.

"I bought something for Liam," he said.

"Oh, tryin to get in with me by bein nice to the boy."

"Something like that," he blushed.

"Liam's waitin for ya. Why don't you go up and tell the sitter she can go home. I'll be up after the rush. I made a little something for you. It's heating on the stove. Now shoo, the boys and me are busy."

Liam looked up from the checker board when Jack walked through the door. Jack could not believe the rush of happiness he felt at the boy's smile.

"Jack, what's in the box?"

"I got you something I think you may be needing soon," he said.

Liam ran over to him and Regan handed him the box. Liam tore off the wrapping, opened the box and looked down. His eyes widened with delight as he pulled the baseball glove out and put it on.

"There's something else in there," Jack said,

Liam looked in the box and pulled out another smaller box. When he unwrapped the package he found a wrist watch compass like the one Jack wore.

"Liam, when you wear the compass you'll always be able to find your way home."

Later when Kate walked in Liam rushed to her and said, "Mum, look what Jack bought me!" He showed her the glove and compass watch.

"Well, I trust you thanked him properly," she said.

"Jack said he would teach me how to play. He told me if you agree we can play this Sunday with his nieces and nephews. Mum, can we?"

Katey looked at Jack and asked, "And where might this game be held?"

"That would be at my folks' place. We have this regular get-together. I think Liam will fit right in," Regan said.

"It's not Liam fittin in I'm worried about," she said.

EIGHTEEN

———◆———

"Detective Ichowitz, Jack, what can I do for you?" The Honorable Bruce Peter Gallo, Mayor of the City of Philadelphia said when they were ushered into his office. Gallo was sitting at his desk and gestured for them to take the leather chairs in front of the desk. As was his custom, the Mayor always assumed what he perceived as the position of power having elevated his desk and chair four inches higher than his visitor's chairs.

"Mayor, thank you for seeing us," Ichowitz replied. "We asked to see you in connection with our investigation of the Megan Larson murder."

Gallo shook his head and sighed, "What a terrible tragedy. She was a lovely young woman."

"Mayor, did you know Ms. Larson very well?"

Gallo paused as if carefully considering his response and said, "Yes."

"Did you see her on June 8th, the night she was murdered?"

He paused again stared at Ichowitz as if trying to discern what the detective knew and said, "Yes I did."

"Can you tell us about it?"

"Megan and I were very close friends. She told me she was staying at a friend's place in Manayunk. She asked if I could stop by and give her some advice about a situation in which she was involved."

"What situation?" Ichowitz asked.

Gallo stared at the detective for a few moments and finally replied, "Well, she had resigned from her job with Dorothy Wiggins, and she was ending their personal relationship. Megan was concerned that Wiggins would react," he paused apparently choosing his words carefully, and continued, "Megan was concerned that Wiggins would be upset, that she would try to dissuade her from moving on."

"Did Megan tell you anything about the nature of her personal relationship with Ms. Wiggins?"

Gallo considered his answer and said, "Wiggins was Megan's mentor. Unfortunately Wiggins wanted their relationship to be more than strictly professional."

"You were aware that Megan had been living at Wiggins' home, weren't you?" Ichowitz asked.

"Yes. But as I told you she had moved out and was staying at her friend's place."

"Mayor, did you know whose place she was staying at?"

"Not until I got there. It happened to be Ari Nooris' condo. Ari, Megan and I had been working on the court house project. That's how I came to know Megan."

"Mayor, did you know that Megan was pregnant?"

Gallo stared back at Ichowitz, obviously surprised by the question. He took a deep breath and said, "No."

Before he could recover from his shock over the revelation of Larson's pregnancy Regan asked, "When exactly did you see Megan on the 8th?"

"It must have been around 8 or 8:30 that night. I'm not sure. It was only for a few minutes. I was in between events. I had been at the fundraiser at the Union League; Jack, I saw you there. I had to be at a meeting with the ward leaders in South Philadelphia at ten. So I couldn't have been with Megan for more than a half hour at the most."

"Was anyone else there?"

"No."

"Mayor, I have to ask you this question." Ichowitz said. "Were you and Ms. Larson in an intimate relationship?"

Gallo blushed and said, "Yes, yes we were. I cared very deeply about her."

"Mayor, would you provide us with a DNA sample? We're trying to determine the identity of the father of Megan's baby."

"Of course."

At their meeting with the DA and her Chief Investigator Charles Ferguson, Regan and Ichowitz told them they believed Gallo had been unaware of Larson's pregnancy. As to his not knowing the nature of Larson's relationship with Wiggins, they were not buying that. Gallo was too shrewd not to have realized that Larson and Wiggins had a sexual relationship. They had checked out his alibi, and Gallo had attended the meeting with the South Philly ward leaders as he claimed. Since Jack corroborated Gallo's attendance at the Union League, it appeared that Gallo was not a suspect in the murder. Besides, as far as they could see, Gallo had no motive to harm Larson.

"Jack, Izzy, do you believe that the Mayor was being honest about his feelings for Megan Larson?" the DA asked.

"Yes. I don't think he's that good a liar," Ichowitz responded.

Romansky laughed and said, "He's a politician, of course he's an accomplished liar. Where are we on the court house case?"

"Vito Senior is on board. Izzy and I will meet him tomorrow to finalize our strategy," Regan replied.

When they had concluded the meeting, Ichowitz asked Regan, "So do we have a strategy for Vito to implement?"

"Not yet, but I'm sure we'll come up with one by tomorrow," Regan said. "First I have to come up with a strategy for Sunday's meeting between my mother and Katey. Got any advice?"

"Introduce them and then go play baseball with Liam and your nieces and nephews. Your mother and Ms O'Malley will take it from there."

"Really?"

"It's the *emess*," Ichowitz said and patted Regan on the shoulder.

The following morning Ichowitz and Regan returned to Vito Coratelli's home.

"Mr. Coratelli, Izzy and I think the best way to proceed, is to…"

Coratelli waved his hand cutting Regan off in mid sentence, "Young man," he said. "I have been handling '*faccio di stronzo*'- what you call low-life bastards, like Gallo and Saunders and the rest of them, since before you were born."

"Here's how we're going to fix these *schifozos*," he said.

For the next forty-five minutes Coratelli laid out his strategy.

Coratelli would start by confronting Mickey Saunders, who he believed was the weakest link in the chain. He would suggest that Saunders' principals were setting him up to take the fall for his son's murder and that the police were already making plans with the DA to arrest him and indict him for Vito Junior's murder. Coratelli would tell him he knew that Saunders could not be involved. After all, Saunders, Chief Justice Bob Fogerty and Coratelli had been friends for over forty years.

"Sow the seed of division, and then we will cultivate them," Coratelli said. "Before he has a chance to react, I will move on to His Honor, and tell him I have been informed that Saunders is about to implicate him in the murder. Let's see how these rats respond."

"Vito, do you really believe they will turn on each other?" Ichowitz asked.

"Izzy, they are all gutless. Neither Saunders nor Gallo actually put the poison in my boy's veins, but they were all guilty. No, it was the Nooris brothers, or someone working for them who did it. We need to scare one of them to rat out the Nooris."

"You'll see. They will be jumping over one another to be the Commonwealth's witness."

Later on, after they set up the time and sequence of Coratelli's meetings with Saunders and the Chief Justice, Regan asked Ichowitz, "Do you think Coratelli will be able to get Saunders to finger the Nooris brothers?"

"Jack, I have watched Vito tear holes in the most solid prosecutions the Commonwealth had ever presented. He can bring a jury to tears even when his client is the most despicable scumbag they have ever encountered. If he can do that, he can convince Mickey Saunders he's going to the needle if he doesn't come forward and make a deal."

NINETEEN

—◆◆◆—

"**M**other, Dad, I asked Katey O'Malley and Liam to join us today," Jack said as they entered the back yard of his parents' home.

The Commissioner and Patricia Regan were standing at the gate.

"Welcome to our home," Commissioner Regan said, as he extended his hand to Kate. "Liam, that's a really nice glove you have there," he said and was greeted with a smile. "It looks just like the first baseball glove I bought Jack when he was around your age. Jack, that's an outfielder's glove. I guess you figure Liam's got the speed and coordination to play out there."

"Dad, Liam's got the makings of a five tool outfielder," Jack replied.

Liam blushed.

"Ladies, if you don't mind, Liam, Jack and I are going to throw the pill around a bit," the Commissioner said, as he took Liam by the hand.

"Hello dear," Mrs. Regan said as she extended her hand to Kate.

"Thank you for inviting us, ma'am," Kate replied.

They watched as Jack and his father introduced Liam to Jack's nephews and nieces who had already arrived. Liam stood next to Jack, who draped his arm over the little boy's shoulder.

"My Liam favors Jack," Kate said.

"And I can see that the feeling is quite mutual," Patricia Regan said. "Come let me introduce you to the rest of the clan."

Jack looked back at Kate and his mother.

"Jack, you can stop worrying about your mother and Ms. O'Malley. That young woman looks more than capable of holding her own. Besides, all your mother wants is for you to be happy," Jack's father said.

Liam was the star of the wiffle-ball game. When Liam and the other kids started to kick the soccer ball, Jack went in search of Katey and his mother. He found them in the kitchen.

"What are the two of you cooking up?" he asked.

"Kate was just giving me pointers on how to prepare the turkey for Thanksgiving dinner," his mother said.

"Mother, I think you'll find that Kate's a whiz when it comes to the culinary arts. She's a graduate of Le Cordon Bleu."

"Is that so, my dear?" Mrs. Regan asked.

Kate blushed and nodded.

"No wonder I heard all the raves about your transformation of the menu at the Grape Tavern. I bet your uncle gave you quite a battle over changing the ambiance of his bar."

"So you know O'Malley pretty well I see," Kate replied with a smile. "I don't think the word 'ambiance' and the Grape were ever used in the same sentence before, Mrs. Regan."

"Call me Patty, dear," Jack's mother said. "Now Jack, you shoo. Go out and play with the kids. Kate and I are talking turkey, and I have to make some notes."

Jack sat down on the Adirondack chair next to his father. The Commissioner handed him a cold bottle of Harp from the cooler. Jack touched the neck of his bottle to his father's and said, "Mother and Katey are talking turkey."

"I assumed the girls were getting along well. I noticed your sister Annie guarding the kitchen door a few minutes ago in case hostilities broke out. I figured that things were going well when she left her post," his father replied. "Kate's a beautiful girl, and that little boy," his father said. "Jack I told your mother that you needed some time to mourn and not to meddle. But you know, she couldn't help herself, and tried to reunite you and Courtney. Does Courtney know about Ms. O'Malley?"

Jack nodded.

"*Oy-vey.*"

"You must have been hanging out with Izzy."

"Since before you were born Jack; Izzy told me that Vito Coratelli Sr. is going to help you with the investigation of his son's death do you think his plan is going to work?"

"Dad, this case seems to be morphing into a conspiracy that could bring down the Mayor, the Chief Justice of the Pennsylvania Supreme Court and God knows who else," Jack replied.

The Commissioner nodded.

"Why don't you give me a summary of what your investigation has uncovered so far?"

Jack took a breath and said, "I became involved as part of a task force looking into municipal corruption by city officials and public employee unions. The investigation led us to the Family Court House project and the possible involvement of the Chief Justice and others. Megan Larson's murder changed everything. She had been a cooperating witness and was going to testify before the grand jury. With her death it appeared that our investigation was going nowhere."

Regan took a long pull on his Harp, and continued, "Then things really got weird when Izzy finds a sophisticated surveillance hook-up at the Nooris condo where Larson was murdered. Nooris and his brother were involved in the court house deal. It turns out that Nooris is a former agent for the Mosaad. Neither Izzy nor I know where that fits in yet, if at all."

"It turns out Homeland Security had been watching Nooris, but they won't tell us why. We had hoped that the surveillance video of the condo would give us a break in the Larson case. As of now, the Regional Head of Homeland is claiming national security prevents him from sharing that evidence. Izzy is working his relationship with the FBI agent assigned to babysit the Homeland guy. We'll see where that goes."

"Then, when we thought we had a handle on things, Vito Junior pulls his publicity stunt with the help of our friend the Mayor, trying to finger you and me and Lt. Mathais. Whatever deal Junior thought he had with the Feds blew up in his face, and he turns to us with evidence that he promised could bring us some indictments in the court house case. Someone murders Vito, the timing is too close to his coming out to be a coincidence. So now we have a potential leak in our organization to deal with as well as everything else."

"Dad, what was originally a probe into public corruption is now a double homicide- no, make that a triple homicide case. I forgot to mention that Megan Larson was five months pregnant when she was murdered. And by the way, our friend the Honorable Bruce Peter Gallo could be the father of Larson's baby."

"So who do you like for the Larson murder?"

"Originally we liked Dorothy Wiggins, Larson's boss. It seems that Wiggins and Larson had more than a professional relationship, and Larson wanted to break it off," Jack replied.

"So?"

"Turns out, the time we have Wiggins leaving the Nooris condo pretty much eliminates her as a suspect."

"Do you have any others in mind?"

"Sure: the Nooris brothers, the Mayor. Problem is nothing seems to fit. And now we have Vito Junior's murder to contend with."

"Sounds like quite a mess," the Commissioner said.

"I guess we'll have to see how Vito Senior's gambit plays out," Jack said.

"Looks like Liam is trying to get your attention," his father said.

"Jack, we need a goalie," Liam said and waived for Jack to join him.

Patricia Regan and Kate O'Malley emerged from the kitchen and watched their sons defend the goal.

Later that night, after they put Liam to bed, Kate O'Malley said, "Jack your family is wonderful. Your sisters were so sweet. They're very protective of you."

"Yes, Annie, Pris and Callie make a formidable front line. I knew you would charm them."

"And your parents could not have been more gracious. O'Malley told me I should ask you about how the son of a policeman from Manayunk and a debutant from the Main Line managed to become the 'First Couple' of Philadelphia. Seems almost as unlikely as a single mother from Dublin and the favored son of what O'Malley refers to as the Royal Regans of Philly can be involved."

"Is that what he calls us?"

She nodded and then he told her his parents' story.

In the autumn of 1969, John Hogan Regan, a recent graduate of the Philadelphia Police Academy, was assigned to foot patrol in Center City. His beat covered a twelve-block area west of Broad Street and south of Market. The beat included Walnut Street from Broad to Twentieth and south to Lombard, which encompassed the exclusive Rittenhouse Square neighborhood. The rookie police officer had survived two tours as a Marine in Viet Nam. He was six foot three inches tall and a lean 225 pounds of muscle. He walked his beat with a swagger that belied his lack of experience as a law enforcement officer.

"Remember, you're not in 'Nam anymore. Just because you graduated near the top of your class at the Academy you still have a lot to learn. No one gives a damn about your pedigree. Don't be foolish."

"Yes, Uncle Joe," Regan said.

Joseph Patrick Regan, was captain of the Philadelphia Police Department's elite Highway Patrol Division. He was the titular head of the Regan family. John Hogan Regan was the third generation of Regans to serve with Philadelphia's Finest. John's father had been killed while on the job when John was thirteen years old. He had decided then, much to his mother's distress, that he would join the "family business" and honor his father's memory.

It was a crisp October morning. The leaves on the trees in Rittenhouse Square had exploded overnight into a brilliant array of colors. It was a far cry from the base at Khe Sanh where his unit had withstood the onslaught of the Viet Cong's relentless attacks last fall. Had it only been a year since he came home? As Regan made his way up Walnut Street he checked himself in the window at 1901, to make sure everything was in its proper place before he strolled past the Junior League consignment shop at 1907 Walnut Street, just in case the beautiful young woman he had noticed smiling at him yesterday happened to be looking out of the window.

Regan nonchalantly turned his head in the direction of the shop and saw a man standing at the counter with his back to the window. He immediately noticed the young woman putting something in a bag. She looked frightened. Regan placed his right hand on his police special revolver and opened the door with his left hand. As Regan entered, the man turned towards him. He was holding a gun in his hand and pointed it at Regan. The young woman screamed, distracting the armed man.

Regan realized that if he discharged his weapon the young woman could be hit by an errant shot. He made a split second decision and lunged at the gun man. Regan knocked the man to the ground just as the weapon discharged. The bullet grazed Regan's right shoulder. Regan knocked the gun out of the gunman's hand with his left hand and simultaneously delivered a right to the man's jaw, knocking him unconscious.

"Are you allright?" he asked the young woman behind the counter.

She nodded.

"Please call the police dispatcher and tell them it's an emergency."

Regan kicked the pistol further away from the gunman. He checked the unconscious man's pulse, flipped him over and cuffed him.

"You're bleeding," the woman said.

Regan looked at his right shoulder where the bullet had ripped through his uniform jacket. In the adrenaline rush of the incident he hadn't realized he had been shot.

He smiled at the young woman and said, "Why, yes I am."

Regan heard the sirens of the approaching patrol cars. Within seconds three cruisers pulled up on the curb in front of the shop. Five police officers, guns in hand, ran into the store.

Despite his protests the EMT insisted that he be transported to the hospital for treatment. He was carted off before he had an opportunity to talk to the young woman. They rushed him to the Hahnemann Hospital ER. When he got there the Mayor, the Commissioner and his Uncle Joe were waiting.

After he had been treated he was told by the doctor to wait until the x-rays confirmed that there was no structural damage to his shoulder.

"Thank God you're OK. Your mother would kill me if you had been seriously hurt," his uncle said. "The Mayor and the Commissioner want to come in and get their photo opportunity with you now. So just smile and try not to say anything stupid. I'll call your mother."

Afterwards, he sat there waiting for his transport back to the District and his debriefing by his commander. He was thinking about the young woman from the Junior League consignment shop. He figured her parents would never let her return there after the incident. He probably would never get another opportunity to meet her.

His uncle came into the treatment room and said, "There's someone here wanted to thank you."

He looked up and there she was. She was even more beautiful than he remembered from their brief flirting of the previous day and the chaotic events at the shop that morning.

"Officer, I just wanted to thank you for what you did," she said and extended her hand.

He extended his arm and winced.

"Oh, you're hurt," she said.

"I'll be all right, Miss…"

"Oh, that's right. We haven't actually met, I'm Patty Maxwell."

"Miss Maxwell, I'm John Regan. No thanks are necessary. I was just doing my job."

An older woman came through the door and said, "Oh, there you are."

"Mother, this is Officer John Regan. He's the policeman who saved my life," Patty said.

"Well young man, thank you. I'm sure my husband will want to add his personal thanks to you as well."

"You're welcome ma'am, but as I was saying to your daughter, I was only doing my job."

"Well, it seems to me you did more than that. Patty, we have to go now. Your father is anxious to see you."

"All right, Mother. But I would like to have a word with Officer Regan. Is that OK?"

Mrs. Maxwell gave her daughter a look and said, "All right, but please make it quick," and left the two of them alone.

"Officer Regan…"

"Please call me Jack."

She smiled and said, "Jack, here's my number, please call me. I'd like to see you again, when you recover from your injury."

Regan blushed. "That would be great."

She leaned over and kissed him on the cheek, and walked out of the room.

A few minutes later, Regan's uncle walked back in the room and looked at him and sighed. "Do you know who just walked out of your room?"

"Patty Maxwell, the girl from the consignment shop."

"Do you know who the Maxwells are?"

He shook his head.

"Mr. Robert Maxwell is the publisher of the *Evening Bulletin*. The Maxwell family came over on the Mayflower. Mr. Maxwell owns paper mills, a bank, you name it. His daughter is a debutant. While I'm sure the Maxwells are appreciative of your savin their daughter's life and all, I don't think they really want the likes of you hanging around their only daughter. Now wipe the lipstick off your cheek and while you're at it wipe that grin off your face."

By the time he got home the front page of the newspaper had several columns devoted to the heroic act of bravery by the rookie police officer, and a full story about the Regan clan and their commitment to public service, including the ultimate sacrifice of John Regan's father.

"Katey, my parents were married within a year. It's the stuff they make movies about."

PART 2.

THE MISSION.

TWENTY

The Strawberry Mansion section of Philadelphia was home to a number of Philadelphia's wealthiest families; however, that was back in the nineteenth century. It eventually became a mixed income, predominantly Jewish neighborhood. Then, since the middle of the twentieth century, the neighborhood went into economic and social decline. Strawberry Mansion is now one of the most dangerous neighborhoods in Philadelphia.

The New Age Mosque is located at 3101 Ridge Avenue, in a building that had originally housed the Shara Zedek Congregation Synagogue. The synagogue had been built circa 1928 when the neighborhood was a thriving middle class Jewish enclave where most of the inhabitants spoke Yiddish and English was their second language. When the synagogue was built its neighbors on the block included a kosher butcher shop, a clothing store, the office of *The Forward*, a Yiddish language newspaper and several lawyers' and doctors' offices.

At present the only occupied properties on the 3100 block of Ridge Avenue, other than the mosque, were a bodega and a laundromat. All of the other buildings had been abandoned and boarded up several years ago. The former synagogue, despite the efforts of its current occupants, prominently displayed the Star of David throughout the faded decorative masonry of the building's façade. The juxtaposition of the Crescent and Star and the Star of David should not, however, be misconstrued as a sign of ecumenical enlightenment. The brand of Islam preached at this mosque would never be characterized as tolerant of their Jewish brothers.

Malik Ben-Ali, the Imam of the Mosque, was known for his fiery excoriations of the State of Israel and the extermination of its people. Ben-Ali had a small but devoted following among the local Muslim community. His flair for the dramatic and his Internet savvy extended his reach far beyond the boundaries of Strawberry Mansion. Ben-Ali was a YouTube sensation. He was handsome and charismatic. He boasted a following of many thousands of like-minded individuals who were dedicated to the destruction of Israel and those who supported its continued existence, including the United States.

Ben-Ali's website rantings also attracted the attention of Homeland Security and the FBI. His activities were likely monitored by foreign agencies, most likely the Mossad and the British MI6 among them. It was rumored that he received financial backing from the Iranians and Hamas. Ben-Ali was accompanied by bodyguards twenty-four seven. He was driven in an armor-enforced Cadillac Escalade from his home in the suburbs to the mosque and back.

FBI Special Agent Rico Valdez, who had worked undercover at the Morales Family Bodega at 1313 Ridge Avenue, immediately noticed the man who was greeted by Ben-Ali's principal bodyguard as someone who had not been at the mosque previously. There was something about the stranger that caught his attention. Valdez noticed the man's slight limp as he made his way into the mosque. Valdez assumed the high speed camera that had been placed on the electric power line affixed to the mosque would provide his superiors with a clear picture of the man's face. Facial recognition programs would reveal his identity. Valdez pulled out his cell phone and made a note of the time the stranger had entered the mosque. He ignored the drug deal that was going down on the sidewalk immediately in front of him.

"*As-salamu Alaykum,*" Ben-Ali said as he kissed his visitor on both cheeks.

"*Wa 'Alaykumo s-salam,*" the visitor responded in the traditional fashion.

"Our friend in Peshawar informed us of your arrival."

The visitor nodded.

Ben-Ali suddenly felt ill at ease as the man stared at him. He found the visitor's penetrating stare unsettling. His green eyes gave away nothing.

The visitor leaned close to Ben-Ali and whispered, "Your mosque has been compromised. They can hear everything you say." He held up his hand - a signal that Ben-Ali was not to respond. Ben-Ali nodded.

"Imam, thank you for seeing me," he said. "I send greetings from the Imam of my mosque. He has watched your webcasts with great admiration. He has sent me to watch and learn."

"It is my honor to be your teacher," Ben-Ali replied. "Please, you will be my guest for dinner at my home after evening prayers."

They continued their innocuous conversation in this manner until the call to evening prayers. Among the small group who had assembled at the mosque for the evening prayers was a relatively new member, Abdulah Mohamed. Since he joined the mosque Mohamed had become a frequent participant at the prayer sessions and was regarded by Ben-Ali as a potential candidate who could be cultivated for more important activities. Like most of Ben-Ali's supplicants, Mohamed was young, poor, unemployed and embittered by what he perceived to be discriminatory treatment of Muslims by the U.S. government and the mainstream citizenry.

Mohamed was not what he appeared to be. He was an agent of Homeland Security, who had been placed at the mosque to infiltrate Ben-Ali's organization. Mohamed immediately noticed the tall stranger with green eyes who was given a prominent place in the sanctuary. At the end of the prayer session, Mohamed positioned himself close enough to the stranger to use the button camera on his shirt to get a full face picture of the mosque's honored guest.

When they were seated in the back seat of his car Ben-Ali asked, "How do you know that my mosque is not secure?"

"Imam, you have powerful enemies. The Israelis and the U.S. Intelligence agencies have you under constant surveillance. I have been advised that there is a traitor inside the mosque as well."

Ben-Ali shook his head. "No. That is not possible," he responded. "My inner circle has been with me since the beginning. New members are carefully watched before we allow them access to our more important activities. How do I know I can trust you?"

The man smiled and pulled up his right sleeve revealing the symbol that had been tattooed on his forearm. Ben-Ali pulled up his sleeve and held his arm next to his visitor. The symbols were identical. They continued their ride in silence.

Special Agent Valdez walked past the security guard at the Federal building at 6th and Arch Streets. His identification badge was hanging from the strap around his neck. The Task Force was working out of an office on the twelfth floor. Howard Keel, the special agent in charge of the Philadelphia office was sitting at the head of the conference table. Three of Valdez's colleagues who worked undercover on the mosque detail were also present.

"Were you able to get a match on the facial recognition program?" Valdez asked his boss.

"Negative. Whoever he is he must have suspected that the mosque was hot."

"Damn."

"Rico, we'll have to ask our friend."

"Boss, I already did. He told me the Imam has not shared any information about the green eyed visitor with anyone except Bahsir, his chief of security. According to our guy, Ben-Ali has been expecting the visitor, whoever he is, for some time."

Salvatore DePalma, a/k/a Abdulah Mohamed, entered the Homeland Security Regional Office at 16th and Callowhill Streets through the service entrance in the alley at the back of the building. DePalma's Semetic heritage and his olive complexion supported his cover identity.

He took the freight elevator to the eighth floor and walked directly into Regional Director Simon Conway's office. Conway had authorized DePalma's undercover assignment, and no one else in the Regional Office had been apprised.

"Director, someone new showed up at evening prayers. I have his picture. I have a feeling he may be someone we should check out," DePalma said as he handed the photo to Conway.

Conway glanced at the picture and said, "That would mean I'd have to disclose to Ossberg the fact that I have you at the mosque. He'd insist that we share whatever intel you provide with the FBI."

DePalma nodded his head. "Director, I understand, but I got a funny feeling about this guy."

Conway waved his hand at the agent and said, "Listen son, for now let's just see what develops. We can share this with them later."

After DePalma left, Conway looked at the photo again and put it away in the mosque file in his credenza and locked the drawer. There's no fucking way he was going to share his intel with the FBI. He hated Ossberg, who he knew had been placed at his agency to spy on him. Conway would bring Ben-Ali down and get all the credit for it. He was not about to allow Ossberg or anyone else to share in his glory.

Had Conway shared his undercover agent's photo with the FBI, the facial recognition program would have revealed that the tall stranger with the green eyes who showed up at the New Age Mosque was Yousef Alawaite. Alawaite was reputed to be one of Al-Qaida's most accomplished bombmakers. Conway's obsession to become the star of the show, his paranoid refusal to share intelligence with his sister agency, would inevitably lead to disastrous consequences.

Ben-Ali's driver dropped Alawaite off near the mosque where he had parked his car earlier that afternoon. The used Corolla was so beat up he knew no one would bother to steal it. He limped over to the car, making sure to keep his face away from the front of the mosque. He had carefully studied the area immediately surrounding the building the day before he made contact. Virtually all of the abandoned buildings that had lined the west side of Ridge Avenue across from the mosque had been cleared. The few remaining buildings on the block did not provide a vantage point for a surveillance camera that would produce any relevant data for whoever was watching.

He figured that whatever agencies had placed equipment at the site would have inserted their cameras on or near the front of the building. The Mossad would have mounted it above the entrance, maybe on the electric junction box that was connected to the building, thus avoiding detection if Ben-Ali had the building swept for surveillance equipment. In any event, he was careful not to allow any clear view of his face when he entered the mosque.

He drove west on Ridge to Fairmount Park. At this hour he could easily detect anyone tailing him as he drove across the Strawberry Mansion Bridge and down the ramp to the Martin Luther King Drive that ran along the west bank of the Schuylkill River towards Center City. As he drove east on the Benjamin Franklin Parkway, he noticed the nearly completed Barnes Museum with the Norris Brothers Construction Company sign on the chain link fence that had been erected around the site.

He drove south on 19th Street around Rittenhouse Square and several blocks beyond, constantly checking to make sure he had no tail. He turned left on Washington Avenue and doubled back twice more until he was satisfied that no one had followed him. He parked his car under the elevated I-95 highway and walked five blocks to the apartment he had rented on 2nd street.

After he checked the apartment to make certain no one had entered it, he placed the call.

"It went well," Alwaite said.

"Good."

"When will we proceed?" he asked.

"The fourth; can you have everything in place?"

"Not a problem."

"Good. And make sure you tell the Imam the date and that he is absolutely not to make any comment about it."

"But you know Ben-Ali is not capable of keeping such a secret."

"That is exactly what I expect."

Alawaite smiled and asked, "Is our man en route?"

"Yes."

TWENTY-ONE

"Vito, I'm so sorry for your loss," Mickey Saunders said has he held Vito Coratelli's hand in both of his. "Junior tried so hard to emulate you. Please sit down. What can I do for you?"

After he took his seat Coratelli stared at Saunders and slowly shook his head. He sighed and said, "Mickey, I believe your condolence is truly sincere. You knew Junior since he was a child. You and I have known each other for over forty years. We have faced off against each other on countless occasions."

Saunders smiled and nodded.

"Because I know you so well, I feel I must warn you that I could always read your tactics in court. You could never bluff me. That's why you never prevailed."

The smile on Saunders' face vanished, "Vito, why are you telling me this now?"

"Because I know you were involved in my son's murder. No, please, don't try to deny it," Coratelli said cutting him off and holding his hand up to emphasize his admonishment. "As I told you, I can see through your lies. So do not disrespect me or embarrass yourself."

Saunders remained silent, his face flushed red and his eyes narrowed.

"Mickey, I did not come here to insult you. I know you did not murder my son. Perhaps you never intended to hurt him. But I do know that you were involved. You need to realize that whatever role you played, you are extremely vulnerable. The District Attorney's people are putting their case together as we speak. They will be placing you under arrest very soon. You need to protect yourself."

"Are you offering to represent me?" Saunders asked.

"No. I'll be a prosecution witness in the case against you. They know you were part of the court house fiasco. Junior left me with documents that will help expose you and the others."

"So what are you saying?"

"You are in this thing way over your head. The others involved will make you the goat, or worse."

Saunders stared at him and finally asked, "What do you mean *worse?*"

"Mickey, they will do to you what they did to my son," Coratelli said as he stood up to leave Saunders' office.

"Vito. Wait."

Coratelli left the room without turning back.

Regan had already obtained a court order to bug Saunders' office; however, unlike the federal agencies, the Philadelphia District Attorney's office did not have the equipment or personnel to deploy the devices in time to capture Saunders' reaction to Coratelli's visit.

"Izz, what do you think Saunders is doing?"

"If Vito is as effective as I believe him to be, Saunders is in full panic mode. He's trying to figure out who gave him up," he replied.

"Do you think he'll come to us?"

"Eventually, but first he'll try to see if he has another play."

"Coratelli is going to see Chief Justice Fogerty next. The Chief isn't exactly known for his testicular fortitude. His reaction ought to be interesting."

Kate and O'Malley were in the bar area evaluating the impact the new menu had on the Grape's bottom line. Between the improved quality of the kitchen and the unique addition of the celebrity bartender, Melody Schwartz, last month's revenues had exceeded all expectations.

"O'Malley, someone told me the food critic from the *Inquirer* was here last week. They want to send a photographer to the place to take pictures of the Fish and Chips and a couple of the other dishes. They also want a picture of Melody mixin her special blue martinis. According to the photographer, the critic is going to give us his highest rating, something to do with bells," Kate said.

"That so," O'Malley replied.

"Yes, and whenever he does that, business really takes off." Kate paused, reading her uncle's less-than-enthusiastic reaction. "What's the problem?"

"It'll just encourage more yuppies to barge into the place like they own it. Ya know the hoity-toity types from Gladwynne and Wayne."

"Uncle Mike, I know you miss some of the regulars. And I realize that the Grape was just a neighborhood bar…"

"What's wrong with that?" he asked.

"Nothin, nothin at all, it's just that this isn't the old neighborhood anymore. This part of Manayunk is changing. Young professionals are moving in, and we have to change to accommodate them, or else."

"Or else what?"

"Or else we're out of business."

O'Malley looked past Kate and said, "Sorry Mister, the bar's closed. We don't open until 12 PM."

Kate turned and stared at the man standing at the door.

"'Lo Katey," he said. "Don't you look pretty in your chef's outfit and all." He smiled at her. "And you must be Uncle Mike."

O'Malley could tell by Kate's reaction that she was not happy to see the stranger. He was tall and lean. His head was completely shaved. His face had that dark stubble that was all the rage. He was handsome in a rugged way, and he had Liam's piercing blue eyes.

"Flynn, what are you doing here? I thought they locked you up for good."

"Now, Kate. Is that anyway to greet an old friend?" he said as he walked into the bar.

"Flynn, we're not friends, and you're not welcome here."

"That so," he said and walked over to where Kate sat, towering over her and no longer smiling.

"Look it, I just happened to be visitin your town and I says to myself, 'Whyn't I stop by and see how Kate and my boy are doin?'"

"We're both doin fine without the likes of you hangin around. So why don't ya jest get out of here and stay away from Liam and me and out of our lives."

He scowled at her and said, "Nah, I think I'll stay around for awhile and see how you and the boy are doing."

"Mister," O'Malley said. Flynn looked up and his eyes narrowed as he focused on the business end of the sawed-off double shot gun O'Malley had pulled from behind the bar and pointed directly at his chest. "My niece said you're not welcome here, so if I were you I'd just turn around and get out while you still can."

"Old man, don't be pointin that thing at me unless you've got the nerve to use it."

"Flynn, or whatever your name is, if you don't get your ass out of here by the count of three, I'll have yer remains shipped in a bag back to Ireland."

Flynn stood there and said, "That's not very hospitable of ya."

"One."

"Uncle Mike, please put the gun down. It will be allright...please?"

O'Malley reluctantly lowered the weapon.

"Uncle Mike, can you give me a moment?"

Kate motioned Flynn to take a seat at the booth near the door. She sat down opposite him.

"Flynn, you promised me you'd leave us be. You agreed it was all for the best."

"Well, things change. Maybe you and the boy should come back."

"No, Flynn. Your family will never change. They'll do to Liam what they did to you. I will not let that happen," she said.

"Kate, it doesn't have ta be that way. You, me and the boy can have a life together," he said and grabbed her hand. "Look at me and tell me you don't still have feelins for me."

She looked directly in his eyes and said, "Flynn, go away and leave us be as ya promised." She removed her hand from his, stood up and opened the door.

"Kate I'll be leavin for now, but I'll be back to see…"

O'Malley cocked the shot gun.

Flynn smiled and turned and said, "And I'll be seein you too, old man," as he walked out the door.

O'Malley watched as the man walked east down Main Street.

"Christ Kate, don't tell me he's Liam's father."

She nodded.

"What in the hell were ya thinkin when you hooked up with the likes of him?"

"It was over nine years ago. I was so young. He was the leading scorer on the Galway United club in the Premier League," she sighed. "The next thing I know I'm pregnant and he's back in Galway. What I didn't know is that his family was involved in the 'Troubles.' They're a dangerous bunch. Uncle Mike, I came here to get away from him. I don't want Liam to have anything to do with Flynn or his people."

"What's he doin here? He doesn't strike me as the kind would come over jest to see his son," O'Malley said.

"I don't know, but I'm sure he's up to no good."

"Well, if I so much as see his smug face anywhere near you or the boy, I'll blow him back to Galway," O'Malley said.

TWENTY-TWO

"Any further developments on the mystery man who visited the mosque?" Howard Keel the SAC asked Rico Valdez who had reported for his briefing.

"No, he hasn't returned to the mosque. According to our friend, Ben-Ali has not made any public comment about who he was or why he was there. However, there is someone we may want to watch," Valdez said as he took a photo from his file and slid it across the conference table to his boss.

"His name is Abdulla Mohamed. He showed up at the mosque around a month ago. Our friend tells me that Mohamed has been a regular attendee at services and asks an unusual number of questions. He fits the profile of someone Al-Qaida would want to indoctrinate. He's young, well-educated and unemployed."

Keel studied the picture and said, "There has been a lot of noise about something big that's about to happen. Ben-Ali's latest webcast even made a reference to the Fourth of July as a national celebration we would find memorable, whatever the hell that means."

Valdez nodded. "Yes you can almost feel it. There's a great deal of activity at the mosque, too."

"You're certain the tall man with the limp has not returned?" Keel asked.

"Affirmative."

"OK, let's put a tail on this guy and see what develops," Keel said as he pointed at the photo of Abdullah Mohamed. "I'll ask our Washington office to check with Langley to see what they have. I'll ask Homeland if they have anything on him too."

V ito Coratelli suggested that the Chief Justice meet him at the club house at the FDR Golf Course in South Philadelphia. The FDR, more commonly referred to as 'The Lakes' because it was a flat links course that frequently flooded, is where Coratelli and Fogerty would sneak on to play a few holes back in the day when they were teenagers. It was also the place young men from South Philly would take their dates for more intimate encounters after dark.

"Chief, thanks for meeting me," Coratelli said when Fogerty approached the booth in the back of the club house at which Coratelli was waiting for him.

"Vito, I haven't been back here since my first campaign for District Attorney; must have been twenty years ago," Fogerty said. "How are you my friend?" he asked as he embraced Coratelli.

"Metz-a-metz. Believe me I know Junior had his shortcomings, but to die like that. I don't know what this world has come to."

"I know, I know," Fogerty shook his head.

"Bob, I must tell you something that you will not want to believe, but that you need to know.

"What?"

"You have been betrayed by your friend Mickey Saunders."

"Betrayed by Mickey? How?"

"Mickey was involved in my son's murder."

Fogerty stared at him and said, "But that's impossible. I thought your son's death was an accident – an overdose. Besides, Mickey has known you for almost as long as we have known one another. Mickey was there when your son made Communion. He could never have been involved in anything like that."

"Bob, it's true. He has not served you well. Mickey is tied up with Gallo and some others. He wanted to make a killing on the Family Court House deal. They were going to set you up to take a fall on that."

"I can't believe it."

"Nevertheless, it is true. The District Attorney will be obtaining arrest warrants very soon. You need to deal with this right away, before the DA moves."

"But how? What can I do?"

Coratelli smiled and said, "I will help you."

A warehouse in North Philadelphia had been leased for Yousef Alawaite to use to meet with the sleepers and prepare them for their journeys to paradise. The warehouse was a former machine shop on Lehigh Avenue near 28th Street. The liquidator hired by the bankruptcy court was unable to unload many of the large milling machines that had been abandoned by the former owner of the facility. They remained rusting away where they had been abandoned when the lights had been turned off. The place still smelled from the degreasers and other toxic chemicals that had not been banned when the business was operating twenty-five years ago.

Alawaite had cleared a section near the rear of the first floor behind a large drill press in front of the filthy windows that faced east. He placed a large prayer carpet there. Alawaite had disabled the overhead lights at the front of the building. The machinery and storage lockers at the front of the warehouse created enough of a barrier that would prevent anyone driving past from seeing what was going on inside the building.

Since Alawaite knew the mosque was being watched, he told the Imam he needed an alternate site at which to train the "volunteers." A devoted member of Ben-Ali's inner circle knew the owners of the warehouse. Ben-Ali assured him they would ask no questions and would not disclose to anyone the mosque's request to lease the facility as a training site for Ben-Ali's army. The anti-Muslim environment in the city required a trained force to defend the mosque against the Jews and the ignorant masses they controlled.

"*As-salamu 'Alaykumu,*" Alawaite greeted the sleepers Bashir Amet, the mosque's chief of security had ushered into the warehouse. Alawaite stood at the edge of the prayer carpet facing them, his back to the eastern wall.

"*Wa 'alaykumu s-salam,*" they responded in unison.

He removed his boots, stepped forward onto the carpet and turned his back to the sleepers. He raised his arms and held his hands palms forward to recite Takbeeratul-Irsam in prayer.

"*Allahu-akbar,*" he began the prayers and the others joined him.

Following the prayers the training began. The five sleepers/volunteers were all men. The youngest was nineteen, the oldest thirty-five. They had been recruited by Al-Qaida. Some of them had been trained in Yemen. They varied in appearance, height, weight and race. Based on his brief encounter with them, Alawaite had determined that there was also a considerable difference in intelligence among the group. The only common trait among them was a fanatical devotion to Islam.

Alawaite patiently explained the plan, leaving out critical details including the date, time and location of the attack. He told them about the device they would use, once again omitting the precise information concerning the nature of the explosives and the triggering mechanism. Although he promised he would provide them with all of the details, Alawaite would never disclose the tactical plan he had devised to any of them.

He would decide over the next several days which of the men would be designated to lead the mission. That individual would be led to believe that he was entrusted with the on-site tactical authority. Such designation was important to create the illusion that they were a unit capable of making necessary changes, even aborting the mission. Of course that would be impossible. No matter what happened, once the men were deployed, the attack would proceed and could not be recalled, regardless of the consequences.

TWENTY-THREE

Rico Valdez was relieved of his mosque surveillance assignment to head up the group assembled to tail Abdullah Mohamed. The SAC assigned him three agents, two men and one female agent. All of them were detached from the Baltimore office. This meant they were unfamiliar with Philadelphia and needed to be briefed on all things "Philly."

Special Agent Julia Farber asked, "Rico, anything you think we should know before we hit the street?"

"Yeah, don't eat a steak sandwich with 'cheese whiz' if you're gonna be on a long stake-out."

"What's a cheese whiz?" she asked.

"I don't know for sure, but it comes in a can and it ain't cheese, and it gives you terrible gas."

Valdez paired her up with Robert Bobrowski, who was an expert in "Black Bag" assignments. He assigned them to insert the surveillance equipment in Mohamed's apartment.

"Remember."

"We know. No steak sandwich with cheese whiz," they replied.

The subject lived on the first floor of a duplex on Upsal Street in the Germantown section of Philadelphia. Bobrowski dressed as a PECO serviceman, rang the doorbell and waited for a response. When he was satisfied that no one could see what he was doing, he placed an apparatus over the lock and accessed the apartment in less than thirty seconds. He knew Mohamed was not at home. He signaled that he had safely entered the apartment. His partner sat in an unmarked car parked across the street from the apartment. She would alert Bobrowski if anyone approached.

Bobrowski checked for security devices and any measures Mohamed may have taken to detect unauthorized entry of his home. There were none. He quickly surveyed the entire apartment. Bobrowski noted the Spartan character of the apartment. There was very little furniture: A chair, a table and a prayer carpet were the only objects in the living room. There was no television, radio, telephone or computer anywhere. The bedroom had a small chest with a few changes of underwear and socks. Three pair of slacks and five shirts hung on wire hangers in the bedroom closet. In place of a bed a futon was folded up against the wall.

The bathroom was similarly devoid of anything other than the barest of essentials, toothpaste, toothbrush, several bars of soap and a spray can of deodorant. A single towel was neatly folded on a shelf.

With the exception of a picture of the Prophet Mohamed there were no pictures hanging on the walls. There were no books and nothing of a personal nature was anywhere to be seen. Abdullah Mohamed left no sign of who he was beyond the Prophet's picture and the prayer rug. Even the kitchen provided no indication of the man beyond the few items marked with the designation of halal preparation.

The apartment was spotless. There were no cobwebs or dust mites. Bobrowski wondered how Mohamed could maintain the apartment in such a pristine manner since the only cleaning materials he could find in the utility closet were a rubber bucket and two rags.

The absence of furniture and personal items limited the places Bobrowski could hide the surveillance equipment. He inserted the devices, checked carefully that he had left no sign that he had been at the apartment and left. Bobrowski had completed the job in less than twenty minutes.

"Rico, we're live," Bobrowski said as Farber pulled away from the curb. "When the subject returns to his apartment you'll have eyes and ears."

"Ski, see anything interesting while you were there?" Valdez asked.

"Rico, it was eerie. I mean, the subject must be the most devout Muslim this side of Mecca. We need to keep a close eye on this bird. Better check his vehicle for weapons. I figure him for a nut job." Bobrowski gave him a detailed account of his observations.

"I'll let the team watching him know what you found."

Valdez hung up and walked over to Keel's office to fill him in.

"Boss, this guy may be the lone wolf sleeper we've been looking for. According to Bobrowski the subject's apartment is more like a cell than a home. There's nothing of a personal nature in the place. No pictures of parents or siblings, no letters, no diary, no computer, nada. We ran his name and picture through all our data bases. There's no trace of Abdulla Mohamed before he showed up at the mosque, five weeks ago. He paid the rent for his apartment along with the security deposit in cash. No credit cards, no bank accounts. His phone is a prepaid mobile, once again paid for with cash. It's like he dropped out of the sky."

Keel nodded and said, "Our Washington office didn't have anything, nor did Langley or Homeland."

"I don't know," Valdez said. "Something about this guy just doesn't feel right."

"Let's put more boots on the ground. I'll assign two more teams. If the subject is a lone wolf, we need to make sure he doesn't catch on that we're watching him," Keel said.

After Valdez left his office, Keel reviewed the file. He figured the cost of the surveillance would run over $50,000 a week. He'd need to run this past his superiors. But with all the noise on the street, and plans for the Fourth of July festivities, he didn't want to be the bureaucrat who disapproved the expenditure of funds that allowed a nut job to go ballistic. If the shit hit the fan, let his bosses take the hit. Keel was in full CYA mode.

Even though her back was to him Regan could tell that Kate was upset the second he walked into the kitchen at the Grape. "Everything OK?" he asked.

She didn't respond. He walked over to her and placed his hand on her shoulder, "What's wrong?"

She turned and accepted his embrace.

"Jack, I'm afraid," she said and buried her face in his chest.

"Afraid of what?"

"Michael Flynn, Liam's father showed up at the Grape this morning. He's a dangerous man."

"Did he threaten you?"

"No. But his being here, I've just got a bad feeling about it."

They sat at the prep counter. "Tell me about him," Regan asked.

She told him that the Flynns were one of the most notorious families from Ulster. Michael's father and grandfather, and all of his uncles and cousins, were members of the IRA. When the violence of "The Troubles" subsided, the family took up more lucrative and equally unsavory pursuits, everything from loan sharking to murder for hire. Of course Katey was completely unaware of this when Flynn, the star of the football club, swept her off her feet.

The Flynns of Ulster branched out into more sophisticated crimes that brought Michael back to Dublin after Liam was born. He became obsessed with their son and wanted to take Kate and Liam back home to Ulster.

"I told him I wouldn't allow Liam to become a part of his family's gang," Kate said. "But he wanted Liam."

The Flynns found out that Liam was Michael's son. His father and grandfather wanted to assure their legacy and made it clear that, with Kate or without her, Liam would be part of the family. Only Michael Flynn's arrest for a botched heist from the Irish Museum of Modern Art in Dublin disrupted their plans. While he was incarcerated Katey fled to the states.

"Jack, I thought that by the time he got out of jail he and his people would have lost their obsession with the boy and left us alone. I even convinced Michael that it was for the best. He was supposed to be in prison for ten years. I can't believe he got released so soon."

"Something doesn't sound right about this," Regan said. "I'll check into it and find out how his sentence could have been reduced."

"Jack, I don't want to get you involved in my problems."

"Katey, it's too late for that. Don't worry. I won't let anyone hurt you or Liam."

Mickey Saunders sat at his desk with his eyes closed. His head throbbed and he felt dizzy. He was afraid if he tried to stand up he would fall on his face. He opened his eyes and the vertigo almost made him throw up. Had Coratelli told him the truth?

When he first heard that Coratelli's son had been found with a needle in his arm, he was relieved. He wanted to believe that Junior had died by his own hand. He was a loose cannon, completely out of control, and sooner or later his reckless ways would have led him to a bad end. But Saunders knew deep down that someone had helped him along, or worse.

Coratelli's warning was probably accurate. He had been blinded by the promise of a big payday. Gallo and Ari Nooris assured him that if he could control Fogerty, they would be able to build the court house on property they owned and his commission would be more than he could earn in a lifetime of practicing law. The bonus would be the satisfaction of exposing Mr. Chief Justice for the fool that he had always been. After all, wasn't Mickey the architect of Fogerty's political career? And what did he have to show for it, some pictures hanging on the wall in his office of him standing in the background as Fogerty was sworn into office, first as District Attorney and later as Chief Justice of the Pennsylvania Supreme Court?

And Dorothy Wiggins would also be taken down by the scandal. Gallo wanted to crush her too. It all started to go bad when the girl Megan Larson was found murdered in Nooris' condo. Who had killed her, and why?

Could he dare turn to Gallo or Nooris? Would he end up with a needle in his arm like Junior, or bludgeoned to death like Larson? Was it too late to ask Fogerty for help, or should he turn himself in and try to make a deal for immunity in return for cooperating with the DA? Saunders was a minor player. Gallo was the big prize. The DA would see that.

He heard a noise in the outer office. Were they coming for him already? He reached for the pistol he kept in the top drawer of his desk.

TWENTY-FOUR

The training went slowly at first. Alawaite patiently repeated every step each of his men had to follow to prepare for the attack. He showed them how to get into proper position to assure that the explosive would create the desired impact. He showed them the triggering mechanism they would use to detonate the device, assuring them they could abort if anything went wrong. His assurance was false, and the triggering mechanism was a dummy. The devices were controlled by timers that would detonate each of the sleepers in the sequence he had planned to create total chaos and mass confusion. The sleepers were merely vessels carrying the devices and nothing more.

Alawaite wanted them to believe that each individual's role was vital to the success of the mission. A single misstep would ruin the mission. If that happened none of them would make their journey to paradise. He read the fear in their eyes when he brought out the vests they would be wearing. He threw one down on the ground and stomped on it with his heavy boots.

"You see there can be no accidental explosion. The device can only be detonated by you," Alawaite said. He could read the relief in their eyes. He had given them a way out if at the last moment any of them had a change of heart. Only one of the sleepers, Farouk, the nineteen-year-old reacted differently. Farouk's eyes still burned with the fire of his devotion. He showed no sign of indecision. He was ready to make the journey.

It was a shame Farouk was too young to be assigned leader. Alawaite would speak with him privately and tell him no matter who was designated to be in charge that he was the true leader.

After four days of surveillance of Abdullah Mohamed, Valdez told Keel they had no indication that the subject was anything more than a religious zealot. Mohamed went to multiple prayer sessions at the mosque each day and returned home. On occasion he would walk, or drive to the Fairmount Park and stroll along the banks of the Schuylkill River chanting prayers to himself. As far as the team could see there were no drops or exchanges with anyone during these excursions.

The surveillance of his home was similarly unremarkable. Mohamed would pray and study the Koran. The only break in his otherwise incredibly devout lifestyle was the effort he put into cleaning his apartment. He was without a doubt the most boring subject the members of the team had ever been assigned to watch.

Valdez's mole at the mosque continued to report Mohamed's active participation in mosque activities. His obvious attempts to earn the trust of the Imam and the inner circle at the mosque had not yet yielded any positive response.

"Rico, this is looking like a dead end," Special Agent Bobrowski said as he finished his shift monitoring Mohamed's apartment. "I mean, I'm enjoying the local fare, I even had a hoagie at Lee's Hoagie House like you suggested."

"The original place, on Cheltenham Avenue," Rico asked.

Bobrowski nodded and said, "I think we should pull the plug."

"Ski, I'm coming to that conclusion, but there's something that just doesn't feel right about this guy. You know, like they say in the movies, there's something 'hinky' about him. Let's give it another twenty-four hours and if nothing happens I'll talk to Keel."

The big break in the case came the next day when Farber and Bobrowski relieved the day shift. Mohamed left the mosque after evening prayers. He started his drive back towards Germantown; however, instead of making a right onto the Kelly Drive to the Lincoln Drive, he made a left and headed into Center City.

"Hello," Bobrowski said. "Farber, call for back-up. Let's see where Abdullah's headed."

"I'm on it."

Mohamed drove all the way to the Art Museum Circle, driving around the circle two times, obviously checking for a tail.

"Uh-oh," Bobrowski said.

"Ski, it's OK. Valdez has him," Farber said. Bobrowski continued east on the Parkway, taking the outer drive and pulling over to wait near the intersection at 23nd Street.

"This guy is definitely trying to make sure no one is tailing him," Bobrowski said. Farber nodded.

Two minutes later they saw Mohamed's car drive east down the center parkway lanes. Valdez was three cars behind him. Bobrowski followed. When Mohamed went around the Logan Circle twice, Valdez peeled off and Bobrowski and Farber picked up the tail. The subject made a left onto 16th Street. He drove north past the entrance to the Vine Street Expressway and parked his car on the street near Spring Garden Street. Bobrowski continued north and asked his partner who was listening through the ear piece, "Does Valdez have him?" she nodded.

By the time Bobrowski parked the car, Farber said, "You are not fucking going to believe this."

"What?"

"Valdez watched Mohamed go in the service entrance to 1601 Callowhill."

He looked at her and said, "So."

"That's the Regional office of Homeland Security."

"What?"

"He's on the job!"

Valdez immediately called SAC Howard Keel. "Boss, sorry to bother you at home, but there's been a development with the surveillance and you're not going to like it. It appears that our subject is a Homeland Security agent."

There was silence on the line for a full thirty seconds.

"Boss?"

"Rico, did I hear you correctly? Did you just tell me that Abdullah Mohamed is on the job?"

"Affirmative."

"Keep your team on surveillance and see if they can get some visual documentation. Meet me in my office in thirty minutes," he said and hung up. Keel checked the directory on his Iphone for Monroe Ossberg, the FBI's liaison to the Homeland Regional Office. He highlighted the number with the cursor and waited for the connection.

He picked up on the second ring, "Ossberg."

"Monroe, sorry to bother you at this hour," Keel struggled to maintain his composure. "Does the name Abdullah Mohamed mean anything to you?"

There was a pause and Ossberg replied, "Isn't that the person of interest at the New Age Mosque your office has placed under active surveillance?"

"That's affirmative."

"Has there been a development?" Ossberg asked.

"You might say that," Keel replied. "You're sure that your only knowledge of the subject is our report of his surveillance."

"Howard, should I know something more about this guy?"

"Yeah, I guess you could say that. Why don't you meet me in my office in thirty minutes," Keel said.

"Should I bring Regional Director Conway?"

"No, let's keep this in house, for the time being."

There are a surprising number of personnel who work at the Philadelphia FBI office at 6th and Arch Streets on the evening and night shifts. That had not been the case prior to 9/11. Regional FBI offices used to work on more or less regular office hours. All of that changed after the towers fell. Ossberg was ushered into the SAC's conference room at 2200 hours by a young female agent.

"Thanks for being so prompt," Keel said. "This is Special Agent Rico Valdez," he said nodding in the direction of the agent who sat to his left. "Please sit down."

Ossberg took a seat on the opposite side of the conference table from Valdez.

"Rico, Special Agent Ossberg has been assigned as liaison to the Philadelphia Regional Office of Homeland Security. Monroe, Rico has been in charge of the detail tailing Abdullah Mohamed. Rico, would you summarize the results of your team's surveillance of Mr. Mohamed for Special Agent Ossberg?" Keel asked.

"Certainly, our surveillance commenced on Monday morning at 0700 hours when the subject left his apartment to attend morning prayers at the mosque. We inserted visual and auditory equipment at his apartment and assigned three teams of agents to follow him."

"Throughout the first four days the subject adhered to a consistent pattern of behavior. He would leave his apartment and attend morning prayers, return to his apartment and read the Koran and clean his place. He would return to the mosque for afternoon prayers. In the afternoons he would either take solitary walks in Fairmount Park until evening prayers or return to his apartment."

"There were absolutely no contacts with any individuals outside the mosque. No drops, nothing suspicious. He appeared for all intents as a devout Muslim whose entire life revolved around his faith. However, this evening after evening prayers the subject broke his normal pattern."

Ossberg waited as Valdez consulted his notes.

"Ninety minutes ago as Team One followed the subject, instead of proceeding directly to his apartment on Upsal Street he drove in the opposite direction on the Kelly Drive towards Center City. I was immediately alerted and as the closest agent on duty I joined the pursuit near the Art Museum Circle."

"The subject took a series of classic maneuvers to detect surveillance. When he was satisfied that no one was tailing him, he proceeded north on 16th Street. He parked his vehicle near Spring Garden Street. We followed him on foot. Once again the subject took appropriate measures to detect surveillance. At approximately 2115 hours I observed the subject enter the Homeland Security Regional Office through the service entrance in the alley behind the building. Team One saw him leave the building at 2135 and tailed him back to his apartment."

Valdez showed Ossberg a series of photos he and his team had taken during the assignment, including stills of the video surveillance from his apartment.

"Monroe, have you ever seen this man at Homeland Regional Office?" Keel asked.

Ossberg shook his head.

"Do you have any explanation for Abdullah Mohamed's visit to the Regional Office this evening?"

Ossberg shook his head again.

"Rico, would you please show Special Agent Ossberg the other photos?"

Valdez removed six photographs from his folder and spread them across the conference table in front of Ossberg.

The room was silent except for the sound of Ossberg's sharp exhale of breath.

The pictures had been taken with a telephoto lens from the roof of the apartment building across 16th Street from the Homeland building with an unobstructed view of the Regional Director's twelfth floor office. The photos showed Regional Director Simon Conway in apparent conversation with Abdullah Mohamed.

TWENTY-FIVE

"Who's there?" Saunders asked.

"It's me," Chief Justice Robert Fogerty said as he walked through the door from the outer office.

"Mickey, you look upset," Fogerty said as he took a seat in front of Saunders' desk. "What's wrong?"

Saunders hesitated, trying to decide how to proceed. He said, "Bob, Vito Coratelli…"

"I know," Fogerty said cutting him off. "That's why I came to see you. He came to see me a couple days ago with some crazy story about you being involved in his son's murder and the District Attorney getting ready to indict you and Mayor Gallo. He gave me the whole spiel."

"And you don't believe him?"

"Of course not; I mean for Christ's sake, you knew Junior since he was a child. There's no way you would have anything to do with any of that." Fogerty sighed and said, "I can only imagine how hard this has been on Vito. I think he's losing it."

Fogerty was following the script Coratelli had suggested to a tee. "Make Saunders believe that he's in the clear. His ego will kick in and he'll go to Gallo and Nooris and boast that he has you completely fooled," Coratelli told him.

"But what about the District Attorney?" Saunders asked.

"Bob, that's just something he made up. Believe me, if the DA was in the process of getting indictments, I would have heard about it," Fogerty said.

Fogerty read the relief in Saunders' face.

"Mickey, even though I don't believe Vito, it's not a good thing for you to have him going around and spreading these rumors about you. I think you need to reason with him. Convince him that he's wrong."

"Bob, that's great advice, thank you. And thank you for your friendship," Saunders added.

After Fogerty left, Saunders realized that there was no way to reason with Coratelli. There was only one solution. He placed the call, "Have you heard what Coratelli is putting out on the street?"

"Yes."

"It must be stopped."

"Agreed."

As soon as he walked out of Saunders' building Fogerty placed the call. "It went just as you said it would. He bought it hook, line and sinker."

"Very good."

"Be careful."

"Of course."

Vito Coratelli hung up the phone. Saunders was such a fool. Vito assumed that Saunders had already set it in motion. They would move against him soon, very soon.

But it would not go down as they believed. He would be ready for them.

Ichowitz did not like Vito's plan. He thought it was reckless, and he was concerned for Coratelli's safety.

"Jack, Vito told me Saunders fell for Fogerty's set-up. But this trap Vito has set with himself as the bait, I don't believe it's going to work."

"Don't you think Saunders is going to report his conversations with Vito and the Chief Justice to his people?" Regan asked.

"Oh no, I fully expect him to react exactly as Coratelli suggested. I'm concerned that Vito has seriously underestimated the capabilities of the killer or killers. I've known Vito a long time. I'm not buying his assurance that he'll allow us to protect him. He's a 'Sidggy.' The Sicilians always want to personally avenge their loved one's murder."

"We cannot allow that to happen," Regan said.

"I hear you. The problem is, does Vito? Jack, is there something else bothering you?" Ichowitz asked.

Regan paused, carefully considering his response. "I really didn't want to bring this up. I mean, with the Larson and Vito Junior murders still open, you already have enough on your plate. You don't need to deal with my personal problems."

"Jack, we're *mishpocheh*," Ichowitz replied. "Tell me what's going on?"

Regan filled him in on the sudden appearance of Michael Flynn, Liam's father.

"Izz, Katey's very worried about him. I asked Mike O'Malley about it. He told me if he so much as sees Flynn near the Grape, he'll blow Flynn's brains out."

"So Kate grabs Liam and runs away when the guy goes to prison, and now he shows up out of the blue in Manayunk and says he just wants to check on his boy?" Ichowitz asks.

"Yeah, it doesn't make a whole lot of sense."

"Let's check him out with Interpol and try to find out why this bird really blew into town."

Following the meeting with Ossberg, Howard Keel contacted the Bureau's Assistant Director William Ross to report the events that resulted in the discovery that Abdullah Mohamed, the subject of his office's surveillance, was an undercover agent working exclusively for the Homeland Security Mid-Atlantic Regional Director. The purpose of his call was twofold. First to obtain guidance on how the Bureau wanted to deal with Homeland, second, and perhaps more important, Keel wanted to make sure his ass was completely covered, both in connection with the expenditure of considerable dollars for what turned out to be a complete exercise in futility in following the agent, and just in case other unanticipated events hit the fan.

"And you believe this Conway guy was operating completely on his own without disclosing anything to our man Ossberg?" Ross asked.

"Yes sir. Special Agent Ossberg has given me a complete rundown on the Regional Director's almost daily acts of stupidity. According to Ossberg, Simon Conway is a greater risk to our nation's security than Osama Bin Laden."

"I've seen some of Ossberg's reports. He's a good man and this assignment could be a career-killer."

"Sir, we need to take some action, and quickly. The Internet is abuzz that something big is going to happen here on the Fourth. Ben-Ali and his mosque are ground zero in this region. We lost a great deal of time chasing our tail on this Abdullah Mohamed fiasco. The Bureau cannot afford any more missteps."

"Howard, I'll discuss this with the director and get back to you."

TWENTY-SIX

The Director of the FBI and the Secretary of Homeland Security agreed that Homeland Mid-Atlantic Regional Director Simon Conway was an unmitigated disaster and had to be removed. The problem was Conway's considerable political connections, primarily the fact that he had married the daughter of the chairman of the House Appropriations Committee, made Conway's removal a matter of significant sensitivity. The Director and the Secretary delegated the responsibility to plan and execute Conway's "exit strategy" to the Philadelphia Bureau office. That way, if there was any political fallout over the incident, neither the Bureau nor Homeland would suffer the consequences. Only the poor bastards at the Regional level would be blamed.

So much for covering my ass, Keel thought upon learning that he had been tasked with the responsibility of relieving the Homeland Security Regional Director of his position.

"Howard, you have the complete backing and support of the Director," Assistant Director Ross told him. "There's no need for you to file a written report."

"Sir, can I anticipate written confirmation of my authority?" Keel asked.

"Howard, off the record, you got the shitty end of the stick on this. Both the director and I realize that. We'll help you anyway we can, but you and your people need to pull this off and make it look like Conway resigned of his own accord."

Two hours later, Keel, Monroe Ossberg, the Bureau's liaison to the Homeland Regional Office, and Rico Valdez were meeting at Ralph's Italian Restaurant on 9th Street near the Italian Market to evaluate their options. According to the menu, Ralph's had been in continuous operation since 1900. A long line of notables and celebrities, among them Theodore Roosevelt, Frank Sinatra, Tony Bennett and Jimmy Durante had frequented the establishment throughout the past century.

Ralph's was also a favorite meeting place for the Philadelphia chapter of La Cosa Nostra. Angelo Bruno, the former head of the "Family," had declared the restaurant neutral turf at which rival factions could dine without fear of attack. Unfortunately, the sidewalk outside Ralph's was not protected, and Bruno's consigliore suffered a fatal case of indigestion when he was shot in the head upon leaving Ralph's one fateful evening. His obituary did mention how much he enjoyed the veal piccante, one of Ralph's classic dishes, as his final meal.

Keel had secured the private dining room on the third floor for this off-the-record meeting with Ossberg and Valdez. "Gentlemen, we have been delegated a sensitive mission by the director," Keel began the business portion of the meeting as the three men enjoyed their espresso and cannoli. In truth, only Keel had been delegated this responsibility; however, he had decided that it was unacceptable that he was the only individual designated and therefore he was not going to suffer the consequences on his own.

"The director agrees with our conclusion that Simon Conway must be removed before he does any further damage. Unfortunately, Conway's political connections eliminate his direct termination by the Secretary of Homeland Security as a viable option. We need to figure out a way to convince Conway that his resignation is the most attractive way for him to move on, any suggestions?"

"Howard, in the six months since his appointment, Conway has been a royal pain in my ass. He fancies himself as a super spy, you know like James Bond or that character on TV who is saving the country from nuclear attack in twenty-four hours. He's always running around town with armed escorts. Conway disappears for days at a time, claiming he's doing special assignments for the Secretary. It's all bullshit," Ossberg ranted.

"What about his personal life? Is there anything there?" Keel asked.

"Well, there was an incident with one of the female agents, a potential sexual harassment matter. She was transferred to DC and the issue was resolved quietly."

"Has he moved his family from Washington, DC?" Keel asked.

"No, he's staying at the Ritz on the region's dime. He told me he doesn't expect to be a Regional Director for too much longer. According to him, something big is in the works, again all bullshit."

"Special Agent Ossberg, so Director Conway considers himself a lady's man," Valdez asked.

"Oh yes."

"Boss, since we already have three teams of agents available with nothing much to do, why don't we tail Conway for a few days? Who knows, maybe we'll come up with something."

Keel nodded. "Monroe, in the meantime please advise Mr. Conway that you have direct orders from the director to assume operational authority over Agent Salvatore DePalma, aka Abdullah Mohamed. If he balks give him my number and I'll ream him a new one."

"Rico, have your guy from Baltimore put his equipment in Conway's suite at the Ritz and in his Mercedes too. Let's stay on him 24/7."

"Boss, do we have a warrant?" Valdez asked.

"Rico, we only need a warrant if we intend to use our surveillance as evidence in court. I have no intention of going through the judicial process. I have a feeling Regional Director Conway left his wife in DC for reasons other than his hoped-for early promotion."

"You think he can't keep little Simon in his pants?" Valdez asked.

"Have you seen any photographs of Mrs. Conway?"

Valdez shook his head.

"Check them out, and maybe you'll get a better idea of what makes him tick."

"I mam, one of your men has apparently decided to abandon the mission," Alawaite told Ben-Ali as they walked along the Kelly Drive.

"No, that is not possible. These soldiers have been carefully prepared for their journeys."

"Nevertheless, Aaban did not show up today. Bashir advises me that his apartment is empty, and no one has any information concerning his whereabouts."

"Can he compromise the mission?" Ben-Ali asked.

Alawaite considered his response and said, "No, he doesn't have enough of the details. But I would appreciate your security finding him and addressing the matter."

"Do you need a replacement?"

"I assumed that the five men were all of the sleepers," Alawaite replied.

"Yes that is true; however, there is a young man who has been with us for several months now. He is passionate in his beliefs and lives his life in strict accord with our Muslim traditions. Would you like to meet him and decide for yourself?"

"What is his name?"

"Abdullah Mohamed."

Ossberg's meeting with Simon Conway was one of the high points of the FBI agent's liaison assignment to Homeland since the Regional Director blew into town. Ossberg walked into Conway's office unannounced, closed the door and sat down in the leather chair in front of Conway's desk without saying a word. Conway scowled at him and said, "What do you think you're doing, barging in here without an appointment? I thought I made it clear to you that you would no longer have unlimited access."

"You did."

"Then have you lost your mind?"

"No."

"Then I suggest you get out of that chair and get the fuck out of my office," Conway said.

"No, I don't think I'll leave just yet."

"I'll have security remove you," Conway said and reached for the phone.

"I don't think that would be a good move on your part," Ossberg remarked.

Conway stared at him. There was something in Ossberg's manner, the calmness with which he responded to his rants that made Conway pause.

Ossberg waited for Conway to put down the phone and said, "The Bureau has found out about your agent at the New Age Mosque. Your unauthorized insertion of an agent there, along with your failure to share the information with the Bureau constitutes a felony. It may well have compromised national security. The Director and the Secretary of Homeland have authorized me to oversee operations of the Regional Office while they evaluate the situation."

"Oh they have, have they? We'll see what the Congressman has to say about that!"

"Well, you can call your father-in-law, but that will only bring attention to the situation."

Conway paused again, evaluating the consequences of such a course of action.

"Here's what I suggest," Ossberg continued. "After we speak with your man, why don't you take some time off? Go down to DC, see your wife. Perhaps after the Director and the Secretary have a chance to cool down, they'll reconsider bringing charges against you. Who knows, maybe I'll be able to turn this thing around and make you out to be a hero," Ossberg smiled.

Conway needed to buy some time. If what Ossberg told him was true, he had fucked up. He had already needed his father-in-law's help to avoid the sexual harassment charge. He realized that going to the Congressman again so soon would be a problem.

"Look, maybe I was wrong, being overly protective of my agent. But, I was concerned that sharing the information prematurely would put him in danger. I'm sure that if you present this to your director he'll agree."

Ossberg nodded and said, "We'll see."

After the meeting with the mole was arranged, Ossberg called Keel and filled him in.

"Monroe, are you telling me Conway bought your line of BS?"

"Howard, Conway's your classic school yard bully. I figured once I got in his face he would back down. Besides, I heard a rumor that the Congressman was not very happy about having to intervene to save Conway's ass when the female agent was going to file charges against him. I think his rabbi is beginning to see his son-in-law as a liability. Make sure Valdez has his people in place. I don't think Conway's going back to DC anytime soon."

"Agent DePalma, Special Agent Ossberg will be overseeing your assignment," Simon Conway told DePalma when he reported to the Regional Office for the emergency briefing.

Ossberg stood up and extended his hand to DePalma, "Monroe Ossberg. I heard you have done some remarkable work here."

DePalma shook his hand and looked at Conway, obviously surprised with the news.

"Director Conway, thank you for setting up the briefing. Agent DePalma and I can take it from here." DePalma noted Ossberg's not-so-subtle dismissal of the Regional Director.

DePalma's eyes widened in surprise when Conway said, "Yes, certainly, I've other important matters to attend to." DePalma also noticed Conway's face turned red and he gave Ossberg a look of pure hatred as he left the conference room.

"You never call, you never write," Isodore Ichowitz said when the receptionist put his call through to Monroe Ossberg.

"Izzy, it's good to hear from you, my friend," Ossberg replied.

"The word's out on the street that Simon Conway stepped on his dick big time. He's out, and you're calling the shots. Is that true?" Ichowitz asked.

"Well, like every rumor you hear, there's some truth to it," Ossberg replied.

"So tell me the emess."

"Izz it's too complicated to discuss over the phone, and right now I'm up to my- you-know-what in alligators. Tell you what, can we meet next week sometime. By then everything should fall into place."

"You wouldn't be shining me on, are you?" Ichowitz asked.

"Izzy, I would never do that to you. We're like '*meshuggeneh*'" Ossberg said.

"You mean '*mishpocheh*,' as in family. '*Meshuggeneh*' means crazy."

"Yeah, *mishpocheh*," Ossberg agreed.

"Monroe, you're *meshuggeneh* if you think I'm buying that line of *michegoss*, or what you would call B.S. you're trying to feed me," Ichowitz responded.

"Izz, I'm not putting you off. I'm all in on this thing right now. It may turn out that by week's end, I may be the one on the way out of town and Conway's back on top."

"Maybe if you let your friends help you it will assure a happy ending,"

"Izz, let me think that over. I'll get back to you tomorrow either way," Ossberg replied.

"The *emess*?" Ichowitz asked.

"The *emess*."

"So what did he say?" Regan asked Ichowitz when he hung up the phone.

"Reading between the lines, it sounds like Conway is on his way out, but the situation's fluid. I think our friend may be in over his head. I offered to help."

"Izz, as far as I'm concerned the jury's still out on this guy. I think he's sitting on the video surveillance of Nooris' condo. I also believe that tape will reveal who killed Megan Larson," Regan said.

"I agree, but I don't understand why he would withhold that evidence from us," Ichowitz said.

"Who knows with the feebies."

"Well, if he doesn't call me back tomorrow we'll know he's hiding something. In the meantime, let's give him the benefit of the doubt."

Ossberg's meeting with DePalma confirmed his suspicions regarding Conway's rank incompetence and complete lack of professionalism. Among the documents in Conway's private file was a photo DePalma had taken that the Regional Director had never previously disclosed to either the FBI or anyone in the region. DePalma told Ossberg that he had provided it to Conway several weeks before. DePalma said he took the photo because the subject, who he had never seen before, had been afforded great deference by the Imam when he visited the mosque. According to DePalma, the subject of the photograph had not returned to the mosque since.

When Ossberg showed Rico Valdez the photo, Valdez told him it was same guy he had noticed limping into the mosque three weeks ago. Valdez told him the FBI was unable to identify him from the surveillance video.

"It seemed to me like this guy is a player with skills. The way he kept his face away from places where it was likely that a video camera might pick him up, you know I just got a vibe about the guy," Valdez said.

"Have you seen him at the mosque since then?" Ossberg asked Valdez.

"Negative."

"Let's put the photo through the facial recognition data base and see if this is someone we need to be concerned about," Ossberg said.

"Did your man have anything else to report?" Valdez asked.

"No, unfortunately despite his best efforts to attract the attention of Ben-Ali and the inner circle at the mosque, he hasn't gained their confidence." Ossberg responded.

"That pretty much confirms what my inside source told me," Valdez said. "I'll let you know if we get a hit on DePalma's photo."

Courtney Wells was restless and lonely. It had been more than a month since she broke off her relationship with Ari Nooris. She was frustrated and perplexed by Jack Regan. Although she acknowledged that

Kate O'Malley was attractive, she didn't believe that the young woman from Ireland was in her league. She was still mystified that Jack had rejected her. Perhaps she should contact Jack's mother and see if another "accidental" meeting could be arranged. She looked at her messages and saw that Ari Nooris had called again. Courtney never had a lack of suitors when she was married. Now only her former lover seemed interested in pursuing her. Oh, what the hell, she thought as she hit his number on the speed dial on her phone.

When she parked her convertible on the street in front of the Old Pickle Works, she could see the sign for the Grape Tavern two blocks away. She quickly dismissed the impulse to get back in her car and camp outside the bar to wait for Regan.

She entered the courtyard and noticed a tall man with a nearly shaved head and a coarsely shaved beard leaving Nooris' condo. He smiled at her as they walked towards each other. He was ruggedly handsome. She could see him take a slow inventory of her as he approached. He nodded and said, "Good day to ya," as he walked past her to the street. Had she detected an Irish accent?

She turned as she got to Nooris' door. The tall man was standing at the entrance to the courtyard. He was staring at her. She felt the heat of her blush and heard him laugh as he walked away.

"Who was that man leaving your condo just before I got here?" she asked Nooris.

"No one important," he said as he took her in his arms.

Michael Flynn was still smiling as he got in the Ford Focus Nooris had rented for him. "Cheap bastard," Flynn muttered as he hit his shin on the steering column. Jaysus, they must have designed this car for midgets, he thought as he put it in gear and pulled away from the curb. So the woman was the reason Nooris had told him he had to cut their meeting short. Couldn't blame him for that, Flynn thought. She was beautiful and sexy. He could tell from the fire he saw in her eyes as he approached her that she would be a worthy lover. He chuckled as he drove past the bar at which Katey worked. It was a shame he had so many things to take care of, or he would enjoy going back there and sayin hello to the mother of his son and that runt of an uncle of hers. He'd get back to them soon; in the meantime perhaps he would ask Ari to introduce him to that sexy lady friend of his.

Special Agents Bobrowski and Farber were relieved the Abdullah Mohamed surveillance had been terminated. Except for the final shift when it turned out the subject was an undercover agent for Homeland Security, the stakeout had to be one of the most boring assignments either of them had ever endured. After chasing their tails for nearly a week, it turned out that the big shots in Philly were just as screwed up as they were in Baltimore. Now they were assigned to watch Simon Conway, the Homeland Security Regional Director responsible for the Mohamed fiasco.

"What a pompous ass," Farber said as she watched Conway strike out again, this time with a woman at least ten years his junior. They had been watching him for the past hour as he worked the bar at the Ritz, the hotel at which he was staying compliments of the Homeland Security Regional Office.

"I bet he's putting his bar tab on the Homeland bill," she said. "There ought to be some law against that, don't you think?"

Bobrowski nodded.

"See that older woman sitting at the end of the bar?" she said. "That cougar's been sending him hot looks all night. I figure after he has another martini or two, Conway will settle for her."

"Bobrowski shrugged and said, "I'm betting on that one over there," he nodded in the direction of a striking woman in a tight short dress who was sitting at one of the bar side tables.

"She looks like a working girl to me," Farber responded. "High class for sure, but still a girl on the make."

"Yep, that's my take," Bobrowski agreed.

"I don't know, I don't even think this guy can get laid if he has the money to pay the hooker," Farber said.

"You may be right, but this beats the hell out of watching Mohamed aka DePalma read the Koran all night," Bobrowski said holding up his bottle of non-alcoholic beer to toast his partner.

Two hours later they called Valdez. "You can tell your boss we got our boy," Bobrowski laughed."

"What's so funny?" Valdez asked.

"This was probably the easiest money that hooker ever made. I don't think the surveillance video is long enough to put on YouTube."

"Really, he got a hooker?" Valdez asked.

"Yeah, but only after he struck out with about ten women at the bar, including a cougar who slapped him for making some off-color remark about what he wanted her to do to him."

"Do you think we have enough to reason with him?" Valdez asked.

"Rico, forget about his father-in-law and wife being upset with his extra-marital misconduct. When he sees what a horrible performance he put on, he'll do anything if we promise not to show the tape to his colleagues."

TWENTY-SEVEN

"**B**rother, the Imam would like a word with you," Bashir Amet the mosque's head of security said to Abdullah Mohamed as he was leaving morning prayers.

"Yes brother," Mohamed said and bowed his head being careful not to display any sign of emotion in reaction to the summons.

"As-salamu 'Alaykum" Ben-Ali greeted him when Mohamed was ushered into his office by the security chief.

"Wa 'alaykumu s-salam," Mohamed responded and bowed.

"Brother Mohamed, your devotion to our faith has not gone unnoticed," Ben-Ali said as he gestured for Abdullah to take a seat. "We know so little about you. Will you share with us," Ben-Ali waved at Bashir and continued, "the details about your life before you came to our mosque?"

Mohamed aka DePalma launched into the elaborate cover story Homeland had devised in the event he was questioned. He was confident that any back check Ben-Ali and his people conducted would completely confirm his story.

When he finished he watched Ben-Ali look over to his security chief and nod. The wordless communication between the two must have signified that they had previously vetted him and his responses confirmed their intelligence.

"Brother, I would like you to meet someone, someone very important to our cause. I will need you to keep all of this between the three of us. Can you promise me you will keep our confidence?"

"Yes Imam."

"Very well, I want you to accompany Brother Bashir. He's going to take you to see our friend," Ben-Ali said. He motioned for Abdullah to come closer to him and whispered in his ear. "In order to assure our friend's safety Bashir will have to blindfold you. Is that all right?"

Mohamed nodded and Ben-Ali patted his shoulder.

When Abdullah Mohamed was led out of the meeting by the chief of security, Escobar Rodriquez, the mosque's janitor, was polishing the floor in the corridor outside the Imam's office. Bashir Amet stared at Rodriquez and motioned for him to allow them to pass. Rodriquez lifted the head phones he wore to suppress the noise of the machine from his ears and asked Amet, "Jeffe, is it all right for me to finish here before afternoon prayers?"

Amet nodded and continued to lead the young man down the corridor to the rear exit.

As soon as he was satisfied that Amet had exited the building Rodriquez picked up a trash bag and walked out the front entrance of the mosque and placed the trash bag with the other refuse that had been staged at the curb for pick-up. He took a bandanna from his back pocket and wiped the perspiration from his forehead. He removed his baseball cap and wiped the head band. Rodriquez replaced the cap with the bill of the Phillies cap backwards and returned to the mosque.

Rodriquez's actions were noted by the surveillance team monitoring the camera mounted in front of the building. His replacing his baseball cap with the bill to the back was a signal that something imminent was about to take place, although the precise nature of the event was not clear. The team reacted when the mosque's van emerged from the rear parking lot and drove past the bodega. Three agents trailed the van in the PECO utility van that had been parked across from the mosque.

The surveillance team immediately contacted Rico Valdez to inform him of their actions. Valdez in turn called SAC Howard Keel. "Boss, there might be something going down at the mosque. My guy gave the warning signal and we're trailing the van. It looks like one of the security men is driving."

The team trailed the van to an abandoned machine shop on Lehigh Avenue. They took photos of Bashir Amet leading a blindfolded Abdullah Mohamed aka Salvatore DePalma into the rear of the building. The lead agent on the detail immediately contacted Valdez for instructions: Should they move in to assure that the agent is not in danger or wait? The decision was to wait.

After a half hour ride a still blindfolded Mohamed was led out of the van and into a building. Bashir Amet removed the blindfold after Mohamed was seated in a chair. The man from the photo was seated opposite him. The man smiled at him.

"Brother," the man said. "I am sorry we needed to blindfold you. The times are perilous and our mission requires such measures."

"I understand," Mohamed responded.

"The Imam tells me you are a devout Muslim."

"There is no god apart from God, and Muhammad is the Messenger of God," Abdullah responded.

"Allahu-Akbar," the man replied.

Abdullah waited as the man studied him. After what seemed to Abdullah as several minutes the man asked, "Are you prepared to sacrifice your soul for your beliefs?"

"If it is God's will."

"Are you prepared to sacrifice others if required?"

Abdullah looked at the man and contemplated his response. He said, "The Prophet said: 'God has no mercy on one who has no mercy for others.'"

The man nodded. "You may go with Brother Bashir."

Fifteen minutes after they had entered the building the FBI surveillance team observed Bashir leading a blindfolded Mohamed/DePalma out of the building and back into the van. The team leader was relieved they had made the correct call and had taken no action to blow the agent's cover. The team waited in place, and shortly thereafter the tall man who had been last seen at the mosque three weeks before limped out of the building and walked west on Lehigh Avenue towards Ridge.

The subject got on the southbound SEPTA Route 34 bus and rode all the way to Broad Street. He took the Broad Street subway line to 15th Street. The surveillance team lost the subject as he made his way through the concourse – he walked down an empty corridor and disappeared.

Valdez reported the events to Keel.

"Boss, this guy's got skills. I figure he caught the tail right away and knew how to give them the slip."

"Rico, any results on facial recognition?"

"Nada. Either the guy had serious reconstruction surgery, or he just fell out of the sky."

"Did the surveillance team go through the warehouse on Lehigh Avenue?"

"Yeah, the place is totally abandoned."

TWENTY-EIGHT

———◆◆◆———

Saunders noticed the woman as he left his office building and made his way to the underground parking lot at 16th and JFK beneath Love Park. She was drop dead gorgeous, tall and exotic-looking. Her dark hair was cut short, setting off her blue eyes and high cheek bones. Every man she passed stared at her. He caught up to her as they waited for the light at 16th and Market Streets. He slowed his pace as they crossed 16th Street. She turned left and walked towards the parking lot entrance. He caught up with her as they both walked down the stairway that led to the garage entrance. He held the door open for her. She smiled and nodded as she walked past him.

As he followed her through the door he caught the scent of her perfume. It was subtle and clean, a contrast to the stale urine odor of the garage. She stumbled and dropped the folder she was carrying. As she fumbled with her pocketbook and the car keys she was holding in her left hand, Saunders bent down to pick up the folder that lay on the ground at her feet. She was wearing six inch high heels, and he could not resist admiring the curve of her shapely long legs. She smiled as he handed her the folder. He almost didn't feel the blade as she plunged it in his ear as he turned away. He was dead before his body hit the concrete surface of the parking lot. She walked away, not bothering to check Saunders' pulse.

Alawaite had already decided that he would need to change locations for the final planning before he noticed the clumsy surveillance team following him from the Lehigh Avenue site. Ben-Ali and his people were even more inept than he had imagined. He warned them that the mosque was being watched, and yet they brought the young man from there directly to his location. Alawaite would have to keep his future contacts with the mosque to a minimum.

As for Abdullah Mohamed, there was something not quite right about the young man the Imam had suggested as a candidate for the mission. He seemed too good to be real. His responses during the brief interview were textbook perfect. Not the way someone who had been blindfolded and delivered to an unknown location would react, unless he was other than what he appeared to be. Should he warn the Imam that Abdullah may be an agent? No doubt Ben-Ali's man Amet would overreact. Alawaite did not want the mosque to create any problems that would upset his plan.

Ichowitz called Regan when he received the report from Interpol. "Jack, Kate's friend Flynn is a bad actor. We may need to take some steps to make sure Kate and Liam are safe."

Michael Flynn was the youngest of seven children of Padraig Francis Flynn aka Paddy and Margret Mary O'Shea of Ulster, Northern Ireland. The Flynns and the O'Sheas were founding members of the Provisional Irish Republican Army. Michael's grandfather, Michael Connor, for whom he was named, and his father and uncles were responsible for numerous acts of violence throughout the "Troubles."

In 1978, Flynn's Uncle Liam had been given a life sentence for his role in a London bombing at Harrods that resulted in the deaths and maiming of several civilians including the three-year-old grandchild of a Member of Parliament from Northern Ireland. While he was serving his sentence at Her Majesty's Prison Maze at the Long Kesh Detention Center, better known among the IRA as the "Maze," he was a key figure in the "Dirty Protest" in which IRA soldiers, who considered themselves political prisoners, refused to wear prison uniforms and wrapped themselves in bed sheets. Their protest was dismissed with distain by then-Prime Minister Margret Thatcher.

The tensions between the warring parties continued to escalate, and Liam continued to agitate from inside the Maze. He died of starvation in the 1981 Irish Hunger Strike. His and his brother soldiers' sacrifice eventually resulted in the Good Friday Agreement and release of "political prisoners." With the end of The Troubles the Flynns took up more lucrative, but no less violent pursuits. Ultimately their criminal enterprise evolved into more sophisticated endeavors, including the theft and sale of valuable works of art. The black market for masterpieces, especially in Russia and the Far East, and the remarkably poor quality of security at museums at which they harvested their treasures quickly made this aspect of their criminal empire the most profitable and easiest of their pursuits.

In March, Michael Flynn had been arrested on charges stemming from the theft of a Picasso from the art museum in Dublin. He was released when the witness who had identified him as the perpetrator of the crime recanted his statement. According to the Interpol report, the authorities believed the witness had been intimidated by "unknown" associates of Mr. Flynn. Of course, these suspicions could not be corroborated. The Gardai, the national police force of Ireland, had no information regarding Flynn's current whereabouts and requested reports from participating agencies.

"Apparently there's no record of Flynn coming through Immigration," Ichowitz said.

"And yet he is here," Regan replied.

"But why?" Ichowitz asked. "I mean, he just doesn't seem like the type of guy who would come all the way from Ireland to Manayunk just to check on his son."

"Yeah, there must be something we haven't picked up on that explains why Flynn's here," Regan said.

"Jack, I'll try my buddy Ossberg at Homeland and see if he has anything. He owes me a call."

"Izz any developments on Saunders yet? If Coratelli's gambit is going to work, we should have had a reaction by now," Regan asked.

"Nothing so far, I'll call you as soon as I have something."

Regan had arranged to take Liam to his baseball game that afternoon while Katey was preparing for the Grape's dinner trade. He was concerned that O'Malley would overreact if Flynn showed up at the Grape Tavern. Regan had asked the district to send a patrol car around on a more or less regular basis, just in case.

"Jack, I think I'm playing center field today. I'm worried that I won't remember where to throw the ball if I catch it," Liam said as they walked over to the park.

"Don't worry. Just catch the ball and listen to your buddy Chris, the second baseman. He'll tell you what to do; and remember, don't react to the sound of the bat hitting the ball. Wait until you see where the ball is hit. You'll have plenty of time to get in position if it's hit your way. You'll be fine," Jack assured him.

Jack watched from the dugout as the game progressed. He suggested that the coach position Liam just a few steps behind the second baseman, assuring the coach that in the unlikely event anyone hit the ball into the outfield Liam had the speed to retrieve it, even if it was hit over his head.

His first time up to bat Liam was nervous and missed the first two pitches by a wide margin. On the third pitch he hit a weak grounder back to the mound and was thrown out at first. When he returned to the dugout Jack called him over and said, "Liam, don't worry about your last at bat. By the time you get up to bat next time the pitcher will be getting tired. You'll have the advantage. Just relax."

Just as Jack predicted, two innings later Liam stepped into the batter's box with two men on base. The opposing coach assumed that Liam would once again swing wildly and make the final out. Liam looked over at Jack and settled in.

"Strike one," the umpire called as the pitch barely crossed the plate knee high.

Liam looked back at Jack who gave him a nod of encouragement.

As the second pitch slowly made its way to the plate Liam waited and hit the ball over the outstretched reach of the first baseman. The ball rolled past the right fielder as Liam rounded second base. By the time the right fielder retrieved the ball, Liam was rounding third. When he crossed the plate he was surrounded by his teammates as the right fielder threw the ball over the catcher's head.

Liam turned and looked out at the crowd, his look of pure joy suddenly froze and he ran over to Regan.

"Liam, what's wrong?" Jack asked.

The boy pointed to the bleachers and said, "That's my Da."

Regan looked over and saw a tall man with near shaved head and a two-day beard staring back at him. Regan held the boy to his side and looked down and said, "Don't worry Liam, he won't bother you." When he looked up the man was gone.

Liam's team won the game, three to one. The unexpected appearance of Liam's father had dampened the boy's excitement over his moment of joy. His teammates were still high fiving each other, completely caught up in their victory as Regan and Liam left the field and walked back to the Grape.

Kate could tell from Liam's expression that something was amiss. She looked over to Regan for some indication. He subtly shook his head.

"Liam, are you OK?" she asked.

"Mum, Da was at the game."

She looked back at Regan; he nodded and the color drained out of her face as she held her son close.

"Izz, Flynn showed up at Liam's game this afternoon," Regan said.

"Did he approach the boy?"

"No. When he saw me staring at him he walked away."

"Can you take Kate and her son some place where they can be safe for a few days?" Ichowitz asked.

"I asked Kate if she would stay with my parents until we find this guy."

"What did she say?"

"She's thinking about it, but I think she'll agree. I figure there's no safer place in the city than the Police Commissioner's house."

"Jack there's been a development in the Coratelli matter."

"Did Saunders ask for a deal?"

"No."

"Why not?"

"He's dead."

"*What?*"

"Someone murdered him last night."

Ichowitz told Regan that Saunders' body had been found at the Philadelphia Parking Authority lot beneath Love Park. At first the EMTs thought he had died of a coronary or that he threw an embolism. When the Medical Examiner conducted the autopsy he discovered the puncture wound in the corpse's left ear. The blade punctured the blood-brain barrier and went directly into the cerebellum. The ME figured he died instantly. He estimated the time of death between approximately 6 and 10 PM last night, probably closer to 6.

"Izz were there any witnesses?"

"None."

"How about security video?"

"There was a security camera at the 16th Street entrance to the garage, but, of course, it hasn't been functioning for at least six months."

"Any theory on why Saunders was murdered?" Regan asked.

"They probably figured he was going to spill."

"Izz this is going off the rails. First Megan Larson, next Vito Coratelli Junior, and now Mickey Saunders. Who's next?" Regan asked.

"Oh yeah, I forgot to mention the Montgomery County detectives called me. Their investigation revealed that there was an agency nurse at the facility the night Junior was murdered. The nursing administrator didn't have anyone scheduled from the agency, but she didn't think anything of it since the paperwork doesn't always come in before the nurse reports for the assignment. Since they're always understaffed, she gave the agency nurse an assignment."

"Anyway, when the paperwork never showed up she questioned her boss, who told her there was no order for an agency nurse that night. The detectives checked the license information the nurse, Selma McIntosh, had left. It was all phony."

"Was there any video?" Regan asked.

"Yeah, but Ms. McIntosh must be a player. No visual of her face. The consensus descriptions provided by the Nursing Administrator and other staff on duty was a tall woman with a bad frizzy blond dye job – you know, black roots – who wore oversized glasses."

"Well at least we know she was tall," Regan observed. "How tall?"

"Glad you asked. It varied from five-ten to six-five." Ichowitz shrugged. "You know eye witnesses."

"Monroe, *Vus Machs Da*? I thought you were going to call me and let me know if Homeland is going to release an unredacted copy of the video of Nooris' condo," Ichowitz said when his call was put through to Monroe Ossberg.

"Izz, you're right. I'm really sorry, but things are crazy over here."

"Well it's nuts all over. Did you hear that Mickey Saunders, one of the characters involved with Nooris in the Family Court House deal, was murdered last night?" Ichowitz asked.

"No."

"That makes three people who were associated with Nooris who are no longer among the living. Monroe, we need to see that tape. It may help us crack the case. It may even prevent another murder."

"I hear you, but I'm not calling the shots over here."

"But I thought your buddy Simon Conway got the sack?"

"Yeah, but I can't make a move without confirmation from DC," Ossberg responded.

"Come on, pal. Can't you give me a peek?"

"Izz, believe me I would, but with the Vice President and the Sec-retary of State due here to get her medal on the Fourth of July, there's more heavyweights from Secret Service, State, Homeland, the Bureau, you name it, looking over my shoulder than you can imagine."

"But I thought we were *mishpocheh*?"

"We are. Just give me some time to work it out."

When he hung up the phone Ossberg looked over at Howard Keel, SAC of the Philadelphia Bureau office.

"Do you think he bought it?" Keel asked.

"Don't think so. Ichowitz has been around the block a few times. He's got a nose for BS."

"Christ, the last thing we need is for the locals to be sticking their nose in our turf. I'll ask the assistant director to bring some heat on the Police Commissioner. Maybe that will keep Ichowitz off your back."

"Katey, you and the boy have to go to Jack's parents' place until that bastard Flynn goes back to Ulster or whatever hell he inhabits," Mike O'Malley told his niece.

She stared back at him, her eyes narrowed and her chin out.

"Now don't be given me that look of yours, girlie. You've got to be thinkin of the boy. Besides, the Regans are good people. They did everything short of donating all their organs to Susan to save her from the cancer."

"Uncle Mike, you know you can't run away and hide from a bully; you have to stand up and fight back. That's what you taught me back in Dublin," she responded.

"Ach woman, I know what I told you. But it's Liam we're talkin about now. I don't know what Flynn's doin here, but surely we don't want your son havin anything to do with the likes of him."

Kate O'Malley knew her uncle was right. There was nothing more important than her son's well-being. But allowing Jack or any man to assume responsibility for their security was a serious commitment. She wasn't sure she was ready to take that step.

"Jack will be here soon to take you and the boy to his folks' place. You're going to have to decide whether you and Liam will be safer with them," O'Malley said.

"I know, I know," she sighed. "If we go there, who's going to be lookin after you, O'Malley?"

He smiled at her and replied, "Now don't you go worryin your pretty head over the likes of me. I've been in a scrum or two in my time."

TWENTY-NINE

The "Welcome America Festival," an eleven-day extravaganza of concerts, parades, fireworks and other events, was the faux tradition with which the city that claimed to be the birthplace of our nation celebrated the Fourth of July holiday. While, in truth, our Founding Fathers had in fact congregated in Philadelphia when they conspired to declare our independence and later reconvened here to draft our constitution, the part about the celebration being a long-standing tradition was exaggerated, unless of course long-standing traditions can be established after only three years.

As always, at least since last year, the festival ends with a concert on the Parkway with the Philly Pops Orchestra and an unbelievable fireworks display over the Philadelphia Museum of Art. This year the penultimate event of the festival is the ceremony in which the Vice President, substituting for the President, will give the Medal of Freedom award to the Secretary of State. The Presidential Medal of Freedom is awarded by the President, "for especially meritorious contributions to the security or national interests of the U.S., or world peace, or cultural or other significant public or private endeavors." In other words the President gave the award to whoever he decided to honor for whatever reason he considered appropriate. Since its inception during JFK's administration, such notables as Colin Powell, Ellsworth Bunker, and John Kenneth Galbraith at one end of the spectrum to Andy Griffith, John Wayne and Frank Sinatra at the other were recipients of the medal. This year's recipient clearly falls somewhere in the middle of the parade of past honorees.

The ceremony was scheduled to take place at noon on July Fourth in front of Independence Hall where the Declaration of Independence was adopted and the U.S. Constitution was later debated, drafted and signed. The Mall between the National Constitution Center at 6th and Arch Streets three blocks north to 6th and Chestnut Street, the site of Independence Hall, will be cordoned off to accommodate the thousands of spectators and dignitaries the promoters of the event anticipate will bear witness. Among those expected to attend are three former presidents, three members of the U.S. Supreme Court, several Senators and Congressmen, the Governor, the Mayor and scores of other prominent local and national business leaders and entertainers. The rumor mill predicted that Oprah Winfrey will also be in attendance and surprise the Secretary with a special gift.

The intense security measures to assure the safety of the principals involved and their distinguished guests led to the inevitable turf fight among the various agencies, national, state and local, as to who among them would be primarily responsible. Rather than coordinate their efforts, the individuals designated to fulfill this responsibility for their respective agencies jealously guarded the actions they had taken individually to keep their charges out of harm's way. The result was a bureaucratic nightmare of potentially disastrous dimensions.

"Commissioner, I have requests from the Secret Service, the FBI, Homeland Security and the National Park Service to give their respective tactical response teams unlimited access to the perimeter buildings that surround Independence Mall for their snipers," his chief of staff greeted John Hogan Regan, Philadelphia's Commissioner of Police when he arrived at his office at the PAB.

Commissioner Regan took a sip of his coffee and said, "Why don't we get their respective leaders together in my conference room, at 1300 for consultation. Don't let any of them know that anyone from any other agency will be attending. That will be our surprise."

"OK , but Commissioner, you better bring a whip and chair if you want to maintain order."

"I think I'll just bring my Smith and Wesson."

When the heads of the various federal agencies involved got over the shock of being assembled without their knowledge, the posturing and infighting got really ugly. Each agency contended that their respective snipers were the only ones capable of assuring the protection of the Vice President, the Secretary of State and other notables scheduled to be on hand at the ceremony. When the petty arguments and insults had reached the beyond rational stage the Commissioner intervened.

"Ladies and gentlemen, I appreciate the sincerity of your contentions and the passion and depth of your commitment to your respective organizations. I also understand the level of your concerns; however, as I'm sure you all appreciate, we need to have a rational and unified plan of action.

"Here's how we are going to handle the security."

Regan explained that since the perimeter of the ceremonial site was not on federal property, the Philadelphia police had sole jurisdiction. Members of the elite anti-terrorist squad had already worked out a detailed plan. Based on Regan's comparison of the PPD plan with those of all the federal agencies, there would be no need for any other agency to be involved in that aspect of the security.

As to the security on the Mall itself, the Commissioner informed them that with the exception of the Secret Service agents that were personally assigned to the VP, the Secretary of State and the former presidents, and the normal park police contingent, the Philadelphia police had jurisdiction to secure the Mall. The Commissioner would permit representatives from the FBI to monitor the tactical command of the operation. This plan had been approved by the Mayor, the Governor and the President.

Before anyone could respond, Regan stood up and left the room.

Ichowitz knocked on Jack Regan's door. "Got a sec?" he asked as he walked in.

Regan looked up from the file he had been studying and said, "Izz, I thought you were going to question Avi Nooris about the hole in his alibi?"

"Yeah, but the ME called me, the DNA results on Megan Larson's baby came in."

"So who's the father?"

"Mayor Gallo."

Regan exhaled sharply and shook his head.

"So boychik, what do you think?" Ichowitz asked.

"Izz, I would have bet the house and the barn that Ari Nooris was the father. Gallo? Really?"

"Emess," Ichowitz replied.

"In truth I never liked Gallo for Megan's killer. I don't see him as wielding anything more dangerous than his mouth. I know he's a treacherous politician, but deep down I never thought he had the cojones to actually kill anybody."

"I agree. Do you think Nooris found out she was Gallo's lover and killed her in a fit of jealousy?" Ichowitz asked.

"Which Nooris?"

"Either one."

"Ari was genuinely upset when we questioned him about Megan's murder. My take is that he didn't know Megan was pregnant. He was also offended when we asked him if he had an affair with her," Regan said as he got up from his chair and began to pace.

"Yeah, he was obviously fond of Ms. Larson and his reaction to a suggestion that the two of them had been romantically involved appeared to be genuine," Ichowitz observed.

"So do you like Avi?" Regan asked.

Ichowitz moved his head side to side and grimaced. "Why would Avi kill Megan Larson?" he asked.

"Jealousy," Regan offered.

"From what we observed, Avi had a thing for younger girls. I don't know. It just doesn't feel right."

"Izz, is your buddy Osberg gonna give us the video? If we had that I'll bet you we wouldn't have to guess who killed Megan Larson."

Ichowitz shook his head and said, "I don't think we can count on any cooperation from my good friend from the Bureau anytime soon."

"I don't get it. I mean what could possibly be on that video that's so friggin important to national security that they won't let us see it?" Regan asked.

"Dunno."

THIRTY

Patricia Hogan opened the door to Jack's bedroom and led Liam and Kate O'Malley in. The small room still looked the same as when a teenaged Jack Regan lived there. On the wall beside the bed was a bookcase where Jack displayed the model airplanes and tanks his father had helped him build when Jack was a little boy. The bookcase also contained the trophies and other memorabilia of his athletic achievements and pictures of the various teams he had been part of, a veritable Jack Regan sports shrine.

Liam stared wide-eyed at the bookcase, especially the model airplanes.

"Kate, Liam can stay in Jack's room, if that's all right with you. It's right next to the room where you and … where you'll be staying," Patricia Regan blushed at the thought of her son and Kate sleeping in the room next door to Kate's son. The awkward moment of silence was broken when Jack arrived with Liam and Kate's suitcases in hand.

"Liam, what did you put in your suit case? It weighs a ton," Jack asked as he set the boy's luggage on the bed.

"Did ya win all those trophies?" Liam asked.

"Yes, but I had a lot of help from my teammates and coaches. Liam, we'll probably have to build a trophy case to hold all the awards you'll collect by the time you graduate from college," Jack said.

"Did ya build those models?"

"Uh-huh. It's something my father and I worked on. In fact there are some kits in the drawer that we never got around to. I bet my father would help us put them together if you're interested. Let's ask him tonight."

With Kate and Liam safe in the bosom of his family, Regan turned his attention to the Larson murder investigation that had morphed into a multiple homicide investigation. Regan and Ichowitz were convinced that all of the murders were somehow tied to the Family Court House scam. Regan was beginning to believe that whoever was the surviving player in that fiasco would be the killer by default. Both of them also believed that the Homeland Security video of Nooris' condo would reveal the identity of Larson's killer.

That night when Regan's father got home, Jack shared his theory that the Larson-Coratelli-Saunders homicides were the work of a single person.

"What does Izzy think?" the Commissioner asked.

"Dad, Izzy thinks there's a connection, but he doesn't believe one person is responsible for all of the homicides."

"Do you have a suspect, someone who had motive and opportunity to have committed all of the homicides?" his father asked.

"No. At least not yet."

"Izzy has been investigating homicides for a long time. I would trust his intuition on this."

"Dad, how are things going with the arrangements for the Fourth of July celebrations? Izzy told me the inter-agency turf fight is quite a kerfuffle."

The Commissioner shook his head and replied, "It's all screwed up, or as Izzy would say, 'It's *frcokt.*'"

"That bad?"

Regan's father told Jack what had transpired that afternoon when he ambushed the heads of all the federal agencies involved and corralled them in his conference room.

"I've never seen so many testosterone-enhanced egos in one room trying to outdo one another at the same time. I should have sold tickets.

It was quite a show. The problem is we have credible threats that some terrorist organization wants to make a spectacle of the awards ceremony. I believe that if everyone would share their information we could come up with a cohesive plan that we could all rely upon."

"What are you going to do?"

"I'm going to rely on our own people and try to keep the rest of them in line."

Josef Alawaite was also considering his plans for the Fourth of July celebration. He had taken the necessary precautions to insulate his operation from the New Age Mosque. The complete absence of discipline of the Imam and his security staff was not unanticipated. Indeed, he had counted on this as part of his plan. He realized that he needed to maintain a sense of purpose and commitment among his soldiers. As the fateful day approached he spent time with each of them individually to reinforce their devotion to the mission.

Alawaite was keenly aware of the need for diligence in covering his tracks. He assumed that some federal agency had followed the mosque's van when Amet brought him the young man the Imam suggested as a replacement for the mission. Alawaite believed the young man was a plant, perhaps someone inserted undercover by some U.S. agency or even the Mossad. He assumed that the chatter on the Internet that the Imam had generated would heighten the scrutiny of the celebration. Once again that also was part of the plan. Regardless, there was nothing anyone could do to stop him.

He checked the sidewalk behind him to make sure there was no tail. When he was satisfied, he limped up the three steps to the front door of his apartment building. He glanced again and thought the van that was parked across the street looked familiar. He would have to relocate. He was glad this would be his final assignment.

Vito Coratelli sat at the oversized desk in the small office in his home. The desk lamp only illuminated the surface of his desk, on which he had placed the list of those he held responsible for the murder of his son. He drew a line through Mickey Saunders' name, and contemplated his next move. He was not surprised to learn of Mickey Saunders' death. The killers were cleaning up the loose ends, and Saunders, who was ready to give them up in return for a lighter sentence, was a loose end. Besides, he got what he deserved. There was no doubt in Coratelli's mind that Saunders had been involved in his son's murder. Who would be their next victim, Gallo? Or would they come after him? If they tried to eliminate him they were in for a surprise.

Ari Nooris was pleased that Courtney Wells had a change of heart and finally returned his call. She was a beautiful woman and a passionate lover. A pity, he thought. He would miss her, but he was quite certain that the future would bring him other beautiful and passionate companions. He found her questions about Michael Flynn amusing. The woman was obviously attracted to men like himself who were not part of the well-bred upper class world she inhabited. Megan Larson had told him that Courtney and Assistant D.A. Regan had once been an item. Lucky for Regan that relationship never went anywhere, he laughed at the thought. Regan was too much of a boy scout; Wells would have destroyed him. Maybe he should set Courtney up with Flynn. Flynn was a heartless bastard; it would serve her right. Nooris needed Flynn to concentrate on his assignment. After they were done, Flynn could have any woman he desired.

He sighed and looked at the picture of Megan Larson he kept in his desk. There was a young woman with promise. She knew what she wanted out of life and she had the guts and determinaion to go after it. What a waste. He wondered again who had killed her and why?

PART 3.

THE MAYHEM

THIRTY-ONE

They removed the chain link fence around the Barnes Foundation construction site on the Parkway, a sure sign that the grand opening of the facility was getting closer. The Barnes' new digs covered over four acres of prime real estate. The foundation's directors believed that relocating to Center City would attract thousands of art lovers from around the world. The city of Philadelphia was also banking on those art lovers dropping millions of dollars a year in hotel stays, meals, etc, into the local economy. A classic win-win for everyone involved, unless you're a fan of the sanctity of last wills and testaments.

The foundation's new home for its famous art collection is a two-story, 93,000-square-foot building the architects designed to display the collection in a way that "replicated the scale, proportion and configuration" of the original gallery in Merion. According to Alfred Barnes' will, any deviation from the unique manner in which he had displayed his works of art was strictly prohibited. Only an army of lawyers and a judge could proclaim with a straight face that the new museum's presentation "replicated" the former presentation.

Regardless, the foundation's curators were preparing the collection for the eight mile move from Merion to Philadelphia. The final plans for the relocation of these masterpieces, whose value had been estimated to be more than three billion dollars, were supposed to be kept under lock and key and only disclosed to those directly involved on a need-to- know basis.

Apparently everyone from the chief curator to the part-time janitor needed to know, so copies of the schedule, the route, etc, were posted throughout the facility. So much for maintaining security!

According to the plan, an unmarked moving van would be parked at the back entrance of the Merion gallery before midnight on July Third. The paintings from the first floor galleries, which had been carefully prepared for transport, would be loaded onto the van throughout the early morning of the Fourth for transport to the Philadelphia facility at 11 AM. The timing of the transport was to coincide with the medal ceremony at Independence Mall. Those involved in setting up the plan had determined that the timing afforded the least amount of interference and traffic during the eight mile trip from Merion to the Parkway.

While the Barnes prepared for the Fourth of July move, the local, state and federal authorities involved in planning the various weekend events were also putting the final touches on their arrangements. The cooperation, or lack thereof, among the various bureaucracies involved continued to create an atmosphere of tension and potential for chaos. With less than a week to go before the celebrations would begin, no one was exactly sure who would be responsible to protect the dignitaries at the Medal of Freedom ceremony.

Detective Isadore Ichowitz stared at the wall in the Fourth District conference room where pictures of the victims and suspects had been put up for the ever-expanding multiple homicide investigation. The murder books on the conference room table were grim reminders of the lack of progress they had made in determining the killer or killers. Ichowitz and Regan had competing theories regarding the murders. Regan believed all of the murders were related to the Family Court House deal and had been the work of a single killer. Ichowitz agreed that the Coratelli and Saunders murders were connected, and possibly the work of the same individual.

Ichowitz did not believe that Megan Larson's homicide was connected, even though she had been involved in the court house scam. He had no hard evidence to support his theory, just the instincts of a veteran homicide detective. Ichowitz put aside his frustration over the FBI/Homeland

Security's refusal to produce the video surveillance of Ari Nooris condo. He decided he would have to break the case by finding new evidence. He sat at the conference room table and began to review the evidence they had accumulated from the beginning of the investigation. He knew from years of experience that the direction the investigation would have to take if it was to be successful would be found there.

"Commissioner, the White House is on line one."

Regan figured the call had to be about his maneuver to remove all of the federal security agencies from the direct security of the mall for the Vice President and the Secretary of State medal presentation event. After a ten-minute conversation with the President's chief of staff, Regan had been persuaded to allow the Secret Service, the FBI and Homeland Security to reassume primary responsibility for security. The Philadelphia police would handle traffic and crowd control.

"Commissioner, I'm sure you understand that our federal agencies have superior resources and far greater expertise than your force," the chief of staff said, condescension dripping from every word.

"I respectfully disagree. May I speak candidly?" Regan asked.

"If you must."

"The pissing contest that your agencies are involved in has created an extremely dangerous situation that compromises the security of the Vice President, the Secretary and everyone attending. Please make sure you convey my reservations to the President."

When the new pecking order was communicated to the PPD tactical division commander and the head of Highway Patrol, and other command-level staff involved in the operation it was met with universal disdain.

"Fellas, no matter what, we have to be ready to pick up the pieces. If the shit hits the fan we need to have a contingency plan in place. Keep our guys on high alert and ready to move in if there's trouble. This is our city, and we have to be ready to protect our citizens if there is a terrorist attack," Commissioner Regan told them.

Josef Alawaite was ready. He was confident that his plan would accomplish the desired result. After carefully checking his route to make sure he had no tail, he approached the bank of pay phones in the Greyhound Bus terminal on Filbert Street. When he was satisfied that no one was close enough to listen in or see him dial the number, he placed the call.

"Is everything on your end settled?" he asked.

"Yes."

"Then we'll proceed," Alawaite said and hung up.

Ari Nooris smiled as he threw the cell phone into the Schuylkill River.

THIRTY-TWO

The moving van pulled up to the gate at the Barnes Foundation at 4:30 AM. The white, unmarked, eighteen-wheeler was identical to the one that was already being loaded at the loading dock to transport the art collection to the new museum. The curator and some of his staff had worked through the night loading the works of art into the trailer. The trailer was about three quarters filled with paintings and sculptures that had been exhibited on the first floor of the museum. It would likely take another two hours or so to complete the loading process.

Harlan Johnson, who had worked a double shift, rubbed his eyes and looked out at the two men in the cab of the eighteen-wheeler that had pulled up to the gate. He checked the clipboard again to make sure he had not missed an entry. There was nothing to indicate that a second moving van was expected. He came out of the guard house and walked up to the gate near the driver's side of the cab.

"Can I help you?" he asked.

The driver said, "Ya can open the gate and let me in."

"But I have no record authorizing entry for your van. What are you doing here?"

"Hey gov, I'm just the driver. I'll show you my manifest. Are ya gonna let me through the gate while we figure out what to do, or what?"

Harlan smiled at the driver and shook his head.

"From your accent it sounds like you're not from around here," the guard said. "I have to check with my supervisor and find out if I'm authorized to let you in."

"All right, mate. Let me give you the manifest and ya can read him the entry," the driver said. He got out of the cab of his truck and walked over to the gate. When the guard reached through the bar to take the manifest from him, the driver grabbed his arm and pulled Johnson's body forward, pinning him against the iron bars. The second man jumped out of the cab and reached inside the gate with a gun and thrust it in the guard's ear.

"Listen to me gov," the driver said. "Don't be foolish. Open the feckin gate and let us in, and no one needs to get hurt. D 'ya understand me?"

Harlan Johnson nodded.

"All right then, I'm gonna let go of your arm. But my mate here is not what I would consider a very understanding fella. He wanted to shoot you as soon as we pulled up to the gate. Matter of fact, he still wants to blow ya away, d 'ya get what I'm tellin ya?"

Harlan Johnson nodded again.

"OK, nice and easy now, open the latch manually right here. I know ya can do it," the driver said and released his hold on the guard.

Harlan Johnson pulled the pin from the lock. The driver immediately pushed the gate aside. The driver now pulled a pistol from behind his back and pointed it at the guard. He motioned to the second man to drive the van on to the property.

"What's your name, mate?" the driver asked him.

"Johnson, Harlan Johnson."

"Harlan, listen to me and do everything I tell ya to do, and no one needs to get hurt. D 'ya understand?"

The guard nodded.

"Good. Now Harlan, are there any more security guards on duty?"

Johnson shook his head.

"OK. How many people are here loadin the truck?"

"The curator, the driver and three others."

"Good. Now you and me and my mate are gonna walk over to the van over there and make acquaintance with your friends. And you're gonna tell them to follow my instructions, or people are gonna get hurt."

They walked slowly towards the loading dock. The driver held the guard from behind, pinning his wrist in a vice lock grip with the pistol thrust firmly in the guard's spine. They walked up the four steps to the loading dock.

"Harlan, who are these men?" a tall elderly man asked as they approached.

"Dr. Abernathy, please don't make any sudden moves and follow this man's instructions," Johnson responded.

"What?" Abernathy asked.

At that moment, the driver released his grip on the guard and pushed him in the direction of the older man. Both the driver and his passenger pointed their weapons at the guard and the man called Abernathy.

"What's the meaning of this?" Abernathy said.

The driver pointed his index finger at his lips and shook his head motioning the man to be quiet. He approached the two men and said, "Are ya the curator?"

"Yes."

"Call everybody here right now, but do it calmly. If you don't, my mate here is gonna shoot you and the guard, and then we'll kill everyone here. Doctor, don't make us do that."

Abernathy's eyes widened. For a moment he looked like he was about to faint.

"Dr. Abernathy, please do as he asks," Harlan Johnson said.

Within minutes, all of the Foundation's personnel were sitting on the loading dock facing the wall with their hands holding the backs of their heads.

"All right folks, here's what's gonna happen. My mate is gonna search each of you one at a time. We'll be takin your cell phones and watches. Don't be worryin, we'll leave them for ya. Now remember as long as everyone continues to cooperate, nobody's gonna get hurt. Don't anyone do anything stupid like tryin to be a hero."

After the gunman collected all of the cell phones and watches, the six individuals were taken to the second van. Their hands were secured behind their backs with plastic ties and they were gagged.

When all six were in the van, the driver said, "Thanks fer your cooperation. Ya see there are plenty of pads fer ya to sit on. Now we'll be shuttin the door so make yerselves comfortable. It shouldn't be too long before someone comes looking fer ya."

Harlan Johnson and the others sat on the pads. The sun light from the early dawn filtered through the cracks of the trailer's doors providing them with limited visibility. Abernathy tried to stand up; Johnson grunted, shook his head and motioned for Abernathy to remain seated. Johnson slowly moved behind Abernathy and placed the back of his head where the gag was tied close to Abernathy's hands. It took the older man close to ten minutes to loosen Johnson's gag.

"Thanks doctor," Johnson whispered. "We need to remain calm, and keep quiet, until we hear them pull the van away. "Now doctor, I'm going to loosen your gag. Is everyone OK?" he whispered. The others nodded. "OK, after I get Dr. Abernathy's gag off we'll work on everyone else. Then we'll work on the plastic ties on our hands, OK?"

Johnson estimated that it took them more than an hour to free everyone. He motioned for them to remain quiet and calm. "We need to make sure they're gone before we try to get out of here," he whispered.

As best he could determine it was somewhere around 7:30. They could hear the gunmen continuing to take the crated works of art to the van.

"I guess they want to fill the truck before they leave," Johnson said. "I'm not sure, but I think they want to stick to the schedule for the transport to Center City. That way they might not attract too much attention," he hesitated and then said. "The thing is how do they know the schedule?"

Johnson knew that according to the schedule, the moving van was supposed to leave the facility around 11 AM. That would mean if his calculation of the time was accurate that they would have to remain in the van for at least two more hours. That was a long time for him to keep everyone calm. The last thing they needed was for anyone to become hysterical and make a racket that brought their captors back.

He motioned the group together and shared his thoughts. "Listen, if they wanted to hurt us, we'd all be dead by now. All they want is the art. As soon as we hear them drive away we'll try to get out of here and alert the police. It's not going to be easy for them to hide an eighteen-wheeler."

Jack Regan was getting used to waking up every morning with Kate O'Malley at his side. He loved the feeling of intimacy, and realized how much he had missed being with someone he cared about.

"Jack, it's time to get up," she said and playfully poked him. He pulled her closer and kissed her.

She pulled away. "No Jack, we can't be doing this in your parents' place."

He kissed her again and she reacted and almost surrendered.

"Jack stop please," she said as she wrestled out of his embrace. "Behave now, and I promise I'll reward you later. I have to wake Liam; he's going with his friend Ryan and his family to the Constitution Center and some ceremony downtown. Liam's really excited about it... What?"

Jack's face tightened and his eyes narrowed. "I know I'm being overly cautious but I'm concerned about Liam and Ryan and his family going there," he said. He told Kate about the website chatter and the steps his father and the federal agencies were taking in response.

"Jack, Liam's really been looking forward to this. I'll call Ryan's parents and let them know what you told me. Maybe they'll postpone the trip downtown to another day. In the meantime, I've got to get the boy up."

Liam was sitting at the kitchen table with Jack's mother. He was eating cereal and reading the back of a box of Captain Crunch.

"We keep this on hand for when Jack stays over." He heard his mother tell the little boy. "It's still his favorite."

Liam looked up at the woman and smiled. "It's really good. I'll tell Mum to buy some so we have it when Jack comes over."

"What are the two of you talking about?" Jack asked as he sat down at the kitchen table next to the boy. "Hey, who told you you could have my Captain Crunch?"

Liam laughed and nodded towards Jack's mother.

"Mother," Jack said and sighed.

Kate walked in the kitchen and motioned for Jack to follow her into the dining room. "I just got off the phone with Ryan's mother. I told her about your concerns. She told me they would just go to the Constitution Center and see the exhibits and then take the boys to the waterfront before the ceremony begins. I think I really scared the poor woman. Jack d 'ya think they'll be safe?"

"Katey, I wish they would avoid the whole area. I'm concerned that some nut-job will do something to disrupt the celebration."

"I'll talk to them when I drop Liam off. Maybe I can convince them not to go. Your mother is going to drive us over to Manayunk. I have to take care of some things at the Grape."

"OK, but call me and let me know what they decide. I have to meet Izzy at the Fourth District this morning. If they decide to go to the Constitution Center, I'll meet them there."

They went back into the kitchen. Jack's mother asked Jack if he would drop off a package at the Barnes. "Jack, you can leave it with Harlan he'll know what to do with it."

THIRTY-THREE

"Izz, it's been nearly a month since Megan Larson's murder and we're no closer to solving it than we were at the beginning of the investigation. For that matter we're no closer to solving the Coratelli and Saunders' murders either," Regan said as he sat down at the conference table and stared at the wall on which they had posted the summary of the investigation and the pictures of the victims and suspects.

The big detective shook his head and replied, "Jack I've been going over the evidence and I think we're closer to solving these murders than you think."

Regan looked at him and waited for further explanation.

"Jack who did you originally suspect killed Megan Larson?"

"Dorothy Wiggins."

"But what about the hole in Avi Nooris alibi?" Ichowitz asked.

"I still like Wiggins. She had a motive. Why would Avi Nooris kill Larson?"

"Jealousy?"

Regan stared at the wall for a moment and said, "I'm not feeling it."

"And who do you think killed Coratelli and Saunders?"

"Someone connected to the court house scam, one of the Nooris', or someone working for them."

"So you no longer believe that one person is responsible for all of the homicides?"

"Izz, I only thought that when we eliminated Wiggins as a suspect for the Larson homicide. Remember, you're the one who told me Gold the

Comcast tech was a reliable witness. Since he left the vic alive and well forty-five minutes after Wiggins had already come and gone I figured there's no way Wiggins was the doer."

"What about Coratelli and Saunders?"

"It's got to be the Nooris' or someone connected to them," Regan replied.

"So maybe we're missing something," Ichowitz said.

"Yeah, like the video surveillance of the condo the night Larson was killed."

Ichowitz smiled and said, "Well, based on my experience when you hit the wall, it's time to go back to the beginning." The big detective saw Regan's look of concern and asked, "What's wrong?"

"Izz, that's going to take considerable time," Regan replied.

Ichowitz nodded.

"I can't start over now. Liam's at the Constitution Center with one of his friends. My father told me all about the buzz on the Internet that there might be some kind of terrorist attack at the awards ceremony today. I have to get down there and get Liam out of harm's way."

"Jack, I'll go over to the tactical HQ we set up near Independence Mall. Do you have a picture of the boy on your phone?"

Regan nodded.

"OK, send it to me. I'll get it out on the street and we'll find him. Take one of the rovers with you so that we can keep in communication."

Regan left the Fourth District with one of the rovers, the hand-held two-way radios the detectives used, but instead of driving directly to Independence Mall, he drove across the Green Street Bridge towards Lower Merion to drop his mother's package off with Harlan, the security guard at the Barnes Foundation.

Harlan heard the rumble from the other truck as soon as the gunmen turned on the ignition. He jumped up, moved to the door, and tried to push it open. There was no give and he figured that the thieves must have secured the door.

He could hear the driver of the rig nearly strip the gears as the van with the works of art maneuvered around them. Harlan motioned for the others to remain still. "We need to wait until someone comes looking for us. There's no sense in screaming yourselves hoarse if there's nobody in earshot. Save your energy."

Harlan put his ear to the back door of the van. He could hear the driver shift gears as the van drove towards the gate. He could tell by the sound that whoever was driving was not experienced at maneuvering a rig of that size.

As Regan approached the entrance to the Foundation he saw an eighteen-wheeler driving east on North Latches Lane towards him. He looked up at the cab and could see the driver look down at him as the van drove past him. The driver stared back at him. Their eyes met for a moment. It looked like Michael Flynn. Maybe it was time for him to have his vision checked, since he was sure that there was no way Flynn would be driving an eighteen-wheeler for the Barnes Foundation. Regan looked up again and the driver who resembled Flynn smiled at him as he drove by.

The electronic gate at the foundation's entrance was open. Regan looked at the guardhouse. It was empty. Regan knew there must be something wrong because Harlan Johnson would never leave his post unattended.

He drove onto the grounds and saw an eighteen-wheeler identical to the one that had just driven past him parked at the turnaround near the foundation's rear entrance. Regan parked his car behind the van. He looked up at the loading dock, and the rear entrance to the building was also open. "Anyone here?" he shouted.

He heard the muffled sounds coming from inside the van and ran over to the trailer. The back door of the trailer had been secured with a chain and lock. He worked the handle on the door to the open position and was able to open the door six or eight inches. Harlan Johnson looked out at him.

"What happened?"

"Someone stole the van with all the art," Johnson said. "Call 911and notify the police. They just drove off less than five minutes ago. They can get …"

Before Harlan could finish they heard what sounded like an explosion.

"What was that?" Harlan Johnson asked.

Regan pulled his mobile phone out of his pocket and hit the emergency number. There was a busy signal. He immediately redialed and got the same result.

"I'll be right back," he said as he ran to his car to get the rover radio Ichowitz had told him to take from the Fourth District.

"Izz, it's Jack. Do you hear me? Over."

"Jack where are you? Over."

"At the Barnes; what's happening?"

"Bombs are exploding at the Mall. I have to help. There's…" Another explosion cut off his transmission. Regan's first thought was, God … please don't let anything happen to Liam!

Regan could hear the sound of multiple sirens approaching from a distance. People from the houses nearby were coming out on the street. Someone approached and shouted, "Is everything OK?"

Regan shook his head and motioned for the man to follow him back to the van.

"What's happening?" Harlan asked.

"I'm not sure. I think there's some kind of attack at the Independence Mall. We need to get you out of there. Is everyone all right?"

"Yes, so far," Harlan replied.

"We need a crow bar or something to break the chain."

Johnson told him where he could find an iron rod he could use. Within minutes Regan, with the help of two neighbors, freed the six foundation staff from the van.

Harlan Johnson told Regan how two armed men had managed to steal the van with the Barnes collection.

"Mr. Regan, they knew the schedule. They got here when we were short staffed and most vulnerable," he said. The frustration was apparent in the clenched manner in which he spoke.

They were still trying to get through on the 911 number to alert the police. Obviously all the circuits were overloaded with calls over what ever was happening at the Independence Mall. Regan realized that with every passing moment the odds of recovering the art were slipping away.

"Harlan, did you hear anything that might indicate where they're taking the art?"

He shook his head, and said, "Mr. Regan, I think we can track the art, at least if we hurry."

Regan looked at him, "What do you mean?"

The guard explained that with the rotation of works in the collection and the world tour a few years before to raise money for the Foundation, his company had electronically tagged the collection to make sure that individual works would not be misplaced. "I'm not certain how far the range of the transmitters will work."

THIRTY-FOUR

M ayor Gallo was running late for the photo op at the National Constitution Center that had been scheduled to begin at 11 AM. Gallo never passed up an opportunity to get some free face time on TV. It was 11:04 when his car pulled up to the no stopping/tow away zone in front of the 6th Street entrance to the center. He nearly collided with a young man dressed in traditional Indian or Pakistani clothing, a kameez, a loose fitting tunic, who was hurrying along the sidewalk directly in front of his car.

As Gallo was about to shout at the man, who was less than three feet from where he was standing, the young man literally vaporized in a violent force of sound, heat, shock and raw carnage. In the instant of recognition before the shock wave and shrapnel from the explosion engulfed him Gallo knew that his life was over. The full force of the bomb blast decapitated the Mayor and lifted his SUV six feet into the air, tossing it half way into 6th Street. The shrapnel from the bomb shattered the glass doors of the Constitution Center fifty yards from the epicenter of the blast, spraying shards of glass on the twenty or more people who had been standing in line waiting to gain access to the building. Before the full impact of the destruction and agony of the survivors had set in, the sound of a second explosion nearby heightened the panic among the crowds that streamed out of the museums and historical sites onto the street.

Sirens and the screams of pain from the wounded, the cacophony from car crashes and blaring horns as drivers tried to avoid the mob that was trying to escape the terror added to the chaos that had replaced the festive atmosphere of mere moments before. Our way of life had once again been changed forever in the cruel micro-second between detonation and explosion.

The reaction of the command centers of the Philadelphia police and the federal agencies assigned to provide security was instantaneous. "We've been hit! We've been hit!" Multiple radio transmissions screamed from the radios of patrolmen stationed throughout the Mall.

Before the PPD command center could ascertain the location of the initial blast, a second explosion, this one so close to the trailer in which they sat that the force of the blast could be felt, momentarily drowned out the radio calls. Commissioner Regan and his command group watched the monitors that provided views from traffic and security cameras that blanketed the six-block area of the Mall and the surrounding streets. The command group acted with complete professionalism as they directed police and emergency personnel to the sites of the explosions. SWAT teams and snipers from all agencies were placed on high alert.

The video from both incidents was instantly reviewed and the information describing the traditional Pakistani clothing the suicide bombers were wearing was calmly relayed on the police frequency. The incidents had occurred within two blocks of each other, the first on 6th Street near Arch at the entrance to the Constitution Center, the second on Race Street near 5th. In both cases the analysis of the actions of the terrorists immediately before the explosions lead to the conclusion that the killers had not detonated the bombs. There had been no obvious sign of any action by either of the men to cause the explosions. Indeed, the location of the second incident on Race Street behind the Federal Reserve Building where there were no pedestrians and no significant property damage opportunity indicated that the killer had not yet reached his intended destination before the bomb exploded.

"Look for young men wearing Salwar Kameez, Sherwani, or Achnan, the traditional Pakistani dress and isolate them," the Command Center alerted the snipers and foot and bicycle patrols across the Mall. The Secret Service had issued its warning to the personal details of the Vice President and the Secretary of State and other notables to divert from the Mall.

Ichowitz, who had stood silently at the side of the Commissioner as the tactical commanders gave their orders said, "Commissioner, the timing of the attack doesn't make any sense."

Commissioner Regan turned to his friend and asked, "What do you mean?"

"The awards ceremony isn't scheduled to begin for another hour. If the bombs were set by a timer, why now?" he responded.

Patrolman Martin Kelly of the canine unit, with Roger, his specially trained companion, was stationed at the southeast corner of 5th and Market Streets watching the crowd looking for any indication of suspicious behavior. Roger began to growl and suddenly became agitated. Kelly scanned the mass of pedestrians now surging away from the Mall, away from the danger. As a young man emerged from the stairs of the Market Frankford subway station, Roger lunged towards him barking and snarling, nearly knocking Kelly off his feet. "Red alert! Red alert!" Kelly shouted into his shoulder microphone.

The young man's eyes widened at the sight of the German shepherd that lunged at him. He smiled and pulled a wire from the jacket pocket of his hooded sweat shirt.

"Drop what you're holding in your hand and put your hands on your head and get down on your knees!" Kelly shouted.

"Clear the area! Clear the area!" a bicycle patrol officer who had arrived yelled out to the crowd that had assembled near the subway exit as he unholstered his glock and pointed it at the suspect.

The young man shouted, *Allahu Akbar!*" and pushed the button he held in his hand. Nothing happened. He pushed the button again and again. His eyes reflected the rage and frustration of his failure.

Kelly, his Glock in hand, and Roger moved on the terrorist, forcing him to his knees. Roger continued to bark and growl. "Cuff him," Kelly directed the bicycle patrolman.

"Bomb Squad! We need the Bomb Squad!" Kelly shouted into his shoulder microphone.

Within minutes a van pulled up and a member of the bomb squad wearing a Nomex suit and ballistic helmet emerged. "Move back," the Unit Leader ordered Kelly.

"Captain, he tried to detonate and failed,"

"Roger that. Take cover."

"Ski, whatdaya see?" the unit commander asked the officer in the Nomex suit as he pointed his riot shot gun at the terrorist.

The bomb squad officer gently lifted the terrorist's sweatshirt and stared at the explosive device strapped to his body. "Not good, no good; it's timed, but I can't be sure if I can kill it."

"Want to abort?"

"Let me try to disable the timer."

The terrorist watched the bomb technician cut away his sweatshirt to get a clear view of the device. John Glochowski, who had learned his craft during two tours of duty in Iraq with the United States Army's Bomb Disposal Unit, gently touched the three wires, red, green and black, that came out of the timer with his gloved hands. He had encountered this configuration before. He carefully separated the wires and studied them as he removed a thin wire cutter from the belt around his Nomex jacket.

"You may want to start praying to Allah for both of our souls," he said to the bomber as he cut the green wire. Glochowski held his breath. The timer stopped.

"Cap, timer's stopped. Bring the blanket, we are hot, repeat hot! Got to make sure it's not booby-trapped."

"Roger that."

THIRTY-FIVE

———◆———

Jack Regan and Harlan Johnson were listening to the KYW radio reports of the suicide terrorist bomb attacks at the Independence Mall as they tracked the art thieves. Regan was nearly overcome by his desire to race to the Mall to find Liam. He realized that going anywhere near the chaos there would likely be futile, but the thought of Katey's son being in danger was foremost in his mind. He had attempted to reach Ichowitz on numerous occasions on the rover. Regan assumed that Izzy had switched to a different frequency in light of the emergency.

"Mr. Regan," Harlan said, pulling Regan out of his reverie.

"Sorry, Harlan."

"Mr. Regan, the signal is getting stronger. I'm not sure, but I think we made the right decision by going in the direction of the Expressway. From what I could hear from inside the van, it didn't sound like whoever is driving the rig is very experienced. A fully loaded eighteen-wheeler isn't easy to maneuver. My guess is he's driving pretty slowly. Maybe we can catch up."

"Have you been able to get a call through to the Barnes?" Regan asked.

"No. The circuits must still be overloaded."

"I wonder if the Lower Merion Police even know about the robbery. I'll try to get Izzy on the rover again."

Regan was approaching the turnoff for the Schuylkill Expressway. "Harlan, which way? East or west?"

"I'm not sure. I can't tell the direction from this monitor."

"I'm going to go east. Let me know if the signal gets weaker," Regan said. When they got on the expressway they saw the traffic in the west-bound lanes was in total gridlock. People were driving out of the city away from the terrorist attack.

"Mr. Regan, it looks like we made the right decision, the monitor shows the truck must still be moving, so it's got to be going east."

One of the adjutants on Commissioner Regan's staff entered the command center and approached Ichowitz. "Detective, I've been monitoring the open frequency, there have been a number of messages from someone named Jack asking for you," he said.

Ichowitz shook his head and said, "I forgot that I gave Jack one of the Fourth District's rovers so that he could keep in touch with me," he told the Commissioner.

Ichowitz immediately switched his radio to the open frequency and said, "Jack it's Izzy. Sorry I was off this frequency. Are you OK?"

"Izz thank god you switched back. Do you know about the Barnes?"

"Know what about the Barnes?" Ichowitz responded.

"Two gunmen made off with a truck filled with half of the collection."

"Say again," Ichowitz replied.

"Izz, they stole the art! Harlan Johnson and I are tracking the truck, we're going east on the expressway. We think the van is going in that direction."

"Commissioner, did you hear that?" Ichowitz asked.

Commissioner Regan nodded. "Ask Jack his location; I'll try to get a cruiser or a helo to assist him."

An art heist and a terrorist attack: a coincidence, or was there some connection? Ichowitz could not see how the two events were tied together, but he could not shake the feeling that somehow these random events were connected.

The reports from officers and emergency personnel on the ground indicated that there had been seven fatalities, including the two suicide bombers and thirty seven injured, ten critically as a result of the attacks. There was an unconfirmed report that Mayor Gallo had been killed in the initial explosion. The bomb squad had a third suicide bomber in isolation. Although they were successful in disconnecting the timing device, they had not yet been able to remove and secure the explosive. The officers were concerned that the vest bomb may be booby-trapped.

It had been forty-five minutes since the initial attack. Despite their best efforts the Mall area had not yet been completely secured. The crowd estimate, immediately before the attack, was that there were more than five thousand people in the area, either at the museums or assembling for the awards ceremony and concert.

As of noon, no one had claimed responsibility for the attack; however, the current working theory was that Al-Qaida was involved, either directly or otherwise. Homeland Security and the FBI raided the New Age Mosque fifteen minutes after the initial explosion looking for the Imam, Malik Ben-Ali and Bashir Amet his chief of security. They were not there, nor were they at their residences or anywhere in the area. There also was no evidence to connect the explosive devices to the Mosque. No residue of C4 or any bomb making materials were found there. The federal agents also had no idea of the whereabouts of the mysterious visitor with the bottle green eyes, who had last been seen limping down a subway concourse after he had interviewed the Homeland Security undercover agent several weeks before.

The federal agents also searched the warehouse on Lehigh Avenue, the last known location at which they assumed the suicide bombers had been trained. Once again, no evidence connecting the explosives to the Mall attack could be secured. All of the suspects were in the wind.

It was the peculiar timing of the attack that bothered Ichowitz the most. From the reports of the frustration of the third suicide bomber over his inability to detonate the bomb and kill the police officer who had confronted him, along with at least two dozen innocent bystanders who were exiting the subway station, confirmed Ichowitz' belief that whoever had planned the attack set the time an hour or so before the Vice President along with the other dignitaries and the highest mass of innocent victims would be present. Why would Al-Qaida, or whoever was responsible, miss an opportunity to cause such devastation?

His radio chirped, indicating another call from Jack.

"Izz, were you able to get Liam's picture out? Has anyone reported seeing him?"

"Jack, nothing. At least he doesn't match any of the victims. Have you caught up with the van?"

"Negative, but the tracker signal is getting stronger."

"What's your 40?"

"Driving north on I 95. Are the police en route?"

"The Commissioner has ordered two units from Highway be diverted to you. You should see them driving south on 95 soon."

"OK. Please let me know if anyone sees Liam."

Ichowitz had been tasked by the Commissioner to coordinate with the Lower Merion Township Police investigation of the robbery at the Barnes. With all the confusion resulting from the Mall attack, and the high alert protocols, it took the police thirty minutes to respond to the 911 call. The detectives had a composite of the two armed men from the hostages. Based on the fact that the armed men arrived in a moving van identical to the van the legitimate movers used, the detectives believe it was an inside job, or at least that the robbers had access to information that provided them the schedule and other relevant details.

According to the statement from the Barnes curator, the estimate of the value of the stolen art works was truly unascertainable. It exceeded any known or quantifiable dollar value. Dr. Abernathy opined that the thieves must be extremely sophisticated if they believed they could sell the art on the black market. He suggested that it was more likely they would make some kind of a ransom demand on the Barnes, like a kidnapping.

THIRTY-SIX

———◆———

Liam and his friend Ryan were waiting in the Hall of Statues at the Constitution Center for Ryan's parents and his special needs eighteen-month-old sister. They promised to behave while Ryan's parents made appropriate arrangements to transport the little girl. The Hall of Statues' exhibit had been set up with remarkable detail by the curators to recreate the scene of the original signers to the Constitution. The curators laid out the exhibit so that visitors could walk among the Founding Fathers, something that delighted museum goers off all ages. The boys were making fun of the curious manner in which Ben Franklin and the others had dressed back in the 1700s and just enjoying life like typical children when the bomb went off.

"What was that?" Ryan asked

"Dunno," Liam replied. The force of the blast was so severe it shook the room.

Within seconds a siren sounded and a voice came over the sound system repeating a warning that an emergency had been declared and everyone had to immediately exit the building.

As the other visitors to the exhibit hurriedly began to exit the museum, Ryan asked, "Liam, what's happening?" Ryan's voice had that plaintive sound like he was about to cry.

Before Liam could respond, a man in a blazer came into the room and said, "Young men, you have to leave the building now. It's not safe for you to stay here."

"But we promised my parents we'd wait here," Ryan responded.

"I'm sorry, but you have to leave now. It's not safe."

Ryan grabbed hold of the Franklin statue as the guard approached.

Before the guard could get to his friend, Liam stepped forward and held up his hand. The stillness with which he held himself stopped the guard in his tracks.

"Ryan, we need to go now," he said.

"But how will my parents find us? We promised to wait here," Ryan said, the tears streaming down his face.

Liam held out his hand to his friend and said, "We'll go to a place that's safe and where they can find us."

Ryan took his hand and the guard led them to an exit. Just as he opened the door the second explosion rocked the building. "Hurry, boys! Get away from here as fast as you can!"

They stepped out of the building into the chaos.

"I want to go back to my mommy!" Ryan cried and tried to open the door of the emergency exit from which they had emerged. There was no handle.

"No Ryan, we have to get away from here!"

"But my mother and father and Keri, what about them?"

"Your Dad will protect them," Liam said and took his friend by the hand, leading him away from the Constitution Center and away from where the sound of the second explosion originated.

The boys ran down the steps. Liam looked at his compass watch and pointed to the street and said, "We need to go west," he pointed.

"Where are we going?" Ryan asked.

"To my Uncle Mike's," Liam replied.

"But how will we find it?"

Liam pointed to his watch/compass and said, "Jack gave this to me. He taught me how to use it. He promised me I would always be able to find my way home. Let's go!"

And the two boys ran west on Arch Street away from the madness.

Jack and Harlan drove North on I 95 past the Allegheny Avenue exit. They saw the flashing lights of the Highway Patrol cruisers approaching from the southbound lanes.

"Mr. Regan, the signal is getting weaker. I think they must have gotten off at Allegheny Avenue."

Jack nodded and switched to the left lane. He saw a break in the road divider about a quarter mile ahead. He ignored the No-U Turn sign and drove to the south bound lanes. The Highway Patrol Officers must have seen his maneuver and they slowed down and let him pass. The three cars took the Allegheny Avenue Exit when Regan got to the end of the exit ramp he asked, "Which way?"

Harlan pointed left towards the river.

Allegheny Avenue dead ended at the Delaware River two blocks east of the exit. The three cars pulled up at a gate to the Tioga Marine Terminal. Regan looked through the chain link fence at the yard and the river beyond it. There was a containerized freighter being loaded at the dock. In the yard were about 500 containers waiting to be loaded. All of the containers looked identical to the white trailer in which the stolen Barnes Art collection had been placed.

Jack called Ichowitz on the rover and filled him in on their location. He explained how they were able to track the van there.

"Jack, do you think the monitor will lead you to the correct container?" Ichowitz asked.

Regan looked over to Harlan who nodded. He conveyed Harlan's response to Ichowitz, who channeled it to the Commissioner.

"Jack, the Commissioner has given you the green light to enter the yard and find the stolen art."

Regan and the Highway Patrol officers quickly devised a plan to enter the yard and search for the container. The police officers called for backup.

"Izz we're going in."

Ichowitz could detect a note of doubt in his friend's voice. "Jack, what's wrong?"

Regan took a deep breath and thought over his response and finally replied, "Izz it's just … I don't know, it just seems too easy."

"What do you mean?"

"I mean the thieves knew everything: the schedule, the type of moving van, the lack of adequate security. How come they didn't know the works of art were electronically tagged?"

THIRTY-SEVEN

I t took Glochowski and his team forty-five minutes to remove the device from the young terrorist. While they performed their dangerous mission, the bomb squad was able to run the young man's prints through VICAP and his photo through the FBI's facial recognition program. By the time he was secured in the federal lock-up at 7th and Arch Street they had a confirmed identification, Farouk Mohammed, birth name Frank Alcott Jr, of Fort Wayne, Indiana. The nineteen-year-old had no previous criminal record. He was not previously listed on any terrorist watch list. A call to the local authorities had resulted in the interview of his parents, Frank Alcott Sr and Mary Elizabeth Alcott. According to the Alcotts, Frank Junior, aka Farouk, was a recent convert to Islam. He had disappeared three months ago. They could not believe that their son could possibly be involved in a terrorist attack.

FBI and Homeland Security decided that Glochowski was the best candidate to conduct the initial interview of Mohammed/Alcott. They believed he had established a rapport with the young terrorist during the ninety or so minutes that elapsed from his capture to removing the device.

"Ski, the feebies think you bonded with that lunatic. They want you to take a crack at him, before they step in. Ya know, maybe you can find out who made the bomb and who sponsored him."

"Cap, you know that's not my thing. I feel safer around IEDs than talking to civilians. I never interviewed a perp before. If ya don't believe me, you can ask my ex," Glochowski replied.

"I know, I know, but the Commissioner thinks it's a good idea, too. Whadaya say?"

Mohammed/Alcott was waiting in one of the interrogation rooms at the federal lock-up. His hands and feet were shackled and he was chained to the table. Glochowski, still wearing his under armor, entered the room and took the chair opposite the young man.

Mohammed/Alcott glared at Glochowski, "You bastard!" he shouted at the police officer.

Glochowski held up his hands in a self deprecating manner and softly replied, "Look it, I told my boss I didn't think it was a good idea for me to be here either. But I gotta follow orders, just like you. So, let me do my thing and then you can do whatever you're gonnna do. I'm going to inform you of your rights now."

"I know my rights!" Mohammed/Alcott shouted.

"I'm sure you do, but I have to do this anyway, OK?" Glochowski calmly replied.

After reading him his rights Glochowski asked, "Do you want to waive your right to counsel and allow this interview to continue?"

Mohammed/Alcott stared at the police officer. "Why should I talk to you?"

Glochowski realized that this was the most critical point of the interview. If he did not handle this correctly, the perp would invoke his right to counsel and the interrogation would have to stop. He took a deep breath and looked directly in the young man's eyes and said, "Listen kid, you're in very serious trouble. You are going to be charged with serious crimes, maybe even treason. You're probably going to spend the rest of your life behind bars. If you cooperate with us and help us prevent another terrorist attack, and save the lives of innocent people, the US Attorney may take that into consideration. If you don't cooperate…" Glochowski shrugged his shoulders.

They stared silently at one another.

Behind the two-way mirror the First Assistant US Attorney, the Philadelphia FBI SAC, the Acting Regional Head of Homeland Security and Glochowski's captain watched the scene unfold.

After staring at him for several minutes the young man sighed. "I know that you are a brave man and I believe that you are also an honest man," Mohammed/Alcott said.

"Thank you."

"I will cooperate with you. But only you."

Glochowski looked up at the camera and shook his head. He had hoped that Mohammed/Alcott would invoke his privilege and relieve Glochowski from further involvement. At least with bombs he could know and understand his risk; working with the suits like this was way out of his comfort zone.

"OK, can I call you Farouk?"

He nodded.

Glochowski pulled a copy of the photograph of the tall man with green eyes that the Homeland Security undercover agent had taken. He showed the photograph to Mohammed and asked him if he could identify him.

"That is Brother Yosef," Farouk said.

"Who is he?"

"Yosef Allawaite, our teacher."

"What did he teach you?"

"He taught us how to detonate the vest."

"Farouk, he lied to you. The vest was on a timing device. The detonator was a dummy switch," Glochowski said.

"No, that can't be true, you're lying to me. The timer must have gone off because the detonator malfunctioned."

Glochowski shook his head.

Farouk's eyes widened with recognition that he had been betrayed.

After an hour of interrogation Mohammed/Alcott had revealed the second location at which the training had been conducted, the dates they had met, and the identities of the remaining suicide bombers.

"Farouk, are you certain there are four of you?"

He nodded.

There was another maniac wearing a bomb running around Philadelphia.

After the interview, Glochowski's captain told him Mohammed/Alcott's identification of the bomb maker was a dead end. Apparently Allawaite had been a well known Al-Qaida bomb maker. He had been killed in a drone attack last year. However, the Speviva Street address at which the training of the terrorists had been conducted did pan out.

"Ski, you did good; we recovered evidence that corroborates the perp's statement. The crime scene techs are collecting all kinds of latents and trace evidence of the explosives the Allawaite imposter used to assemble his killing machines. The FBI told me they got a bite from the Brits on the facial recognition search. They're still waiting to get the skinny but they think he's got some tie in with the Mossad."

"What's that?"

"The Israeli Secret Service."

THIRTY-EIGHT

K ate O'Malley was frantic with worry and guilt over allowing Liam to accompany his friend to Independence Mall. If she had followed Jack's advice, Liam would never have been anywhere near the terrorist attack in the first place.

"Kate, stop beating yourself up over lettin the boy go with his friend," Mike O'Malley said. "There's nothing to be gained by it. Liam's a smart lad. He'll find a way to get out of danger. You'll see."

"Do ya really think so, Uncle Mike?"

He nodded. "Have ya heard anything from Jack?"

"He told me that all the police have Liam's picture. They're lookin out for him and other kids who were separated from their folks after the bombing."

"What about Ryan's folks? Have ya talked with them?"

"Yes. They're beside themselves with worry too."

"Look, I know it's a hard thing to wait for news about someone you love. The clock seems to stand still from the weight of the worry. But we have to have some faith that Liam will be alright. He's wise beyond his years."

Two hours had passed since the initial bombing. Liam and his friend Ryan were out there, somewhere, alone. Kate O'Malley could only speculate on the dangers two nine-year-olds could encounter in the wake of the terrorist attack. Her Uncle was right about Liam. He was clever, but he was only a boy.

It took Jack and Harlan and the Highway Patrol Officers less than a half hour to find the trailer with the Barnes' art treasures in the Tioga Marine Terminal lot. They secured the crime scene while they waited for the technicians to arrive. Jack could not believe the thieves could be both so sophisticated and foolish at the same time. The robbery had obviously been well planned and had been flawlessly executed. The failure to know about the electronic tags was an oversight that ran counter to everything else about the caper.

After a careful search of the premises, there was no sign of the two thieves. Why had they abandoned their prize?

In what had otherwise been a brutal day for the law enforcement community, the recovery of what might have gone down as the greatest art heist in history was a stunning victory.

"Jack, even the President made note of your achievement during his remarks about the terrorist attack. It reaffirmed his belief that the federal and local authorities would find those involved in this cowardly attack on innocent victims and bring them to justice. You and Harlan Johnson are going to receive a special Presidential Citation for what you did," Ichowitz told him when he arrived at the terminal with the techs.

"Izz, the only thing I want is to find Liam and his buddy," he replied.

"I know, Jack. It's only a matter of time until we find the boys."

"Izz, can you imagine how scared they must be?"

It had taken Liam and Ryan about an hour to walk the twenty blocks to the path that ran along the Schuylkill River.

"Ryan, see the art museum?" Liam said as he pointed up river at the building that looked like a Greek temple that sat high up on a bluff overlooking the Schuylkill River. "Once we get there we'll be close to home. Jack and Mum took me to the park near there a couple of times. There are plenty of water fountains along the way. We'll be at my Uncle Mike's before you know it. I bet ya my mum and your parents will be there waitin for us."

Ryan, still shaken by the violent events that had separated him from his family, stared at his friend. He hadn't spoken a word since the two boys ran away from the Constitution Center.

"Here, take the compass. You can navigate us to home," Liam said as he removed the watch/compass from his wrist and handed it to his friend.

"Really?"

Liam nodded and the two boys walked beside the river towards the museum.

While the crime scene techs conducted their analysis of the rig and the precious cargo in the trailer, Regan could not keep his attention on the proceedings. He was worried about Liam and his friend Ryan. More than four hours had passed since the attack, and they were still missing.

"What do you think, Jack?" Ichowitz asked.

"Sorry, Izz, what were you saying?"

"No problem, I was just saying the thieves must have been wearing gloves. The techs weren't able to find any latents in the cab or on any of the boxes in the trailer. Except for the eye witness description of the thieves, and the fact that one of them spoke with an Irish accent, we really don't have a line on who these guys are."

Regan shook his head and said, "Christ, I thought I told you I saw the driver. He looked like Michael Flynn ... you know, Liam's father. I thought my mind was playing tricks on me, but if the witnesses said one of the thieves spoke with an Irish accent, do you think he could have been Flynn?"

In the chaos of the aftermath of the terrorist attack Regan must have forgotten to mention this.

"Jack, maybe it was Flynn."

Regan nodded.

"How the heck did Flynn get involved in this?"

"Izz, at least it explains why he came here. I never really thought he came here just to see his son. But there's just something about his involvement in this that doesn't feel right," Regan said.

"Well the Interpol report said the Flynns have been involved in a number of high profile art thefts. This surely would have been one of the biggest heists ever."

Regan stared at the trailer and turned to Ichowitz. "Izz, are we certain all of the art is still in the truck?"

Ichowitz shook his head.

"Harlan, do you know how many paintings and sculptures were supposed to be trucked over to the new museum?" Regan asked.

"Mr. Regan, the bill of lading should indicate the number of crates. I'm pretty certain Dr. Abernathy also had a chart that identified the art by the numbers on the crates."

Ichowitz called the Lower Merion detectives at the facility and within minutes he was provided the number of packages that were supposed to be trucked over. The Crime Techs counted the crates and reported that the truck was ten short.

"Izz, could the thieves have left them in Lower Merion?"

"Negative. All of the art that had been packed for shipment is gone."

"Then Flynn and his accomplice somehow took ten works of art from the truck," Regan said.

"But according to the guard, the truck went through the gate less than ten minutes before you and Harlan got here. And according to the guard no vehicles left the facility after the truck with the art got here," Ichowitz observed.

"So that means either the ten missing packages are still here, or they never got here," Regan said.

"*Boychik*, we have a real mystery on our hands."

Ichowitz instructed the crime scene techs to search the terminal yard using Harlan Johnson's monitor, just in case the art works had been stashed in another container. Ichowitz reviewed the records to see if any containers had been loaded on a freighter after the truck arrived. Both searches came up dry.

"Izz, there just wasn't enough time for them to move the ten crates from the truck after they got here. So they must have stashed them before they left Lower Merion."

"Do we know what was in the missing crates?" Regan asked.

"Still working on it."

"This just doesn't make any sense. Why would they take the truck here, if all they wanted to steal was ten paintings?" Regan said. "I mean, why run the risk of getting caught with the eighteen-wheeler?"

THIRTY-NINE

Michael Flynn sat at the bar at Brynes' Tavern at East Westmoreland and Richmond Streets, six blocks west of the Tioga Marine Terminal. He nursed the half and half the bartender with a snake's head tattoo peaking out of the skimpy tee shirt she was wearing from the top of her left breast had served him. She leaned over the bar to wipe away a phantom spill in front of where Flynn was sitting and smiled at him.

"Darlin, if you don't stop flashing those bodacious tatas at me, I'll likely spill my entire pint," he said as he raised his glass in her direction. "Besides, it looks like your regulars are startin to tire of all the attention you've been favorin me with. Here," he said as he placed a fifty dollar bill in her cleavage. "Give the boyos a round on me and favor them with your luvly presence for a bit and keep whatever is left for your tip."

"I saw you staring at the snake's head. Would you like to see the rest of him?" she asked as she leaned closer to Flynn.

"Aw darlin, I surely would luv to see it in all of its splendor. But your customers must be served," he said and nodded at the three men at the other end of the bar who were giving him the hard look.

She pouted as she walked away.

Flynn was killing time until his ride arrived. He had walked out of the terminal minutes before Regan and the police showed up. Except for Regan's unanticipated arrival at the Barnes facility, the rest of the plan had worked flawlessly. The original plan was to wait until the scheduled change of the security guard at the facility and to drive the art away with the monitors chirping. He found Regan's involvement a little bonus. Katey's new boyfriend had been just a tad too cocky. He would have liked to wipe the smile off his smug face, but that would have to wait for another day. At least he had the pleasure of taking Regan on a wild goose chase.

Flynn looked up at the flat screen above the bar. The news report of the aftermath of the terrorist attack was jarring. Seven dead and thirty seven wounded. He was appalled at the extent of the damage and injuries reported in the media. He had been assured the attack was only supposed to be a noisey diversion for the heist. Obviously, he had been misinformed. He figured that by now Regan and the police had probably discovered that ten of the paintings were missing. They were likely stewing over how he had gotten the paintings off the truck in the few minutes between his pulling the rig into the terminal and their arrival. He thought to himself, "I bet they think we're a feckin Houdini act," as he took a long pull on the pint.

Flynn looked up at the television behind the bar at the breaking news report. "We have received a report that a fourth bomber is still at large," the somber faced reporter said. She was standing in front of the bomb-damaged entrance to the Constitution Center. The camera panned across the Mall as she said, "Somewhere out there is another dangerous terrorist. If you see any suspicious activity, immediately report it to the authorities."

That news would surely keep the authorities busy for some time to come, when John Q Public starts reporting sightings of suspicious-looking Muslims lurking around Center City and God knows where, he thought. Jaysus, at least they won't be blaming the Irish. Flynn looked at his watch, finished the last of his pint, smiled at Ms. Snakes' Head and left the bar.

L iam and Ryan walked up the stairs that lead from the canal path to Main Street two blocks east of the Grape Tavern at 4:45 PM. Despite being exhausted from their ordeal, they ran the remaining tenth of a mile.

"Liam, oh thank God you're safe!" Kate O'Malley shouted as the boy rushed into her arms. "Uncle Mike, call Ryan's folks and tell them the boys are here," she said as she held both boys in her embrace. "Ryan, your parents and sister are safe. We were all so worried about you."

Within minutes the Kellys arrived and both mothers would not let their sons out of their embrace.

"Will you let the boys breath? I'll bet they're hungry. Want something to eat?" Mike O'Malley asked. Both of the buys nodded. "Kate, get the boys something. We'll make sure they don't leave our sight."

Kate reluctantly released her hold on her son. "Would you like some fish and chips?" She asked.

Both boys nodded.

"All right then, but I want to hear what happened and how you got here."

Liam and Ryan alternated in providing their accounts of the journey from the Constitution Center to Manayunk.

"Mum, we used the compass Jack gave me to get here. It was just like he said; with a compass you can always find your way home. Ryan and me took turns," Liam said as Ryan nodded his agreement.

"I have to call Jack and his parents and let them know you're both safe," Kate said.

Jack was relieved and grateful to learn that Liam and his friend were safe. He marveled at the manner in which Liam had reacted to the chaos with which he had been confronted in the wake of the bombing. His ability to maneuver out of harm's way was impressive and demonstrated abilities that grown men did not possess. All of this from a boy, not yet ten years old!

"Kate, I was so worried about Liam, I found it nearly impossible to focus on the robbery from the Barnes." He filled her in on his unanticipated involvement in the art heist. "Kate, you need to go back to my parent's house, you and Liam. It's really important."

"Jack, don't you think we'll be OK with Uncle Mike?"

"Kate, we think the guy driving the rig with the stolen art was Michael Flynn. If it was he's still around, and he's dangerous. I need you to take

Liam to my folks. I asked Izzy to send a unit from the Fourth District to take you there. I'll meet you there as soon as I can get out of this. Please do this for me. The unit should be there any minute."

Kate realized that had she followed Jack's advice this morning Liam would never have been in the terrible predicament and danger he had endured.

"Alright Jack we'll be there."

FORTY

———◆◆◆———

Among the dignitaries invited to attend the awards ceremony was Sheikh Nazeur ibn Aziz, third cousin to King Abdul-Aziz of the House of Saud, the King of Saudi Arabia. Nazeur was one of the most influential advisors to the King. He had been educated at Harvard and the London School of Economics. Nazeur, like many of the Royal cousins spent the majority of his life away from the Kingdom. Unlike many of the King's cousins Nazeur had amassed a fortune as an options trader and oil broker. He was not financially dependent on the Royal Family's largesse. Also unlike many of the 15,000 members of the family, he was a devout Muslim who refrained from the outrageous behavior and excessive lifestyles that often brought disgrace to the Royal Family.

Nazeur, although a man of faith, was not a complete ascetic. His great personal wealth afforded him a lifestyle beyond the imagination of even the vaunted one per cent of the meritocracy in the United States, or the aristocracy of Europe and the newly-minted capitalist/criminals of Russia. His traveling entourage often numbered over fifty. His personal security force sometimes as many as fifteen bodyguards were all trusted members of his family. He always traveled in his own luxury custom jets and yachts.

Nazeur's yacht, a ninety-meter beauty powered by 8 electric generators with two heli-pads, and security features that rivaled those of a US Navy destroyer, was docked on the Delaware River at Penn's Landing. With the exception of the Battleship New Jersey and freighters discharging containerized cargo, Nazeur's yacht was the largest seafaring vessel in the port.

His great wealth also afforded him the luxury to indulge his passion to acquire works of fine art. Nazeur had over the years amassed the single greatest private collection of post-impressionist paintings in the world; and the publicly reported works in his collection were only the tip of the iceberg. Nazeur's private collection also included dozens of masterpieces that had been obtained by other-than-legal means.

Michael Flynn was escorted by one of Nazeur's cousin-guards to the pool and lounge on the top deck at the stern of the yacht. His colleagues, the Nooris brothers and Shona, greeted Flynn, and Nazeur embraced him.

"Michael, I can't thank you enough for bringing all of us together," Nazeur said as he released Flynn from his embrace.

"Your Highness, when Ari first approached me I realized that you were the only person in the world who would appreciate the opportunity to possess the best of the best."

Nazeur smiled, and said, "And likely the only person in the world with the assets to finance the operation and purchase the art."

Seated near the end of the bar was a lean man who quietly observed the gathering. His most arresting feature was his green eyes. His stare was almost penetrating.

"Michael, I don't think you had the opportunity to meet my colleague Nochem Rabinowitz," Ari Nooris said, pointing at the man with green eyes. "The two of you were without doubt the most important members of our team."

Flynn walked over to the man and extended his hand. "So you're the mystery man who fooled the Imam and his Afghani sponsors, masterful job, mate."

Rabinowitz nodded silently as he shook Flynn's hand.

"Don't talk much, do ya?" Flynn commented.

"Michael, Nochem has been undercover for so long I don't think he's gotten used to the fact that he no longer has to play the part of an Al-Qaida terrorist," Ari Nooris responded.

Flynn and Rabinowitz continued to stare at one another.

"Michael, would you like to see the Cézanne? I couldn't keep it in the hold any longer," Nazeur said taking Flynn by the arm and leading him into the lounge.

There under the lights in an alcove was "The Card Players," one of Cézanne's greatest works. "You know, some months back another version of the "Players" went for $225,000,000 at auction. This would likely yield over $300 million," Nazeur said.

"Your Highness, I would say you got yourself quite a bargain, considerin the entire lot only cost you $900 million," Flynn observed.

"Michael, you are forgetting the considerable risk I assumed in agreeing to sponsor your project. My cousin the King would never understand how I could collaborate with former Mossad agents and expose my brothers to the outrage that will surly follow in the wake of the 'terrorist' attack," Nazeur said barely concealing the smile.

The value of the ten works of art Nazeur had obtained was incalculable, conservatively several billion dollars. Not that he would ever sell them. The fact that these treasures would no longer be available for the world of art lovers to enjoy was in his perverse view far more valuable – a thought that Flynn found depressing.

"My friend, will you be joining us when we weigh anchor?"

"No, Your Highness, I've some unfinished business to attend to," Flynn replied. "I trust you've wired my commission to the usual location."

Nazeur nodded.

"Michael, how will you get back to Ulster?" Nooris asked.

"I've made appropriate arrangements. And you?"

"His Highness has graciously arranged for our passage on this beautiful vessel to Curacao. From there we will make our way home from Venezuela."

"Ari, what about your family and your business interests here, are you just going to abandon everything?"

"Michael I'm touched by your concern. I've made provisions for my family. As to the business, between the market collapse and real estate downturn, what's left isn't worth the trouble. Our share of the proceeds from this operation assures that all of us will live comfortably for the rest of our lives."

"Lady and gentlemen, I'm sure you have things to discuss, you must excuse me as I prepare for evening prayers," Nazeur said as he withdrew to his private quarters.

"Ari, the media's reportin there's a fourth bomber unaccounted for," Flynn said.

Nooris smiled and said, "Yes, there is. It ought to keep the federal and local police on edge for some time. It should keep them focused on the Mall and other public sites while we make our escape."

Flynn took a notepad from his pocket and wrote, 'Our host has eyes and ears on all of us, so be careful what you say,' and handed it to Ari Nooris who nodded.

Nooris and Flynn walked to the stern and looked out across the Delaware River at the Battleship New Jersey.

"That was some distraction your man created," Flynn whispered.

Nooris shrugged, "It isn't an exact science, and it had to look authentic. He did manage to get one of the vests to blow up where no civilians could be hurt," he responded.

"I heard the news report on the boy who was taken into custody. Will he be a problem?"

"Shouldn't be, Nochem tells me he wasn't the sharpest knife in the drawer, and Nochem never broke his cover."

"What about the Imam?" Flynn asked.

"He's in the wind. Why so worried? Are you getting a conscience?" Nooris asked.

"Nah, it's just your entire operation was so messy with all the loose ends with your real estate deals and all."

"I told you I cleaned up the mess, besides there's nothing that links any of this to you; nothing for you to worry about. Am I missing something?" Nooris asked.

"Nah, nothing I can't take care of myself."

"Are you sure you don't want to sail down to Curacao with the rest of us?"

Flynn shook his head. Nooris patted him on his shoulder. "Seems like His Highness likes the art," Nooris said.

"That tool will hide it in one of his mansions never ta see the light of day. He's what your people call a scmuck."

"You mean a *schmuck*."

"Yeah."

"Well he's a very rich *schmuck*."

FORTY-ONE

———————

There had been 150 calls reporting suspicious-looking individuals logged in by 911 dispatchers after the local newscasters announced that a fourth terrorist bomber was unaccounted for. None of them panned out. Ichowitz was starting to wonder if the statement the captured terrorist had given to Glochowski about another suicide bomber was accurate. Although the feds believed that Farouk/Alcott was telling Glochowski what he believed was the truth, it could be misinformation that had been fed to the gullible young man.

There were so many aspects of the attack and the art heist that did not add up, maybe this was another attempt to distract them. Despite the apparent incongruities of the crimes, Ichowitz believed the two events were connected; however, at this point in the investigation he was unable to figure out how.

The only common thread between the two events, aside from the timing, was the fact that both crimes had inexplicable elements of both brilliance and incompetence. The terrorist attack had obviously been carefully planned. The suicide bombers had been selected, trained and armed by an individual, or individuals, with great sophistication and substantial financial and organizational support. This had been no fly-by-night operation.

That being the case, the execution of the plan was shoddy and largely ineffectual. With the exception of the explosion near the entrance to the National Constitution Center, the attack caused minimal property damage, and in consideration of the potentially catastrophic losses that could have occurred if the suicide bombers were stationed near the awards ceremony when the Vice President was making the presentation, the human carnage would have been devastating. Seven dead and thirty four injured, although significant, was nowhere close to the body count that might have otherwise occurred.

As to the theft of the art, once again the planning of the robbery was impeccable. The thieves knew when the paintings and other art treasures would be packed and ready for transport, and when security would be slack. The failure of the thieves to account for the electronic monitoring was beyond careless. Why would such a carefully-planned caper result in abandoning a truck filled with some of the most magnificent works of art in the world in a parking lot? If the objective was only to steal the ten missing paintings, why go to all the trouble of stealing the entire truck-load in the first place?

Neither the FBI nor Homeland Security had any evidence that the crimes were connected. Both agencies were working under the premise that the terrorist attack was the work of Al-Qaida and that the art theft was the independent act of criminals that just happened to take place at around the same time. Jack Regan, like Ichowitz, found the coincidence too convenient. To Regan, the entire sequence of events was telling. In fact his happening upon the Barnes at the time the thieves were driving away was the only piece of the puzzle that didn't fit. The involvement of Michael Flynn added a whole new dimension to the matter that made it personal and even more alarming.

"Izz, have you heard from your buddy Ossberg?" Regan asked.

"No he's managed to insulate himself from any unwelcome interruptions from the local authorities," the detective replied. "I'm happy to hear that Liam and his buddy are safe. Those kids are really something. Did the unit from the Fourth District pick up the boy and his mother and take them to your parents?"

Regan nodded.

"At least we won't have to worry about their safety for the time being. How do you think Flynn fits into all of this?"

"Izz, I've been trying to figure that out for hours with no joy."

"Let's sleep on it and see if we can figure out some connection in the morning."

The Flynns had long and deep connections with the American Irish community dating back to the time of "The Troubles." IRA soldiers on the lam from the British authorities were often sent to the States until the heat cooled off. In some cases they married and took up permanent residence, and the connection with their brothers who remained in the homeland further strengthened the ties between their families. It also enlarged the criminal enterprises on both sides of the pond.

The bartender at Duffy's Tavern on 2nd Street near Girard Avenue in Northern Liberties looked up from the glass he was cleaning when Michael Flynn entered the bar. With a nearly undetectable nod of his head he directed Flynn to the door at the end of the room. Flynn smiled and made his way past the patrons seated at the bar, none of whom acknowledged that he was there.

He knocked on the door and waited as someone on the other side looked through the peep hole. He heard a muffled exchange and the door opened, allowing him access to the room. An old man sitting at the head of a conference table, whose wrinkled face told the story of the hard life he had endured, smiled at him. "Jaysus, would you look at what the winds of fate have blown our way," he said to the others who flanked both sides of the table.

Six men, whose ages spanned several decades, but all of whom looked hard and dangerous, stared silently at Flynn.

"Gentlemen, this is Michael, the young man I was tellin ya about, who traveled from the Isle to our fair city on a mission of undisclosed purpose. Michael, how's your family?" Daniel Duffy, the patriarch of the Irish mob in Philadelphia asked.

"Duffy thanks for seein me on such short notice. My family is fine and my father sends his regards to you and yours," Flynn responded as he continued to stand awaiting a signal from his host to take a seat.

The old man said, "Take a load off," and pointed to the vacant chair at the opposite end of the table. "Quinn, get our guest something to take the taste of the road off his lips so that he can share his story with us."

The youngest of the men got up and walked over to the bar. He brought a bottle of Jamison's and a tumbler over to Flynn and poured a generous portion of the whiskey into the glass.

"*Slainte*," Flynn said as he raised his glass to his host and drank the whiskey.

"And will ya be tellin us the purpose of your visit?" Duffy asked.

"I was just hopin for your hospitality for a short spell so I can finish my business," Flynn replied.

"Would your business have anything to do with the botched job I've been hearin about concerning certain works of art from one of the museums?"

"Well, ya can't believe everything you're hearin about certain things being botched and all," Flynn replied.

Duffy stared at his guest silently. He was aware of Flynn's involvement in the Barnes robbery since the Flynns had sought permission to operate in his territory, provided they would agree to pay appropriate compensation for the privilege.

"Well boyos, me and Michael Flynn have some things to discuss so why'nt ya give us some privacy, if ya don't mind. Have a good night and stay out of trouble," he said, dismissing them.

When the room had cleared Duffy motioned Flynn to move next to him. Flynn got up and brought the whiskey bottle and poured both of them two inches of the rich amber whiskey.

Duffy drank his whiskey and wiped his mouth with the back of his hand and whispered, "Michael lad, don't tell me ya had anything ta do with that mess at the Mall today."

"All right, I won't."

Duffy stared at him, "Jaysus that was fooked up."

Flynn nodded.

"Did ya know what they were gonna do?"

Flynn shook his head.

"Are ya gonna do anything about it?"

"I'm workin on it."

"Will ya be needin any assistance?"

"Na, but thanks for askin," he paused and said, "There is something though; do ya know Vito Coratelli?"

Duffy nodded.

"Do ya think ya could set up a meetin for me tonight?"

"Consider it done," Duffy replied.

"Oh, and there's something else. Do ya know a Michael O'Malley?"

The old man looked at him, "O'Malley the runt who runs a bar in Manayunk?"

"Yeah, that's the one."

"Whaddaya want to trouble yourself with him for?"

"Duffy, it's a personal matter, nothing ta do with our business," Flynn replied.

The old man stared at him and said, "O'Malley is a man who keeps his word and pays his debts, if ya get my meanin. If I were you, I'd leave O'Malley alone. He might not look like much, but back in the day he was quite the brawler. Pound for pound he was one of the toughest welterweights ever to come out of this town. I saw him nearly beat a man to death at the Blue Horizon."

"Duffy, that was years ago. He looks ta me like he's seen better days," Flynn replied.

"Flynn, jest because a man has some age on him doesn't mean he's no longer dangerous. My advice to you is to leave O'Malley be."

FORTY-TWO

———◆◆◆———

The police found the fourth vest bomb in an abandoned yard in Kensington at 11:45 PM. One of the hookers who plied her trade on Frankford Avenue saw it when she brought her John to her private place for their date.

"It was the easiest twenty dollars, I ever made," she said. She smiled at the detective flashing the gold capped front tooth in a suggestive manner at the young man. "When I was about to give him...well you know, oral sex he saw the vest and ran away. I looked behind me to see what scared him off and saw it. I figured it was what the fuckin Aarabs must have used at the Mall," she paused and leaned closer to the detective and said, "Officer, is there any reward money?"

He shook his head.

"Well then, is there anything else I can do?" she asked leaning closer and running her tongue over her lips.

He shook his head again as he tried not to gag on the overpowering smell of her cheap perfume.

The bomb squad was immediately dispatched to the area and quickly determined that the vest was not armed. The squad reported that in all other respects it was identical to the vest they had removed from Farouk/Alcott and the remains of the vest bombs that had been recovered from the two explosions.

Across town in South Philadelphia, Michael Flynn was sitting in Vito Coratelli's tiny study. The only light in the room was a desk lamp that cast its illumination in such a manner as to leave Coratelli, who sat behind his desk, in shadow.

"Mr. Coratelli, thanks for meetin with me on such short notice," Flynn said.

"Mr. Flynn, Danny Duffy and I go way back. I know him to be an honorable man of serious intention. He assured me that the purpose of your meeting was a matter of critical significance, so I felt compelled to meet with you. How can I be of assistance?"

"Mr. Coratelli, I've seen you on the tele tellin the reporters that you know your son didn't commit suicide and that he was murdered. I know where the people who are responsible for your son's murder can be found."

Coratelli leaned forward into the light and stared at Flynn as if trying to discern if his visitor was being candid.

"They're the same bunch responsible for the attack at the Mall today," Flynn continued. "They're also behind the theft from the Barnes. Them and the art are in the same place, but they won't be there for much longer."

"Mr. Flynn, who murdered my son?"

"Shona Cohen."

Coratelli stared at him and asked, "Who is Shona Cohen?"

"She works with Ari Nooris and poses as his receptionist."

"What would she have to do with my son's murder?"

"Mr. Coratelli, she's no receptionist. The woman's a Mossad-trained assassin. She's a cold hearted killer."

Coratelli thought that through for a moment and asked, "Did she also kill Mickey Saunders?"

Flynn nodded.

Coratelli, the accomplished trial attorney, showed no reaction to Flynn's declarations.

"Mr. Flynn, why are you telling me this, shouldn't you be speaking with the police?"

"Well, ya see there's a bit of a problem with me meetin with the authorities," Flynn replied.

"And what exactly would that problem be?"

"Ya see I was the one who stole the art from the Barnes. So I don't think meetin with the police would be such a grand idea, if ya get my meaning."

Coratelli smiled and said, "Mr. Flynn, do you have a dollar on you?"

Flynn nodded, reached into his pocket, pulled a dollar bill from his billfold and placed it in Coratelli's hand.

"Now that I have been officially retained, whatever you tell me will be subject to attorney-client privilege. So, where exactly can these people be found?"

For the next forty-five minutes Flynn provided Coratelli with all of the particulars regarding the whereabouts of the Nooris brothers and their associates, their wealthy benefactor and the stolen works of art.

"Do you know when Nazeur's yacht will be leaving for Curacao?" Coratelli asked.

"Nah, for all I know it already left. But I put one of the tracking devices from the paintings on the stern of the ship before I left. It's the same device the police used to track the truck I left at the marine terminal. I'm sure the police will be able to track the vessel if they get on it soon."

Coratelli picked up the receiver and placed a call.

"Ichowitz," the recipient responded.

"Izzy, sorry about the hour, but I just became aware of some information that I believe you need to know."

Coratelli wasted no time in summarizing Flynn's story.

"Vito, this is the *emess*?" Ichowitz asked when Coratelli had finished.

"Izzy my friend, would I give you anything else?"

By 2:30 AM, Ichowitz, Jack Regan, the Commissioner and the commander of the PPD SWAT team along with his tactical group leaders had convened in the Commissioner's conference room at the PAB. Also in attendance was Monroe Ossberg of Homeland Security.

"According to the Harbor Master and the Coast Guard, Nazeur's yacht, 'The Haij' is scheduled to depart from Penn's Landing at 1000,"

George Restrum, SWAT Team Alpha leader informed the group. "If the vessel experiences a problem when it enters the main shipping channel, we can arrange to respond to a May Day and tow the vessel to a location where we can deal with Nazuer's guests and the cargo. Two members of the Team who were Navy Seals are on standby to 'assist' in the operation."

"Commissioner, don't you agree that Homeland and the FBI are better equipped to deal with this?"

"Mr. Ossberg, it's too late to get anyone else involved. If we don't move on this now, our window of opportunity will close. The Barnes collection and the people responsible for the attack on the Mall will be out of our reach," the Commissioner responded.

"Look, we'll make sure your agencies get full credit for cooperating in the operation."

"Then do we have the green light?" Restrum asked.

"Affirmative," the Commissioner replied.

FORTY-THREE

"May-Day! May-Day!" the captain of the *Haji* shouted into the microphone. The vessel had lost all power just as it entered the Delaware River's main shipping channel. The channel was only 400 feet wide at the Beckett Street Terminal. It would be directly in the path of the freighter laden with Chilean fruit that was scheduled to dock at the Gloucester Marine Terminal within the hour. Captain Hansen could see the freighter approaching from the south through his binoculars.

"What's wrong? Why aren't we moving?" Sheikh Nazeur asked as he entered the vessel's command center.

"I don't know, Your Highness. Everything was checked out last night. When we weighed anchor this morning there was nothing wrong. But as we entered the channel we lost our main power. We need to be towed back to shore," the captain calmly replied.

"Ahoy, *Haji*," they were interrupted by the loudspeaker from the Coast Guard cutter that approached from the stern. "What is the nature of your emergency?"

"We've lost all power," Hansen responded and waived out the window at the Coast Guard officer who stood near the bow of the cutter.

Within fifteen minutes the Coast Guard had the *Haji* in tow. With all the action at the bow of the vessel, no one on board took any notice of the rubber raft that followed the *Haji*. As the *Haji* passed through the shadow of the Walt Whitman Bridge the raft darted up to the stern of the vessel. Someone from the raft threw a rope with a grappling hook onto the *Haji* and three men silently boarded the ship in less than ten seconds, dropping the line into the Delaware as the raft peeled off, remaining in the shadow of the bridge.

Restrum's men split up upon boarding the vessel and made their way from the stern to the bow, making sure that no one could surprise their team when the operation commenced. An eight-man squad on board the Coast Guard Cutter would board the ship and take the crew and guests into custody, and the three-man team would assure that no one on board could disrupt the assault.

With the element of surprise on their side, the capture of the *Haji* proceeded without a hitch. The Coast Guard towed the ship to an abandoned pier at Fort Mifflin. The fort was located on Mudd Island near the confluence of the Delaware and Schuylkill rivers. As early as the founding of Philadelphia, Mudd Island had been reconigzed as strategically important for the defense of the settlement. In the War of Independence the British army bombarded it and captured the fort as part of their conquest of Philadelphia in the autumn of 1777. Once again the Philadelphia police would use the site as part of their war against the terrorists who had attacked their city.

"What is the meaning of this?" an outraged Sheikh Nazeur ibn Aziz screamed at George Restrum as he was lead into the makeshift interrogation room that had been set up in a restricted area in Fort Mifflin.

Restrum stared at Nazeur and calmly replied, "Mr. Nazeur, you are in a great deal of trouble. Among the passengers on your ship are individuals who are suspected of masterminding and carrying out the terrorist attack on Independence Mall yesterday. We have also removed from your ship valuable works of art stolen from the Barnes Foundation. I suggest that you cooperate with our investigation unless you want to be immediately transported to Guantanamo Bay for a less civilized interrogation."

"I know nothing about these crimes," Nazeur responded with faux indignance.

"Please don't insult me," Restrum replied.

"I demand counsel and an opportunity to consult with the Kingdom's Consul."

"Sheikh, perhaps you do not fully understand the seriousness of your situation. You are suspected of complicity in multiple acts of terrorism. As such, you have no right to an attorney and no right to communicate with your Consul's office. Unless you cooperate with me, I will turn you over to my colleagues at Homeland Security. Believe me you do not want that to happen."

"And what will happen to me if I cooperate?" Nazeur asked.

Restrum shrugged his shoulders and said, "That's not up to me. My superiors will make that call."

Restrum showed him a picture of Shona Cohen and asked, "Do you know her?"

Nazeur nodded.

"Where is she?"

"I do not know. She left the Haji early this morning. Ari Nooris told me she would make her way to Venezuela on her own."

"How about him?" Restrum showed Nazeur a picture of Michael Flynn.

"Yes. That is Michael Flynn the art thief. He's the one who introduced me to the Israelis."

For the next ninety minutes Restrum questioned Nazeur about his involvement in the plot. The interrogation session was observed by Commissioner Regan, Monroe Ossberg from Homeland Security and FBI SAC Howard Keel.

"Sheikh, one last question. We recovered nine of the missing works of art from your yacht. You told us Nooris and Flynn delivered ten paintings, is that right?"

"Yes."

"Was the George Braque oil, "The Pitcher" one of the works they stole from the Barnes for you?"

"Yes it was."

"What did you do with it?"

Nazeur stared at his interrogators, obviously confused by the question. "Sheikh?"

"It was in the hold with all of the paintings except the Cézanne."

"No it wasn't."

"But that's impossible! I personally inspected and supervised the storage of my paintings. There must be some mistake."

George Restrum smiled at his prisoner and said, "Sheikh it looks like you're the victim of a crime. Someone stole the painting you stole from the Barnes."

"Gentlemen, do you want to check with Washington to decide how to handle the Nooris brothers and Rabinowitz?" Commissioner Regan asked Ossberg and Keel.

"How about His Highness and the missing painting?" Ossberg asked.

"I think we've gotten everything we can from him. As to the painting, maybe Flynn took it. Who knows?" Regan replied. "Anyway, perhaps DC can use Nazuer as a chip in exchange for something from the Saudis."

"Commissioner, we'll consult with the Director and the Secretary and let you know what they decide. You and your men did good work. Sorry we gave you such a hard time," Keel said as he extended his hand to Commissioner Regan.

FORTY-FOUR

I t was a quiet night at the Grape Tavern. No one seemed to be in the celebratory mood in the wake of the attack on the Mall, so O'Malley figured he would close early. After the staff finished cleaning up, he moved a stool to the corner of the bar and counted the till. The moment O'Malley saw Flynn walk through the door he reached for the sawed-off shot gun he kept behind the bar. He smiled as he felt the buckshot enter the chamber as he pointed the ugly weapon at his uninvited visitor. He had warned Flynn to stay away from the Grape and leave his niece and her son alone. Flynn flashed him a smile and held up his hands and said, "Don't be pointin the gun at me, O'Malley. I'm not here lookin for trouble."

"So then why are ya here?"

"I've come to talk to you about the boy."

O'Malley pointed the gun at Flynn and said, "I told ya that if you bother Kate or Liam I'd send ya back to Ireland in a box."

"That you did," Flynn said and nodded in agreement. "But I didn't come here to hurt Kate or my son."

"Then what are ya doin here?"

"O'Malley, I'm going to reach into my pocket and show you something, so don't shoot me, OK?"

O'Malley nodded but continued to aim the weapon at Flynn. Flynn pulled an envelope from his back pocket and said, "Can I approach the bar and explain what this is?"

O'Malley nodded.

Flynn walked towards the bar and said, "This envelope contains information and the password for an account in a bank in Switzerland. I set up an account for Liam and designated you as the guardian. There's 500,000 Euros in the account. I figure that ought to be enough to assure that Liam has everything he needs for his education and to take care of anything else that might come up."

O'Malley stared at Flynn. "Ya know Kate won't be takin any of your money."

Flynn nodded and said, "That's why I'm givin it to you. Danny Duffy told me I could trust you to do the right thing by the boy."

"But what do ya want from Liam in return?"

"Nothin. You can tell him and Kate where the money's from if ya choose to or not. Whether Kate likes it or not, the boy's a Flynn, and we take care of our own."

"And you won't be comin around and botherin Liam and Kate?"

Flynn smiled and said, "Old man, I don't think I'll be steppin foot in this country ever again. You'll take care of this now, won't ya?"

O'Malley nodded.

"Then I'll be on my way. I trust ya won't be shootin me in my back as I leave," he said as he turned and walked out of the bar.

O'Malley looked at the envelope and sighed. He reached for the bottle of Tullamore Dew and a tumbler, poured himself two inches of the whiskey and took a generous sip. He felt the warmth of the drink and shook his head. He had figured Michael Flynn for a black-hearted bastard. Had he been wrong? Surely Flynn must have some ulterior motive. Flynn had known that Kate would never take the money from him. But a half a million Euros! He would have to figure out how to get Kate to understand that this would assure Liam's welfare for the rest of his life, and maybe for another generation or more.

While he figured out what to do, at least he could let Kate know that Flynn was no longer a threat to her and Liam. They could get back to their normal routine and move back to the third floor apartment. O'Malley shook his head as he realized how much he missed having Kate and the boy around.

They had placed the Nooris brothers and Rabinowitz aka Josef Allawaite in separate holding cells at Fort Mifflin. Ari Nooris and Nochem Rabinowitz, the seasoned Mossad agents they were, sat stoically and waited for the forces beyond their immediate control to decide their fate. Avi Nooris was an entirely different story. He was not a trained agent. He found the thought of being incarcerated terrifying. He paced the cell looking without success for a means of escape.

George Restrum and FBI Special Agent Rico Valdez watched the monitor as Avi Nooris deteriorated before their eyes. "Special Agent Valdez, do you think Mr. Nooris is ready for interrogation?"

Valdez smiled and asked, "Have the white shirts given the OK?"

"Negative."

Valdez shrugged his shoulders. "You know, we really don't have any evidence tying Avi to the attack on the Mall. He may have been involved in the Barnes heist. If we get a shot at him, we may be able to turn him. You know, 'Mr. Nooris, if you cooperate we may be able to save you from a trip to Gitmo,' that kind of thing."

"You think he's dumb enough to buy that line of bullshit?" Restrum asked. Valdez nodded.

"You think our bosses are smart enough to give us a crack at him?"

Valdez gave Restrum a thoughtful look and said, "I don't know about the Commissioner, but my guys have their heads so far up their asses that it's highly unlikely we'll get any opportunity to squeeze that dobolu."

"Jack, George Restrum's guys have taken the Nooris brothers and the Allawaite imposter into custody," Ichowitz called Regan with the news. "Nooris' receptionist Shona and Michael Flynn are still in the wind," he continued.

"Izz, was this from Coratelli's tip?"

"Yes."

"So who do you figure is his informant?" Regan asked.

"Well, could be some disgruntled associate of Sheikh Nazeur. Vito won't divulge his client's identity."

"Too bad," Regan replied.

"How are Kate and Liam?" Ichowitz asked.

"Between Kate and my mother, they won't leave the boy alone for a second," he said and laughed. "So what do you think Shona and Flynn are up to?"

"Beats me; I know Flynn's not exactly a gentleman, but somehow I don't figure him as involved in the Mall attack. Besides, since you saw him at the Barnes when the bombs went off…well you know that more or less eliminates him from direct involvement in that," Ichowitz observed.

"Yeah, unless it was all part of the plan he devised."

"True. I'm more concerned with Ms. Cohen. She well could be the mystery woman behind the murders of Vito Junior and Mickey Saunders."

Kate walked into the room as Jack was hanging up.

"The boy's finally asleep," she said as she sat down on the sofa next to Regan.

"He's quite a young man," Regan said as he put his arm around her shoulder.

"Yes. He won't take his compass watch off. He told your mother that he wants to be a lawyer, just like you when he grows up," she said and kissed Regan.

"Will you be comin up to bed now?"

"I want to talk with my father. You need to get some rest, I'll be up soon," he said and kissed her.

FORTY-FIVE

———◆◆◆———

Regan was gasping for breath as he struggled to get to the surface. He could see the light high above him. He felt the chill enter his body and knew that his death was imminent. He kicked with all of his remaining strength. He could make out the features of his killer. She was a beautiful woman. She smiled at him as she pushed his head under the surface one final time.

"Jack, wake up," his father gently patted his shoulder.

It was only a dream. But it seemed so real. He looked around feeling disoriented. He must have fallen asleep in the living room.

"Dad, what time is it?"

"It's 4 AM."

"Did you get anything from the Nooris brothers?"

"Well, we did get a statement from Avi Nooris, but his brother and the other Mossad agent Rabinowitz are stonewalling," the Commissioner yawned.

"So?"

"Avi said he didn't know anything about the attack on the Mall. He was only involved in the Barnes heist. He thought the explosions were supposed to be a distraction. He swore that he had been assured no one would be hurt. He claimed the plan to steal the art was all Michael Flynn's idea."

"Do you believe him?"

The Commissioner yawned again and said, "I believe some of it. Restrum and the feds are going to analyze the video of his statement later this morning. They'll probably interrogate him again. In the meantime, they'll try to get Ari and the other agent to cooperate, but I doubt that either of them will break."

"How about the rich Saudi?" Jack asked.

"He also claims he was only interested in the art. He had no knowledge of, or part in the attack."

"Do you believe him?"

The Commissioner shook his head.

Jack could see that his father was tired. "Dad, get some sleep. We'll talk about this later."

So if Avi Nooris was telling the truth, Michael Flynn was the mastermind behind the Barnes robbery. Jack felt somewhat relieved to know that Flynn had not come all the way from Ireland just to try to convince Kate to return with Liam. He still felt that Flynn was someone to be concerned about, especially since the robbery turned out to be a bust. How did the robbery and the faux terrorist attack on the Mall fit in with the Coratelli and Saunders murders? Was any of this connected to Megan Larson's murder?

Jack would have to talk it out with Izzy. In the meantime he needed to make sure that Kate and Liam were safe.

Shona Cohen assumed that something must have gone wrong when Ari Nooris failed to contact her at the prearranged time. The plan was for Shona to wait for final instructions from Ari before cleaning up the remaining loose ends and leaving the country. The Mall attack had been badly botched. It had never been intended to result in the carnage that had occurred. This was not the West Bank where collateral damage – dead Palestinians – could be easily dismissed as battlefield debris.

Without contact from Nooris she would have to decide on her own whether to abandon the mission. Shona had been carefully trained in her craft. She was methodical and unemotionally analyzed the consequences to herself and the others of leaving the mission. She stared at her reflection in the mirror of the womens' restroom at the 30th Street Station. She could take the next Amtrak to New York and make her way to the Canadian border and disappear, or take the regional rail or a bus to the safe house. She figured she could wait twenty-four hours before making her decision. Perhaps in that time she would find out what had happened to the rest of her team. The absence of any further word from Ari and no media report of arrests were a strong indication that Nooris had been taken into custody.

The thought of Ari Nooris in custody was inconceivable. Ari had been her mentor for more than a decade. He found her in an orphanage in Jerusalem when she was twelve years old. Abandoned by her junkie mother in Moscow, she had been rescued by an Israeli relief organization and brought to Israel. For the first several months after she made "Aliyah," she refused all efforts to integrate her into the culture of her new homeland. Only Ari Nooris was able to see what the psychologists and doctors at the orphanage failed to realize. Shona had been so badly abused as a child that she had been irreparably damaged. Ari showed her the way to channel her pain and extract her revenge. For this, she was forever in his debt.

Her thoughts returned to the present. If Ari and the others had been arrested, how could the authorities have known that they were on the Saudis' ship? There must have been a leak, but who, and why? Patience was the hallmark of spy craft; in time she would find out, and when she did she would deal with whoever was responsible in her very unique fashion. She would do it for Ari. She owed him that much.

In the meantime she needed to remain free. Among her other talents, Shona was a master of disguise. She could dramatically alter her appearance from glamorous cover girl to old hag, with minimal use of cosmetics or other devices. From her years in the field she knew that her best move was to hide in plain sight. She would go back to Manayunk. If anyone was looking for her that was the last place they would think she would go.

Jack spent the rest of the sleepless night trying to figure out if there was any way to tie the Larson murder to the Nooris-Flynn art heist/ Mall attack. In the madness and mayhem of the attack and the theft it seemed to him that the Larson murder investigation had been more or less abandoned. Even though he didn't believe there was a direct connection between the crimes, he would ask his father if he could arrange to allow him and Ichowitz to interrogate Avi Nooris. Jack would also ask Izzy to try to get Ossberg to give them the unredacted copy of the security video of Nooris' condo.

After an hour and a half of consultation between the Philadelphia Police Department and representatives from the FBI and Homeland Security, Jack and Ichowitz were given access to Avi Nooris.

Avi Nooris was lead into the room by two armed federal agents. He was handcuffed and his feet were shackled. Nooris had not tolerated his incarceration well. His skin was sallow and he appeared to have shrunk from the overly muscled physique of which he was so proud a mere thirty-six hours before. Nooris' eyes constantly moved back and forth between Regan and Ichowitz.

"Please remove the handcuffs and shackles from Mr. Norris," Ichowitz asked the guards.

When the restraints had been removed and Nooris was seated, Ichowitz addressed him.

"Mr. Nooris, the federal authorities have allowed us to interview you about the three homicides we are investigating. Neither me nor District Attorney Regan believe that you were directly involved in the terrorist attack. However, we both believe you know more about the homicides than you told the FBI. Mr. Nooris, as I see it, the only way for you to avoid being held under the federal anti-terrorist laws is if you cooperate with our investigation," Ichowitz said.

Nooris silently stared back at Ichowitz. A bead of perspiration from his forehead slowly worked its way down his cheek.

"Mr. Nooris, do you understand what I just told you?"

Nooris nodded.

"Will you answer our questions?"

He nodded again.

"Alright then, District Attorney Regan will begin," Ichowitz said and looked over at Jack.

"Avi, before we get to the homicides tell me, how did you get the ten paintings from the Barnes to Nazeur's yacht?"

Nooris turned his gaze to Regan and smiled. "Flynn told me that if you ever found out that the art got to the Haij it would drive you crazy."

"He was right about that. So how did you?"

Nooris shrugged and said, "It wasn't a fucking magic trick. Shona showed up with a van, and we took the paintings Nazeur wanted to his boat."

"So you weren't in the truck when Flynn took the rest of the art to the Tioga Marine terminal?"

"I was out of there hours before that."

"Tell me something, why did Flynn take the eighteen-wheeler with art and then abandon it?"

Nooris smiled again and said, "It was all to divert your attention from the ten paintings the Arab wanted."

"And did you deliver all of the paintings to the yacht?"

Nooris nodded. Based on his response Regan assumed he had no knowledge that one of the paintings had been taken from the yacht.

"And the attack … was that supposed to be a diversion too?" Regan continued his inquiry.

Nooris nodded again, "Except for the fools who put on the vest no one else was supposed to get hurt; just a lot of noise."

"So what went wrong?"

"I don't know," he said and sighed.

Regan looked at Ichowitz and shook his head.

"OK Avi, let's talk about the murders. Who murdered Vito Coratelli?"

Nooris stared at Regan and said nothing.

"Avi, you need to tell us what you know and you need to tell us now."

Nooris told them that the murders of Coratelli and Saunders were part of his brother's exit strategy. Both of the victims knew more than Nooris felt comfortable with leaving them in place when the Nooris left town. Coratelli was a junkie and a flake. Ari realized that Coratelli's attempt to shake him down over the court house deal would never end. So he waited for the best opportunity to eliminate the problem.

"So who killed him?"

Nooris shook his head and sighed. "If I tell you they will kill me."

"If you *don't* tell us the feds will send you to Gitmo. Your choice," Regan replied.

Nooris sat stone still and stared back at Regan. He shook his head and said, "Shona."

"The receptionist?"

He nodded.

"How did she know Coratelli was at the rehab?"

"I don't know; someone leaked the information. That's all I know about that."

"How about Saunders?"

"Shona."

"Why?"

"Again, Saunders was unreliable."

"How do you know that Shona killed both of them?" Regan asked.

"I was there when Ari told her to do it."

"Did Shona kill Megan Larson?"

Nooris shook his head and said, "No. Why would she do that?"

"Ari could have told her to," Regan said.

He made a face and waived dismissively and said, "No. Ari had no reason to have Megan Larson killed. Megan was no danger to Ari or anything Ari was doing."

"Where is Shona?"

I don't know, I swear to God I don't know. I hope you find her before she finds me," he replied.

"OK," Regan said.

"What's going to happen to me?" Nooris asked.

Ichowitz shrugged his shoulders and said, "We need to review what you told us with the Commissioner. In the meantime, we'll ask the guards to allow you to wash up and change into clean clothes. We'll get back to you very soon."

After the guards had taken Nooris back to his cell, Ichowitz turned to Jack and asked, "So do you believe him?"

Regan nodded and asked, "What's our next move?"

"We need to find Shona Cohen, and we need to find out who leaked Vito Junior's location to Ari Nooris," Ichowitz replied.

"Izz, if Shona didn't kill Megan Larson, we need to get that video of Nooris' condo from your buddy Ossberg."

"There's a Detective Ichowitz on Line One for you."

Ossberg was expecting the call. He figured Ichowitz would be looking for quid pro quo since the Philadelphia Police had generously allowed Homeland and the FBI to assume custody of the Nooris gang and Nazeur. He wouldn't have blamed the locals if they had frozen them out in consideration of the hard time the feds had given them over the entire Mall security fiasco. The local police had done more to secure the area and apprehend the bad guys than the combined forces of the FBI, Homeland Security and the Secret Service.

"Izzy, I was expecting your call," he said.

"Then I'm glad I didn't disappoint you. Monroe, I think you know why I'm calling," Ichowitz replied.

"I'll have the video delivered to you later this morning. Izz, it's like I told you, it doesn't reveal who killed Megan Larson."

FORTY-SIX

———◆◆◆———

J
ack and Izzy met in the Fourth District conference room they had used for the murder investigations. The room looked just as it had when they left on July Third, before all hell had broken loose. The tumult of events, the terrorist attack at the Mall, Liam's miraculous journey to safety, the Barnes robbery and the apprehension of some of the perpetrators of the crimes – so much had transpired since Jack had last been there. He took a quick inventory. The pictures of the victims and suspects were still pined to the wall, the murder book lay unopened on the table, empty coffee cups and sandwich wrappings overflowed from the trashcan; it was all just as they had left it. Despite the fact that so much had transpired in the seventy-two hours since they had last assembled there, including Avi Nooris' statement implicating Shona Cohen as Coratelli and Saunders' killer, Jack realized they still had no break in the Megan Larson case.

The disc of the Nooris condo Ossberg had provided had turned out to be the dead end the federal agent had described. Regan and Ichowitz sat through an accelerated ninety minutes of the condo's back wall with no shot of either the victim or her assailant. As Ichowitz removed the disc from the laptop he said, "Well, at least we know something for certain now that we didn't know before."

Regan shook his head and asked, "What do we know?"

"*Boychik*, think about it. Why would the feds invest their time and effort to install sophisticated surveillance equipment in Ari Nooris' condo and yet have absolutely no evidence of the Mall attack or the Coratelli and Saunders murders?"

"Because they're a bunch of incompetent assholes," Regan replied.

"Too obvious; why would they stonewall us and stall before turning over this worthless video?"

"Because they didn't want us to realize they're a bunch of incompetent assholes."

"Once again too obvious,"

"So what am I missing?"

"They're hiding something from us," Ichowitz said.

"What?"

"The identity of the killer."

Regan stared at his friend and asked, "Why would they do that?"

"Because there's something more important to them than Megan Larson's murder," Ichowitz said as he placed the worthless disc back in its case.

"Izzy, what could possibly be more important than a murder?"

"That I do not know. But if we can figure that out we should be well on our way to cracking this case."

"So what do we do now?"

"Let's hope we can locate Shona Cohen."

"Uncle Mike, can ya give me a hand putting the produce in the cooler?" Kate asked as she struggled with the crate of lettuce.

O'Malley picked up a carton of broccoli rabe and followed his niece into the walk-in box. As he placed the produce in its proper spot on the shelf he said, "You'll never guess who dropped by the Grape last night."

"Was it the Queen or maybe His Holiness the Pope?" she gave him her stock response to the 'never guess who' questions he had frequently asked her when she was a child back in Ireland.

"Nah," he said with a shake of his head.

She turned and smiled and asked, "Well now, don't keep me in suspense any longer, who then?"

"Michael Flynn."

The mere sound of his name instantly removed the smile from her face.

"Before ya start, let me assure ya there's nothin to be upset about. I mean I didn't shoot him or anything like that, although I did keep him at gun point for most of the visit."

"So what did he want?"

"He told me he wouldn't be comin around again botherin you and the boy."

"And did ya believe him?"

"That I did," O'Malley replied.

"Well Uncle Mike, Flynn's a liar for sure, so why would ya believe anything he had to say?"

"Well, he gave me something to hold for Liam that more or less made me think he was on the level."

"And what might that be?"

"A Swiss bank account with 500,000 Euros."

Kate stared at her uncle and opened her mouth but found herself unable to utter the fresh retort she had planned to say.

"Cat got your tongue?" he asked.

She was still speechless.

"Come, let's get out of this cooler and discuss this over a cuppa tea," O'Malley said leading his still speechless niece out of the walk-in box.

They sat in a booth without speaking as they drank the rich tea Kate had brewed. "Uncle Mike, I won't be taking any of Flynn's money. God only knows how he amassed that fortune. I'm sure he came by it in some illegal manner."

"Katey girl, ya don't know that for certain. And besides, the money's not fer you, it's fer Liam."

"But Uncle Mike, there's sure to be strings attached. No one gives anyone a sum of money that large without wantin something in return."

"I know. I know, that was my first thought too. But when I asked him why he was doing this and whether he'd be hangin around, he said he would never set foot in this country again. He said, 'Flynns take care of our own.'" O'Malley took another drink of tea and continued, "Anyways he told me Danny Duffy told him I could be trusted to hold the money for Liam. So I went to see Duffy first thing this mornin. I told him about Flynn comin by and all, except for the amount of the gift. I figured he didn't need ta know all that. Duffy wasn't at all surprised to hear of it. Nor did he question my concern that Flynn would want something in return."

"So Duffy says, he doesn't expect to be seein Flynn back in the states anytime soon, if ever. When I asked why, he gave me one of them looks like it was none of my affair. Then he said if Flynn wants to provide for his son it's a blessing for sure and for us not to act so high and mighty like a bunch of toffs. Duffy's a hard man fer certain, but he owes me and he's always done right by me. If Duffy says we've nothing to be worried about from Flynn, I'd bank on it."

"I don't know Uncle Mike, with great fortune comes great complications," she said and sighed.

"Well we've time enough to decide what to do about the money. But fer now, you and the boy can come back home and we can start putting our lives back in order. Kate, can you tell me how a level-headed young woman like you could get involved with the likes of a man like Flynn?"

She told him about the Michael Flynn she had fallen in love with – a young man who desperately wanted to break away from his family and live an honest life, like normal people. His talent on the pitch was his way out. He promised Kate they would be married and he would take care of both her and their son.

"So what happened?"

"The Flynns would not let him go. Uncle Mike, they broke his leg so he couldn't play football. They wanted to insure that he would honor their tradition. We agreed that I needed to leave before they took Liam to Ulster. His family would never allow the boy to escape his destiny. When he showed up here I was afraid he changed his mind."

Shona Cohen checked the papers, the local TV news, and the Internet for reports about the arrest of those responsible for the attack on the Mall. Except for a sketchy story about a botched attempt to steal art from the Barnes Foundation, there was nothing that she could find that shed light on what had happened to Ari Nooris and the rest. The lack of news spoke volumes to her that they had been taken into custody. The Barnes story did not elaborate on whether all of the art had been recovered. It was still conceivable that Nooris and the masterpieces were sailing their way to Curacao. She knew in her heart, however, that if that were the case Ari would have found a way to let her know.

If Ari and the team had been taken into custody, the authorities were probably looking for her. She had been carefully trained for such a contingency and was confident that she could move about without any real threat of capture. She smiled at her reflection in the mirror. Her long red hair had been shorn and dyed a deep black. The special contacts she wore had changed her green eyes to brown. The rimless eye-glasses and eyebrow piercing all combined to create a tough-girl, butch feel. She would fit right in at the 12th Air Command on Samson Street later tonight. She had been told that the club accommodated a more mature clientele and that it was likely she would be able to hook up with her quarry there. Shona had decided that Ari would want her to complete the mission, likely her last before she left.

FORTY-SEVEN

———◆———

When he left the Fourth District Regan drove over to the Grape Tavern to check on Kate and Liam. He could hear Kate singing as he entered the kitchen. She was sitting at the counter with the pastry bag in her hands decorating the chicken pot pies with 'GT' dough initials that graced one of the Tavern's signature dishes. She turned and smiled at him.

"What's wrong? You look like you lost your best friend," Kate asked as he entered.

"Oh nothing really, I thought we were about to get a big break in the murder investigation Izzy and I have been working on, but we hit another stone wall. But you seem to be pretty chipper," he said as he sat down on the stool next to her.

"That I am," she nodded still smiling at him.

"And to what do you credit this display of contentment?"

"Liam and I can move back here. We won't have to be intruding on your parents' hospitality any longer."

Regan was taken aback by Kate's declaration and asked, "Kate, are you sure that's a wise move? I mean, aren't you concerned about your and Liam's safety? Believe me you're not an imposition, if that's your concern."

"No, no. Your parents, your entire family have been wonderful. It's not that at all. It's just we have nothin to fear now."

Kate told him about Flynn's visit with O'Malley and O'Malley's follow-up with Danny Duffy. Regan knew that Duffy was the head of Philadelphia's Irish mob.

"So you believe that Flynn is going back to Ireland, never to return," Regan said.

She nodded.

"But how can you be so sure?"

"That's the thing I wanted to talk to you about. You see Flynn left something for Uncle Mike to hold for Liam, and I'm not altogether sure about how to handle it. Ya know, whether to keep it or not."

"What exactly did Flynn leave in O'Malley's safe keeping for Liam?"

"A Swiss bank account with 500,000 Euros."

Regan whistled and said, "That's a lot of 'I'm sorry I missed being a better father to you guilt money.'"

"I know," she replied. "I'm concerned about the amount of the trust fund and where it likely came from. Flynn's a scoundrel and God only knows what he's done to amass such a fortune. O'Malley told me not to be hasty and jump to conclusions that might turn out to be unfounded and all."

"So what are you going to do? Are you going to return the money?"

"Well, as O'Malley has already pointed out, it's not up to me. Flynn named him the Trustee, 'don't ya know,' seems Danny Duffy, who both O'Malley and Flynn hold in high regard, vouched for O'Malley's good character. Can ya imagine that? Anyway, I wanted your advice. I'm not comfortable with any of this; I don't want Michael Flynn having anything to do with my son. I especially don't want Liam beholden to Flynn, even if he remains an ocean away."

Jack shook his head and replied, "Seems to me we have some time to think this through. For now, I'm not so sure I feel comfortable with you and Liam moving back here, at least until we confirm that Flynn is gone. Besides, I like having the two of you with my family and me."

"You do, do ya?"

He nodded. She leaned over and kissed him. "Well, we don't have to move back to the Grape, we could move in with you. If that's allright; I mean I don't think Liam would mind."

Ossberg and Keel, his counterpart at the FBI, had been given clearance by their superiors to transport Ari Nooris and Rabinowitz to Gitmo for more comprehensive interrogation. Good luck, he thought. There was no way either of those two would break, regardless of the methods the CIA would try. They were hard case professionals who would never let their guard down. Avi Nooris would remain in their custody for the time being. Perhaps he could provide them with more useful information that could lead to the apprehension of the assassin Shona Cohen. Ossberg still found it hard to accept that the attack on the Mall was nothing more than a distraction for the Barnes robbery that had gone terribly wrong. But why would former Mossad agents plan a terrorist attack on U.S. soil?

The State Department had plans for Nazeur. He would be used to barter with the Saudis. Nazeur's involvement in a number of sophisticated international financial transactions created complications for both countries. Ossberg was more than happy to hand him over to the diplomats. He had more than enough on his plate.

He turned his attention to the other hot file on his desk, an investigation involving the Carrington Group, a multi-national hedge fund. He was looking for a reason to remove the classified status Homeland had designated for the investigation. As far as he could tell the allegations surrounding the Carrington Group's various enterprises as a money-laundering operation for Al-Qaida had not yielded any hard evidence. The Carrington Group invested in and sometimes operated a vast array of businesses throughout the world. Its latest ventures involved trash recycling operations that converted human waste into energy pellets.

Carrington, through various questionable business arrangements, had secured long term deals with municipalities throughout the country.

When they targeted Philadelphia as the site for its next super recycling plant, the Carrington advance team brought its well-funded operatives onto the scene looking for corrupt politicians and others, in this case crooked municipal employee union leaders, to bribe to obtain the requisite approvals and to clear away the opposition. Carrington had hired none other than Dorothy Wiggins as local counsel, no doubt for her contacts among the local unions and politicians who could be helpful in securing the contract.

Homeland became suspicious of Carrington when an incident in Detroit exposed a potential for mayhem on a catastrophic scale. The Detroit operation, either intentionally or otherwise, included a group of Al-Qaida sympathizers who tried to convert the recycling operation into a delivery device that could disseminate toxic waste into the municipal reservoir. Luckily the infrastructure of the municipal water system was in such dire shape that the state government was already in the process of assuming responsibility for the utility.

When the state authorities began the inspection process they immediately discovered what the terrorists were trying to accomplish. Homeland and the FBI set a trap and quietly eliminated the threat. Now that Carrington was on their radar, Homeland and the FBI were carefully monitoring any new ventures in which it became involved. The Philadelphia operation was no exception. As far as Ossberg could see, it followed the same pattern as other municipal takeovers.

The players in this market were, once again, a handful of corrupt politicians and union leaders. Ossberg's predecessor claimed to have an "insider" who had been providing him a steady stream of what appeared to Ossberg to be worthless information. There was absolutely nothing that resembled a terrorist threat as far as he could tell. If he could convince his superiors that there was nothing here, he could declassify the file and turn it over to the local authorities. The file included a surveillance video that would have significant impact on more than potential criminal indictments for public corruption.

FORTY-EIGHT

———◆———

Regan rushed out of the courtroom in which the preliminary hearing on one of the top prelates of the Archdiocese of Philadelphia had been convened. Monsignor Peter Polanski had been charged as the architect of the cover-up of rampant child abuse that had been recently exposed in the Philadelphia church. Philly, like many other dioceses throughout the country and beyond, was dealing with the problem that had been ignored for decades. In this case, the egregious nature of the crimes and the Church's response was almost too much for Regan, a former altar-boy, to comprehend.

During his cross examination of the defendant he received a text from Izzy Ichowitz to contact him immediately. Ichowitz had never texted Regan before. Regan wasn't even aware that his friend knew how to text, so he figured whatever Ichowitz wanted to discuss must be pretty important.

He stuck his hand in the path of the closing elevator doors and heard someone say, "Jesus Christ couldn't you wait for the next elevator!" When the doors opened he saw the only occupant in the car was Dorothy Wiggins. Wiggins smirked at Regan and said, condescension dripping from every word, "Assistant District Attorney Regan, guess you must be involved in vitally important business on behalf of the Commonwealth."

Regan stared at her for a moment and said with an equal measure of sarcasm, "Ms. Wiggins, it's always such a pleasure to see you."

294 MURDER AND MAYHEM IN MANAYUNK

Wiggins' face turned scarlet with the affront and responded, "Pretty cocky for someone who hasn't been able to come up with a suspect in the Meagan Larson murder."

"Oh, we have a suspect," he replied.

"You do- who?"

He turned to face her and said, "Ms. Wiggins, you know I'm not at liberty to share that information with you. I'm sure you'll find out in due course."

They rode down the six floors in silence. When Regan got out of the elevator and was certain Wiggins was not within earshot he called Ichowitz.

"Izz, what's up?"

"Jack, Ari Nooris and Nochem Rabinowitz escaped."

It took Regan a few seconds to process Ichowitz' message, how could that have happened? "Izz I thought the feds were shipping them to Gitmo!"

Ichowitz told Regan that the two Mossad agents walked away from their FBI escorts while they were being transported from the temporary confinement at Fort Mifflin.

"So three dangerous former Mossad agents, Nooris, Rabinowitz and Shona Cohen are on the loose?"

"Uh-huh."

"*Oy-vey*," Regan said.

"You can say that again, *boychik*. I'm at the PAB. Why don't you come over and join in on the fun?"

The ease with which Nooris and Rabinowitz had escaped from custody stunned Howard Keel, the Philadelphia FBI SAC. He knew that if the two former Mossad agents-turned-terrorists were not quickly apprehended, it would mean the end of his career. He cursed himself for summarily dismissing the local authorities' offer to assume custody of the suspects they had captured on Sheik Nazeurs' yacht. He now realized the hubris of assuming that his agents were superior to the local police.

The so-called joint federal and city task force was assembling at the Philadelphia Police Administration Building, everyone but the police referred to as the "Round House," to try to come up with a strategy to re-arrest the two escapees and apprehend the others involved in the attack/ art heist.

After the FBI and Homeland agents 'responsible' for the escape had completed their report they were excused from the meeting.

"Commissioner, your department has more assets available to help us find these individuals. Can you fill us in on the PPD's actions?" Keel asked.

Commissioner Regan described the comprehensive dragnet his department had set up to find the terrorists. Six hours had passed since they had escaped custody. The Philadelphia Police had recovered an abandoned vehicle that Nooris and Rabinowitz had used that they had stolen from one of the Philadelphia Airport long term parking lots. The fingerprints taken from the vehicle confirmed that the escapees had stolen the vehicle. The Police also found the yellow jump suits the FBI had clothed them in when they were taken into custody that they had left in the stolen vehicle.

"We found the Mercury Mountaineer on Kingsesseing Avenue, about five miles from the Philadelphia Airport. Our canvass of the neighborhood failed to uncover any leads. We issued an APB for both men. We had already issued one for Shona Cohen. So far none of our personnel have had any luck," Regan reported. "Photos of all three have been released to local media outlets."

After he had completed his report and the meeting broke, Keel waited as the rest left. "Commissioner, can I speak with you privately?" Keel followed Regan into the Commissioner's office. He sat down on the leather club chair in front of Regan's desk and sighed. "Looks like we...I mean *I* really stepped on my dick," he said.

Regan shrugged his shoulders in a "what can you say" kind of gesture. "Do you think we have any realistic shot of recapturing these guys?"

Regan stared at the ceiling as he contemplated his response. After a moment of silence he said, "Howard, we know a great deal about Ari

296 MURDER AND MAYHEM IN MANAYUNK

Nooris. He's lived in this area, on and off, for twenty years. He knows the city, and he's well known in this town. That cuts both ways. We have our people on high alert. Who knows?"

"How about his family?"

Regan shook his head. "They left for Israel before any of this. We asked the Lower Merion police to check on their residence, just in case."

"Anything show up on the surveillance cameras?"

Regan shook his head and smirked, "The late Mayor Gallo paid some pal of his over $17 million to install this state-of–the-art surveillance system in Center City and in high crime areas. They were supposed to provide us with 24/7 coverage at a fraction of the cost of beat patrol officers. Turns out, half of the cameras never worked, and the other half only work half the time. All that money could have been used to hire an additional 100 officers. What a waste!"

"So I take it you're not optimistic," Keel said.

Once again Regan responded with a shoulder shrug.

Keel sighed and said, "I should have taken you up on your offer to take custody of those two 'gonifs.' Is that what your man Ichowitz called them?"

Regan smiled and nodded. "Look, there's no percentage in second guessing yourself. We're covering every escape route we can. If they try to leave the area ..."

"John, don't kid a kidder. They're in the wind and likely will never be caught."

"Howard, can I ask you something?"

Keel nodded.

"What can you tell me about Homeland's surveillance of Nooris' activities?"

Keel stared at the ceiling as he composed his response and shook his head. "You didn't hear this from me."

Regan nodded.

"Homeland is acting on the Agency's behalf. Nooris and his people had been the subject of the CIA's interest for quite some time. They suspect Nooris as the muscle behind some international hedge fund, the Carrington Group. Although Carrington has a number of legitimate businesses, it's really a money laundering operation on an international scale. They're also involved in black ops."

"But why would Nooris get involved with Flynn and the Saudi in the art heist?"

"Ego, hubris, who knows? Nooris went rouge when he was passed over for the top spot in the Mossad several years ago. Apparently he backed the wrong side in the Israeli elections. If you think our brand of politics is a dirty game, I hear it pales in comparison to the hardball they play over there. They play for keeps," Keel smiled and said, "Here the losers become pundits and go on television or write books and turn into millionaires, over there they end up in prison or worse," Keel said and shrugged his shoulders.

"How about Rabinowitz, what's his story?"

"Rabinowitz and the girl Shona Cohen, were Nooris' assets back when he was in the Mossad. They are completely loyal to him. He selected them, trained them and both of them would take a bullet for him."

"Are you telling me that Nooris put Rabinowitz in deep cover just to use him for the Barnes job?" Regan asked.

Keel thought over his response and said, "Probably not; my guess is he had Rabinowitz in place for something else, but when the opportunity to use him for his personal gain came up, he took advantage of it."

Regan stared at Keel and asked, "So what's going to happen to you?"

Keel shook his head and said, "Someone has to pay for the screw up that left three killers on the loose. I'll either be reassigned to some back-water post never to be seen or heard from again, or retired."

Regan shook his head and said, "Howard, just thank your lucky stars this isn't Israel."

Ichowitz filled Jack in on the status of the manhunt for the escaped ter-rorists. Despite the manpower of the Philadelphia Police Department and the FBI, there was no trace of either man. The consensus opinion of the authorities was that they had fled the area, perhaps even the country.

"Izz, I know everyone believes that Nooris and his associate are long gone, but my gut tells me that they're still here," Regan said as he handed the summaries of the dragnet reports back to Ichowitz.

"Why would they remain in Philly?" the detective asked.

"Ari Nooris has lived here on and off for most of his life. He knows this town like the back of his hand. He has to know that his picture has been given to every local and federal law enforcement officer up and down the east coast. Where better to wait until the heat is off?"

"So if we can figure out where he may be holed up, you think we may be able to recapture Nooris and Rabinowitz?" Ichowitz asked.

"Yeah, and maybe Shona too."

FORTY-NINE

———◆◆◆———

The Arts Condos, formerly the Sylvania House at 1324 Locust Street had seen better days. It had survived the down decades before the neighborhood east of South Broad Street had been given a tony new name, "West Washington Square," and the gay community had moved in and began the gentrification process that had transformed the area into a cool and desirable place to live. The Arts Condos would eventually benefit from the energy and money the young professionals would spend on renovating their apartments. At present the building still looked more like the old Sylvania House, in need of a major facelift. Many of the units were still vacant. The economic downturn had halted, for the time being, the inevitable restoration that would eventually make millionaires of the urban pioneers and real estate speculators.

Ari Nooris and Nochem Rabinowitz, now Ed Mankowitz and Harry Oshansky, waited for the rental agent to complete the lease agreement for the two bedroom unit on the second floor. "You're sure you don't want the unit on the thirteenth floor with the view of the Kimmel Center? It's already been renovated and it's only $500 a month more," he asked Nooris/Mankowitz.

"My companion is very superstitious and would never think of staying on the thirteenth floor," Nooris/Mankowitz said as he placed a protective arm around Rabinowitz/Oshansky. "Would you Harrila?"

The two men had transformed themselves from their former persona to a flamboyant gay couple. Rabinowitz had shaved his head bald and cut his beard to a stylish goatee. He wore a pair of oversized emerald earrings that matched the ring on the third finger of his left hand. He wore the new skinny jeans and a tight tee shirt that emphasized his well toned body. He smiled at the rental agent and the gold cap on his front tooth sparkled in the sunlight that filled the room.

Nooris/Mankowitz had dyed his hair silver and added blue highlights. He wore heavy stage make-up to create the impression that he was trying to look younger than the middle age look he had affected with the cosmetic bags under his eyes, puffed up jowls and false teeth, all of which had added a good ten years to his appearance. He also wore an emerald ring on his finger that matched his companion's ring.

They paid the agent the two month's rent and a security deposit in cash. Since the entire transaction was less than $10,000, the rental agent did not have to report the cash to any authority. Nooris assumed the agent would not report the transaction, or at least the entire amount, to the condo unit's owner either, and that was fine with him. The less people who knew about their arrangement the better he liked it.

The unit they had selected fit their needs to perfection. It was at the rear of the apartment building near the fire escape. Nooris and Rabinowitz fixed the emergency exit door so that they could enter and exit the building without having to use the lobby entrance on Locust Street. The emergency exit opened to an alley between the apartment building and a ten foot high wall of a parking garage. Rabinowitz cut the wire to the overhead lamp outside the exit leaving the alley in near total darkness at night.

They watched the local news reports of their escape from the federal authorities. They looked nothing like the mug shot images that flashed across the screen. One of the broadcasts included an interview of Vito Coratelli who agreed with the assessment of how dangerous the escapees were, and dramatically ended the interview by emphatically claiming, "They murdered my son!" as he pointed at the camera. Nooris assumed that Shona now knew of both their apprehension and escape. He would leave her a message revising their original plans, if it wasn't already too late. They had escaped eight hours ago. If everything went as planned they would leave the country within forty-eight hours.

He needed to find out who had leaked the information to the authorities that had led to their arrest. Nooris was certain that the old detective Ichowitz, or his sidekick the Police Commissioner's son, would know. There would be considerable risk in getting to either of these men in the time frame he had in mind. A third less high risk option was Coratelli, the father of the junkie Nooris had eliminated. There was something about his performance during the televised interview that bothered Nooris. Although Coratelli was more accessible, Nooris wasn't sure that he knew who had provided their whereabouts to the police. His other option of course was to just walk away. After all, he had the Arab's money. It had been transferred from one of Sheik Nazeur's accounts to Nooris' Cayman Island bank before they had been taken into custody. But to just walk away was not his nature.

"Looks like your pal Nooris and his accomplice who's the spittin image of Osama Bin Laden, broke out of jail," Danny Duffy said as he nodded at the flat screen television above the bar in the back room of his tavern.

Michael Flynn nodded.

"Flynn, is there anything I should be concerned about?"

"Nothin at all, I've got it covered; don't you be worryin about the likes of them," Flynn replied.

The older man stared at him as if he was looking through him and said, "That sounds like a line of malarkey to me, boyo. Ya know we have ya ready to ship outta town tonight. Should we be revisin the schedule so that you can take care of any onfinished business?"

Flynn turned away from the newscast and responded, "Duffy, I'd appreciate the gesture."

"Should I be warnin O'Malley to keep an eye out as well?" Duffy asked.

"I don't know if that's necessary. I mean, why worry the old man and Kate? They've been through enough when the boy went missin for all that time after the attack and all."

Duffy stared at Flynn and said, "Well here's how it's gonna be. I'll have some of the boys keep an eye on O'Malley and his niece and your son. Here, take this."

He handed Flynn a bag. "What's in the bag?" he asked.

"It's a fully loaded Smith and Wesson M&P .357 revolver with the serial number filed off and an extra magazine."

"I'm an art thief. Why are you giving me this?"

"Just in case; ya never know what ya might encounter," Duffy said with a shrug of his shoulders.

Flynn lifted his pint and said, "Thank you."

Duffy gave him a knowing look and said, "We take care of our own."

S hona was relieved to learn that Ari and Rabinowitz had escaped. She assumed they had been arrested when Ari had not contacted her as previously arranged. She had checked the drop earlier that day. There was still no message. She was confident that as soon as Ari was sure it was safe he would reach out to her. Until she received orders to the contrary, she decided that she should go ahead and complete the mission.

Ari had told her he had been contacted by certain people who needed to eliminate a certain party in Philadelphia. It all had something to do with a recycling plant. The "why" never was an issue for her; the "who" was all she needed to know.

She checked out her appearance to make certain that she had struck the perfect "butch-bad girl on the make" look. She wore a black leather jacket over a tight black hooded sweatshirt and tight black jeans and leather boots with high heels. The bouncer at 12th Air Command waved her in ahead of a number of ladies who were already lined up at the entrance. She turned and stared down one of the more vocal objectors who had called her a "skinny bitch." The bouncer shrugged his shoulders and smiled as he held open the door.

Shona saw her sitting alone at the bar. She took the stool next to her and told the bartender, "I'll have a Jack and Coke, and put it on her bill," and nodded at the woman to her left.

"What the fuck," Dorothy Wiggins said.

Shona gave her a seductive smile and said, "I heard you're a bulldog in the courtroom. That true?"

Wiggins gave her an appraising look and watched as Shona took a sip of her cocktail. "And who told you that?" she asked.

Shona shrugged and replied, "It's what they say about you Ms. Wiggins."

"Do I know you, Miss…?"

"Brittany. Brittany Stone," Shona said extending her hand to Wiggins.

Wiggins took Shona's hand in hers and held it for an extended moment.

"And why is it that you need an attorney, Miss Stone?"

"I hear there's a warrant out for my arrest; something to do with hacking into some corporation's computer system, or something like that."

"And I assume that you are innocent, and know nothing about these allegations," Wiggins replied.

"Ms Wiggins, if I was innocent and knew nothing about the charges I wouldn't need a lawyer now, would I?"

Wiggins lifted her martini in a mock toast and said, "My, my, an honest woman. That's something I'm not accustomed to encountering in my line of work. Miss Stone, since you apparently have heard that I'm a, how did you refer to me?"

"A bulldog in the courtroom," Shona replied.

"Yes, how flattering. Anyway bulldogs like me don't work for doggie treats," Wiggins said.

Shona leaned over and stuck her tongue in Wiggins' ear and said, "I think we may be able to work something out. Don't you?"

FIFTY

chowitz realized that with every passing hour the odds of recapturing Nooris and his associates were diminishing. He believed that Avi Nooris, Ari's half brother, had told them everything he knew about his older sibling's various enterprises, both legitimate and otherwise. Ichowitz had concluded that Ari must have decided long ago that his brother neither had the intellect or the capacity to carry out the criminal activities in which he was involved. Avi had been intentionally kept in the dark concerning the full scope of the Mall attack and the rest of his brother's endeavors.

The detective knew that Ari's smartest play was to get as far away from Philadelphia, probably out of the country, as quickly as possible. As an experienced former Mossad agent, Nooris must already have at his disposal the necessary resources and a comprehensive escape plan in place. Ichowitz could not, however, dismiss out of hand Jack's gut feeling that Nooris was still in the area, although he could think of no rational reason to support this conclusion.

Ichowitz was trying to let his young friend have some quality time with Kate O'Malley and Liam. He could see that Jack had finally allowed himself to move on with his life. The detective was still concerned that Michael Flynn, the art thief who had played a pivotal role in the foiled Barnes Foundation robbery, was a continuing threat to the O'Malley family. Although Vito Coratelli refused to disclose the source of the information that had led to the Nooris gang's capture and the return of the missing

306 MURDER AND MAYHEM IN MANAYUNK

masterpieces, Ichowitz was convinced that Flynn was somehow involved in this aspect of the case as well. Once again, however, Ichowitz could not come up with any rational explanation for this conclusion either.

And who had murdered Megan Larson, and why? All of this began with the murder of the young woman who was going to be Jack Regan's star witness before the Grand Jury in the Dorothy Wiggins municipal corruption case. What had initially appeared to be a simple homicide investigation had morphed into a multiple homicide, terrorist attack, and an international art heist. If the information Avi Nooris had provided the authorities was accurate, with the exception of the Larson case they would be able to successfully prosecute all of those responsible for all of the other crimes, assuming they could capture the actors. Once again, Ichowitz believed that the evidence that could solve that mystery was available, but for reasons he could not understand, his friend at Homeland Security was withholding information that would reveal the identity of the individual, or individuals involved in the Larson homicide.

He decided that he would take another shot at Vito Coratelli. After numerous battles in many different courtrooms in countless cross examinations over nearly three decades, they had become friends. Ichowitz was more than a little concerned that Vito would try to avenge his son's murder; it was, after all, the Sicilian way. If Nooris was involved in the murder, and if he was still in the area, any attempt by Coratelli to extract "justice" could be extremely dangerous. Ichowitz would need all of his skill to convince his friend to be forthcoming as to the identity of his source. The only way to assure that those responsible for his son's murder and the other crimes were brought to justice was to re-apprehend Nooris and his gang.

"Kate, you seem distracted. Is there something wrong?" Regan asked. He had been looking forward to a pleasant evening with Kate and Liam at his place. In all of the turmoil that they had been through in the wake of the attack on the Mall, this was the first time he felt that Kate and Liam were safe. Kate had been so excited about returning to Manayunk, and yet now her discomfort was palpable. Was Michael Flynn back in the picture, or had Jack done something to bring this about?

Jack had waited until Liam went to bed to ask her what had gone wrong. She was standing in front of the fireplace staring at the picture of Susan that still sat on the mantel. "Jack, were you and your wife thinking of having a family before she became ill?" she asked in response to his question.

"Yes, when Susan completed her training. Why?"

She turned and looked at him there were tears in her eyes. "What's wrong, honey?" he asked as he took her in his arms.

"I'm pregnant."

"You're pregnant?"

She nodded.

"Really?"

"Yes."

"That's wonderful. I mean that's great! We're going to have a baby! When are we going to have a baby?"

"In about six months or so."

She looked at him as if he were crazy. "How can you be so happy about this?" she asked.

Now it was his turn to look at her as if she was daft and replied, "Because I love you, and I love Liam, and we can become a family."

"So you don't think I trapped you?"

"Katey, I want to marry you. I want to adopt Liam. I want us, all of us, to be together. Isn't that what you want?"

She nodded.

"Then you'll marry me?"

"Yes."

"Can we tell my family and O'Malley?"

He kissed her and said, "We're going to have a baby!"

Ichowitz' phone chirped as he was turning onto 8th Street about six blocks from Coratelli's home on Christian Street. He could see from the caller ID that it was Jack.

"Boychik, I thought I told you to take the night off and have some fun with your Kate and Liam," he said.

"Izz, I have some great news to share with you. Kate and I are getting married and we're going to have a baby!"

"Jack, that's wonderful news. I'm so happy for you and Kate and Liam. You'll make a perfect family."

After they discussed all of the details of his impending marriage and baby, Jack asked, "Izz, where are you? Aunt Ida told me you went out on some urgent business. What's going on?"

"Nothing to worry about; I thought I would try to reason with Vito Coratelli and see if he would tell me his source. I just have a feeling that Nooris and his friends are still hanging around. Maybe if we find out who gave Vito the tip that led to their capture we could get lucky again."

"Do you really think Nooris and his associates are still here?" Jack asked.

"They probably flew the coop; but just in case, I thought I'd give it a shot." "Izz, don't do anything crazy. I mean, these people are extremely dangerous."

"Jack, you sound just like Ida. Don't worry. I'm too old to go after the bad guys. I'm just gonna schmooze with Vito and see if he'll give up his source."

"OK, promise me you'll call me tonight and let me know how you made out," Regan said.

Ichowitz sighed and replied, "Yes, Mother."

FIFTY-ONE

━━◄••►━━

9:30 PM

The valet drove Dorothy Wiggins' Mercedes to the front of the 12th Air Command where Wiggins and Shona/Brittany were waiting. Shona/Brittany lightly ran her fingers down Wiggins back and across her buttocks. She brushed her lips across Wiggins' ear and whispered, "I think that's your car."

Wiggins nodded and reluctantly stepped away as Shona/ Brittany laughed. They rode in silence as the young woman lightly stroked the older woman's arm. Wiggins was completely under her control. Wiggins pulled into her parking space in the underground lot of her condo building, The Residences at the Ritz-Carlton. At forty-eight stories the Ritz was the tallest residential tower in the in the city. It had been built on the site of the former One Meridian Tower that had been seriously damaged in a fatal fire in 1991. Ironically, Wiggins' penthouse unit cost $10 million, roughly the amount of her fee in the class action settlement of the litigation she had brought on behalf of the victims in the One Meridian Tower case.

Wiggins turned to her passenger. She smiled and as she was about to speak, the young woman shook her head, put her fingers on Wiggins' lips and placed her middle finger in Wiggins' mouth. Wiggins sucked on Shona/Brittany's finger and the young woman laughed again.

Shona/Brittany leaned closer and whispered, "Let's go up to your place," and she lightly bit Wiggins' earlobe. Wiggins exhaled heavily and nodded. As they waited for the elevator the young woman positioned herself so that Wiggins blocked her face from the security camera above the elevator door. When Wiggins turned to speak, Shona/Brittany shook her head and pressed her finger to Wiggins' lips and whispered, "We can talk later."

They stepped into the elevator and rode up to the forty-seventh floor in silence. Once again Shona/Brittany used the older woman to shield her from the camera in the elevator car. The young woman stood directly behind Wiggins thrusting her body at the older woman's buttocks, fondling her breasts and licking the back of her neck as they rode up to the penthouse apartment. Wiggins was wet with anticipation when the elevator doors opened. Shona gently pushed Wiggins out of the elevator.

As they stepped directly into the foyer of Wiggins' apartment, Shona removed her hands from Wiggins' breasts and took the older woman's head in both her hands violently snapping Wiggins' neck to the left and right, instantly killing her. She gently dropped Wiggins' body to the marble floor in front of the Louis XIV gold filigreed credenza.

She removed a cloth treated with a chemical fabric cleaner that she had placed in a plastic bag from her back pocket and wiped Wiggins' body. After she removed the key fob and access card from Wiggins' pocket she checked herself in the mirror.

She removed the piercings from her nose and above her right eyebrow and pulled a blond wig out of her jacket pocket and put it on. She wiped the lipstick and make-up from her face with a wet and dry she had brought with her and put on a pair of rimless eye glasses, changing her appearance to that of a much younger person. She took off the leather jacket and smiled at her reflection one last time before turning back to the elevator. Using the specially-treated cloth she pressed the button to recall the elevator. Before the elevator door opened, she pulled the hoodie over her head. She never once looked at the body of the dead woman that lay less than three feet from the elevator.

She kept her head down and away from the camera and rode the elevator down to the underground garage. She drove Wiggins' Mercedes out of the garage onto Penn Square and turned right on Broad Street. She drove three blocks south and made a left into the multi-story self-parking lot adjacent to the Hersey Hotel at Broad and Locust Streets. She parked the vehicle in a space near the rear of the fourth level and left the lot by the back stairway. Shona stepped out on to Locust Street and blended in with students from the Academy of The Arts who were parading up and down Broad and Locust Streets.

Shona slowly made her way to the Broad Street Subway station at Broad and Walnut Streets. She boarded the southbound train to Pattison Avenue and lost herself in the crowd leaving the Citizens' Bank Park, where the Phillies had just completed a sweep of the Pittsburgh Pirates. Shona never gave a second's thought to her actions in the preceding hour and a half. She had completed her mission and would check in the morning to see if Ari had left her any further instructions. If not, she would leave the city and the country.

10 PM

Ichowitz and Coratelli were sitting at the small table in Coratelli's kitchen reminiscing over their many courtroom encounters. The kitchens in South Philadelphia row houses, despite thousands of dollars in upgrades, still looked much the same as they had when the parents and grandparents of the current occupants owned the homes. The linoleum floors and white appliances may have been replaced with imported Italian tile, granite countertops and stainless steel appliances, but in the end there is only so much you can do with the limited space available. The Coratellis' kitchen, although tastefully remodeled, was no exception.

Coratelli's wife Loretta was spending the week with their daughter in North Wildwood, New Jersey, or "down the shore" as the locals refer to the South Jersey beaches, so the two men had the rare occasion to hang out in her domain.

"Izz, more Limoncello? I made it myself," Coratelli asked as he poured himself another shot.

"Vito, I have to drive home. I'm not the best driver when I'm sober. Another shot of your hooch and I'd probably get pulled over for a DUI," Ichowitz replied.

Coratelli downed the shot of the chilled sweet liquor and sighed. "Izzy, my friend. While it is always a pleasure to sit and talk with you, I assume you're here for more than an old-fashioned bull session."

Ichowitz nodded.

"Let me guess," Coratelli continued. "Since the feds somehow managed to let Nooris and his associate escape from custody and you know that one of my clients provided the tip that led to their arrest, you probably think my source may have in his possession information that could lead to their recapture. Is that right?"

"Counselor, do I have to answer with a yes or no, or can I elaborate?" Ichowitz replied.

Coratelli smiled. "Well?"

"Vito, these are really bad guys. They need to be put away. If you can help in any way, you would be doing a great service to the community."

"Izzy, you know I can't divulge my client's identity without his authorization. Besides, I haven't heard from my client for several days. For all I know he's no longer in the city, or even in the country. Tell me something. How did those jibones get loose?"

Ichowitz filled him in on the details of how Nooris and Rabibowitz had escaped.

"Are you kidding me? You mean the two FBI agents stopped at a Wawa to get coffee and the prisoners just walked away? That's the *emess*?"

Ichowitz nodded. "Vito, I know you're bound by attorney-client privilege. But can I ask you some hypothetical questions?"

The lawyer nodded.

"Hypothetically speaking, did your source have anything to do with the robbery at the Barnes Foundation?"

He nodded.

"Once again, hypothetically, did your source claim that he had nothing to do with the attack at the Mall?"

Coratelli nodded again.

"Did you believe him?"

"Do you mean hypothetically?"

Ichowitz nodded.

"Yes I did."

"Can you think of any hypothetical reason why your source wanted Nooris and his gang arrested?"

"I suppose he was convinced that these individuals were reckless and dangerous and that their crimes should not go unpunished, hypothetically."

Ichowitz nodded, agreeing with the lawyer's conclusion. "Vito, I know that your source is Michael Flynn. Avi Nooris implicated him in the Barnes heist. He more or less told us that neither he nor Flynn had anything to do with the fake terrorist attack. My guess is that your assumption that Flynn was genuinely upset with Nooris' reckless disregard for the safety and wellbeing of innocent people was the reason he stepped forward, so to speak."

Ichowitz stopped and asked, "Did you hear that?"

Before he could say another word the back door was kicked in. Nooris and Rabinowitz were standing in the kitchen pointing Glock 45 caliber automatic pistols at them.

FIFTY-TWO

———◆◆◆———

10:15PM

"What's wrong?" Kate asked Regan who was once again looking at his watch and checking his cell phone. At her count this was the sixth time he had done that in the last hour.

"I'm sure there's nothing wrong, it's just that I asked Izzy to call me and let me know how his meeting with Coratelli went," Jack answered.

"He'll probably call ya in the morning," she said.

He nodded.

For the past hour or so they had been discussing their future life together. Both of them were looking forward to telling Liam that they would soon become a real family. "Are you sure Liam will be OK with all of this?" Jack asked.

"Oh Jack, Liam idolizes you."

"How about your uncle?"

"O'Malley will gladly walk me down the aisle. He'll figure I'll finally be out of his hair and let the old codger return the Grape Tavern to its former state of bad food and ill repair; fat chance of that happenin. What about your folks? D'ya think they'll want the likes of me in such 'la de da' society?"

Regan laughed. "You know my father told me that the Maxwells weren't very keen on the idea of their daughter marrying a lowly policeman from Manayunk. They did everything in their power to break them up. They sent my mother away on a trip around the world. They even threatened to disinherit my mother if she went through with the marriage."

"So what happened?"

"My parents ran away to Elkton, Maryland and got married."

"But I thought they had a grand party at some large estate your grandparents owned. Your mother showed me the wedding pictures."

"They did, after my mother told them she was pregnant. So I don't think my parents will have any objection. Besides, you heard my mother when we called her this evening. She's genuinely thrilled."

Jack looked at his watch again. It was 10:30.

"Why don't you call his cell phone? He's probably on his way home."

"I left him a message less than an hour ago. He hasn't returned my call," Regan replied.

10:25 PM

Michael Flynn had decided to drop in on Vito Coratelli and ask him to pass on another tip to the police. Flynn knew the location of two of the houses Nooris had used when they were preparing for the Barnes robbery. If Nooris or any of his gang were still in the area, they might be using one of those locations to hide out until the manhunt cooled off.

Flynn noticed the two men standing outside Coratelli's house as he walked south on 8th Street. There was something familiar about the men that made him slow his pace. He bent over as if to tie his shoelace and watched as the taller man, whose bald head shone in the light from the street lamp, walked towards the back of the house. Flynn noticed his limp and immediately realized that the bald man was Nochem Rabinowitz. He assumed his companion was Ari Nooris. He was amazed at how the two men had altered their appearance. Rabinowitz had shaved his head and trimmed his beard to a goatee; Nooris had somehow managed to look much older. While Nooris and Rabinowitz were preoccupied with their scrutiny of the Coratelli property, Flynn, the accomplished art thief that he was, silently moved into the shadows in a space between two parked cars and continued to observe the two men.

From his vantage point he could see Rabinowitz signal Nooris to join him at the rear of Coratelli's house. Flynn checked his surroundings to see if anyone else was in the vicinity; there were no vehicles on either 8th or Christian Streets and no pedestrians anywhere in sight. He heard a loud crashing sound from the rear of Coratelli's house and he quickly and silently made his way to the back of the building, always making sure to remain in the shadows.

He crouched behind the large plastic trash container that stood fifteen feet from the back door. The shattered glass and splintered wood from the door-jam was scattered across the small concrete landing and down the three steps to the bricked-over yard. He would have to be careful not to step on the debris if he attempted to get any closer. The noise would alert Nooris and Rabinowitz that someone was approaching.

He inched closer to the partially-opened door. He saw the two men standing with their backs to the door, pointing guns at Coratelli and another man who was sitting at the kitchen table.

"Rabi. How convenient," Nooris said. "Mr. Coratelli and Detective Ichowitz, the very two gentlemen we wanted to see, are both here. Rabi, please relieve the Detective of any firearms he may have in his possession. As to our host Mr. Coratelli, he's a lawyer. I assume the only dangerous weapon he's packing is his mouth."

Coratelli nodded and smiled, "Mr. Nooris, Detective Ichowitz just finished telling me all about your daring escape from the FBI." Coratelli looked at the broken door-jam and said, "You know if you wanted to retain me, all you had to do was call. I gladly would have made time to see you without all the theatrics."

Rabinowitz gestured for the Detective to stand. He removed the Smith &Wesson 40 caliber M&P Shield from Ichowitz's shoulder holster and quickly patted him down, finding no other weapons on the detective.

"Gentlemen," Nooris said, motioning with the Glock. "Why don't we move to the living room where we can more comfortably discuss our business? Mr. Coratelli, if you'd be so kind as to lead the way," Nooris smiled, still pointing the weapon at them.

"Rabi, why don't you check around the property to make sure there's no one around to interrupt our discussion?"

Flynn silently withdrew from the back yard before Rabinowitz had exited the building. He watched as the gunman limped from the back yard to the perimeter of the house and returned after making certain no one was there. Flynn decided that his best course of action was to leave and try to find a pay phone and make an anonymous call to the police.

As Flynn crossed Christian Street he saw Jack Regan getting out of his car. What the hell was he doing here? If Regan barged in, there could be disastrous – possibly fatal – consequences. Flynn grabbed Regan's arm, preventing him from slamming the car door shut. Regan's eyes widened with surprise when he realized it was Flynn who had stopped him. Flynn held his hand to his lips, pointed towards Coratelli's house and pulled Regan down so that the car blocked them from anyone in the building's line of sight.

"Your partner the big detective and Coratelli are being held at gunpoint by Nooris and Rabinowitz," he whispered. "I think ya'd be makin a big mistake if ya were to barge in there and make a fuss."

Regan had still not fully recovered from the shock of Flynn's sudden appearance.

"What..."

Flynn signaled Regan to lower his voice, once again gesturing towards the house across the street.

"What are you doing here?" Regan whispered.

"Not important. Can ya summon the police? I think your friend's in danger," Flynn said.

Regan nodded but before he could pull out his cell phone there was a loud crashing sound and shouting from inside Coratelli's house.

"Too late," Flynn said. "Call the police and wait here." He silently ran towards the house, crouching low and remaining in the shadow of the vehicles parked in front of the house.

Regan thought he saw Flynn holding a pistol as he ran.

FIFTY-THREE

10:28PM

"**G**entlemen, if you would kindly be seated," Nooris said and pointed at the plastic covered sofa in front of the picture window in Coratelli's living room.

Ichowitz and Coratelli sat side by side and stared at the gunman.

"What do you want?" Ichowitz asked.

"Information," Nooris responded.

"Mr. Nooris wants to know who told the police that they were on Sheik Nazeur's yacht. Isn't that right?" Coratelli said.

Nooris nodded.

"Why?" Ichowitz asked.

"I assume he would like to extract some form of revenge from whomever it was that betrayed him. Isn't that right, Mr. Nooris?"

Nooris nodded again.

Ichowitz shook his head.

"Detective Ichowitz, you seem disappointed, or is it *disdain* you are exhibiting?" Nooris commented in response to the detective's reaction.

"It's neither disappointment nor disdain. I just think you're *meshugheh*."

"Mr. Coratelli, can you explain to your friend the significance of revenge?" Nooris asked.

"Izzy, it may seem, how do your people put it, like nonsense?"

"*Narishkeitt*."

"Yes *narishkeitt* to you, but avenging a wrong, say for example, the killing of a loved one, or giving the police information that leads to one's apprehension, can serve many purposes. It can signal to the world that you are not a person who can be taken lightly. It also can cleanse the soul by relieving a person of the burden of unrequited hatred," Coratelli explained.

"Precisely," Nooris observed.

Ichowitz looked at both men and shook his head.

"And your companion agrees?" Ichowitz asked nodding in the direction of Rabinowitz, who stood silently taking in the scene with no apparent reaction.

"Enough small talk, I need to know who betrayed us." Nooris said.

There was no response.

Without saying another word Nooris shot Ichowitz in his left knee. The detective screamed in pain and fell to the floor knocking the floor lamp to his left to the ground.

"Mr. Coratelli, Detective Ichowitz, the next bullet will be aimed at one of your heads. Now tell me. *Who betrayed me?*"

As Nooris aimed the Glock at the fallen detective, there was a loud gunshot and he crumpled to the ground. He had been shot in the back by someone in the dining room. In that instant, Coratelli pulled a pistol from his pocket and fired a bullet at Rabinowitz who had turned to return fire from the unknown assailant. Flynn shot Rabinowitz and kicked the weapons away from the gunmen.

"Are ya hurt bad?" he asked the detective.

Ichowitz shook his head.

"You?" he asked Coratelli.

"No."

Flynn thrust a piece of paper in Coratelli's hand.

"What's this?"

"Places Shona Cohen may be hidin."

Jack Regan ran into the room from the dining room. He saw the two gunmen and his friend on the floor.

"My God! Izzy!"

"I'm OK."

The sound of approaching sirens broke the silence.

"I'll be goin then," Flynn said and left the room. They watched as he walked out the back door and disappeared into the night.

Within minutes of Flynn's departure, two police cruisers screeched to a stop in front of Coratelli's house, clearing the small crowd of neighbors who had been attracted by the sound of gunshots being fired. Officers with weapons drawn approached the front door. Regan opened the door before they could knock and announce their presence.

He held up his ID and said, "Detective Ichowitz has been shot. Call the EMTs!"

"Officer down! Officer down!" one of the officers shouted into his shoulder microphone as he ran through the door.

Within an hour Regan's father, the Chief of Homicide and several other high- ranking officials of the Philadelphia Police Department were waiting outside of surgery with Ida Ichowitz and Jack Regan. The initial diagnosis from Bradley Oppenheimer, Jefferson Hospital's Chief of Orthopedic Surgery, was that the bullet had entered Ichowitz's left leg above the kneecap. That was the good news. The fact that he had been shot with a hollow nose 45-caliber bullet from close range made it impossible for the surgeon to know the full extent of the injury until they opened the wound.

At the same time, both Rabinowitz and Nooris were also being operated on at Hahneman Hospital for the injuries they had sustained in the shootings at Coratelli's house. Jack Regan and Vito Coratelli had given their statements to the Third District Chief of Detectives. The Department put an APB out for Michael Flynn. His picture was already out on every local newscast and website.

"Jack, are you telling me that Flynn saved Izzy's life?"

"Dad, he stopped me from going in the Coratelli house. Mr. Coratelli said Nooris was about to shoot Izzy in the head when Flynn shot him."

Commissioner Regan shook his head and said, "When we arrest him, I don't know if we should charge him or give him a medal."

"Dad, I'm betting you'll never arrest him."

FIFTY-FOUR

———◆◆◆———

"**W**ell, would ya look what the wind blew in, boyos. We have here a genuine hero, don't cha know," Duffy said as Flynn walked into the back room.

Flynn smiled and handed Duffy the gun Duffy had given him several hours before and said, "Thanks for the piece. It came in handy."

"Michael lad, yer friend Vito Coratelli is all over the tele extolling yer virtues. His only missgivin is that ya didn't kill those two villains. Were they the ones who killed his son?"

Flynn shook his head and said, "Nooris gave the order, but someone else killed Vito Junior.".

"So there's another killer still on the loose?"

"A woman, Shona Cohen, I gave Vito the addresses of a couple safe houses Nooris had used when we were planning the Barnes job. I assume the police haven't found her, so she must have left town."

"Well it's a lucky thing for Coratelli and that policeman ya happened to stop by," Duffy observed. "Anyways, it's time fer you to be leavin our fair city. In truth I'll be missin all the excitement of havin yer company. Fergus will be escortin ya to Detroit and across the border to Canada. I'm afraid you'll have to ride in the back of the truck with the furniture part of the way."

Duffy signaled for the glasses to be filled, raised his glass and said, "May the road rise to meet ya,

May the wind be always at yer back,
May the sun shine warm upon yer face,
The rains fall soft on yer fields and,
Until we meet again,
May God hold ya in the palm of his hand."
"*Slainte*," Flynn responded.
"*Slainte*," they all replied and drank the whiskey.

chowitz was in surgery for over five hours. A visibly tired Dr. Oppenheimer, still wearing his scrubs, walked into the waiting area and approached the group that now included Matt and Ben, Ichowitz's sons, Ida and Jack and his father, who had been anxiously waiting for the doctor's report.

"Mrs. Ichowitz, folks, your husband is a very lucky man. He came through the surgery remarkably well."

The doctor sat down next to Ida Ichowitz and placed a diagram of a knee on his lap, pointing at it as he explained the surgery. "The bullet entered your husband's leg about three millimeters above the patella, the kneecap, and exited his thigh, just missing his tibia. It nicked the anterior cartilage, partially severing the collateral ligaments that help stabilize the knee and also partially severing the ACL, the anterior cruciate ligament, the ACL connects the tibia to the femur. We reconstructed the ACL.

"Detective Ichowitz will have to go to rehab. He'll probably walk with a slight limp for the rest of his life, but a millimeter one way or the other and, well… Anyway, he's in recovery; Mrs. Ichowitz, he wants to see you. He said he may need police protection because he knows you're going to kill him for going to that meeting without back-up like you told him to."

Ida looked at the doctor and said, "He's a real comedian, that one. Boys, let's go see your father." She pointed at Jack and his father and said, "You too; you're mespokha."

Jack and his father left the hospital while the Ichowitz family tended to their patient. It had been a long night. "Jack, we'll give you a lift home," Commissioner Regan said. "You can get your car later."

They sat in the back seat of the Commissioner's sedan. "Commissioner," his driver said, "There's a call for you from Homicide."

Commissioner Regan picked up the car phone. It was Larry Jackson, the Chief of Homicide, he listened to the call, sighed and hung up. "Jack, we need to make a detour. It appears that Dorothy Wiggins' body was discovered in her apartment. The preliminary investigation indicates it was a homicide." The long night just got longer.

There were a half dozen police cruisers, the medical examiner's van and the crime scene truck parked on the driveway in front of the entrance to the Residences at the Ritz Carlton. The police had cordoned off the area. Vans with television antennae and reporters with videos on tripods were set up on the City Hall sidewalk across the street from the luxury condo building. News of the Wiggins' homicide had already leaked out, no doubt from someone on the condo's staff.

Regan and his father ignored the questions the reporters yelled out from across Penn Square as they signed in with the officer controlling the crime scene. A visibly shaken Howard St. Claire, the Ritz' Concierge, stood in the lobby with one of the police officers.

"Commissioner, nothing like this is supposed to happen at the Residences. I say this is supposed to be an oasis - a safe haven from the violence. How could you allow this to happen?" he spoke with a refined British accent.

After the Commissioner assured the concierge that the police would do everything possible to keep the "madness" at bay and minimize the disruption to the residents, they went up to the forty-seventh floor and logged into the crime scene for a briefing. Homicide Chief Larry Jackson told them the body had been discovered by the night maid who was replacing the flowers on Wiggins' foyer credenza with fresh flowers at around 1 AM. She immediately contacted her supervisor, who called the police. The preliminary report of the Medical Examiner indicated cause of death, a broken neck, by manual manipulation; time of death less than six hours prior to the maid's discovery of the body.

"Based on the time Wiggins and her companion accessed the property and whoever used Wiggins' card to leave the parking garage, Wiggins had been murdered between 9:45 and 10 PM. The surveillance video of the elevator at the underground garage and on the elevator shows a woman accompanied the vic to her apartment. There was no view of the woman's face. She was obviously aware of the location of the video cameras. We're dealing with a pro here," Jackson observed.

"Wiggins' car is missing. We suspect the assailant drove it out of the parking lot. The body has been taken to the ME. The autopsy is scheduled for later this morning."

"Chief, could you get any idea how tall the woman was from the video?" Jack asked Jackson.

"Negative. Why?"

"I'm thinking that the murderer was Shona Cohen, Nooris assistant. The woman Avi Nooris told us killed Vito Coratelli Jr and Mickey Saunders. I've seen her and she's tall ... I would say close to six feet."

"Why would she murder Dorothy Wiggins? For that matter, why would she even still be in Philly?" Jackson asked.

"I don't know," Jack replied.

"Well, with Wiggins' history there will probably be a long list of suspects. According to *Philadelphia Magazine* she was the most hated lawyer in Philly. And that's quite a distinction, no offense," Jackson said nodding at Jack.

Jack smiled and replied, "Chief, none taken."

FIFTY-FIVE

L ater that morning Jack Regan called Monroe Ossberg to let him know that his friend Isodore Ichowitz would recover from the shooting. Regan also let him know that Nooris and Rabinowitz had been treated for their injuries and would be returned to federal custody when the local authorities were finished with them. He suggested that, for the time being, the FBI and Homeland assume a subordinate position. This was appropriate protocol since the Philadelphia Police had arrested them for the felonies in connection with their home invasion and assault on Coratelli and Izzy.

"Mr. Ossberg, the District Attorney is going to indict them for Assault with Intent and other charges. Since one of the victims was a prominent member of the PPD, you can assure FBI SAC Keel that the department will not allow either of these men to escape custody."

Ossberg accepted the rebuke graciously. After all, the federal authorities had badly botched the relatively easy transfer of the prisoners that allowed their escape and the near-fatal consequences that followed.

"Jack, is Izzy able to see visitors?" he asked.

"Mr. Ossberg."

"Jack, please. The formality is not necessary."

"Monroe, you'll have to check with his wife. She's running the toughest security screening I've ever encountered. Izzy's my godfather and she practically strip-searched me before she let me see him. I had to promise not to mention anything about the Wiggins murder."

Ossberg laughed. "So what happened?"

"One of the officers standing guard had already told him about it." He paused and said, "You know if you see him he's going to ask you about the Larson case. He thinks you're holding out evidence that might help us close the case," Jack commented.

"I know. Do you have any leads on Wiggins' murderer?"Ossberg asked.

"No, but if I were a betting man I'd lay long odds on Shona Cohen. Monroe, do you have evidence that would shed some light on Megan Larson's killer?"

"Jack, I ..."

"Forget it," Regan cut him off.

Regan and Ichowitz had exhausted every possible angle to come up with a logical explanation for why the feds would withhold information about the Larson murder. In the wake of everything that had transpired since, even if the feds originally had a legitimate reason to withhold evidence, it didn't seem that there could be any plausible justification at this juncture. Regan had reached the conclusion that they had nothing. Izzy still believed they were holding something back. Regan pitied Ossberg. He was certain Izzy would put Ossberg on a super guilt trip when he visited him at the hospital.

Shona Cohen watched the early morning local newscasts that widely reported the shootings at Vito Coratelli's house. She had never trusted Michael Flynn. Ari must be slipping. He should have let her eliminate him when she asked. She realized that both Ari and Rabinowitz were beyond her help now. It was highly unlikely that they would be able to escape a second time. It was also equally unlikely that the authorities would break either of them. She assumed the half brother, Avi, already gave up what little information he knew about his older sibling's dealings.

It was time for her to move on. She had ample assets, including the stolen painting from the Barnes, and the skills to evade the authorities. She had completed her mission. She felt no remorse over anything she had done. It wasn't a matter of personal preference or emotion. It was an assignment, nothing more. Nooris had trained her well. She would miss his mentoring, but she would carry on without him. Their relationship was not what anyone would think of as a friendship. It was far more complicated than that. Whatever it had been, now it was over, and now it was time for her to shed her skin and take on a new persona.

She boarded the Bolt bus to New York City. She had dyed her hair blond and fashioned the blond hair extensions into a pony tail that she placed through the back of a faded Phillys baseball cap. She wore tight blue jeans, Ugg boots and a sweatshirt with Pratt Art Institute on the front and carried a large rectangular canvas bag that art students use to transport their projects. Among the sketches and drawings in her carrier was the priceless oil painting by Georges Braque that Ari had instructed her to take from the Arab. Looking like the other college coeds returning from a weekend at home, she twittered away on her smart phone, occasionally laughing at the response, as she waited in line to board the early morning bus.

Jack Regan sat beside Ichowitz's bed in the chair in which the detective's wife had stationed herself following his surgery. She reluctantly suspended her vigil at her sons' insistence that she rest at home. They assured her that the police would stand guard throughout the night and keep their father safe from any harm.

"Jack, you look like you're the one who took a bullet. Go home, let Kate cook you some breakfast and get some sleep," Ichowitz told him.

"Izz, I will, I just wanted to give you an update on the investigation of the Wiggins murder."

After filling Ichowitz in on the progress, or perhaps better described, lack of progress, he asked, "Izz, I hear that your buddy Monroe Ossberg dropped by to see you. So does he have anything to share that may help us on the Larson case?"

Ichowitz sighed and replied, "He swears that he didn't withhold any evidence."

"But you don't believe him?"

Ichowitz shook his head.

"Well, my boss says the Larson investigation is going to go to cold case status. We have nothing firm to go on in the Wiggins murder other than our belief that Shona Cohen is the doer."

"Did we check out the addresses Flynn gave us?" Ichowitz asked.

Regan nodded his head and said, "No joy."

"I see Vito Coratelli has been all over the morning news casts extolling the bravery and decisiveness of the art thief Michael Flynn. His description of Flynn's exploits makes the likes of both the federal and local authorities out to be like the 'Keystone Cops.' We could really use a break on the Wiggins investigation."

Regan shrugged his shoulders.

"Go home, get some rest. Who knows? Maybe something will come up tomorrow," Ichowitz said.

"You get some rest too. I'll see you tomorrow. You need to get back on your feet real fast. You're going to be my Best Man. I can't have you walking down the aisle using a walker."

They both realized the Larson case would remain unsolved.

FIFTY-SIX

———◆———

Monroe Ossberg realized that he had let his friend, likely his only friend in Philadelphia, Isodore Ichowitz, down. He could sense that the big detective knew he was not telling him the truth, the "*emess*," when he claimed Homeland had turned over everything in its possession that could shed light on the Megan Larson murder investigation. Ossberg had conclusive evidence that revealed the identity of the killer. The "Top Secret" designation on the file, however, precluded him from even discussing, let alone releasing the evidence. If he were to do so, not only would his career come to a swift and unhappy conclusion, he could also be prosecuted under the Patriot Act, and various other federal statutes.

The Larson case and the chaos that followed in its wake had already likely derailed the career of Howard Keel, the FBI Philadelphia SAC, despite his efforts to deflect responsibility for the consequences that had resulted principally from the unimaginable stupidity of Ossberg's predecessor, the political appointee Simon Conway. Conway never disclosed his mole in the New Age mosque of the now-missing radical cleric Malik Ben-Ali. Keel had directed around-the-clock surveillance of the Homeland agent, believing him to be a sleeper terrorist. Despite the fact that Keel's agents discovered the mole, thousands of dollars had been wasted and lives had been lost. Someone other than the well-connected political appointee had to take the fall.

Ossberg had submitted numerous requests of Homeland to declassify the Carrington file. Most recently when he received word of Wiggins' murder, he asked the Assistant Secretary if he could have permission to release the disc of the Nooris condo surveillance. He received the same response he had received the five previous requests: The case was too sensitive to allow local authorities any information about Homeland's investigation. Ossberg had also requested that he be relieved of his temporary assignment to Homeland. Once again his request was denied on the basis of his efficient stewardship of the Regional Office, at least until another politically-connected appointee could be found to replace him.

What Ossberg had been prevented from telling Ichowitz is that Homeland had placed a second surveillance camera in the Nooris condo. This camera gave an entirely different view of the first floor of the unit – a view that provided a full account of the murder, including the identity of the murderer. Homeland's contractor had removed all traces of the camera before Ichowitz could send any of the Philadelphia Police Department's technical unit back for a second, more comprehensive search of the condo.

He placed the disc in the player and once again watched as the scene revealed the horrific images of Larson's final moments. The silent video showed the victim's passionate embrace of a male. As the two lovers moved towards the door, the camera revealed Mayor Gallo as Larson's lover. Less than a minute later Larson is back in the shot moving towards the back of the unit. She approaches the door and after what must have been an exchange with whomever was outside Larson opens the door.

A visibly agitated Dorothy Wiggins enters. The soundless video shows images of what must surely have been a heated exchange between the two women. Wiggins reaches to embrace Larson who violently pushes her away. More words are exchanged and Larson appears to laugh at Wiggins. She turns away from Wiggins as if moving towards the front of the room. Wiggins looks around and grabs the andiron from the fire place. She strikes Larson repeatedly with the andiron. The blood spray from the back of Larson's head splashes across the assailant's face and body as she continues to beat the victim.

Wiggins drops the instrument of crime at her feet, looks down at the body and says something and turns and runs out the back door. The video shows the motionless body of the victim with the expanding pool of blood lying on the floor of the condo.

Ossberg removed the disc from the player and returned it to the safe. He wondered again what could possibly be so important to prevent the Federal Government from disclosing the identity of the young woman's murderer.

EPILOGUE

When Shona Cohen got off the Bolt bus at 34th Street and 9th Avenue in mid-town Manhattan she immediately walked over to the James A Farley Post Office on 8th Avenue. As she climbed the stairs to the main entrance she read the famous inscription on the building's colonnade: "Neither snow, nor rain, nor heat, nor gloom of night stays these couriers from the swift completion of their appointed rounds." She made her way to the basement where the post office boxes were located and walked down the long corridor to Box 1674, checking to make sure no one was watching her. She accessed the box and removed its contents, discarding the accumulated junk mail and keeping only a single envelope addressed to No Risk LTD. She placed the envelope in her backpack and left the building.

She leisurely walked the six blocks and two avenues to Bryant Park at 40th Street and 6th Avenue again checking to make sure she had no tail. She purchased a falafel and bottle of water from the street vendor on the corner and sat on a bench that looked out onto 5th Avenue. After she finished her snack she removed the envelope from her back pack and opened it. The envelope contained a single sheet of bond paper on which the following appeared: "The thief, the detective and his lawyer, and the father."

She smiled and tore the document and the envelope into pieces, threw the scraps of paper along with the wax paper in which her sandwich had been wrapped into the enclosed recyclable trash container and walked west on 40th

Street towards 7th Avenue. She checked her wristwatch. If she hurried she could catch the next Amtrak from Penn Station back to Philadelphia. Perhaps everyone on the list was still there. She smiled thinking that, like the inscription over the entrance to the post office building, she could swiftly complete her appointed rounds.

THE END

ABOUT THE AUTHOR

Neal Goldstein was born and raised in Philadelphia. He lives with his wife in Haverford, Pennsylvania. A graduate of Temple University and Temple University School of Law, he currently practices law in Philadelphia representing labor unions and employee benefit plans.

Made in the USA
Charleston, SC
12 July 2013